# NELSON'S CASTLE

# NELSON'S CASTLE

## *A Bronte Fairy Tale*

*Susanne Petito-Egielski*

Amuninni Press
18 Division Street
Suite 512
Saratoga Springs, NY 12866

ISBN-13: 978-0-9894711-0-7
LCCN: 2013914350

Cover Photo by Susanne Petito-Egielski
Cover Design by Mary Ross
Typeset by Jenni Wheeler

*Printed in the United States of America*

For my grandmother, Nunziata Salanitri Lupo

For my mother, Maria Teresa Antonetta Lupo Petito

And for Robert who climbs beautiful mountains for me

# ACKNOWLEDGMENTS

The writing of this work could not have been accomplished without the kindness, love and support of two phenomenal women: my dear friend and writing buddy, Shakti Chris, the most positive force in my life, who, in our "office" at Starbucks, inspired me with her wisdom and insights, and my "sister" and life-long friend, Janet Myers, who never wavered in her friendship and faith in me, even when I monopolized our Saturday morning catch-up calls with gossip about people who only existed in my mind.

To Pinky Haley and Chiara Montalto, my Saratoga Springs and Brooklyn readers and cheerleaders, thank you for your time and encouragement. Thank you, Molly McKitterick and The Word Process, for expert editing and heavenly patience. Thank you, Saratoga Springs Public Library, Kimberlie DeSilva, her Higher Grounds Caffè and my table with a view, Arthur Tobias who always gave me a reason to carry on and, most of all, Angela Sheck, my reader, my critic, my friend.

Thank you, the Lupo family of Brooklyn, especially Aunt Mil, who, ever since her baby-sitting days, spun tales which transported all her nieces and nephews to the most fantastic of worlds. Thank you, too, the Lupo family of Bronte, especially Nunzio, whose knowledge of his homeland remains unsurpassed. I would be negligent if I did not express my overwhelming gratitude to the men and women of Bronte whose labor of love, *Bronte insieme*, provided me with inspiration and a wealth of information pertaining to history, cultural traditions, aphorisms, dialectal and orthographic peculiarities and so much more but also my sincere apologies to them for any and all intentional (and unintentional) historical and geographical deviations.

To Dr. Josephine Danna, our "Jo," who always gave the best writing advice and Cynthia Patterson, our "Miss Montreal," who always gave so much more than friendship, your loving spirit shines in all of us. To the Italian American Writers Association, The John D. Calandra Italian American Institute, The Calandra Writers Group and, most of all, to the exceptional writer and teacher, Anthony Valerio, I am forever grateful.

Lastly, my heartfelt gratitude to the coolest husband on the planet. Thank you, Robert, my Bob E.-Guitar, a million times over, for the time and space you graciously afforded me and for lovingly embracing the "girl" on her journey.

# Contents:

**1 May 1877** ..............................................................1

**Part I: The Town** ....................................................3

Mountains never meet other mountains. ......................5

Little and nothing go hand in hand. ...........................12

A house without a man is a house without a name. ......24

A bird in the cage sings not from love but rage. ...........32

When the pear is ripe, it must fall on its own. ..............44

Laugh on Friday. Cry on Saturday. ..............................56

With or without the rooster, the sun shines. ................63

From a rose, a thorn. From a thorn, a rose. ..................70

The one with the salt makes the soup. .........................78

**Part II: The Castle** .................................................89

A man shows himself by his word. An ox by his horns. ...............91

Only those that do nothing never make mistakes. ........100

The dog always chews on the pauper. ..........................107

With a doctor comes pain. ...........................................121

What you despise today, you may desire tomorrow. ......135

**Part III: The Dwelling** ...............................................145

Death is not the worst thing. ...................................147

Good times and bad times never last. ........................162

One nut in the sack makes no noise. ..........................171

When fortune turns her back, so do friends. .............182

**Part IV: The Party** ...................................................189

A man born round cannot die square. .......................191

The door only opens from the inside. .......................215

When the Devil flatters you, he wants your soul. ........237

God protect me from my friends. .............................253

**Part V: The Forest** ..................................................291

To love the one who does not love you is a waste of time. ............293

**1 May 1880** ...........................................................309

Whoever is born is reborn. .......................................311

# 1 MAY 1877

# PART I: THE TOWN

*Mountains never meet other mountains.*

Long ago, my Papà told a tale of the long, blue hallway in the Castle where paintings of the Admiral Nelson hang. *The First Duke of Bronte* was what the Nelson heirs carved 'neath the Admiral's paintings. And hero, too. *Hero.*

I tap at the walls of the lava cave that sheltered me all these years, my mind's eye seeing my own likeness hanging in the darkest chambers and, 'neath it, the words, *The Great Coward.* And near such a likeness, Alfiu Saitta's likeness, too, and, 'neath it, the words, *The Brave and Mad Cousin.* I slap at the insects scurrying 'cross my legs and let out a laugh, my mind's eye seeing such a chamber where the likenesses of fools and cowards hang. The small creatures laugh, too. I shout and laugh and shout and laugh, choking for breath. I scratch at the loose folds of flesh on my thighs, there, where insects make their bed for the night. I pound the earth, and, this, to frighten them away. But who pays mind to a coward? Not the small creatures in my lava cave and not Alfiu.

Eighteen hundred and sixty. That was the year the general Garibbaldi landed on our island and Alfiu was shot and I fled Bronti. That was the year my brave, mad cousin took to haunting me.

Night after night, like a dogged beggar, Alfiu Saitta chases me through my dreams, a smoking ball of light cupped in his hands. And when he blows the smoke away and the light shines a bright white, he moans his rasping tune. *The girl, the girl. She's lost her way on others' paths.* Night after night, year after year, in his ball of light, he brings her to my view: a baby baptized; a child in a heavy brown shawl; a young girl, Alfiu's knife, bloody in her hand.

Last night in my dreams, Alfiu moaned out a new tune. *The girl, the girl. Cousin, keep her safe from harm.* He blew the smoke away. In his ball of light, I seen her and her Mamma, Alfiu's mad wife, Agata. The girl, small, bony, pale, she knotted the heavy brown shawl 'neath her chin. When her lips stopped their trembling, she blew a kiss to her Mamma.

I seen it float 'cross the small cottage, a gentle kiss of silk and light. It brushed the black walls and the low roof and the marriage bed where the Mamma wrestled in a fitful sleep. The girl smiled, her kiss safe on its journey. It hovered near the Mamma's cheek, a coward kiss, fearful to brush the flesh. The Mamma swatted the air. The kiss sighed, falling lifeless on the ground. The girl wiped her eyes and took in a breath. "Mamma," she whispered, "when I kill the one with Nelson blood, you'll hold tight to all my kisses."

A thousand times and more I seen the Mamma snatch away the girl's joy and heard the girl's mad talk of vengeance for Alfiu. No more! *Basta*! I shouted, and, slow, slow, the cottage and the girl and the Mamma faded and the ball thickened with smoke. Alfiu faded, too, 'though his rasping moans lingered. *The girl. The girl. Cousin, keep her safe from harm.*

I struggled to laugh. I was sick of crying. "No, Alfiu," I shouted, "you always been the brave one! *You* keep her safe in your pretty ball of light!" With that, I shook myself awake and swore last night never no more to sleep and never no more to see Alfiu Saitta in my dreams. I slapped my brow, bristling that such vows been so late in coming.

Now, my belly cries out for food. What calls me more? A full belly or a good night's sleep? I spit on the hard earth I call my bed and ready myself to search for food, the long, shuddering lizards, the brown spotted grasshoppers of winter, all what I kill in the dark of night before the wolves hunt in silence.

I am of great height, but height alone won't stave off the wolves. I look down at my long arms and my long legs, once firm with muscles, now a limp target for the pack. My fingers sink in the hollows of my cheeks. My hair falls long on my chest. How long! How white! And white and thick the curls of my beard.

How old I am. Old and tired and filled with hunger. I crawl to the mouth of the cave, my head low to the earth, smelling and tapping for food. Good fortune smiles on me. Bare outside, I come 'on the stripped carcass of a hare that stronger, swifter creatures already feasted on. I drag it back inside the cave and crunch on the bones, hoping for a taste of flesh to ease my hunger. I stuff them in my mouth and let out a choking laugh, bringing to mind my wife that, time and again, scolded me when I stuffed in more food than my mouth could hold.

And while I suck the long bones clean, I see her in my mind's eye, my good and holy wife, there, in our cottage in Bronti, her round rump lapped over the stool by the fire, bundling the plants she gathered that day, and, me, my arms 'round her fleshy waist and kissing her arms and neck and face, and, her, laughing so sweet, and, me, sobbing that fortune shined so bright on me.

I throw the bones to the earth and wrap myself in the coarse green cloak she made me, threadbare after all these years, but still it keeps me warm. My body yearns for sleep, but I fight it off with a heartsick prayer. "O, my Sicilia, island of the poor, island of the conquered! O, my Sicilia! O, plains and pastures and hills and mountains that God gave us, but the foreigners took away! O, my Bronti, quivering at the feet of the most feared and beautiful mountain! My Bronti, quivering at *Mungibellu's* feet! My Bronti, downtrodden by bloodsucking Nelson heirs! Bronti, where is your glory? Bronti, where is mine?"

All through the night in the dark of my cave, I whisper my heartsick prayer with the small creatures that whir and hum 'neath rocks and stones. Grasshoppers race 'cross my feet and join in the prayer. Can these be the grasshoppers of spring, their bodies long and lean, their bodies, part grey, part green, so tasty in spring? Can it be spring?

What year is this? What month? What day? How long I been away from Bronti! A peasant's life I led there, laboring on land stolen from us time and again. *Caps* we called ourselves. Caps were all we had the right to wear. Caps, banding together, peasant standing strong with peasant.

What am I now? I threw away my cap long ago and ran to mountains far from Bronti soon after revolution smoldered and peasants went mad. Now, I hide in Bronti's shadows, bearing the mark of a coward, with no fight in me for nothing no more.

None but sleep can rid me of such thoughts. But sleep won't bring me peace, not when Alfiu Saitta... I slap my cheeks and shake the sleep out of me. I pat my belly. A great hunger still gnaws there. I grab sharp twigs and a small jagged rock and crawl to the mouth of the cave, but a flash of light sends me reeling back. I throw my hands 'cross my eyes. Slow, slow, I spread my fingers, my cloudy eyes peering at blue waves of light.

I stumble back. My teeth rattle. My knees knock loud, but louder are my cries. "No! No! No!" Out from the light, a dark hand beckons me. Out from the light, the spirit of my cousin issues forth.

There, at the mouth of the cave, Alfiu Saitta bows. Alfiu dressed in his marriage clothes, a young boy once more, a broad smile 'neath a king's moustache and dark hair smelling of olive oil. Do I dream with eyes open? Do I dream 'though wide awake? I jump up and rub my eyes. "Alfiu!" I cross myself. "Alfiu, by all what's good and holy, you got no right to be here!" At the sound of my words, his black eyes fill with water. "Alfiu, *ppi piaciri*, please, leave me be!"

"*Muntagna*," he clasps his hands and moans. Muntagna he calls me, Muntagna, like we're boys once more, wielding our phantom swords up and down Corsu Umbertu. "Muntagna, are you a mountain of a man this night?" He makes a fist. He opens his hands and blows away the smoke. There, captive in a small ball of light, I see the girl and the Castle.

I fall back down and scuttle to the deepest chamber of the cave. "Alfiu, you do wrong to bring such magic here."

He holds out his palms where a knife shines bright in the ball of light. "The girl. Look where the paths of others lead her…keep her safe…keep her safe…"

I shield my eyes and tap my way to the mouth of the cave. I breathe in the cold night air to shake free of the spell. "You want her safe? Go to Bronti!" I shout. "Shine your ball of light at the girl's *cummari*…she'll keep her goddaughter safe. Sì, go to her! Go to my Vin…my Vin…my *Vin… cen…zaaaa…*"

Vincenza. I scratch at my lips 'til they bleed, unworthy lips that now cry out my wife's good and holy name.

"Not Vincenza—*you!*" Alfiu's breath, strong and mad like the foreign wind, it blows me back to the deepest chamber of my cave.

"No! *Vigliaccu*…coward…that's what the Bruntiszi called me. *Va ben'*. Coward I been in Bronti and coward I stay in the wild. But breathing I am!"

"And the girl? Who got to keep her breathing?"

I pound my fists on the earth. "She got none to do with me!" I race from the cave, stumbling over lava rocks, running 'til my legs cry out for rest. I throw myself on the earth and look up at the black heavens where Alfiu's ball of light bolts 'cross the sky, its beams aiming straight to where I huddle. Quick, the warm beams pelt my body and fill me with the girl's desires. I jump up and twirl 'round like the spider dancers to rid my blood of all her sorrows and yearnings.

"Muntagna," Alfiu whispers, him by my side, "now, she got *all* to do with you."

Dizzy, I fall to the ground.

"Cousin, no more of your foolishness. Get up. This day marks the day of her birth and…"

"The day of her birth?" I slap my brow and fall back down. "The first of May? The day…" My mouth waters now that I bring to mind the bounty of chicken and pig and warm lemon cakes, the feast the Nelson heirs made for their Bronti peasants but once each year. Is there still such a feast for them? I raise my fists high in the air. "But where is my feast, Alfiu? Thanks to you, I fled Bronti, and, now, my feast is none but grasshoppers!"

I pound my chest 'til deep red marks rise up on my flesh and, this, to frighten his spirit and rid me of him for good. Alfiu waves his hand 'cross my body, and, quick, all the markings fade from view. I forage through the dirt on my chest for signs of pain. "Alfiu, where do you get such powers to heal me?" I slap my hand 'cross my mouth. "Alfiu, what demon world do you now call home?"

"A glorious and forgiving world it is, and gifts I bring you from there." He cradles me in his arms. I feel the strength of his muscles 'round me. *But how?* The arms of a spirit with no flesh or bones, arms of shining light that burn and blind me. He eases his hold. I break away and roll in the dirt to cool my body. "Get up and know the nature of all the creatures of the wild. Take their strength and swiftness and cunning. Take their sight and smell and hearing. Muntagna, take their gifts to make your blood brave."

"Brave! No power in the heavens or on the earth or in your demon world makes a coward's blood brave!" I swat the air to keep his gifts at bay, but try as I might, the power already takes a hold in me. I fall 'cross a mountain of a rock. With the strength of a hundred men, I pick it up and throw it at Alfiu. "Glorious saints! What happens in this old man's body that, but a moment past, rattled with the weak bones of near fifty years?" I look to the north, far north, and far west to my Bronti. "An old man's body," I sob and throw myself 'cross the cold earth, "an old man's body that withered away in far-off caves where no holy Vincenza fed it or clothed it or soothed it in her bed."

Alfiu takes in a breath and blows out all what's inside him, a smoky, blue breath that throws me back to my cave and makes my legs light and strong. Strong, too, my eyes. So keen and strong they are now that in the deepest chamber of my cave, I eye the tasty grasshoppers, part grey, part green, of early spring. I leap to snatch them, five in all, and stuff them in my mouth. "What happens here?" I try to shout, but my mouth fills with the sounds of a wild dog.

Alfiu smiles at the mouth of the cave. "What happens, Muntagna? The power and nature of all the creatures of the wild."

"But I am still a man!" I rush at him and dig my wrist in the sharp edge of a rock. "Or am I?" The rank odor of blood fills the air. "Or am I?" I shake my wrist, the warm rank blood splashing on the rocks. "Take it, Alfiu, this strange demon blood and all your demon magic coursing through me!"

"Blessed gifts they are but not for the giving back." He grabs my wrist and mouths a prayer. The deep cut fades…but, more, slow, slow, my back hunches…and, more, slow, slow, the flesh on my feet and hands stretches thick and tight.

I try to stand straight and tall. "*Ahi! Ahi!*" I cry out, crouching low to the earth, restless, with a sudden urge to run. Like a mountain cat, quick and far I run, leaping 'cross jagged rocks with no pain and no mark of wounds or gashes.

I pound my chest, a strength and power in me like never before. "Good gifts," I shout with an ease in my breath that takes me by surprise, "but not for…"

"Use them," Alfiu whispers, him by my side once more. "Use them for the girl."

I slump on the earth. "Good gifts, Alfiu, but not for a coward."

"Muntagna, what got to frighten you now? There's none to fear but the Devil himself, and he stays in full sight 'though he wears the mask of a gentleman."

"Gentleman? There's but one place to eye a gentleman in Bronti…"

Alfiu makes a fist and opens his hand. There, in his ball of light, I see the Castle.

*Ppù! Ppù!* I spit on the earth. "Now, cousin, now it all comes to light. What you ached to do all those years ago, I got to do now. There he goes, they got to say, the coward of Bronti, storming the Castle, wielding his sword at the Duca of Bronti and piercing his heart. There the coward goes, they got to say, piercing the heart of a Nelson heir 'til he drains it clean of Nelson blood! But the coward, they got to say, piercing the Duca's heart? Never! they got to say." A low growl rises in my throat, "Alfiu, even if I wanted to… the Duca, he's back in his homeland. He left the Castle long ago."

"Not the Duca."

"Not the Duca? Who, then? The son?"

"Muntagna, we lose time. Soon, it will be light…"

I look up. The dark heavens are bare of stars and moonlight. Still, I see the smoky swell of clouds in the east. 'Cross the land, the shadows of mountains come in view. All what Alfiu says is true. Soon, it will be light.

"Muntagna, my time here comes to an end. Help the girl on her journey. Keep her safe from harm."

"And risk my own life…for…" I pounce on Alfiu and pass right through him and land flat on the earth. "Risk my own life for…the sake of a ghost!"

Alfiu makes a fist and opens his hand. There, in his palm in the small ball of light, I see the girl kneeling, a pistol at her chest. "Basta! Muntagna, your tongue twists and turns and puts off all what your body got to do. Give me your word before it's too late. Help…the…girl." His arms reach out to me. I cup my mouth at the sight of them, once dark and mighty, pale and limp they are now and fading far from view. He opens his mouth wide, but his voice is bare a whisper. I pull at my ear and take in all his blessings.

I shut my eyes and bless him, too, but when I open them, Alfiu is gone. The air is still and silent but for the shadows that dart from caves, creatures of the wild that, quick, come 'on me. They sniff and circle me. I show my teeth and circle them, too, me, the strong and swift and cunning one, the biggest beast they ever seen, with hair and beard now long white fur and hands and feet now sharp and clawed. They scatter, the lot of them, but a small hare, I am quick to snatch. Without a spit, without a knife, I pounce on him and fling him 'cross a rock. I hold him tight. His big, brown eyes fix on mine. His hind legs flutter in the air. When the trembling stops, these once robust legs hang lifeless on my chest. A good meal I'll have this night. A feast. And for such a feast, I got to thank Alfiu. I hear him still. Or is it the foreign wind I hear that blows my cousin's words back to earth? *Be brave…be brave.* I clasp my hands, if hands I call them still, and say a prayer for all his gifts. I shout out the prayer, more a promise than a prayer, but all what rises in my throat is a howl, loud like the foreign wind. "I give you my word," I howl. "Alfiu Saitta, I give you my word to keep the girl safe from harm!"

*Little and nothing go hand in hand.*

I race down the rugged mountain, leaving my lava cave and the world of an exiled man. Far in the distance, high on a rocky slope, I see two wolf pups biting and licking each other. In the grey of the morning, I see their Mamma, the grey and yellow and black of her coat. I hear the pups, their whimpers loud like thunder. I see the Papà, shining his teeth and standing straight and still while the others in the pack look down the rocky slope. I see them! I hear them! I smell them, too, the tender meat of a fox still on their breath. At such a distance, do they see me? If I am their early morning meal, they got to catch me first. They rush at me. They are swift. I am swifter, on two feet, on four. Quick, like a bolt of lightning, I reach Bronti. I turn 'round and laugh at the wolves with their tongues hanging, panting from the chase, and, me, like it's the Lord's Day, and I been resting all day, my tongue in my mouth, my breath calm and steady. Calm and steady, I crawl to the Saitta door.

I press my cheek on the splintered slats and eye the girl near the cooling ashes of the hearth. She sleeps on a black pig's belly, her arm resting on the marriage bed. What a sight they are, the small black pig and the girl, still like holy statues, and the Mamma in the marriage bed, ripping at the sheets. The three moaning, but the girl, deep in her dreams, she moans the loudest of all. "Mamma," she cries out, "see how I slash the Duca's throat!" She waves the phantom knife in the air, her small body shaking, her head pounding on the pig's belly 'til he wakes with a cry.

The girl, she wakes with a shudder. "*Sst…sst,*" her finger to her mouth, "be quiet or we wake Mamma." She crawls 'cross the small cottage to the sack on the wood table and tosses the squealing pig the last bit of ground-up wheat that his mouth catches before it reaches the earth. "See what you done," she whispers to the pig now that the sheets rustle on the marriage bed where the Mamma, in a fitful sleep, throws out a nest of curses and shakes herself awake. The girl whimpers and buries her face in the crook of her arm, all but her eyes she hides from view.

Pale eyes she got, pale eyes that give the evil eye. Quick, I turn away from those eyes, the shape of almonds, the color of gold, that cross her from Bronti to some magic world. Pale eyes, the kind that cast a spell on all that look 'on them like the pig that looks up, the Mamma, too, 'til the girl fixes her eyes on them, and the cottage falls silent.

She creeps to the door and pulls it open. I leap behind a pile of stones. "Bad girl I am to sleep so long," she whispers, pointing to the Star of Dawn that already lights the heavens. She rushes back inside and throws on a loose brown blouse, a brown-laced bodice, a full brown skirt and a long, brown apron folded like a sack at the waist. Dressed in the color of the earth, she sets about sweeping up ashes and piling old kindle in the hearth.

When she's done with the chores, she taps 'neath the marriage bed for her plaything of binding twigs. She kisses the small *limuni* head speared on a long, gnarled twig, a small lemon head now dried and spotted with the years. "Be a good daughter," she whispers and cradles the plaything back 'neath the Mamma's bed where it brushes a shawl and *u pisciaturi*, the brown clay pot filled with the night's wastes. She pulls the pot out from 'neath the bed, the fringes of the shawl tangled in its handle.

She taps her head and whips her legs with the fringes. "Bad girl I am to leave this cursed head uncovered!" She pulls at her hair, the loose braid tumbling down her back and on to the dirt floor. I jump back at the sight of all what Alfiu spared me in his ball of light, the girl, draped in brown, with eyes, the color of gold, and hair, long past her bare feet and red, red like the beautiful mountain's fire.

She makes a tight braid and covers her hair 'neath the heavy brown shawl and knots the shawl 'neath her chin. "Be good to Mamma," she whispers to the pig and pats his head. He races 'round the table, squealing for more ground-up wheat, his hunger cries stirring the Mamma 'til she throws off the sheets. I gaze at her face, and my own face burns with tears.

Agata, Alfiu's dear wife. Alfiu's mad wife, Agata. Where is the beauty now? *Bella, bella*, we called her on the day she married. Beautiful, beautiful Agata, our Agatuzza, with the long, dark curls and the brown, plump flesh. Who is she now? A mad woman of five and thirty years, with clumps of white hair that weigh down her rawboned shoulders, with swollen eyes and round, red knuckles. What is she now?

'Neath Agata's bed clothes, on the loose flesh of her belly, the girl folds two leaves of the rue plant, part blue, part green. "To calm the spasms, Mamma, and calm the head. Chew them even if they let out a stink. 'A z'a Vincenza says what's not pleasing to us can still do us good." She kisses her Mamma's brow. Agata slaps her face. "All loathe the smell of *ruta*," she whispers, grabbing tight to her Mamma's hands, "that's what 'a z'a Vincenza says. But, Mamma, who don't taste the cures? Sleep, Mamma, sleep. I'm your good daughter."

I let out a sigh, more a yip than a sigh, crouching behind a pile of stones, Alfiu's stones, for the bigger cottage and the bigger hearth he never built. The third night of August in the year eighteen hundred and sixty, Alfiu and me, we drank wine behind his stones. That was the night, desperate and drunk, he cursed Garibbaldi.

"Traitor of a general that gave us nothing and made pacts to protect the Castle and Nelson blood! So, here's what I say to Garibbaldi and his promise for the great united l'Italia!" And he ripped the scarves, the red and white and green scarves the lot of us waved, all with the general's likeness on them. "How long we got to wait to profit from the land? Come on, Muntagna, *amuninn'*! No Duca of Bronti and no Garibbaldi can stop us from taking back our land! Amuninn'! Amuninn'! Come on! Come on!"

he shouted, barreling through the roads of Bronti, spitting at the feet of lawyers, innkeepers, Notaries—all the men that wore the hats. *Hats* we called them. *Hats*, Bruntiszi through and through, that profited from their own deals with the Duca.

"*Vurimmu 'a terra*! We want the land! We want *our* land!" he shouted. "You there, wearing your fancy hats, give us back our land, so we can wear hats, too!" The third night of August in the year eighteen hundred and sixty, all the peasants raged with Alfiu, and their rage exploded in madness.

"Come on, Muntagna, amuninn'!" Alfiu shouted, rushing back to me. The church bells rang three times, the toll of the Agony. "Cousin," Alfiu shouted after each long, solemn knell, "are you brave and strong and a mountain of a man this night?" At the last knell, he picked up a knife and threw it at my feet. "A brave man always finds a weapon. It's what that traitor Garibbaldi preached. So, now, here's yours!"

I grabbed my belly and keeled over. I moaned that the wine was bad and crawled to my cottage and bed. I threw the pillow over my face that night, but, still, I choked on the bitter smoke of burning inns and cottages. I cupped my ears, but, still, I heard the swells of madness, the shrieks and cries of men that wore the hats when Alfiu and his kind ransacked their homes and ripped the rich men from their hiding places—the cupboards, beds and dung heaps. But the cheers, they were louder and more sorrowful than all the cries. They were the cheers of Alfiu and his kind when they set homes and men on fire and slit throats and reveled in the blood that spilled through all the roads of Bronti.

'Neath the sheets that August night, I was safe from peasant madness. 'Neath the sheets that night, I was a coward through and through.

I howl and hurl Alfiu's stones in the road, cursing them and that night of madness 'til the girl stumbles on the smallest stone and lets out a cry and shakes me from my dark thoughts.

"*Ahi!*" She rubs her feet and hoists the clay pot on her hip, holding tight to it now that the foreign wind picks up strength. How hot the gusts! How strong it blows! How far it journeyed from desert lands, whirling the dirt of the road up through the air and straight in the girl's eyes! Shielding them the best she can, and, her, near on her knees, she staggers through the neighborhood 'a Maronna ri Loretu, past the stone cottages that crowd one on the other, past the church and the square. "*Ahi*!" she cries out when her feet bleed on the steps stone cutters chiseled, then abandoned, when, like the wind, the Bronti council changed its course. "*Ahi*!" she cries 'til she stumbles on the last rugged step that takes her to Corsu Umbertu, the dirt road winding north and south and straight through the heart of the town.

South on Corsu Umbertu she staggers in the wind to the ditch where all peasant girls empty the night's wastes, pinching her nose now that the hot foreign wind blows with no mercy and throws the stench of the ditch back to the town. "No more! No more!" she cries out, but a mighty gust flings her to the ground.

"Leave me be!" She swats the thick, brown air and struggles to stand and steady u pisciaturi back on the flat of her small hip, but the pot slips and a murky wetness drips down her skirt. "Mamma," she turns 'round and 'round, sobbing, "how can I find my way in such darkness?"

I whimper and yip and bark. She flicks her head. Through the thick, brown air, she understands my speech, if speech I call it still. Soft and low to the south I whimper so she knows I mean no harm, but long and steady 'til she pushes herself up and knows where to follow.

In the thick, brown air on Corsu Umbertu, her eyes shine like tiny oil lamps, heeding my whimpers that lead her south, straight to the end of town. But what is this? The girl stops, with all the chores she got to do, the girl stands still, there, on the empty road, where peasant girls with dark hair soon got to gather on the way to the ditch and players soon got to take up their shiny horns and rehearse the march for the first of May. What can I do to keep her safe from the lot of them if she stands in the road like a holy statue?

What if the dark hair peasant girls see her? What if they look away and crook their finger at the girl with gold eyes and red hair and turn the evil eye back on her? What if their Mammas see their daughters running, and, quick, they look away and crook their fingers and turn the evil eye back on her? What can I do when they curse her 'neath their breath and the curse takes hold? Safe I got to keep her from all what got to do her harm. I got to howl like a wild dog, that's what I got to do, and frighten the lot of them away.

I ready myself to howl, but, for what? The girl's alone, still and silent. Caught in a spell, she gazes at the high hills of Bronti and the neighborhood Santu Vitu that rises up with a church and a square, the square where a firing squad stood rigid on the tenth day of August in the year eighteen hundred and sixty and Garibbaldi's lieutenant sat on his horse and shouted out the order, "*Caricate. Puntate. Fuoco.*"

*Fire…*

"Papà!" the girl cries out like she's there, in the square all those years ago before her own eyes seen the light of day. Like she's there and sees what the Bruntiszi seen, Alfiu, tried and punished for his madness, his body slumping to the ground. "A just eye for eye…Alfiu Saitta!" the girl shouts. But what is this? She turns her back on the foreign wind and climbs up the road. That's not where the ditch is. That's not where she got to do her chores. Up on Corsu Umbertu…that's where the wind drives her. North…where seeds of trouble grow.

"A just eye for eye!" Quick and steady she marches, her fist in the air, up Corsu Umbertu she marches and reaches the low lava road north and west of the town, the road the Bruntiszi peasants trudge in the dark of morning when they work the Duca's land.

When my Papà's Papà was but a boy, the foreign king built the low lava road and all the roads on our island, and all for none but his army. 'Round Bronti, such roads are none but paths with sharp inclines and bends. *Trazzere* we call them, mule tracks that none but a mule or a small cart travels on. The low road the girl marches on, it's a mule track with small mounds of lava, a road more rock than dirt, a road more abandoned than cleared, the low road that whispers, *This is all what the Bruntiszi merit.*

A loud noise shakes me from my thoughts. I turn 'round. The grey-green waters of *u Simetu* crash on shining rocks. How far the girl journeyed! I look up at the pale morning sky. How far she journeyed and how quick! Over the river noise, she shouts her farewells to the far-off town and marches to the end of the low lava road. At its end, the new carriage road with the smooth stones and mighty oaks stretches out before the girl.

*Old like an oak.* That's what the Bruntiszi say. But the oaks the Duca's men planted on this new carriage road, they're not old. "Bella, bella," she whispers like they're the most beautiful trees she ever seen. She steadies u pisciaturi back on her hip to take the first steps on the new carriage road, her bare feet, quick and nimble, soon gliding like sea birds over the smooth stones.

She races through the trees 'til she comes 'on a lone white flower near a small rock. But what is this? She crosses herself and yanks the flower from its home. "Little flower, know I mean you no harm. *Kill the small,* Mamma taught me, *'til you harden your heart to kill the big.*" She throws the flower on the ground and presses her toes in its heart. "And you are small, and I got to…I got to…"

No sooner the petals break free and scatter 'cross the smooth stones of the road that she runs after them, sobbing. She grabs for a small white petal. "Heartsick I am that I killed you," she whispers, "but I got to harden my heart…" She takes in a breath and spits at the petal. "Sì, harden my heart…" She makes a fist, opens her hand, her fingers spread wide and pointing straight up at the trees' crowns. "Harden my heart to kill the big!"

The leaves on all the oaks tremble. The warm morning light shines through.

She gazes up. "But how? But how?" she whispers.

Behind a thick trunk, I shudder. *But how?* I wonder, too.

"Grazii." She marches up the road, the light splashing on her small, thin face, and sings out a nonsense tune. "Grazii, Magic that makes my blood brave."

*Signori 'nglisi,* the English Gentlemen, they made the new carriage road for none but Castle folk, not for a peasant girl singing nonsense tunes and hoisting u pisciaturi high over her head and…and…what is this?…not for a peasant girl hurling the pot's wastes on the new carriage road. Glorious saints! A peasant's wastes on the road that leads to the Castle, the Castle where Nelson blood thrives!

"*Two are powerful,* you taught me, Mamma, *the one with everything and the one with nothing.*" The girl throws u pisciaturi far in the air, all what remains in the pot soaring and diving like small dark birds. "Take it, *Voscenza,* Your Excellency, Your *Great* Excellency. *Tè*! *Tè*! Take that and that and that! Take it all. It's all what Mamma and me got, and all what Mamma and me give you."

She stands brave and strong and shouts blessings to her Mamma and curses to the Duca and all the Nelson heirs to come 'til a mighty gust pegs her to the ground and buries her 'neath a rush of leaves. She shakes the leaves off and holds the shawl down the best she can, but the knot 'neath her chin breaks free. The shawl whips past her. From out of nowhere, magpies swoop down and aim their dark sleek heads at the red crown.

"Mammita!" She makes a fist, opens her hand and spreads her fingers wide. Quick, the birds lose interest in their booty and scatter back up to the sky. "But how? But how?" she whispers.

*But how?* I wonder, too.

"My shawl!"

The big, brown wings flap in the distance, the shawl, none but a trembling bird lost in flight. She runs for it and jumps for it, the wind blowing strong, her red hair flying 'round her. So strong the wind blows that I got to wrap my limbs 'round a young oak to keep my own self from soaring away. The girl, she looks for none to hold on to, the wind flinging her this way and that, her hands high to the heavens, reaching, with no good fortune, for the brown fringes. "Alfiu," I cry out, "help the girl!"

Quick, I say the prayer. Quick, Alfiu hears it. The oak trees cease to shed their leaves. The wind quiets down. The girl looks up, the shawl drifting to her open arms. She knots it tight 'neath her chin and races up the new carriage road, taking a breath but when she comes 'on an orchard of small fruit trees, their leaves covered with fine white hairs.

"Bella, bella. Beautiful, beautiful." Soon that she nears the smallest tree, a bud blossoms. She strokes the bud. It opens, and five fair petals fall in her palm. She taps the edges and folds the petals back in her palm, struggling to hold her fist tight. A small green fruit pushes through. She breathes 'cross her knuckles and, slow, slow, pries away her fingers. "But how? But how?" she whispers and eyes the fruit, part apple, part pear, turning yellow in her palm.

*But how?* I wonder, too.

She warms the fruit 'til it's soft to bite and stuffs it in her mouth, the yellow flesh hanging on her small teeth. She throws her head back, her palm wiping clean the mix of juice and dirt dripping down her neck.

She licks the sticky mix and shudders. She knows the taste of dirt. What peasant don't know? But the bitter sweet of fruit jolts her body, and the girl twirls 'round like the spider dancers 'til she falls in a bed of leaves. She scoops them up in the bones of her arms and flings the leaves with their fine white hairs back to the branches. "Mamma," she shouts and spits the yellow flesh of the fruit to the heavens, "*u cutugnu*! Mamma, u cutugnu!"

U cutugnu. I seen it in Alfiu's ball of light, the quince orchard near where the Duca's son takes his early walk. The fruit the girl warmed in her palm offers proof. U cutugnu…part apple, part pear…the fruit offers proof. This is the road. This is the orchard, bare of fruit 'til harvest time— or 'til the girl makes her magic. All the town knows. Now the girl knows if she stays on the road, she got to come 'on him, the Duca's son that stands tall and pale over his Papà's peasants and shares in their desire, or so he says, "for none more than a morsel of bread, a morning prayer and a day of hard labor."

"For you, Mamma." The girl rips open her blouse. There, on her chest, with nails sharp like her Mamma's, she scratches tiny crosses. "Blood for honor and blood for vengeance for the great Alfiu Saitta, my Papà! *U sangu vori u sangu*, the way you taught me, Mamma. Blood wants blood."

Far away in the town, I hear the brass band play a march from ancient times, a march to rally peasants against their foreign rulers, a march Alfiu heeded to his death. But this is the first of May, a day for celebration. And even if Alfiu lived to hear the horns this first of May, lived to take up the cry for justice and lived to arm himself with a knife and a fist or, now, like the peasants do, with papers shuffled like cards in court; even if he fought for what he always fought for, the forest and the farmland that was and is the right of all Bruntiszi, no fight waged against Nelson blood ever been won.

The Notaries see to that. They tighten the noose of taxes 'round the peasants' necks and wave old documents with raised gold seals and open their mouths wide to make their speeches in court. *Look, see, it is written and stamped and signed by the Bourbon king. Granted he's no more our king, but he gave this land to the hero Nelson, the first Duca of Bronti, and all entitled by Nelson blood.* That's how the fourth Duca of Bronti still holds all on our land. *Possessions*, he calls them, like the oak trees, the small orchard of fruit, the oranges from the fertile groves, the snow from the beautiful mountain, the brass band tunes, the peasants and the town. All possessions of the fourth Duca of Bronti and, when he dies, the son. And all ripe for one battle to change the tides of fortune.

North of the oak trees and the orchards, the girl readies herself for such a battle. North, she shoots past solemn rows of cypress trees that line the end of the new carriage road. At the last tree, she bows low and spits on the earth. She wields a phantom knife and cries out, "*Voscenza*, Your Excellency, your *Great* Excellency, this is what we say to your road. *Ppù! Ppù!* And this is what we say to your son. What you done to the brave Alfiu Saitta, now I do to you!" She beats her chest. "See, Mamma, see? I do all what's in our hearts! See? I *am* your good daughter!"

With a boom in her voice that got to surprise even her own self, she holds her hand high and shouts, "I take on the ways of our brave hero, Orlannu, the bravest knight in Carlu Magnu's court, conqueror of all infidels. And, me? I conquer you! You stand before me, *Voscenza*, Your Excellency, Your *Great* Excellency. I show you no mercy. On your knees, I show you no...I... show...you...no...*sst...sst...*" She puts her finger to her mouth and flicks her head. She crouches, the way brave men do when they ready themselves for the enemy.

I hear them, too, the enemy sounds deep in the earth that put an end to her brave speeches. So near! So loud! The pounding of hoof beats, a thousand of them! The Duca's horses all with the Duca's men astride. Come for the girl, and, me, behind the thickest tree, they got to find me, too. My legs too rigid to run, I howl, but the poundings mock me. "Alfiu!" I cry out. "Save me! Save me!"

Loud are my pleadings, but louder still is the roar of laughter that fills the air. Alfiu come to mock me, too! I look 'round for him and his mad ball of light, but all I hear is the laughter and all I see are four white feet that lap 'cross the earth. A lamb's feet...that's all what's on the road. None but a lamb rushing at the girl, wild strands of fleece flying in the air.

The lamb is young but already bears the mark of the island's breed. Her body hunches and a white tuft furrows down the middle of her long brown face. And, then, there are the eyes, the sad brown eyes that stare out from the edges of her face that all but brush her soft, lopped ears.

Some say the breed straddles two natures. When the Duca's son seen them on his first visit to our island, he was but a boy. "I want to ride a fine horse like that when I grow up," he told the Duca. When the Duca laughed that they were none but sheep, the boy said they wasn't right. Even the peasants say the breed's not right. On our island, there are breeds brought over from the Duca's land, the lot of them tended by the Duca's loyal shepherds. For this breed, there is but one shepherd. Of this breed, none but a few remain.

The Duca prizes the last of this kind. I seen it all in Alfiu's ball of light. Before the Duca left for Lundra, these were his parting words, "I take leave of you, my son, on this last day of June in the year eighteen hundred seventy-four. Obey my orders until Her Majesty releases me from all obligations in London." But the son, prizing the sheep more than the Papà done, he disobeyed the Duca the day he left and set them free, untying them from the solemn cypress trees where the Duca said "they serve as a prelude for our guests' amusements and curiosities at the manor.

This one has no Mamma. The Duca's men seen to that when, 'neath a starless sky, they tried to snatch the lamb. The ewe shook the suckling lamb free and pushed her behind a small grassy mound. In the dark, the Duca's men tripped and fell on each other. With their knives held high, they slashed each other. The ewe waited in silence. Her sorrowful eyes gazed out in the night 'til the Duca's men cried for vengeance.

They took turns slitting her throat.

The lamb bleated her cries. The hornless ram took it for a sign. Coward that he was, he raced to the highest hills and never showed his face again. The ewes stayed behind but did not suckle the lamb and did not love her.

Alfiu showed it all to me. I shudder when I bring it to mind, but the lamb, she flies up the new carriage road, clover brimming from her mouth, a creature free of all sorrows. A boy runs after her, wielding a long cane in the air, a boy of great height with bones of twenty years, no more, and dark, wet eyes and, 'neath his loose white shirt, a boy wanting for muscles.

The lamb rushes straight at the crouching girl, knocking her to the ground, the two, shaking and stunned. The boy, near out of breath, he sways over them, steadying the girl's pisciaturi in his arms. But what is this? He wears a long, brown stocking cap and presses the tail to his cheek. Glorious saints! If he's the boy I knew in Bronti, if he's the boy all grown that still bears the mark, then, he got much to hide. Five hunchback sheep circle him. He swings the cane over their heads and hits one of them. "Forgive me," he whispers and slaps his own thigh to make amends.

"Grazii for my lamb," he says to the girl, his voice low, his eyes to the earth.

The girl eyes u pisciaturi and grabs it from his hold.

"It's yours?"

She nods.

"Good fortune shines on you this day. I found it past the oak trees. When do my sheep ever seek food or comfort on the Duca's road? But the lamb this day, she broke free of the others and up the Duca's road she ran." He sweeps the lamb up and cradles her shaking body in his arms. "I got no life without her," his sleeve soaks up the last of his tears, "and she got no life without me. I couldn't protect her Mamma, but I got to protect her. The other sheep don't want nothing to do with her. They cast her aside for no good cause…so, I got to be like her Papà. See? I been chasing her all over, and, now, good fortune shines on me. But look at her. She wants the liberty 'til she tastes it. She's like all of us, we want what brings us joy, and, then, we come near to all what we want, and it don't bring us joy…"

The girl tightens the knot 'neath her chin and crawls past the hunchback sheep, her brow near scraping the ground. The sheep gaze in her eyes, and, one by one, they smile, I swear on my eyes, they smile, joyful to be near her. She tries to pull herself up, but they circle her, nuzzling her cheeks, nibbling at her shawl and pulling it down with each small bite.

"No!" She pushes them back. They bleat loud and wild and race 'round the boy 'til their white feet tangle in the legs of his loose brown pants.

The girl struggles to her feet. "I'm in your debt," the boy calls out. She flies down the road past the solemn cypress trees and the orchard and the oak trees 'til she reaches the low lava road, u pisciaturi clanging on the rocks.

*A house without a man is a house without a name.*

I wait for the girl at the Saitta cottage behind Alfiu's pile of stones. In my mind's eye, I see my own cottage, and small that it was, it was a castle with Vincenza by my side.

Always three days past the Lord's Day, I'd wake from happy dreams to Vincenza standing over me. "Pretty dreams you dream this night," she'd whisper. "Va ben' that you dream. But me? I got no time for pretty dreams." With a stick in her hand, she'd beat the casings of the mattress 'round my legs. "It's your doing that I got to fuss with all this work. You, with your big muscles, you flatten the straw and cloth out like bread before it rises." She'd squeeze her lips in a small *o*, holding back a smile the best she could, and I'd feel the warmth of pride course through me.

"I know what you tell the others," I'd say leaping out of bed and throwing my arms 'round her thick waist. "This is what you say: *I swear on my eyes, with all I got to do, I got to beat the casings harder and harder each week, but what do you expect, cummari? No maritu is so strong as mine.* Vincenzina, is this not what you sigh to all the Bruntiszi wives?"

She'd shake her head and throw out her cheek and wait for a kiss. "Now, get an early start," she'd say out of breath and near burst from joy when she'd turn the mattress over and eye all what my strength and bulk flattened out. Such a chore she done, such a joy she held in her heart, like all Bruntiszi wives, three days past the Lord's Day when all dreams of the night come true. But where is Agata Saitta's chore? Where is her joy?

The girl opens the door. Agata rocks in her marriage bed, her red swollen lids jutting out from the sheets. Rest, Agata, Rest. There's no cause for you to rise early no more and turn a mattress or beat the casings or make a pretty bed with sheets of fine spun linen and threadwork of clover and crosses. What good do they serve you now? Bunched at the foot of the bed is all your handiwork—the linens of your dowry and the pillows you stuffed on your marriage day.

You seen to it all that day, and so did Alfiu with the beams and boards he nailed and the trestle he built to make your bed on the day you married. One to the other is what we said of you, two broad beans grown together on the same vine. And, now, what would you give, Agata, to beat the casings and turn the mattress, but one more time?

The girl stands at the threshold, her hand gripping the latch. She brushes the lamb's feast of clover from her skirt, crosses herself and steps inside. She throws kisses to the wood cross hanging over the bed, the cross I carved for the Saitta marriage. In the bed, her Mamma pounds the mattress. "Be still, Mamma," the girl whispers. "Be still and rest."

"Where is the print of your muscles?" Agata cries out. "Where is the smell of oak on your broad, beautiful chest? Where is your deep, strong voice that prays to Santu Giuseppi to keep our household safe from harm? Safe from harm, Alfiu, my ruler, my life! Safe from harm!"

The girl strokes her Mamma's face. "Be still, Mamma, no dream can undo the past."

Like the blood of all the grieving, Agata Saitta's blood courses with regrets. If Alfiu paid mind to his head and not his heart; if he tended the lava soil like a patient man and not fought for a piece of the Duca's fertile land; if he wore a cap with a long tail to cover his face, the kind Agata knitted for the shepherd boy; if Alfiu's shirt not been stained with the blood of the Duca's Notary; if all that, then, three days past the Lord's Day, Agata Saitta, like all good Bruntiszi wives, would beat the casings and turn the mattress, and all her dreams would come true.

And she'd rise early with her *maritu* before he labored on the Duca's land. And they'd work their own lands and dig near lava rocks, there, where none ought to grow. And they'd graft branches and plant trees, the way she done when she was a young bride. And she'd wait with her maritu ten years for the trees to bear their fruit, and if it took five years more, she'd not lose patience. In time, the red husk would give way to white and, inside the husk, the shell, and, inside the shell, wrapped in purple skin, the green nut would issue forth, the color of a king's bright jewel. These were Alfiu's dreams. Agata's, too. Poor, sorrowful Agata. Like all that grieve, Agata Saitta now dreams to undo the past, and that is the well of all her sorrows.

"Rest, Mamma, rest." The girl presses down the Mamma's bed clothes and slides u pisciaturi 'neath the bed near her plaything of binding twigs that Vincenza made when the girl was but a child. I seen it all in Alfiu's ball of light, the way Vincenza bound the twigs and sewn the dress of blue cloth and tied a crisp white apron 'round it and whispered "bella, bella," when she speared the lemon head on the long, gnarled twig 'til the girl whispered it was beautiful, too.

The girl cradles her plaything and sings a lullaby. "*Figghia mia,* I am your Mamma, and you are my good daughter." She throws old branches in the hearth and lights the fire. "Warm yourself by the fire but stay clear of it. A good Mamma got to keep her daughter safe from harm. A good Mamma…got to…*love* her daughter."

Agata waves her arms in the air and swats away the girl's lullaby, singing out her own song. "*Figghia ru diavulu…*" Soon that her Mamma whispers the words, the girl crosses herself and lets down the folds of her apron, the plaything hiding 'neath it. "Figghia ru diavulu…" Daughter of the Devil. Such a cruel song Agata sings. With a voice that crackles like old wood in a fire, she fills the air with her hateful song.

I howl to shake Agata from her poison spell. Captive in her dark ways, she breathes no fear. But the girl, she shudders at the sounds of a wild dog so near the cottage. She crouches 'neath the table, her plaything breaking free and rolling on the hard dirt floor. "Z'a Vincenza," she whispers, her hands clasped in prayer, "help me keep Mamma safe from the creatures of the wild."

"Figghia ru diavulu…daughter of the Devil…figghia ru diavulu!" Agata cries out.

"And, ppi piaciri, z'a Vincenza, help me keep Mamma's curses at bay."

The foreign wind flings the door wide open and whirls Agata's words through the dark cottage. When the stone walls can no more hold them, they fly in the air like the stench of u pisciaturi straight to all the cottages of Bronti where now all got to know what the daughter is. But, Alfiu, good, kind Alfiu, the Papà she knows through her Mamma's dreams, brave Alfiu that wielded his knife like the hero Orlannu wielded his sword. Alfiu, the clever one. Alfiu, the mad, senseless one. *He* is her Papà. And *he* is not the Devil.

The girl crawls back to the hearth and reaches for her Mamma's hand. "No, Mamma, I been good, and good's not the sign of the Devil. I done good for you, Mamma. I been on the road to the Castle. Ppi piaciri, say I been good."

Agata paid no mind to the howling, but at the sound of the word *Castle,* she opens her eyes wide, like a sick one healed with prayers and blessings. She takes in the hearth, the black walls, the dirt floor, the thick knotted branches where the aprons and bed clothes hang. She takes in the cupboard, the small jug of olive oil and the small bowl of salt behind the tin plate, the tin cup, the wood fork, the wood spoon. She takes in the loom where she wove her marriage dress. And she takes in the marriage chest Alfiu carved, there, at the foot of the bed where Agata's marriage dress and Alfiu's marriage vest tangle 'neath a bloody shirt. And, then, she eyes her daughter. She turns away and crooks her finger. She pulls at her white clumps of hair and waves them at the girl.

"Cover yourself, girl!"

"Mamma, I been there, on the Duca's road. I threw the pot high in the air, and I cursed him…on his road, I cursed him for you."

"Cover yourself and hide what's got to be hidden."

"I done it for you."

"You wear the Devil's color in your hair, but, wait…he got to come for his fox soon enough. Fire to fire, blood to blood, blood that got to pour out of you. When it does, he got to call you home and make you his bride. And I got to be rid of you for good."

"Mamma, look. See? I hide all what got to be hidden." She wipes the wet from her cheeks with the fringes of her shawl and tightens the knot 'neath her chin.

"You're of his blood and his nature."

"I been on the road. I done all what you asked of me."

"You're not one of us."

"'A z'a Vincenza says…"

"*His* blood! *His* nature!"

The girl hides her face in her hands. "But 'a z'a Vincenza says…"

Vincenza, my Vincenza, with the soft, round face and the hands that hold the secrets of the plants. Vincenza with the soothing voice that needs no foreign wind to carry its sweetness through the land and reach the hardest hearts. My Vincenza. Who is to say, if she'll bring the neighbors Saitta her brown bread and broad beans, and, who is to say, if this day, Agata will sit at the table and call for her daughter to sit by her side.

"Who's the one you call *Mamma*, the coward's wife or me?" Agata presses her lips tight and waits for the girl to bow her head. "*Ven aca*, girl. Come close." With her round, red knuckles, she tucks a strand of hair back 'neath the girl's shawl, her hand falling on her daughter's cheek.

The girl shudders. So strong and wild are the shudders that more strands fall 'cross her face. Agata's knuckles tuck them in. "*Nanna ninna ninna… nanna ninna ninna,*" she sings a soft lullaby. The girl throws her hand over the smile spreading 'cross her face and shakes her head. Again, the strands fall. Again, Agata tucks them in. Again and again, the girl's head shakes; again and again, the Mamma's knuckles tuck in the loose strands, the two in their quiet dance 'til Agata slaps her own face and frees herself of the tenderness. She reaches 'neath the pillow and eases the knife off the bed and drops it in the lap of the kneeling girl while she sings soft a new lullaby. "*Nanna ninna ninna…a just eye for eye….Ninna nanna ninna…kill the small 'til you harden your heart to kill the big.*"

"Mamma, no!"

"This day's a good day, sì?"

The girl takes in a breath. "Sì…Mamma."

"Figghia mia?"

"Mamma!" The girl throws her body 'cross the sheets, her face bright, the knife falling to the ground. "Sì, Mamma, I *am* your figghia. I *am* your good figghia."

"You reach the age this day, sì?"

"I reach the age in years."

"Ten years?"

"And six more. But 'a z'a Vincenza says I'm still a child."

"The coward's wife! She got to come soon." She points at the small black pig curled by the fire. "Kill him!"

"Mamma, no!"

"Kill the small 'til you harden your heart to kill the big."

"Ppi piaciri! Please!"

"Kill the pig!"

"But he's my friend."

"Friend? You got no friend, not man, not beast." Agata leaps from her bed and kicks the plaything on the dirt floor. She grabs it by its lemon head and rips the dried fruit from the long, gnarled twig and waves the body of binding twigs at the girl. "*This*, this is your friend?" She hurls it in the fire where its arms and legs and blue marriage dress crackle and curl in the sharp flames. "Where is your *friend* now?" The girl shakes her head, her eyes fixed on the fire. "Gone, that's where. Now, there's no more friend to rattle the hatred inside you. Where did it go, girl? The hatred for the one that killed the great Alfiu Saitta?"

"It's in me," the girl whispers, her body trembling. "Mamma, I swear on my eyes, it's in me."

"I see the teacher got to make her lesson again. So, girl, who killed the great Alfiu Saitta?"

"The Duca, that's what you told me. And all what you spoke, I took for truth and buried what 'a z'a Vincenza told me long ago. But this morning, I brought to mind all what 'a z'a Vincenza told me of the lieutenant in Garibbaldi's army that came to Bronti and brought the rebels to trial and, this morning, I gazed up at the neighborhood Santu Vitu where he gave the orders, where 'a z'a Vincenza said Papà was…"

Agata spits on the dirt floor, hissing out her curses. "If the coward's wife fills your heart with one more lie about the great Alfiu Saitta, I'll kill her!"

"No, Mamma!"

"I'll kill her!"

"No! 'A z'a Vincenza was wrong to tell such a lie. You spoke the truth. You said the Duca killed the great Alfiu Saitta in the Castle, and he done it. Mamma, he done it. Not no lieutenant. It was the Duca. The Duca, Mamma."

"Wheeere?" Agata stammers.

"Don't do no harm to 'a z'a Vincenza," the girl whispers.

"Wheeere?"

"Where you told me, Mamma. He killed the great Alfiu Saitta in the Castle. In the Castle!"

"Va ben'. Va ben'. And what rattles your hatred now?"

"None rattles it, Mamma. It's in my heart, good and pure, all the hatred for the Duca and the Castle."

"It got to beat in you strong like a great longing. If it don't, you show your Mamma the hatred you spare the pig."

"No, Mamma, no!" The girl takes the knife and waves it 'neath Agata's eyes. "I swear on my eyes, no! Mamma, if you ask me to hate the pig, I got to hate him. If you ask me to…"

"Figghia mia…"

"Figghia mia, figghia mia. These are the bright words that shine in my heart. Sì, Mamma…I am your daughter…your good…"

"Kill him! The pig was sick. You made him strong. When the one that heals is the one that betrays, then and only then is vengeance pure."

"…then and only then is vengeance pure." The girl tucks the knife 'neath the waist of her apron and sneaks up on the pig. She lets out a gasp like the ones the dying make when they fight with quick, hard breaths to stay on the earth. "Forgive me," she whispers to the pig. He squeals at the gold eyes shining down on him and races out the open door.

The girl rushes after him. There he is but past the threshold. I swear on my eyes, he waits for her. She kneels and taps her lap. He curls in it. She crosses herself and raises the knife high. "Forgive me," she whispers. With eyes to the heavens, she stabs the pig and makes a cut on the low side of his rump. The pig flies from the girl's lap and races 'round and 'round, squealing his tale of betrayal and trust. "Forgive me," she whispers and throws the knife down. "Forgive me," and makes a fist. She opens her hand and spreads her fingers wide. "Magic, heal the pig! Heal the pig!" She grabs her belly and crouches in the road. There, in the dirt road, sobbing, she opens her mouth and throws out the bitter and sweet juice of the orchard fruit, part apple, part pear.

*

"Done?"

The girl kicks the door and crawls to her Mamma. She nods and holds out the bloody knife, the new stains mixed with the old.

"Sì, figghia mia, well done. Wipe your eyes and sit by my side. Now, you'll hear a tale of a figghia that wasn't good like you."

"Once there was a woman that had no figghia. She prayed to 'a Maronna 'a Nunziata for a good figghia, if not of flesh and blood, then of clay, that she could call her own. 'A Maronna 'a Nunziata heard her prayers, and a brown clay pisciaturi fell in the woman's lap. This was the child that the woman longed for. She was filled with joy and took u pisciaturi everywhere she went.

"Her neighbors invited her to their children's marriage celebration, and she brought u pisciaturi with her. The young boy and girl were from wealthy parents. The food was plentiful. At the sight of u pisciaturi, the guests could eat no more. The Mamma of the boy pleaded with the woman to hide u pisciaturi from sight. The woman took u pisciaturi to the young couple's room and put it on the marriage chest, then went about the business of enjoying herself at the celebration. U pisciaturi stayed on the chest 'til the bride came in. The young girl took off all her jewels. One by one, the rings and bracelets clinked inside the belly of u pisciaturi 'til the pot could hold no more. When the couple fell to sleep, u pisciaturi jumped out the window and came running home.

"'Mamma, open the door. Look all what I brought you!' The woman sat down. U pisciaturi poured out all the jewels.

"'Figghia mia,' the Mamma cried, 'such a good daughter! Now, go back and bring me more fine gifts.'

"And, so, u pisciaturi went back to the couple's room. This time the young married boy put u pisciaturi 'neath the marriage bed where it served him well through the night for he ate much food and drank much wine. In the morning, u pisciaturi's belly could hold no more, and, so, the pot jumped out the window and came running home.

"'Mamma, open the door. Look all what I brought you!'

"The woman opened the door and sat down and tapped her apron. U pisciaturi jumped up and poured the gifts in the Mamma's lap.

"At the sight of her apron filled with all what the boy emptied in the pot, the woman shouted the curses of the Devil and flung the brown clay pisciaturi out the door. 'Out, pisciaturi! Out! From this day, I have no more figghia!'"

Vincenza told me the tale a hundred times and more, holding out my hands, pouring the phantom booty in my palms, throwing out her legs and rocking side to side, laughing that she was u pisciaturi waddling down the road. Who can say how many times Vincenza told the tale to the girl? But Agata's tale, it's not Vincenza's joyous one. With no smile on her face, she shaped the tale to suit herself. "I have no more figghia! I have no more figghia!" Again and again, she shouts out the words, so loud that me and the girl got to cup our ears to deaden the sound of them.

"Mamma, I got to be your good daughter… your good figghia."

"Figghia mia," the Mamma whispers and rocks the girl in her arms.

*A bird in the cage sings not from love but rage.*

I hear the brass band play a slow and solemn march high on Corsu Umbertu. I see the red, white and green flag that united l'Italia for good and bad and the large chipped statue of 'a Maronna 'a Nunziata on a platform that men with broad chests balance on their shoulders. Patri Radici leads the procession and whispers prayers from the Sacred Book. The peasants and their noisy bellies follow him. I hear them. I see them. And…what is this? I smell *finucchina* leaves and hot baked bread. Glorious saints, I see her! I see her with the leaves in her hand and the bread in her basket! I see her! Grazii, Alfiu, grazii! Gifts to help the girl you give me, but gifts that serve me, too. I see her! I see my Vincenza shutting our cottage door, making her way down via Grisley and taking in a breath on each stone step 'til she reaches Corsu Umbertu where the flag and the statue and the priest and the peasants pass her by.

The procession passes winding roads that jut off from Corsu Umbertu. Blessed and protected by neighborhood shrines, these roads open up to courtyards huddled far from view. On one of these roads, east of Corsu Umbertu, there, on via Leanza, Vincenza turns off. My head spins. My chest pounds. So close to me she is now, passing 'neath the low, round archway of the neighborhood 'a Maronna ri Loretu.

'Neath the archway, Vincenza leans on the small shrine cut in the stone. She kisses her fingers and squeezes them up through the iron grill past the flowers to pat the statue's feet. She stops at the first cottage in the courtyard, crosses herself and opens the door. Through a mouth of chipped dark teeth, she smiles at Agata and the girl. The small black pig runs through her full legs, tips the basket in her arms and rushes to the straw near the hearth where he curls, sleepy and healed. There, the fire blazes. There, on a stool, Agata rocks her daughter, eyes the pig and, quick, pushes the girl to the dirt floor. "Figghia ru diavulu!"

"No, Mamma! I'm not *his*…"

"Help me to bed," she crooks her finger at the girl, "or does the Mamma ask so much of the daughter?"

"I do all what you ask of me."

"*Zzu, zzu!*" Vincenza pushes the door wide open and sweeps away a swarm of pigs. "*Maronna mia!*" Her thick fingers wedge in the slats of the wood door. She yanks her finger free and kisses the small gold band of a marriage ring. "*Si biniric'*," she says near out of breath.

Agata twists the sheet in her mouth, smiling when no blessing breaks through.

"Si biniric', z'a Vincenza," the girl whispers back. On hands and knees, slow, slow, she makes her way to the young finucchina leaves that brush Vincenza's full black skirt. The girl spreads her fingers, and the smell of blood and fruit, part apple, part pear, fills the cottage. *A finucchina washes clean the body stench.* Always Vincenza said that of the fennel. The girl reaches for the sprig of bright feather leaves, but Vincenza grabs the small fingers and holds them tight in the air 'til the girl lets out a cry.

"The greens won't wash clean what fills the cottage. The smell of the Duca's orchard and the smell of blood, they hold to your hands like death in a room." She squeezes the girl's fingers and lays hard kisses on them. "You begin to learn the gifts in your hands, sì? But what do you use them for? To satisfy your own longings."

Vincenza tears off a small sprig and puts it in the girl's hand. "No, z'a Vincenza," the girl rubs it on the tips of her fingers, "they are not *all* my longings."

"All what I teach you…and how do you live the lessons? You do things… you go places…"

"*Things…places…z'a* Vincenza, you know where I go. And you know what I got to do. I am the feeble servant that fails to do the bidding of her lady. But I will. I got to!" She kisses the hem of Agata's bed clothes. "Mammita, forgive me."

Agata smiles and spits.

Vincenza rushes to the bed and wipes the spittle running down Agata's neck. "Cousin, basta! You make the child sick with all your carryings on. No, do not turn from me. No more of this. Now, get up and let me dress you."

Agata crawls to the foot of the bed, not like a playful *buttana*, the kind what rubs her chest and spreads her thighs and kneels by the river's edge where she waits for traveling merchants and their coins. Her nails scratch and tear at the sheets. From the look in her eyes, all what she wants got none to do with joy.

"Basta! Enough and enough and enough!" Vincenza breathes hard. Eye to eye, brow to brow, she whispers to Agata. "Cousin, heed my words. We got to dress you. You don't take joy in a feast for the first of May? Va ben', we don't make a feast for the good of the spring, and we don't share in the Nelson bounty. But we got to make a feast for the girl."

"Feast?" Agata spits again. "For the one that brings me shame?"

"Basta! She's a good girl and brings no more shame than you or me."

"Look at her! She longs for the Devil. She heals, but when does she betray? Where is my daughter? Here! Here!" She cups her palm 'neath her eye. In the tears she gathers, she makes tiny crosses and rubs them on her belly like a sacred oil. "Here! Here's where she is. Here, in my belly…the little what remains of her!"

"Agata!"

"I had but one daughter…one daughter. What the Devil left me, what *he* left me, I got no use for!"

Vincenza cups the girl's ears. "Child, say the prayers I taught you. Keep your Mamma's words at bay. Throw them back to the wind, but do not let them fill your heart." She pushes a wide mouth jug near the girl's feet and wipes the girl's eyes. "Now, bring us water from the beautiful mountain, and let this be an end to all your broodings."

"Z'a Vincenza, it's too late to go to Mungibellu."

"Sì, the sun already shines, but that's no cause for worry. The field guards don't stand watch this day. They're in town for the feast, ready to snatch food from a peasant's plate and fill their bellies with all what the Duca offers us this day. Child, worry about the field guards on the morrow."

"Va ben', Z'a Vincenza, but if you need the water quick, I can go to the fountains and..."

"No, child. Heed my words: *The end of the journey for our neighbor is but a resting place for us.* Our neighbors fetch water at the fountains in the squares. And, that, for them, marks the end of their journey. How many times I got to tell you? There, the water's warm and heavy, and it breeds a poison none can see or taste. Go farther than the fountains. My child, you got to journey to the beautiful mountain for the pure water. It's the only way we'll keep the sickness from your Mamma's home. Heed my words: *None but pure water got to enter the home.* Now, go. Your Mamma and me, we got to speak of things."

"Things, z'a Vincenza? Things I done bad?"

"No, child, things your Mamma done, and things she got to do."

"She's sick, and you taught me we got to turn a blind eye to all things she done in sickness."

"Sì, child, she's sick with too much grief. She mourns, but it's long past the hour of grief. Soon enough her eyes got to dry, and, then, none got to seek her out, and, then, where are the coins? And what becomes of her and what becomes of you? Now, go, child...your Mamma and me, we got to speak."

*

Vincenza nears the marriage bed. She holds out her hand. Slow, slow, she strokes Agata's cheek. "Dear cousin, look at me. You got to shake the grief off, and, when you do, you got to find new ways to earn for you and the girl. How do you pass your days and nights? You sleep, you grieve, and when a feeble strength courses in you, you leave your daughter's side and roam the roads in threadbare clothes to find a cottage in mourning. And, there, the grieving welcome you, and you weep for all what died, and you weep for the living. How much more can you weep?"

Vincenza speaks the shameful truth. Long ago, I seen it in Alfiu's ball of light. The girl was but a child when the shadow of a bird flew in Agata's eyes. Vincenza took it for a sign. There, in the young widow's black eyes, Vincenza seen a magpie with a withered heart. Vincenza said it was the sign of all the sorrows buried deep in Agata's heart. And when the sorrows showed themselves, Vincenza said that was a good sign, for, soon, the sorrows had no means but to wither and die.

"What do you know of sorrows?" Agata shouted at Vincenza. That was when she eyed her small child with the bright red hair stroking the plaything of binding twigs. "Like the Devil, like the Devil!" she shouted and spat on the earth. She grabbed a heavy brown shawl and wrapped the child's hair in it. "More like the Devil each day." She pushed the child away and crooked her finger. "Evil! Evil that's what she is! With eyes that give the evil eye!" That's when Vincenza kissed the child's brow. That's when her smoky breath near whispered out the child's name.

Agata seen the tenderness and threw herself on Vincenza and slapped her lips. She snatched the plaything from the screaming child and hurled it at the pig hiding 'neath the table. "The Devil's child got our souls to play with. She got no more need of playthings. And I got no more need of you!" With that, she pushed Vincenza out the door. "Say her name? You gave your word. And I gave mine. Say her name, and I'll do all what I said I would." That was the one time Vincenza stayed away for days. And, Agata, she crouched by the hearth for near as long, gazing at the fire, her eyes swollen with tears.

It wasn't the way Vincenza said it'd be. I seen it all in Alfiu's ball of light. When the shadow of a magpie flew in Agata's eyes, her sorrows didn't wither and die. They turned to madness. The young widow threw off her work at the loom and paid no more mind to the loom or the chickens or the eggs or any earnings she ever hoped to gain. In time, Vincenza brought food, all what she could, and taught the child prayers and the secrets of the plants, all what she could, Vincenza, her own good self still sick with sorrow.

The seasons passed, and Agata Saitta grew pale and thin and cried and cursed day to night 'til one winter's night an innkeeper took notice of the widow wandering through the dark roads, pulling at her hair and wailing, the cross-eyed lunatic of Bronti by her side. The innkeeper brought her home to a big room where chairs with seats of rope from wild agave lined the walls. There, his Papà's lifeless body lay. And, there, all the mourners seen Agata Saitta throw her own body on the ground and cry and curse and rip at her hair. Late that night, the innkeeper gave her three shining coins.

And, soon, when death came to their cottages, the Bruntiszi sought her out, the young widow with swollen eyes wailing *u reputu* at the bedside of the rich and the poor, the young widow, with bones of bare twenty years, white-haired and sorrowful, the great mourner of Bronti.

*

"Weep no more for strangers or for your own self," Vincenza whispers and kisses Agata's hands. "The past cannot be undone. Bless the living. Bless the girl."

"Bless the girl?" Agata leaps from her bed and tightens her fingers 'round Vincenza's throat. I bark and shriek, but she pays me no mind. "Figghia ru diavulu. The child of the Devil lies with the Devil!" She shakes Vincenza 'til my Vincenza falls. "Where are the blessings? Where is the joy?" She grabs the knife with the fresh blood of the pig shining on the blade. "Here! Here is the joy!" She spits on Vincenza, an act so cruel and vile I can take no more.

*Keep the girl safe from harm,* that was all what Alfiu pleaded. But what of my Vincenza? I got to keep her safe, too. I leap up on the low roof of the cottage and howl like a wild dog to shake Agata from her madness. Vincenza lets out a cry, but, Agata, she lets out a laugh and her own mad howl. I leap back down on the road. "Get out, Vincenza!" Agata grabs Vincenza's face and buries her nails deep in her cheeks.

I lunge behind the pile of stones and hurl the lot of them at nearby cottages. Such a loud ruckus I make, but I don't care who hears or sees me. I ready myself to storm the cottage and tear the widow limb from limb, grieving or not, cousin or not, but Vincenza, she crosses herself, and, quick, in a spell, the anger eases out of me. In calm, I watch the fire spread 'cross Vincenza's face and watch the flesh rise like small, plump cakes and watch her stroke and soothe her cheeks the best she can.

"Agata, I'm not going home."

Agata points to Vincenza's cheeks and lets out a soft cry. "What did you do, Vincenza?"

Vincenza shakes her head.

"Me? What I done? Vincenza, no! I done what the Devil made me do… what the Devil made me do…" She strokes Vincenza's cheeks and plies them with small kisses. "All what the Devil made me do time and again…"

"Agata, calma, calma. Heed my words. Your maritu and my maritu, they were cousins," she pats her swollen cheeks, "we got to forgive all what we do to each other."

"Forgive? Before you speak, Vincenza, chew on your words."

*

How long I watched Agata and Vincenza, who can say? Unshielded near the Saitta cottage now, I pay no mind to the peasants rushing at me, my Bruntiszi that eye me for the beast I become and the beast they got to kill. They throw rocks at me and wave knives in the air. A jagged rock hits me in the chest. Now that I am down, a few brave peasants slash at my legs. "Alfiu, Alfiu!" I howl. With that, the peasants grab one to the other. I howl again and watch them run like scared rabbits back to their cottages. Me? I limp away alone on the road and hide near my own cottage in via Grisley behind a pile of rubble where small black pigs rummage for food.

I ache to go inside and sleep in my bed and wait for my Vincenza. My body is heavy with sleep, but it hurts to sleep, and it hurts to stay awake. 'Though, quick, Alfiu healed the wounds on my leg, it hurts to touch these legs, these arms, this new body of a man that's now no more a man. It hurts but not from pain. I reach out and touch the stones of the cottage I once called my home. It hurts to be so near to my Vincenza and, still, so far.

And the foreign wind hurts, too. It picks up strength, throws me in its thick brown sack of air and flings me here, there, all the way to the west of Corsu Umbertu, and, I swear on my eyes, it calls out my name. "Leave me be!" I shout, but a gust blows me near a fountain where dark hair peasant girls fill up their jugs. A deep laugh trails away, and I know this is all Alfiu's doings. Behind a cottage I hide and wait for the girl while the dark hair peasant girls tell their tale of the shepherd boy and his brown stocking cap and their tale of the cross-eyed lunatic and his Lady of the Castle.

How loud they tell the tales 'til the girl nears and they fall to silence, turning away and crooking their fingers to hold off the evil eye. But with their eyes to the earth, they still turn this way and that to show the girl their bright spring colors for the first of May, their red skirts and green blouses and yellow shawls. They cross themselves the way their Mammas taught them and give the girl their blessings to weaken the evil eye.

But the girl don't give back the blessings or wave her shawl in the air. What's there for the girl to show off? Her brown skirt, her brown apron, her heavy brown shawl? She keeps her head down and presses her lips tight like her Mamma when she holds back her blessings.

The young peasant girl with burnt fingers that tried to hug the fire in the hearth when she was but a child, so happy she was to be warm that winter night, she's the one that whispers first. "If the fox don't give God's blessings, *His* are not the blessings the fox desires." The girl tightens the knot 'neath her chin, lowers her head and creeps past the peasant girl with burnt fingers and all her friends. "Well, now we know," the one with burnt fingers lets out a laugh, "a fox don't fetch water. If she got no chores to do this day, does she got time to hear the tale of how she become a fox?" The others giggle. "Amuninn'!" the one with burnt fingers shouts to her friends. "Come on!" And, soon, all the dark hair peasant girls put to the side their chores and run after the girl while the one with burnt fingers shouts out the tale of the fox.

*

"When the one-eyed monster slept and the Bruntiszi crowded on the road to watch Mungibellu's black smoke and shooting flames, when the forest animals screeched and wailed and rushed from their homes and flooded the town and slipped through open doors, when a small red creature found shelter by a marriage bed where a hammock hung and a baby slept, when the baby with long, black curls waved her hand and the small red creature leapt on the marriage bed and licked the baby's hand, when the baby giggled and the creature slipped in the hammock and licked the baby's lips, that's when the miracle happened. 'A Maronna 'a Nunziata wakened the one-eyed monster that roams in Mungibellu, and he snatched the fire from the beautiful mountain's throat and cradled it back to her belly. The town was spared, and the peasants made their way back to the cottages.

"When the Mamma crossed the threshold, the small red creature fled. She rushed to the hammock and, falling to the ground, the Mamma cursed the creature and wailed her mourning cries, for what she once cradled in her arms was no more. There, the baby lay, happy and giggling, but with gold eyes and sleek red hair flowing down her back like Mungibellu's fire."

*

Who can say how much of the tale the girl heard? The dark hair peasant girls ran after her taking turns telling the tale of the fox, but soon grew tired of their cruel chase and made their way back to the fountain, giggling and telling more tales. High up on Mungibellu's precious flank, that's where the girl climbed. Now, she sweeps the wide mouth jug in the smooth sheet of snow, making a path 'round her. "None but pure water got to enter the home," she whispers. She pushes the snow in the jug, lifts it and rests it on her shoulder.

For years I seen the girl on Mungibellu in Alfiu's ball of light. She climbed the beautiful mountain far up in spring and summer past the melting snow. In winter, clumsy and slow in Alfiu's shoes and cloak, she trudged where snow draped down from Mungibellu's precious flank, and, still shivering, she climbed the more. In all the seasons, she filled the jug with pure water. And always in the scant morning light before the field guards came on watch. But, this morning, she took too long on carriage roads she never got no right to be on, and, soon, the Angelus bells got to ring.

Good that the Duca's men don't guard the mountain this day. The first of May's a feast for them, too. They pray and feast with Bruntiszi peasants, like they're all of the same kind, but, on the morrow, they'll punish any peasant that breaks a rule they say is law. Always with a scowl on their faces, always squatting on donkeys at the foot of the beautiful mountain, they wave old documents with raised gold seals, proof, they say (but who can read it?), of the Duca's rights to Mungibellu and her snow.

We call them *i camperi*, a stew of rich and poor men and all with no scruples, thieves and thugs the lot of them, that defend their master at all costs, or so they say. All the town knows the field guards take their own liberties and reap their own profits when they guard the Duca's land. All the town knows this tax on snow been outlawed years ago, but in the name of the Duca, these men still wait at the foot of the mountain for payment and all for their own selves. No peasant girl can battle the lot of them.

*

At the foot of the mountain, I wait for the girl. She flies down the precious flank, down rocky slopes and near lava rocks where I hide. She races down roads east of Bronti and winding roads that lead to the town. She passes square after square and fountain after fountain where dark hair peasant girls stop their chores to crook their fingers at her.

At the threshold of the cottage she crosses herself and whispers a blessing for her Mamma. She opens the door and smiles at the sight of Vincenza sitting on a small, wood stool, her round rump lapped over the sides. There, near the marriage bed and the hearth, Vincenza rocks side to side while she sings a lullaby to calm Agata. Losing herself in her own song, she rocks so hard that a leg of the stool breaks off. She throws her arms out, grabbing for the small mouth jug near her. It tips over when she falls to the ground.

"Z'a Vincenza!" the girl cries out, the wide mouth jug of pure water bouncing on her hip.

"Calma, child, calma, all is good," Vincenza shakes her fleshy toes of the water spilling at her feet, "but the jug…"

"Sì, I brought you the pure water from Mungibellu," the girl pushes the wide mouth jug near the hearth. "I done all what you asked of me."

"No, child, not that jug. This one, *u bumburu*, the small mouth jug, it's still full."

Agata stirs from her calm and lets out a mad laugh. "The girl done it! All the evil in Bronti, the girl done!"

"Calma, Agata, calma. Now, slow, slow, tell me, Agata, what did you do with the greens? The jug's full. I brought you greens last night. You gave your word the girl would make the minestra with them. How do you make the minestra with greens but no water?"

"We lose…"

"Agata, the water's still here. Where are the greens?"

"All what we lose, we lose great."

"The jug's full. Where are the greens I brought you?"

"'*A virdura*? You want to know where *they* are? They're here, for all to see, all in the pig's belly. Look how he grows fat and healthy."

"Va ben' that the pig's fed and stays healthy…but your daughter…"

"The girl's a coward, vigliaccu like your maritu."

"Basta with what's done and can't be made right. The minestra *I* can make right. Rest now. No more talk. Rest. I got to make the minestra for you and the girl." She takes the girl by the hand and brings her to the marriage bed. "Child, stay close to your Mamma. Rub her belly to calm her. Wash her face with the water from the wide mouth jug. Let her sip the water to quench her body. It's the purest water we have this day, but save some for the dough."

"Z'a Vincenza, what of the water in u bumburu?"

"We'll use the water in the small mouth jug for the cooking."

In the hearth, a pot rests on an iron stool. Vincenza grabs twigs and branches from the corner of the hearth and puts them on the fire. She lifts the belly of the small mouth jug, cradles it like a baby in her arms, tips it on the pot and pours out the water so careful that not one drop splashes in the fire. She waits for the water to boil.

The girl raises her Mamma's head and helps her drink from the tin cup. She sighs when Vincenza scoops out a handful of broad beans from her apron and spreads sprigs of 'a finucchina on the table. "A better meal the Duca and his son'll never eat."

"*Sst…sst.* The rest we got to do in quiet. Your Mamma's calm now and resting good." She holds her finger to her mouth 'til the water boils. When it does, she takes the tin cup from the girl and ladles the water in it. She pours the broad beans in the pot with the rest of the water 'til their skins wrinkle. Then, she adds salt for the taste and for the bellies to take in the food better. She lays yellow flower buds near the tin cup. "To make your Mamma rest, child."

"The flower buds to make Mamma rest," the girl whispers, "but not to sleep." Vincenza nods to the small sack 'neath the table, and, with that, the girl leaves her Mamma's side and digs her hands inside the sack. She sprinkles out wheat on the table and makes a small ring. In the center of the ring, she pours the pure water. She kneads and rolls the wheat and water 'til she makes a dough. With small, round stems of grass, she shapes the dough in sticks for *i maccarruni* that soon got to make its way in the boiling water. "The flower buds to rest," the girl whispers when she's done, "but not to sleep."

"Sì, child, your Mamma got to dodge the sleep to stir i maccarruni that you made so good. One yellow bud added, one yellow bud forgotten, and all changes the calm inside your Mamma. Now, tell me what your hands bring to mind."

The girl scoops the flower buds in her palms. "How much to fill the cup."

"And tell me what your heart brings to mind."

She crosses herself. "The prayers to say."

"Good, child. Now, put the flower buds in your Mamma's tea." Vincenza smiles when the girl sprinkles five flower buds in the cup and mouths a prayer. She nods again, and the girl goes back to work, tearing the sprigs of 'a finucchina from their tiny bulbs and reaching behind the plate for the small jug of olive oil.

"Z'a Vincenza, Mamma don't got to stir i maccarruni. I can do it."

"You won't be here," Vincenza whispers, "not when we got a celebration to…"

"But Mamma says I got to stay far from all Bruntiszi."

"You and me, we won't be celebrating the first of May with them," Vincenza throws a kiss to the girl, "we'll be celebrating the day of your birth."

The girl lowers her eyes. "No one in Bronti celebrates such a day. All Bruntiszi celebrate their saint's day. But, me, I got no saint to…"

"The day of your birth was a holy day, child. Now, tell me, what can your z'a Vincenza offer you this day?"

The girl holds her chest and lets out a sigh. "You know what I want."

"I cannot heal your Mamma, child, not when grief's got a hold of her. But if I got the power to give you…"

The girl takes in a breath. "You got the power, but you won't."

"Child, if I have the power, I will."

"Va ben', I have but one desire," she fixes her eyes on Vincenza, "say my saint's name."

Vincenza's eyes fill with water. She falls at the girl's feet, clasping her hands to the heavens. "I can no more count the times you ask this of me. One day, child, I got to shout it out for all the island to hear."

"Shout it out this day, z'a Vincenza, shout out my name, and I'll know my path in life! Ppi piaciri, z'a Vincenza, please. I know the path Mamma wants of me. And that's the path to bring her joy. But there's something in me, these months it grows in me, it calls to me, another path…"

"The path to healing…"

"That's your path. And Mamma's is the path to justice. But what of mine? I'll know it but when I know my name. Z'a Vincenza, shout it out this day!"

"I will, one day, I will, but for now it stays a whisper in my heart, a strong whisper, child, that grows in strength each day. Let that be enough for *your* heart. Now, serve your Mamma her tea. It's time to start our journey."

*When the pear is ripe, it falls on its own.*

Vincenza leads the girl south on Corsu Umbertu and out of town, slow, slow, up the lava roads, her basket of plants and baked bread swinging on her arm. They walk in silence, their eyes to the earth, the two smiling with who knows what happy thoughts 'til Vincenza slows her pace at the foot of *'a bacca,* the boat-shaped mountain, and, so the name. She grabs the girl's hand. "Look up, child."

"*A muntagnella!*" the girl cries out, calling 'a bacca the *small mountain* for that's what she is, too. The mountains Mungibellu gave birth to when she spewed forth her lava and rock, they're great in height and girth and got monsters in them, too, that guard the fire in their bellies. And, when the monsters sleep, these great mountains spew forth their own lava and rock and stay huddled 'round the beautiful mountain like children too frightened to leave their Mamma's side. But not 'a bacca. Far from all the great mountains, this one's proud to stand alone. This one with her own ways holds all the fire tight in her belly and never spews forth her ashes or sand or lava or rock. This one's a kind mountain, like no other.

As little ones, Alfiu and his friends raced up and down all the great mountains and wielded their phantom swords, and, me, older and bigger than the lot of them, I trailed behind, my long arms and my long legs battling the wind and my ears taking in all what the boys shouted when they turned 'round and laughed at me. *Did your Mamma bed the Arab giant what straddled u Simetu? Is that how you got so big?* And that was when the strength grew in me, and I caught them and pushed this one and that one down, but the small ones, like swarms of bees, they always overtook me and always got the better of me. *Coward* they called me when I ran for safety. *Brave* they called themselves. Brave warriors the lot of them, them that raced up and down all the great mountains, but this weakling of a mountain, this one they mocked and never climbed.

"Child," Vincenza waves her arm in the air, "this day, on this mountain where the brightest flowers grow, I offer you a day of peace."

The girl looks 'round. "Z'a Vincenza, there are no bright flowers here. But, for peace, each day I'm with you, I'm at peace." She grabs Vincenza's hand and kisses it. "So much you do for me. So much you know."

Vincenza snatches back her hand and lets out a laugh. "And what do I know?"

"All there's to know of the plants and how to help Mamma…and, this day, if I'm good, you got tell me all there's to know of…of the chickens."

Vincenza clasps her hands in prayer and shakes them, a bright smile on her face. "Maronna mia, what flies in your thoughts now?"

"When I was a little one, I woke up each day to Mamma when she called the chickens, *cci, cci* she called to feed them, *sciu, sciu,* she cried out after their meal when they swarmed 'round her skirt and she tried to break free. Out in the sun they rolled in the dust and scratched for their food. But one day, I heard no more scratching, and I seen no more dust thrown up to the sky, and that was the day I ate no more eggs. Z'a Vincenza…where are Mamma's chickens? I'm so hungry for eggs."

Vincenza takes the girl by the hand. "Come, child, we have a ways to go."

"I'm so hungry. We had so many, and they gave us the biggest eggs, fine to the taste. Mamma said they were blessed by her own Mamma and Papà and her own self 'til…and now they're gone."

"The chickens were a gift, a gift from your Mamma's Papà to Alfiu Saitta on the day he took your Mamma for his bride. When your Papà worked the fields, your Mamma set out to all the squares with two big baskets in her arms with hopes to sell all the eggs…and she done that good. But when your Mamma sold no more, the chickens were of no more use to her. *Help yourselves as I help you* the Savior says, and one night the chickens were gone. Who helped himself to them, a weasel or a peasant, who can say? This I *can* say: they were no more good to your Mamma. She left them all alone, and, now, they are good to another."

"But they were good to me. And, Mamma, she…Z'a Vincenza, no one came to take our chickens. They died when curses filled Mamma's heart, and nothing good could grow 'round her."

"But you are good."

"And you are good," the girl slips her arms 'round Vincenza's neck, "but, then, how does Mamma and how do the *cummari* treat you in such a bad way? You that do the good, and no woman shows kindness to you. Do they hold to what your maritu done, and that a coward's way falls to his wife?"

"A coward's way falls to his wife? Child, learn to speak your own words."

"I speak what Mamma…" The girl falls at Vincenza's knees and hides her face 'neath Vincenza's apron. "Forgive me, z'a Vincenza, forgive me."

"Basta, child, basta. Get up. Walk with me. Now, how can I make you understand? The moon shines full and bright, then it disappears, but it comes back, and when it does, it's but a shard in the sky. It changes. Everything in the world changes, even a cummari's heart. Any heart can change. A cummari's. A coward's. This I got to believe 'til my dying day." She shakes off her shawl and quickens her pace. "Hurry, child."

Vincenza rests her foot on the sandstone base of the mountain. She crosses herself, closes her eyes and sweeps her foot 'cross a rock. At her touch, warm grass springs forth. She waves her hand, and thick grass covers the mountain from crown to foot. She sweeps her foot 'cross the grass, and a path issues forth, a path thick with bright, sweet-smelling flowers.

"Flowers! So big! So bright! But how? But how, z'a Vincenza?"

"Is this not the same question you ask your own self when magic takes a hold in you?"

The girl bites her lip and nods, her eyes to the earth.

Vincenza rushes up the path. "Welcome your gifts and use them for the good. This day, the gifts I welcome bring you peace."

Vincenza waves for the girl to follow, but her small feet dig deep in Vincenza's prints and linger there. "The earth's so soft and warm," she closes her eyes and takes in a breath, "the air's so sweet." She lets out a cry. *Si-si-si-si-si-si-si-si-Si-si-si-si-si.* But what mode of cry is this? She pulls at her throat, rubs it, looks 'round. It's laughter, I know the sound now. How strange the laughter. Shy. Trembling. Is this the first time she ever laughed?

She throws her arms to the sky and races up the mountain on the path of white and red and yellow flowers. In her joy, she throws off a sweetness that sends the island bees in swarms all 'round her. Their small wings buzz 'round her head. Their dark bodies dive 'round her face. But, still, the girl laughs. I let out a high pitch yip to frighten them away, but these are island bees, wild and restless.

The girl laughs. Vincenza, too. The girl waves her arms. Vincenza, too. Vincenza's breath is sweet, a sweetness that rivals any flower on the island. The bees swarm 'round her. Vincenza swats with all her might, but the biggest of the lot, she eyes my Vincenza's plump cheek, and, there, she jabs her poison needle.

"*Ahi!*" Vincenza cries and throws herself 'cross the earth. She cups her cheek 'til her hand can no more hide the swelling.

"The basket, z'a Vincenza. Quick!"

The girl digs her hand in the basket and pulls out a sack folded on a bed of myrtle leaves and shakes it out. Some rope and a knife fall in the grass. She grabs the knife, grips it by the handle and waves it high the way the angry peasant does.

"No!"

"For good," the girl whispers. "Good to good." She lowers the knife and lays the blade on Vincenza's cheek. "Iron to iron," she says and, with that, the stinger makes its way up through the flesh. The girl pulls it out. She rummages through the rootstalks in the basket 'til she finds the shoot of the rue plant that she rubs on Vincenza's cheek. She crosses herself. "We use many parts of the ruta plant for many cures," she whispers, "but the tops of the young shoots, that's where the greatest virtues lie. I got no means now to make the proper cure, but this got to take away the pain and make you happy again."

Vincenza's eyes fill with water. She grabs the girl's hand and kisses it a hundred times and more. "This is a strange world when the teacher whispers *grazii* to the child." She wipes the wet from her cheeks and fixes her eyes on the girl's fingers that rub up and down the blade. Quick, Vincenza yanks the knife from her hand and throws it down. "No!"

"Z'a Vincenza, I done no harm!"

She kisses the girl's palms. "In your hand is not where a knife got to rest. Child, my child, you were but a baby when I put a worm in your hand. I prayed in your mouth, and that was when you understood. In your heart, you understood the secrets of the plants and the secrets of the worm charmer. And, more, deep in your heart, you took on the ways..."

"Z'a Vincenza, is this the kind of peace you bring me?" She grabs her belly and sobs. "I done no harm for a punishment. I took the knife, but I done no harm."

"*Sst...sst...*"

"But there's a thing sudden in my belly..."

Vincenza tears off a piece of brown bread. "Here, wipe clean your hunger and listen well. You were a baby when your Mamma put the knife in your hand, but I put a worm in it. Your fingers let your Mamma's knife fall to the earth, but they held the worm tight. Your Mamma's eyes turned blind to the sign, but I knew. And when you picked yourself from the ground and walked your first steps, that was when I took you to forgotten places and taught you the healing ways of the plants."

Vincenza rests the knife on the sack near the basket where a thick red stalk sways in the warm wind. She wraps her fingers 'round it. "Peace for you this day, child, but, always, with a lesson."

On grassy slopes and lava rocks and at the edge of the forest, these are the places where Vincenza finds the plants that heal. These are the places where the girl learns the secrets. Alfiu showed it all to me in his ball of light. But, now, on the small mountain Vincenza covered with grass and flowers where clover fills the air, here, on Vincenza's mountain, the girl sits silent rubbing her belly like she never learned nothing.

"*Ahi!*" she cries out and tightens her hands 'round her belly now that a bright wetness eases down her legs. "Z'a Vincenza, what happens to me? Can it be a spell the Devil casts?"

"*Sst...sst...* Now is not the time for foolishness." Vincenza wraps her arms 'round the high stems of plants with wisps of leaves and white petals and a bright yellow heart. "You know the plant and its magic. Does it bring harm or good?"

The girl spreads her skirt and blots the sticky wetness that runs down her leg. "Harm or..."

"Child, you know the plant. You knelt by my side when it worked wonders a hundred times and more."

The girl rips out the stained grass and hurls it at the sky. "Harm! The magic brews from the evil one. And it brings harm, and *I* bring harm this day."

"Child, what foolishness!"

"Look at me!" She lifts her skirt and shows Vincenza the wet dripping down. "Look what I done! I bring blood, z'a Vincenza, blood, red like the blood on Papà's shirt!"

"Basta!"

"Blood, blood Mamma says got to pour out of me when the Devil takes me home."

"Basta! You speak words that are not your own." Vincenza lifts the girl's chin and points to the sky. "Look, a gift from the Savior, and the Devil's got none to do with it." She rubs the girl's belly. "And, you, you're a gift from the Savior, too. All this is the Savior's *magic*. And it is good."

On distant slopes where I hide, the melody of Vincenza's words drifts to me. 'Cross the mountain, the melody of Vincenza's words drifts to the lopped ears of a lamb, clover brimming from her mouth. She pokes her head up at the gentle sound. The lamb races down the slope and straight to the girl. "I know you, little lamb," the girl rests her hand on the lamb's head, her fingers sinking in the soft wool strands. I swear on my eyes, the lamb smiles when she nuzzles the girl's leg and licks the blood and wipes the girl clean the way a ewe wipes clean her baby lamb.

Vincenza throws the girl behind her. "When the wound opens, we seek no one and nothing, and no one and nothing seek us out."

"Wound? Z'a Vincenza…death comes to me this day, so soon? And, me, with no path in life?"

She spins the girl back 'round and folds her small hands in prayer. "It's the wound of all women, child," and presses the girl's hands tight, "and this day, it makes me call you *Signurina*."

"*Signurina*?" The girl nuzzles the back of Vincenza's hands.

"Sì, and, when it happens, that's when no one and nothing seek us out, and we seek none to stay by our side."

"None…to stay by our side…" The girl pushes the lamb away, but the tongue, stubborn the way it is, it fastens to the girl's ankles.

"Forgive me," the girl whispers. She throws the lamb to the ground and fights her way through the thick grassy slope up to the wide mouth of 'a bacca, far from the lamb that grows tired of the chase and heads back to her feast of clover.

"Child…my child…wait for me…"

How far Vincenza's sweet voice carries through the air! How quick the girl obeys! She digs her feet in the earth and stands rigid like a field guard 'til her legs start to tremble. When they can no more hold her, she drops to the ground, there, at the mouth of an ancient dwelling where stones lay one on the other, an abandoned dwelling for shepherds and thieves. She crawls inside. In the corner at the mouth of the dwelling, she crawls past a thin wood flute and a wide mouth jug jutting out from a green blanket that gives off the wet wool smells of a shepherd and his sheep.

When the bright red sun drifts behind the mountains, Vincenza reaches the girl. She leans on the stones inside the dwelling, bare a breath in her. "Watch…what…I…do," she huffs, ripping her apron in long, wide strips.

I hide close by behind piles of stones that once were roofs and walls for ancient dwellings and ready myself to howl at the man or the beast that happens 'on Vincenza and the girl. Soon that Vincenza lifts the girl's skirt, I turn my back on what no man got no right to see.

"Knot the strips one to the other," Vincenza whispers to the girl, "and all 'neath your belly like a corded belt. Pull the wide ones from back to front. Drape them over the knotted strips. Tie their ends to the long strips."

"All what you tell me, I do," the girl whispers, "but I never seen no cloths like this."

"Child, the other peasant women, they never seen it, too. They bleed in their clothes, but that's not pure. And when they wash the clothes by the river, or, some lazy ones, by the fountains when no one sees, that's not pure. This I taught your Mamma and now I teach you."

"But I never seen Mamma wash…"

"Child, when grief got a hold of your Mamma, it dried her out and took away all her fertile ways."

"Z'a Vincenza, if I don't go by the river, where do I wash them?"

"When you go back to your Mamma, wash the strips of cloth after the hour of the Vespri with all what remains of the clean water you fetched that day. Let the strips soak through the night with the ash from Mungibellu. Gather lots of it. It makes the cloths clean. But do this where none can see you. Do this 'til the wound heals. Heed my words: throw the water far outside the town in the ditch where you empty u pisciaturi. Nothing unclean got to make way near the cottage."

"Z'a Vincenza, it's done." With that, I turn back 'round. Straight inside the dark dwelling I peer, my eyes taking in the trembling girl. "Z'a Vincenza, I got to go back home to Mamma," she whispers and spreads out her skirt and pats it down.

"No, child," Vincenza sighs, "your Mamma with her talk of the Devil and his ways…if she sees all what happened this day…no, child. Ppi piaciri, please, don't look at me with such eyes. It's for the good of all that you stay here this night. Now, wrap your body inside the shawl. Here, high up in the mountains, the air's not so gentle."

The girl shakes off the shawl. She loosens the braid and lets her hair fall. She lies down and curls her body 'neath the red blanket of hair.

"Va ben', child, you find the warmth we all seek, and you find it in your own way." Vincenza strokes the girl's hair and kisses it. "Put the shawl 'neath your head like a pillow. Here, like this."

"Z'a Vincenza, when I sleep with the pig, I got to make a pillow for him, too. Then, he got to forgive me for when Mamma…for when I near killed him."

Vincenza presses her lips tight, breathing out all the air inside her. "Child, such thoughts of sorrow got to stay outside in the cold night air. Now, sleep. *Bon riposu.* Before the Mattutinu bells ring, I'll come and take you home."

The girl lets out a sigh. "Va ben', I'll stay this night. But when I go back, I got to tell Mamma. If I don't tell, and she finds out…"

Vincenza presses the girl's small bones in her arms. "Who knows the secrets of the plants?"

"No one. I tell no one."

"Who will know of the path of bright flowers this day?"

"No one. I give you my word."

"Mamma?"

"No, z'a Vincenza, she never heard the secrets of the plants. And she'll never hear the secret of your magic."

"And she'll never hear the secret of your wound. Va ben', *Signurina*?"

"Va ben', z'a Vincenza."

"I got to go to your Mamma now. She got to be worried sick. Look, now, how the light scarce guides me. Heed all what I say…before the morning bells, I'll come back with more cloths and with water from the beautiful mountain, pure water to drink and to wash the cloths. Bon riposu. May 'a Maronna 'a Nunziata keep you safe from harm."

Vincenza makes her way down the grassy slope. Slow, slow, with each step she takes, the grass turns to rock behind her. It's 'a bacca, once more, that weakling of a mountain, bare of grass and bright flowers now that Vincenza heads home. I howl soft and low 'til the sky turns black. I watch the girl, the way her body rocks side to side to the sounds I make. Soft and low I howl, but I ready myself to howl loud and wild now that two foreigners with lanterns in their hands struggle up the rocky slope near the cave where the girl drifts off to sleep and dreams.

*

"Are you familiar with the painting *Portrait of an Unknown Man*?" asks the woman foreigner. She wears a long, red dress made of shiny cloth with no sleeves and a neck low and daring. No peasant woman ever been so shameless. To make amends, the woman hides her body 'neath a skirt with more draping than I ever seen on one dress. I swear on my eyes, if it's not two dresses, two skirts, to be sure. The one on top is big as a marriage bed and draped with shiny cloth pulled up and trailing behind. The skirt 'neath it has more pleats and frills and ruffles than all the dresses in Bronti and got to be heavier than the lot of them, too. The woman wears short red gloves and a black velvet ribbon tied 'round her neck that hangs down her back. In the cold night air, she shudders like a big, red flower in the wind.

"*Portrait of an Unknown Man*? By the master Antonello?" asks the man, the surgeon of the Castle that I seen a hundred times and more in Alfiu's ball of light, him in his high black hat with a line of scars on his face and neck, him with a tight smile pressed on his face. "I am quite familiar with the portrait."

"Then, dear doctor, you know that much has been written on the subject's smile, one which hides a world of mystery. Is the bearer of this smile a nobleman or a murderer? A painter or a thief?"

"Pray tell, dear lady, what does our enigmatic subject have to do with this night's festivities?"

"It has a world to do with *you*. I know so little about you, my dear enigmatic doctor…"

He waves the lantern near the woman's face and smiles. "I, on the other hand, have more than educated myself as to the Duke's lovely guests whether their visits be of a brief or of a rather protracted nature. In your case, dear lady, I hope for something quite extended."

"Dr. Gale! As I was saying, I know so little about you," and, with that, she brushes his arm, "save that I suspect you conjured up this mountain to keep me from the festivities."

"If I did…?"

"Did you?"

"My dear lady, I did, indeed. Do you like my magic?"

The woman rubs her bare arms and shudders. "Dr. Gale, I appreciate *all* magic. Yet, I have not quite ascertained from whence your magic emanates, from heaven or from hell. I pray the former."

"Dear lady, you suspect the latter."

"On the contrary, Dr. Gale, I pray you are an angel of a gentleman sent down from heaven to guide me back to the other guests. If you deign not guide me, then, I implore you, conjure the manor with your magic."

"The peasants refer to the manor as the *Castle*. When in Rome, my dear lady, or, as befits our situation, when in *Hades*."

"*Castle, manor*, Dr. Gale…shall you help me to that safe haven or not?"

"And should I not?"

"Then, what would the Duke's son say regarding the disappearance of one of his beloved guests?"

The man lets out a laugh. "The *boy* has been preoccupied all evening with his *delicate* Elizabeth and her stomach malady. I doubt he's taken notice of anything or anyone else."

"Dr. Gale, I must return to the others. Answer me, now. Shall I journey on perilous roads with no companion?"

"My dear lady, I am insulted by your lack of faith in me…and my *green fairy*. We shall both see you back to the manor, but why such haste? With the Duke too long away from us, the manor lacks a certain warmth and conviviality," he puts his mouth to her ear, "the son, after all, is not the father."

The woman cups her hands and breathes in them. She walks 'round the man, puffing out clouds of cold night air that trail behind her. "Dr. Gale, where are we?"

"Let us enjoy the mountain air."

"Dr. Gale," she swings the lantern to the north and the south, "are we close to town?"

"Would, dear lady, we were farther still."

"You are harsh."

"I speak the truth. Bronte, or, as the peasants say *Brontiiii*, is a disaster of a town, and the Bronte peasant, simply put, is lazy and a thief. If there were a way to return to my beloved England, I would, however, not before destroying that town and every one of its worthless peasants." The man stands straight and brushes his boot on a rock at the mouth of the dwelling where the girl sleeps. "I am prepared," he shouts out and raises his arms to the heavens, "to seize all manner of lightning and thunder which the

Cyclopes forge for me! Unlike earthquakes and volcanic eruptions which have tried and failed, my own forces of nature shall destroy Bronte for all time!"

Only a Devil makes such vile speeches. But wait…speeches in a foreign tongue that now I make sense of! Alfiu, he got to be the one that sent me such a gift this night. And now that I see the cruel ways and hear the cruel speeches of the surgeon of the Castle, a man that vows to heal, I got to rip this Devil apart before he does more harm, me, stronger than any creature in the wild. *Use the powers for the girl*, that's what Alfiu whispers 'cross my heart. I eye the dwelling and take in a breath and ready myself to howl like a wild dog if that Devil of a man dares disturb the girl in her sleep. But what is this? He shakes his head and scratches the line of scars on his face and neck.

The woman waves the lantern near his face. "I suspect the night air stings and does little to soothe your wounds." She tips his hat back and touches the scars on his face.

The man grabs her hand. "Dear lady, Pandora paid for her curiosity." He presses it hard 'til she lets out a small cry. "Shall you pay in kind?"

"I meant no harm."

"No harm, indeed. Nonetheless, I should ask you to counteract my hurt feelings with a kiss, the location of which I have yet to determine." He swipes his hand 'cross his chest and belly and thighs. "However, that, dear lady, shall have to wait. You seem quite out of sorts."

"I am chilled and quite uneasy here. Good night, Dr. Gale, I have no recourse but to manage my way back to the manor without you." The woman turns 'round, picks up her pleats and frills and ruffles and taps her way down the rocky slope, the lantern in her hand, the shiny red dress swishing behind her.

"Wait, dear lady," he rushes after her, "the donkeys are close by, and I shall strive to make our descent pleasant, more pleasant, indeed, if you allow me to make a private toast courtesy of my other delightful companion, my *green fairy*, which remains ever so close to my heart." He reaches for a small jewel flask from the pocket in his vest. She pulls away and stumbles over a small rock. He seizes her in his arms.

"No!" The woman breaks free. "My dear doctor, you and your *green fairy* shall have to wait. First, you must take me far from this God-forsaken corner of your world. And, then, and only then, shall I be obliging."

*Laugh on Friday. Cry on Saturday.*

I thank Alfiu for the powers he gave me. What men don't see in the dark and the distance, I see. What men don't smell, I smell. And I run, I run faster than any peasant. And I howl, a howl that frightens the rich and the poor. These are the blessings and the curses...sì, the curses. What men don't hear, I hear, and this night I'm cursed to hear a girl crying out in her dreams for a Mamma to love her.

The girl moans with such a deep longing that my throat grows thick with sorrow. Tears soak her red blanket of hair, but no such tears disturb her sleep. Not the two foreigners that mark their way back to the Castle, not the soft, low howls of the night, nothing disturbs her sleep, not even the boy that nears the mouth of the dwelling and, with his cane, strikes the stones and strikes the girl's ankle, all 'cross the hard and the soft of her foot. I try to howl, but my throat is still too thick with sorrow.

"*Ahi!*"

"Who goes there?" the boy shouts out and sweeps the cane in the air.

"*Ahi!*" A small creature with bright eyes races over the girl's toes and dives to safety 'neath the green wool blanket.

The girl opens her eyes. Like the creature's bright eyes, her own eyes shine in the darkness. She piles her hair up, wraps it in the heavy brown shawl and crawls to the green blanket near the bright-eyed, trembling creature that flies out in the night. The girl, trembling, too, she huddles at the mouth of the dwelling.

"Stay!" The boy taps his way to the shining light of the girl's gold eyes. "Stay, if you mean no harm."

"No," she whispers, "I mean no harm. 'A z'a Vincenza said I got to stay in this dwelling, but now that you are here, I got to leave or none stays pure."

The boy opens his sack and takes out a tin cup, a small jug of olive oil, and a sulphur stick. He pours oil in the cup, takes a piece of flax, salts it, rolls it, puts it in the oil and lights the dry end of the flax. The smell of warm oil fills the air, reaching far-off rubbles of stone roofs and walls, there, where I hide.

"It's you," he waves the cup 'cross her face.

"You know of me?"

"You saved my lamb this day."

She knots the shawl tight 'neath her chin. "Ppi piaciri," she holds out her hand. He passes her the tin cup. She waves it 'neath his face. Quick, he presses the long tail of his brown stocking cap to his cheek. "Shepherd boy, it's you."

"It's good you are here. Speech no more comes easy to me, the way I live alone day to night. But with you, the speech comes easy. And I got to savor it 'til the morrow for now you got to rest. Bon riposu. 'Til the light of day, when I'll bring you a good meal for your journey." He takes the tin cup and holds it 'neath her face. "Maronna mia, your eyes…"

"My cursed eyes," she whispers and bows her head.

"Your eyes…sì, they tell me you got to journey far."

"What more, shepherd boy?"

"What more?"

"Shepherd boy, you stand brave and look me in the eye. Mamma says, 'pale eyes give the evil eye.' But, you, how don't you crook your finger at the sight of me?"

"Crook my finger? You saved my lamb!"

"She found me."

"That was all what she needed. Now, I got to help you. Fortune brings gifts when we pay our debts. Tell me, how do I call the girl I got to pay my debt to?"

She lets out a sigh. "One day, I got to shout it out for all the island to hear. One day, when I know my path in life. But not this day."

The boy kneels and rests the tin cup on the ground. "And when I know my path in life, I'll shout out my name, too, for I am not, in truth, a shepherd boy." He bows and lets out a laugh, his eyes raised, fixed on hers.

"You are kind, shepherd boy. You are kind. But even if you're not the shepherd boy, even if you're the Devil come here to bring bad fortune, the sin I carry stains both the blessed and the cursed. For that, I got to go."

"No. Take my blanket and rest in warmth this night."

She pats her head. "I got all to keep me warm…"

"Va ben', but stay." He reaches for the green wool blanket and the thin flute. "Stay."

She falls to the ground. Caught in a spell, she lies there quiet with her eyes closed 'til he takes his leave.

'Neath the spotted shadow of the moon, the sheep circle the boy and ready themselves to pass a quiet night in sleep and dreams. The boy, too, he readies himself for sleep and lays his head on the soft wool strands of the lamb's belly. He takes off his cap, touches the bright red mark in the hollow of his cheek. "But who can know," he whispers, "who can ever know all our sins?"

The light in the tin cup fades from view. In the dark of the dwelling, the girl, wrapped in the warm blanket of her hair, hums the joyless tune the shepherd boy plays 'til she falls fast to sleep. The sad, long tones of the flute slip in her dreams. So, too, the tales of the dark hair peasant girls, the tales and tones weaving through the girl's dreams like flax on a loom.

*

Long ago, the dream whispers, *there lived a shepherd and his wife. The two were very happy, but they longed for a baby boy that would one day tend the shepherd's flock. Now, the one that leased the land where the sheep grazed gave the shepherd fifty sheep to feed and fatten, and when it was time to bring them to market, he shared a tiny profit with the shepherd. It was hard work and small profit, but the shepherd was happy and happier still now that his wife was with child.*

*On the first of May, she climbed the mountain to bring her maritu bread she baked for him that very day. But the wife, a forgetful woman, forgot that bread baked on the first of May brings bad fortune. When she climbed the mountain, she forgot soon enough even the cause for her visit. This she forgot the moment she seen a beautiful round baby lamb, the most beautiful lamb she ever laid eyes on. All the other lambs bore the mark of the island's breed, but not this one.*

*The wife stroked the lamb's soft wool strands, and that was when the longing got the best of her. In all the world, she desired none more but to eat a lamb.*

*Lamb for the rich, lamb for the titled. Not for their marriage, not for any feast, did the shepherd and his wife partake of lamb. But, on this day, her longings were strong. She hid the lamb in her basket and blessed her maritu and climbed down the mountain.*

*All day the wife looked at the lamb. All day she parted the lamb's soft wool strands. All day she rubbed the lamb's belly. All day she prayed to taste the tender lamb 'til the evening prayers when she threw off the temptation and come to her senses. Troubled by his wife's strange ways, the maritu left his sheep and came home that night. She threw her arms 'round him and begged him to take the lamb back to the mountain. Tired and craving sleep, he refused 'til he could take no more of her begging.*

*Now the shepherd held to many superstitions. "Tell me, tell me," he shouted out, "did you touch the lamb?"*

*"To put her in the basket."*

*"Did you rub her belly?"*

*She gave herself a slap on the cheek, and not a gentle one at that, and, quick, her cheek flushed in pain. "What gives you such ideas?" she asked in the voice of an innocent one and spent the night rubbing her cheek 'til the redness faded.*

*When the shepherd's wife gave birth, and the shepherd heard the baby's first cries, he was filled with joy. "A baby boy!" the midwife shouted to him. But when she seen the baby's face, she rushed out of the cottage, pulling at her hair and wailing.*

*"How could I know?" the shepherd's wife whispered to her baby boy and rubbed his cheek. And, there, in the shape of a broad bean and raw like the lamb's belly, a bright red mark hollowed in the baby boy's right cheek.*

*The boy grew up to be a very fine shepherd. When the Savior called his Mamma and Papà to paradise, the shepherd boy climbed a mountain far from the world where he tended the Duca's prized flock. He ate soft white cheese and bread and olives. He ate oranges in the spring and fruit, part apple, part pear, at harvest time, and, on the first of May, chicken and pig, all what the Duca and his son provided. He slept in a cave of lava stones and learned the secrets of forgotten plants and flowers. He believed himself a most happy soul 'til the day he found true joy when he fixed his eyes 'on a young girl in a heavy brown shawl sleeping in the hollows of his dwelling…*

"And that's how the tale of the shepherd boy ends."

All through the night, the girl dreamed the tale and, in her bliss, whispered the new and joyful end. Now, slow, slow, the morning light breaks through dark streaks of clouds. Flocks of magpies fly 'cross the sky. Behind the beautiful mountain, rays of light let off a soft glow, and, still, the girl whispers and dreams. I look 'round. The rocks and stones flicker with light. So, too, the dwelling where the girl, at long last, wakes from sleep. Soon that the boy taps his cane at the mouth of the dwelling, she throws her hair 'neath the shawl and knots it tight.

"The sun shines, and you still dream," he smiles and lays brown bread at her feet.

"It's three days past the Lord's Day. What we dream this day got to be true." She cups her mouth, but the words slip through her fingers. "It *is* true. It *is* how the tale of the shepherd boy ends."

"Now is not the time to talk of tales or dreams. Now is the time to give our blessings and eat. Our blessings to the Duca and his son for this meal."

Quick, the girl jumps up and spits on the ground.

"What is this? The blessings are for all that prepare and, *sì*, for the one that provides."

"Shepherd boy, my Mamma says the one that *provides* eats all what we harvest, and, more, too, she says your Duca is a murderer."

The boy kneels and fills his mouth with the soft white cheese that sinks in the valleys of the brown bread. When the bread crunches in his cheeks, the girl's belly moans. This makes the boy smile. "Only fools choose not to eat when food is for the plenty." He takes another bite of the crusty bread. Pieces of soft white cheese break free. They drift in the air and fall in the weave of her shawl. She picks them out and sneaks them on her tongue. "Light," she whispers, "like Patri Radici's bread…" Light and fresh like the holy bread she sneaked but one time, the bread Patri Radici pressed on Bruntiszi tongues to satisfy the hungriest on earth.

*The hungriest on earth,* that's what Patri Radici called the Bruntiszi when he started his sermon that day, not *good people of Bronti,* but *you, Bruntiszi, the hungriest on earth.* That was the day Agata flung herself on her daughter's small body and cursed her and all the earth. I seen it all in Alfiu's ball of light. He showed me how Vincenza tried to calm Agata that day. She threw the yellow flower buds in the tin cup for Agata to drink. Her lids grew heavy, and that's when Vincenza rushed with the girl to the sanctuary 'a Maronna 'a Nunziata. There, Vincenza leaned on the bell tower, gained back her breath and crossed herself at the sandstone portal. Hand in hand, Vincenza and the girl passed through the bronze doors and hid to the side of the brown marble altar table when Patri Radici started his sermon.

On that morning, Mungibellu blew out her breath. The grey breath soon turned black and hid Mungibellu in her own thick smoke.

Over his long white tunic, Patri Radici wore a white silk cloak of fancy embroidered bands of gold thread with no sleeves and open at the sides. The peasants whispered when they seen it. They knew the Duca sent the priest that gift and that it come all the way from Roma, in trade, to be sure, for the priest's praise of him at each sermon. Patri Radici, flicking specks of dust from near the shoulder, paid no mind to the signs, the shaking of the ground and the fire that crawled down the beautiful mountain like a big, red snake. He ended his sermon the way he always ended them, in praise for his namesake, the great Sant'Eupliu, the martyr that chose death over a life of pagan worship.

"Sant'Eupliu!" Patri Radici sang out the martyr's name. The peasants looked 'round at the candles and the statues shaking in the sanctuary and trembled in silence. When the statue of Sant'Eupliu crashed to the floor, the peasants cried out. Patri Radici cried out, too. He slipped off his white embroidered cloak, bowed to the crucifix on the altar table, kissed the wood floor and rushed down the aisle. Without crossing themselves, the peasants toppled their low wood chairs and rushed behind him. They pushed each other out the doors, Vincenza, pulled and pushed with the lot of them. An old cummari shoved her down. Vincenza's hand slipped free of the girl's.

The girl crawled between this foot and that, hid behind this chipped statue and that 'til the sanctuary emptied out. That was when she climbed 'cross the white linen cloth that covered the brown marble altar table. She looked up. Above her, the eyes of 'a Maronna 'a Nunziata and the angel messenger gazed down, but the girl paid them no mind.

*The hungriest on earth* is what Patri Radici called the Bruntiszi that day. The girl whispered his words. On the brown marble altar table, she dug her hands in the gold cup where the warm holy bread piled high. More and more she stuffed the pieces in her mouth 'til her puffed cheeks could hold no more.

The one-eyed monster that guards the fire in Mungibellu cradled the smoke and fire back to her belly. He made no more noise, and the earth was quiet. Slow, slow, the peasants made their way back to the sanctuary, Patri Radici leading them. They pushed through the bronze doors and stopped 'neath the sandstone portal of chiseled angels and demons, the peasants pointing and wailing, Patri Radici, wailing the loudest of all.

There, for all to see, a girl's head naked in God's holy house. There, for all to see, a girl's hair, red like Mungibellu's fire, spread 'cross the altar table. The cummari wailed at the sight of the girl's hair, all but fainting when they neared the altar table where the girl lay patting her belly, holy bread in her hand, spittle dripping down her chin.

Patri Radici sobbed, and his tears near filled the gold cup. "For her *Nanna*, we welcomed the girl. All of you know it was Signa Agata's Mamma that made the hosts from the very wheat she denied herself. Why did she do this? Bruntiszi, she did this for her church and for her Savior. Signa Agata is sick. Why, Bruntiszi? The girl, she is the cause of all her sorrow."

With that, Vincenza snatched the girl and rushed past the curses of the faithful without kneeling or even crossing herself, taking a breath only when the girl fell on her knees at the sanctuary doors. "Come, z'a Vincenza," the girl whispered, "kneel the way you taught me."

"Pray, Bruntiszi," the priest shouted out, and the wind howled his words through all the roads of Bronti, "pray that no Devil's child ever enters this holy house again!"

The girl picks out the last bit of soft cheese from the weave and licks the fringes of her shawl. "You got to leave, shepherd boy. 'A z'a Vincenza says this day I got to stay far from man and beast."

"Eat," says the shepherd boy and smiles. "Eat."


*With or without the rooster, the sun shines.*


Vincenza, my Vincenza, you made your way down 'a bacca and back to the Saitta cottage. You left the girl in an ancient dwelling and calmed Agata the best you knew how with your yellow flower buds. I seen it all in Alfiu's ball of light, how Agata ranted on the first of May that the Devil took the girl and now she won't never welcome her back home. And, you, my dear Vincenza, you kept the girl safe, far from her Mamma and her rantings. For so long you kept the girl away from her Mamma and from your own self. And how each day your heart bore the sorrows!

I left the girl to comfort you. "Calma, Vincenza, calma," I howled, day to night, soft and low. "The girl is safe. The shepherd boy gives her food and teaches her the secrets of the plants." But what sense did you make of all my howls, Vincenza? You were frightened and prayed for the *evil creature* to go back to the wild.

You stayed with Agata and done her chores. I stayed with you. You climbed the beautiful mountain and brought back the pure water. You climbed so high, and, now, you hold your chest to take your breaths. Rest, Vincenza. The girl's safe. The shepherd boy and the girl, they found a new dwelling far from 'a bacca, that weakling of a mountain. But, know, Vincenza, know, the girl's safe.

"Alfiu, forgive me," I pray, "I left the girl. Time and again, I left her, but it was all for my Vincenza. Now, she needs me more than ever. Alfiu, there she is, making her way on a narrow mule track. And there *he* is. Maronna mia! My dear and holy wife on a trazzera with the one more dangerous than any creature in the wild!"

Red for Mungibellu's fire. Red to ward off evil. On two red wheels, the size and color of the setting sun, the painted cart bounces down a trazzera south of Bronti. In the cart, pots and jugs clang, and baskets weaved from the thin stems of the *ligara* plant, what foreigners call the *old man's beard*, they jostle on the wood planks. 'Long the sides of the cart, the ruffles of fancy dresses swish over the bright panels of infidels battling the brave Orlannu. A child could carry such a load on his shoulders, but the white mare huffs like she drags Mungibellu and all her mountains behind her. The mare calls to mind an old buttana that still fancies herself a young whore made up the way she is in her crown of drooping red feathers and bands of red tassels that near cover her face, made up the way she is with bells and mirrors that hang from the breast straps and harness to weigh her down like a suit of armor. With all this to bear, who can fault the poor creature that pants and drags her hooves when the short man with hollow eyes and a black beard pulls on the reins?

With a jolt, the short man's body reels back, the soles of his boots flapping in the air like small brown mouths come over with laughter. He wipes his brow. Through his long, brown teeth, he turns 'round to sing out his greetings in the high pitch of a girlish voice. "Gooood Mooooreeen." Vincenza keeps her eyes down and pays no mind to how he greets her, but I do. I swear on my eyes, that girlish voice is a rightful sign of danger. Who but Vincenza don't see and hear the sign?

She nods. "Mastru Nonziu, forgive me, the sun's not been kind to me." She wipes her own brow and digs her feet in the earth.

The man opens his mouth wide. His jaw clicks and makes the sound the Notaries do when they end their speeches in court. "Wait! *Clicca…clicca*. I know what you're looking for…*clicca…clicca*…and I have it…right here!"

He dives through the clay and straw goods 'til he unties the one item he says no Bruntiszi can live without, a pair of leather-laced boots, swinging at the back of the cart. "None like the soft shoes you got to wear," he says, "when you crush the grapes for the Duca's fine wine. No, these are new boots for a promeeeeenade made for the delicate feet of a king…or a queen…or you." Same *new* pair swinging at the back of the cart from the time the carter first waved them 'cross our eyes when he sobbed that with such bargaining the shrewd Bruntiszi would sure to put him out of business.

Long ago, a field guard spoke of swarms of vendors on the west of our island that crowd the roads and gather in the squares to hawk the wares that fill their baskets. Vendors of dishes and herbs, rosaries and holy pictures, sulphur sticks and baskets, and spoons and forks and knives. Here, at Mungibellu's feet, there is but one vendor that sings out but one tired song for all his wares. One vendor that wears a lava cross 'round his neck and kisses it a hundred times and more each day 'til he wets it smooth like a river stone. One vendor that comes from that dark town north of Bronti where they build their churches with black lava stone.

Sì, he comes from the north where all trouble starts and from the north he blows his way to Bronti with the stench of bargains and flattery on his lips. He passes his days 'long the trazzere, the narrow and rocky mule tracks that lead to the towns at Mungibellu's feet, a carter by trade, a gossiper by nature, 'til the hour of the Vespri prayers when he *happens* on the new carriage road that leads to the Castle and the stables, hedging for grain and shelter for the old mare, Chiazza.

*

I kept my eyes on him for years in Bronti, and, long after I fled the town, I seen him, time and again, in Alfiu's ball of light. The Duca seen the carter for the conniver he always been, and, so, what invitations to the Castle that slipped through, they were thanks to the twists and turns of the carter's tongue and not from no regard the Duca held for him. When the Duca sailed back to Lundra, that's when the carter took to tricking his son.

For years now he *happens* on the Duca's son, on the new carriage road, at the Vespri hour. At the first sight of him, he leaps from his cart and bows and blesses him. And when the son gets his fill of flattery, he asks the carter to "continue our discourse" over food and drink, and that's when that girlish voice of his sings out. "Dinner? If you insist, Your Excellencia. Va ben', but just a small bowl of minestra. Va ben', but just a scrap of hard bread. Va ben', but just a sip of peasant wine." And before who knows what, the carter gobbles down plates of meat and gulps down the finest wines, then warms himself by the fire, with more bowings and blessings and flatteries, all while slipping out news of this peasant and that peasant 'til the gold clock strikes the late hours and the son got no way out but to beg the carter to stay the night.

*

"Mastru Nonziu, si biniric'…"

"And blessings to you, *Madama of the road…*"

"*Madama. Madama.* What foolishness. I got no time for your foolishness this day."

"The Duca's son teaches me the foreign tongues and the courtly ways and all for my counsel. If Madama of the road takes none of my goods, let her take a good deal of my counsel."

"Then, counsel me. Counsel me. Days to weeks now, I gave my cousin a tea to calm her. Two places I had to be, but I chose one place for the other. Two hearts I had to soothe, but I chose one heart for the other. Counsel me, Mastru Nonziu. Last night, my cousin called for the girl. She wanted her back home. Last night I looked for her, there, in the dwelling on 'a bacca where I left her. But she's gone. The girl, she's gone! Where do I go? How do I find her?"

"It's *you!* Signa Vincenza, it's *you!*" the carter shouts out. "Who casts such a spell on me to make me see and hear the phantom Lady of the Castle? Signa Vincenza, it's *you!*"

"Mastru Nonziu!"

"Madama, I believed you were the *Lady,* the *Lady* worshipped by the cross-eyed lunatic, but…glorious saints! Now that you stand before me, I see you are more beautiful than any *Lady* of his dream."

Vincenza clasps her hands in prayer and shakes them to the heavens. "Maronna mia, more foolishness! And, for this, I got no patience."

"Patience? You live your life a patient woman…patient you wait for your maritu, 'til he comes back from who knows where…"

"I got no more patience! This morning, I took liberties with the flower buds to cut away my cousin's sorrow. One more, one less, and that makes the change. I know better. I'm a grown woman, an old woman. I know better for her. Now, she sleeps with a wide grin on her face. A strange sleep she sleeps. I'm ill at ease at what I done, but I got to find the girl."

"Your cousin's sorrows, she got them good, but what of *your* sorrows, Madama? Who is the one to cut away your sorrows? Am I the one, my dear Madama?"

"I got no more time. No more time. *Eat the minestra or throw it out the window.* Help me or… "

"Madama, with all my heart, I got to help you, and, then, you got to be thankful to me, and, then, I got to take you for my…"

With that, I howl like a wild dog 'til the carter's feet shake in his laughing boots. "Madama, you hear all what's 'round us?"

"I hear yapping from the wilds and more yapping from you!"

"Madama, I got to protect you." With that, he holds out his arms, but Vincenza slaps them away.

"The girl, Mastru Nonziu."

"The girl? Va ben', the girl. I got to help you find her. This day, good fortune is my friend. I got to help you find her, and, then, you got to be thankful to me, and, then, I got to take you for my…"

The carter pulls on his black beard, a short, full beard. But a beard on a man long past his forty years, how it got no sign of white in it, I don't know. What makes a man happy? His beard, his wife and his money. The carter can keep his money, stolen or earned, and he can keep his foolish beard, but he'll not take my Vincenza!

Vincenza stomps her foot on a smooth patch of earth. "I lose time with your foolishness, and I got no more time to lose. Blessings to you on your journey, Mastru Nonziu."

She stands there and waits for his blessings. He crosses his hands over his heart and whispers, "Madama, my dear Madama, *stay…*"

She lowers her eyes, and, what is this? She stumbles on a lava rock on the mule track she walked a hundred times and more. But, now, she stumbles? Now, she falls? Like a bolt of lightning, he leaps from his bench and kneels at her side, his thick hands wrapped 'round hers.

"Mastru Nonziu, who are you?" She tries to break free of the hold. "Are you the man I pray you are, the one that brings old kindle and sulphur sticks and sacks of wheat to the Saitta cottage when Signa Agata and the girl sleep, the one that brings paper cones filled with green nuts the girl finds on the table in the morning? Are you the kind and good one?"

He leans in and smiles, his long, brown teeth so close to her they near brush her chin.

"Are you the one to find the girl?" She fixes her eyes on him. "Are you the one to bring me peace?"

"And if I am that man, Madama, that good and kind man, then…what will you do to thank me?"

She pushes him away and stumbles to her feet. "Leave me be, Mastru Nonziu, I am still a…married…"

"Madama…"

"No more of this. No more, Mastru Nonziu," she runs past the cart, "now is not the time…"

"When?"

Vincenza throws her head back and lets out a sigh. "Mastru Nonziu, the girl… she's like no other."

"Stay, and you can tell me all of the girl."

"I got to find her. With or without you, I got to find…"

"So, that's how it goes? *With or without the rooster, the sun shines.*" He throws out his chest and slaps his leg. "But, with the rooster, the sun shines brighter." He takes her arm and helps her up on the bench. "Madama, be it the answer to your prayers or a prayer you dare yet whisper, this day you got your rooster. You got your rooster! Together, we'll look for the girl."

*

For two months now, behind the beautiful mountain, the sun rose in the heated sky more times than the girl knew how to count. The spotted shadow of the moon showed itself but once each month, two spotted shadows of the moon the girl counted from the night Vincenza left her. At the start, she feared she'd dry herself out with all the tears she shed, missing her Mamma and her z'a Vincenza the way she done. The shepherd boy done all he could to comfort her, soothing her with tales of lost ones finding their way back home but only when it was *time*. She knew that, too, she told him back, for her dreams were of such a nature, and 'though she ached to see her Mamma and her z'a Vincenza, there was growing inside her, and this she whispered to herself and dared not tell the shepherd boy, there was growing inside her a desire to stay and never leave.

Through May and June, the girl's heart filled with wonder each time the boy showed himself behind this rock or that grassy mound, and, always, she said, bathed in gold light the way the Savior shone or so Patri Radici said when she seen him act out the story of the Savior that rose from the dead. At night she slept in their mountain dwelling north of 'a bacca and nearer to Bronti than she dared to know. *It is you* she whispered in her bliss each night. *It is you that brings me life.* When the wound opened, she didn't heed Vincenza's words to stay far from man and beast for the shepherd boy said his own words, and they soothed and healed her, and they made her body shudder, words like *good* and *kind*.

Always at night, she asked the boy if he heard the weeping of women. "It's none but a creature in the wild," is the way he answered, and, quick, poured her wine to wash clean her thoughts and served her bread and 'a ricotta, sweet and satisfying the hungriest on earth. Always, he talked of red flesh oranges he wanted her to taste in late winter. Always, she smiled and told him one day she'd cook for him, food like a good maccarruni with broad beans and greens she knew to season with salt and oil, the way Vincenza taught her. Always, he told her his belly yearned for such delights.

When he reached for the last piece of bread, that was always when their fingers touched and pulled back and touched again and lingered for a small while. When he grabbed his flute, she knew their time that day neared the end. Always, she shook her head 'til strands of hair broke free from 'neath the shawl. Always, his finger moved to tuck them in. Always, a shudder filled her body, and she sighed. Always, he sighed, too.

"Your majesty," that was when he bowed and took his leave.

"My lord," always she hid her eyes, guarding his face in her visions, she whispered, 'til she slept and dreamed.

All the days in May and June, the hunchback sheep grazed in pastures far from the boy and his dwelling. But when his shadow was long on the hill, he called them back home. And when the sun made its way behind the mountains and the first stars shone in the sky, they waited for him outside the dwelling in the chill night air, biding their time to circle 'round him and drift in peaceful sleep.

Only the lamb stayed close to the boy and girl, day to night, her snout blackened with buzzing flies. When the spotted shadow of the moon settled in the sky and the girl's wound opened, always the lamb licked the girl's legs and ankles clean. And when the girl cradled the lamb to pray for her Mamma and her z'a Vincenza, she no longer seen their faces, she whispered to the lamb, for, now, in her mind's eye and in her heart, she seen but the shepherd boy, the one that none named for *beautiful.*

Beautiful? The shepherd boy got no beauty, not when the beast sleeps inside him for all to see. That red mark, in the shape of a broad bean and raw like a lamb's belly, it hollows in the boy's right cheek. A beast he got inside him. It little matters if it's gentle like the lamb or wild like the mountain cat. It's a beast...a *beast.* And when he crossed to the beast's world, he gave up his soul, and that's how he came to live with beasts and make his home far from Bronti. He knows, we all know, the beast can swell in him and take over the ways of a man. I shudder when I bring to mind the power coursing through him. Who can say if it's greater than mine, but to keep the girl safe, I ready myself to howl, and, if I got to, to fight him, and, if I got to, to kill him, when the beast takes over the shepherd boy.


*From a rose, a thorn. From a thorn, a rose.*


On a searing morning in July, the girl wakes to the light that shines on all the gifts the shepherd boy brought her through the night. She taps the soft bedding, the small pisciaturi, the jug of pure water from Mungibellu and tells herself, no, this is not a dream. "My Savior, my sorcerer," she whispers, "you got to journey far to find such treasures. My Savior, my sorcerer, good fortune shines on me for you bring these treasures home to me."

A leaf from the *ficarindia* rests at her side, a long, wide leaf from the prickly pear bush. The shepherd picked out all the spines. The care he took makes it more prized than any fancy dish in the Castle. On the leaf, there's a piece of brown bread and soft white cheese. This makes the girl smile. "It's you, my Savior, my sorcerer. It's you that I…" She bites her lips to keep the word she longs to say at bay.

He calls to the lamb. She takes the last bite of bread and the last sip of water and tightens the knot 'neath her chin. He presses the long tail of his stocking cap to his cheek, and they set out to where secret plants thrive, to unknown lands, not far-away at all, lands that brush the chin of Bronti, and she'd know, too, if she but cast her eyes from his gaze.

He wipes his brow with his full white sleeve and pats the sweat dripping down his neck. "We journeyed to far-off mountains but a day past." He strikes his cane on a rock and smiles when the lamb races to them. "What did you learn there?"

The July sun beats down on their heads. She pats her face and neck with the fringe of her shawl and climbs behind him up a small mountain. "Flowers," she says, "so many of them, shepherd boy, with long, spreading petals curling back. A deep pink color they were, but you cared more for the stems, and you taught me a good use for them."

"The stems are where we get the juice. A little water is all what we need. Then, we stir it up to make…"

He points to a smooth patch of lava earth. She kneels and lays his sack near small leaves pushing from the narrow openings of black rocks. "We stir it up to make the froth to wash all what needs to be cleaned, our clothes, our bodies…even our hair."

"But this day we got to learn of other plants, the unknown and forgotten ones that nourish us, too." The boy tears off a small leaf from the narrow opening of the black rock and hands it to the girl. "This is where Mungibellu and all the mountains keep their secrets."

"And when you find their secrets, shepherd boy, fortune smiles on you."

"I was born the first day of the year. That's the day my Mamma said brings good fortune. For so long, that was not true." He lowers his eyes and presses the long tail of his stocking cap to his cheek. But, now, you are here. And this is the first I know of good fortune." She sighs. He sighs, too, and pats the warm earth and waits for the girl to fold her skirt and sit by his side.

"You show me all what the plants know, and, for that, I am thankful. But 'a z'a Vincenza, too…she teaches me such things. Still, now, she teaches me 'though she's not by my side. Last night she came to me in dreams and told me of the plant that got to heal the fright in the girl like me, but not me, and, then, she said it was time."

"Time?"

"Sì, shepherd boy. Time…to take me *home*." The word breaks free from her small lips. The boy mouths it, too. He grabs his throat like it's on fire. He swallows the word whole. He grabs his chest, but it does no good to try to stop it, not when words take hold and sear our hearts.

He rips a head of yellow flowers from their stems. "Signa Vincenza is not wise. She married a coward, u vigliaccu they call him. She chose him. We choose the one that's like us."

"That's what Mamma tells me, but 'a z'a Vincenza isn't a coward…"

The boy points to the north, to the town with the crowded clay roofs and cottage stenches. "Ask your Mamma down there if I don't speak the truth."

Slow, slow, she raises her hand, her finger pointing straight to Bronti. "Mammita!" She slaps her cheeks and pinches her arms to shake herself free, she says, of the incantation the shepherd boy cast in her in May and June and, now, July. "Mammita, I'm here! Here!" She rocks back and forth and holds out her arms and pulls at her shawl like the women mourners.

"No, no, do not weep. Bronti isn't so far. Blessings on your Mamma and Signa Vincenza. Blessings on all the women and their men and on all what labor for the Duca."

"The Duca? Mamma says the Duca…"

"*Mamma says.* Sorrows, sorrows for all what know but with their ears."

"Mamma says…"

"Basta!" The boy flings a fistful of stones at the town. "*Mamma says… 'a z'a Vincenza says…* Down there, you know with your ears. Here, you know with your eyes and nose and mouth." He grabs her hands. "And these. These hands got to tell you all the truth 'round you."

"What truth?"

"When the pear's ripe, it got to fall on its own. But first you got to find the fertile soil and know the seedlings' needs for sun and water. Where's the fertile soil in Bronti? Down there, the tree can't grow. And, then, where's the pear?"

"But Mamma says the Duca…"

"And I say *basta!*"

He throws the petals at the girl. They strike her cheek and fall in the fringes of her shawl. "We forgive," she whispers, soft and sacred the way Vincenza prays, "we forgive all what we do to each other." But, soon, the holy words fade, and Agata's curses fill the air. "May you have a heart so knives can pierce it! May the Devil welcome you with open arms!" The lamb bleats a slaughter cry. The boy jumps up, grabs the lamb's legs and swings them 'cross his arms.

"And I say the Duca's back in his homeland, and I say his son turns a blind eye."

"So, now, I got to thank the son? The way his Papà thanked my Papà, the great Alfiu Saitta?" She cries out Alfiu's name, her eyes to the heavens. I look up at the heavens, too. Mountains of dark clouds huddle in the sky. I look 'round. Flowers shake in the rising wind. The lamb's soft strands whip 'cross the boy's face. Gusts blow 'round the girl, ripping the shawl from her head, throwing her to the ground. Gusts blow 'round the boy, flinging the long tail of his stocking cap behind him.

The foreign wind rages. The boy holds tight to the lamb the best he can. The wind blows harder. The boy holds tighter. With a jolt, the lamb digs her feet in the boy's shirt and tears the stitchings on his shoulder. He loosens his grip. She spirals out of his arms and runs for shelter right when a powerful gust hurls the boy to the ground, his cap flying behind the rock where the wind cast the girl's shawl.

"What happens here?" the girl cries out and rips off her apron and throws it over her hair.

"Bad things. Look at us. We are naked and sinners to the world, and, for our sins, we got to pay. Me, with no cap. You, with no shawl. We let the world see all what we are, and, now, we got to pay." He throws his hands to the heavens. Up to the heavens, the girl throws her hands, too, and makes a fist and spreads her fingers wide. Slow, slow, the wind quiets down. The boy raises his eyes and fixes them on the girl. Like in a spell, he slips the apron from her head and ties it back 'round her waist. With the back of his hand, he strokes her hair. "Where is *your* sin? You hide all what you are. But all what you are…is *beautiful*."

The girl holds tight to the apron. She falls to the ground, hiding her face there. "Beautiful. Beautiful," the boy whispers, him, on his knees. He lifts her chin and smiles.

Small pink stars flush her face. "But look at you, shepherd boy," she sobs. "Where is your sin? *You*, you are beautiful."

He kisses the girl's hands.

She throws her arms 'cross her chest. "O, how my heart cries out for you each night, shepherd boy, when you sleep outside the dwelling like an animal, not the good boy, the fine lord, I know you to be."

He holds her face in his hands. She shudders. He shudders, too. She places her hand on his shoulder, her fingers catching in the torn stitchings of his shirt. It rips wide open. He shudders. She shudders, too.

He wraps her in his arms. Her ear brushes 'long his chest. "I hear your heart," she whispers. "It rises soft like the tune you play when the moon shines."

She curls in his chest, her hair spread over him. He smiles and drifts to sleep in the calm of the storm.

"When Mamma turns away and crooks her finger, I look 'round," she whispers. "I want to see another girl like me. I pray there's another girl Mamma fears more and curses more. Another like me, but worse than me, not with the eyes of a fox, but with the eyes of a mountain cat. But, no. It's me, always me, the fox Mamma fears and curses. But, you, when you look at me, shepherd boy, you don't turn away. The day we met, there was no fear in your eyes. There were no curses on your lips. 'A z'a Vincenza says I am like no other. But, you, *you* are like no other."

The boy, lost in sleep and dreams, hears none of her speech 'til the girl nudges him awake. "My lord, can you hear it? Listen. Listen to all what fills the air."

"It's the wind," he sighs, shaking off the comfort of his bliss.

"No. These sounds are not from nature. *Child, my child,* they call out. Can you hear them?"

Before the boy says *sì* or *no*, Vincenza, wild like the girl's Mamma, pounces on the boy. "Curses on your cursed life!" Aided by a sudden mighty gust, she throws the boy behind the rock near the cap and the shawl. She rushes at him and slaps his torn shirt, "This is how you hide the sins of your Mamma? Cover yourself! You bring evil to the girl. She don't know to hide from a boy with such a nature. She's not like the others." She kicks the long tail of his stocking cap. "Cover yourself!"

The boy strikes his cane on the rock. The sheep scatter. He reaches for the cap and the shawl. "Signa Vincenza, you are not wrong." He shuffles to the girl and lays the shawl at her feet. "The girl," he fixes his eyes on her, "the girl is like no other."

He holds out his hand, but the scent of yellow flower buds rises in the air and draws the girl behind the rock and straight to Vincenza's open arms. "Z'a Vincenza, he gives me life!" The foreign wind blows the smells of the boy through the air, his grass, his wool, his sweat smells, his kind and sorrowful smells, all mixing with the scent of yellow flower buds. The girl gulps them in. "He gives me life, z'a Vincenza...life!"

The carter rushes to Vincenza with a small jug of water. "Madama, you and the girl drink. The water's fresh and good. It will calm you. Drink, but let us hurry." He looks up at the heavens and shakes his face free of the first drops of rain. "Glorious saints!" He gasps at the changing colors of the sky. "It's green!" A torrent of rain pours down on him. Far in the distance, I crouch behind a rock that shines like a black polished jewel and shakes with each boom of thunder. Water splashes everywhere, soaking my Vincenza and the girl, but, still, I let out a laugh when the rain drips down on the carter's beard, washing it clean of the black tinge.

"I made this happen, Mastru Nonziu. I lingered too long in the cottage."

"No, Madama, you are far from guilty. You are pure and good, but now's not the time to sing your praises." He holds the dripping jacket over her head, but the wind whips it from his hand. It soars through the sky like an owl's trembling prey. "Quick, Madama!"

She wipes the girl's brow and pats her cheek. "Amuninn'! Amuninn'! Come on, child! Don't linger no more!" Vincenza pulls the girl from behind the rock, but soon that the girl eyes the shepherd boy, her small feet dig in the muddy earth. "Va ben', child, say your farewells to him, if you got to, but, in truth, he merits none of your kindness."

The carter stomps his foot in a deep puddle. "We're losing precious time!" The rain water splashes back in his face and drips down the sides of his nose. "Madama," he shakes his head like a horse that got ticks in his ear, "the storm rages, and you stand like a holy statue!"

He rips off his vest and shelters Vincenza 'neath it. Like a bold suitor, he takes her arm and leads her down the mountain flank to the cart where Chiazza snorts and blows and shakes free from her crown of soaking flowers. There, in the rainstorm, they wait for the girl.

*

The sun burns through the dark clouds and strips the earth of the smell of rain. It dries Vincenza's soft, plump skin. It dries the painted panels of the cart and all the scenes of battles the brave Orlannu fought. The carter rolls back the tarp weighed down by a belly of water. He kisses the black lava cross 'round his neck and helps Vincenza up on the bench. The girl jumps in the back where she crouches near the fancy dresses.

"Weep not, Mamsella. The storm's past." He sings his nonsense tune of the little wood dove, and Chiazza settles in a steady gait. "Weep not. This got to make you feel better: whatever you desire in my cart, take it. It's a gift from me to you."

"With gifts come obligations," Vincenza says. "Bring to mind, Mastru Nonziu, the *gift* Garibbaldi got from the 'nglisi and the *gift* Garibbaldi gave back to them when he landed on our island. *You land here, you come to unite, we give you no problem. You chase out foreign kings, Garibbaldi, we give you no problem. But the signori 'nglisi, the English Gentlemen, they got to stay at the Castle. You land here, Garibbaldi, and unite l'Italia, we give you no problem, but Nelson blood got to stay in Bronti.* Bring to mind the pact they made and all what profited Garibbaldi and the Duca, but where were the gifts for the Bruntiszi?"

"What's this?" the girl asks cradling a small white box in her palm. "Once Mamma told me of a box where peasants hide all what they earn. Is this such a box?"

"Mamsella, does it look like a money box made of clay? No, it's of a fine bone china, that's what the Duca's son told me. See how smooth and round it is like a big, bright moon? No peasant could save up for such a treasure, and, to steal one, he got to be stabbed before he makes his way out his neighbor's door. No, this is a box where we keep our jewels and our most loved possessions. The Duca's son gave it to me on my last visit to the Castle. It's from the Duca's city of Lundra and a gift from one that holds my loyalty in high…Mamsella, regard the clasp…it's gold."

"Good men were killed that August day, Mastru Nonziu. The girl knows, and you know, too, how the general and his army betrayed us to keep the ones in the Castle safe and in power."

"Madama, the girl knows all the sorrow you and her Mamma teach her, but what of the pleasure? *Ripe fig, fall in my mouth.* Mamsella, what sense do you make of the wise words? Madama, look at her, she don't know…do you? No? Then, I got to tell the two of you all the gifts that fall from the Duca's son right in my mouth. Oui, Madama, gifts! A gift of feasts he offers me each day, tender meats, warm lemon cakes and the finest wines. A gift of rest he offers me each night in a soft bed the cross-eyed lunatic rants is his right alone. Through my loyalty, *I* have earned the right. And through my loyalty and through my counsel, the ripe fig always finds a way to my mouth."

The girl throws the box at the clanging pots. "Eat all the figs your mouth can hold, Mastru Nonziu, but your belly soon got to moan!"

"Stubborn girl! That's how you show your thanks to me? You're like all the Bruntiszi, stubborn like the trees that grow in lava rocks. And, you, with one more stubborn root from the women that raised you. A gift I give you with *no* obligations. Take the box to put your rings in and hair ornaments, too, for your marriage day." He turns 'round and eyes the girl wrapped in her heavy brown shawl. "Well, not all girls got to marry. A better thought is to give it to your Mamma. She can put her rings inside."

"Mamma wears but one ring, her marriage ring. She wears it day to night."

"No…no…that's not what I…" His jaw clicks, and he sings a bungled tune of a carter and his good fortune. "No," he whispers when he got no more words to sing, "a pot *clicca…clicca…*got to be the precious gift for you."

He turns to Vincenza. "Before I speak, I got to learn to chew on my words. You see here a starving man that swallowed his words whole with no good seasonings." He leans in and waves a finger near Vincenza's mouth. "Madama, wait…what's this I see? A smile? A smile to blind and weaken me? Sì, a smile. A precious gift from you to me that I got to hold close in my heart 'til my dying day. See how the sun now shines. A precious gift from the heavens to me. Fortune is the true friend of Mastru Nonziu this day."

*The one with the salt makes the soup.*

Agata stands at the threshold of the cottage, her hands, feet and hair bathed in olive oil, her white hair pulled back and tied with a red ribbon. She wears a string of blue beads 'round her neck, and 'round her waist, an apron tied tight and clean of stains. She wags her finger and opens her mouth wide, showing off all her small, dark teeth. She lets out a laugh and tells her daughter she's late.

She bows and kisses Vincenza's hands and bows to the carter, too. "*Vurimmu 'a terra,*" and leads them inside. "That's all what my Alfiu cries out each night." She lets out a sigh and strokes the stones of the hearth, her black eyes shining in the flickering light of the fire. "And, you, Mastru Nonziu, do you want the land, too? Are you brave enough to join my Alfiu and his mountain of a cousin this night to sing out their song and give the Duca and his Notaries their due?"

"I…"

She waves to the hearth. The carter and Vincenza pull up stools by the fire. "I took liberties with the flower buds. It was the only way I could leave my cousin and look for the girl," Vincenza whispers to the carter, "and now you see the cost my cousin pays."

"What do you say of this, Mastru Nonziu?" Agata pushes the girl aside and reaches for a brown cap on the marriage bed. "A new one I sewed this day. A cap for my Alfiu. A cap he wears. A cap he'll always be. 'Down with the hats,' he'll cry this night, 'you, there, wearing your hat, the hour of justice draws near.'"

"Madama Agata…"

"*Madama? Madama?* We wash clean such nonsense words with laughter before they turn to madness in our hearts." She spits in her hands and throws the spittle back in her mouth. She laughs, a cackle of a laugh. They mix in her mouth, the spittle and the laugh, making their way in gurgles to the back of her throat, snaking down her belly to the small mound of flesh 'neath her apron that she pats and rubs.

"Madama," the carter pinches Vincenza's arm, "and what if the laughter long ago turned to madness?"

"Sst…sst… Mastru Nonziu, a grieving woman stands before you that melds the here and now with all what's gone before."

"Ppi piaciri, Madama, I'm not at ease. Please, let us take our leave before your cousin…" Vincenza shakes her head, but the carter, he jumps up, grabs her arm and pushes her out the door.

*

The girl kneels by the fire. Her Mamma, sitting on the stool, stares in silence at the low flames. "Mamma," the girl whispers, but Agata swats the word away. The girl slips her arm 'round Agata's waist and brushes her cheek 'cross Agata's round, red knuckles. "Mamma, I lived a most beautiful dream."

"And, me, I dream the most beautiful dreams, but only when your sister keeps vigil." She squeezes the girl's chin. "I got to tell you each and all of them."

"I know your dreams, Mamma. They cry out to me each night."

"How many dreams I dreamed of her…"

"I know."

"She was too good for the earth…"

"I know."

"Do you know where she is?"

"Mamma, all this I know."

"Do you know the cause?"

"The cause? Sì, I know the cause, Mamma." The girl licks her palms, and the boy's smells, the grass and wool and sweat smells, the kindness and sorrow smells, they all come alive in her hands. They fill the cottage, and when the stone walls can no more hold them, they fill the air on all the roads of Bronti. "The boy told 'a z'a Vincenza. 'The girl,' he said, 'is like no other.'"

Agata moans with laughter. "Such nonsense words."

"No. I speak the truth."

"The truth? The truth?" Agata clasps her hands, the blue beads catching in them. She throws her hands up to the heavens with such might that the beads break free from their cord. *Plinca. Plinca. Plinca.* They pelt the iron pot in the hearth and scatter on the ground. "What truth? The truth that you screamed and frightened her?"

"No, Mamma." The girl picks up the blue beads, one by one, and keeps her eyes to the earth. One by one, she whispers *no* to all what her Mamma asks.

"The truth that, quick, she followed you, so the midwife had to pull her from my belly?"

"No, Mamma."

"What truth?" The woman throws kisses to her belly. *"Nanna ninna ninna.* It wasn't your time, figghia mia. *Nanna ninna ninna.* You left me. The one that stays is *his* child. I got no use for her."

"Mamma, this is what you dreamed last night?"

"This is what I dream each night."

"I know. Mamma, I know. This is all what I hear when you cry out in your dreams."

"I done my part, but when the midwife screamed, the cummari rushed in. They seen your sister and pulled at their hair and wailed."

"I know."

"'Curses to the cursed,' they cried at her round face, sacred and beautiful, save for the one…"

The girl throws the beads at the stone wall. "I know! Mamma, I know! I know!"

"You know none of it! Your sister was sacred and beautiful and weak. She needed milk. I gave it to her. The weak got to be fed and loved. I fed her. I loved her. 'Curses to the cursed!' the cummari cried. Your sister with the round face…sacred and beautiful…save…"

The girl falls at her Mamma's feet and strikes her ears 'til they're red like fire. "Mamma, ppi piaciri! No more!"

"…sacred and beautiful…*save*…"

"No more," she whimpers.

"…*save* for the one black eye…"

"No more…no more…no more…"

"…where an eye ought not to be!"

The girl licks her fingers and waves them 'neath her nose. "O, Holy Savior, where is your sweet smell to save me?" She runs outside the cottage, runs back in. "O Holy Savior," her fists to the heavens, "where are you to save me?"

"*Savior?*"

"Mamma, he's gone. He's gone, and I'm weak."

"Who are you to speak of the Savior? He seen you and abandoned me."

"Sì, Mamma, he abandons me, too. All what you say is true."

Agata holds out her hand. The girl picks up the blue beads and piles them in her Mamma's palm. "Now, you know, girl. All what we lose, we lose great."

"Sì, Mamma. All what we lose, we lose great."

"*The one-eyed monster* the cummari called her. But she was beautiful. And she was blessed. What is the blessed name I gave her?"

"I hear you call it out each day you pray it."

"Shout out your sister's name for all of Bronti to hear and pray with us."

"Maria Nunziata!"

"Maria Nunziata?"

"The angel! The angel! Maria Nunziata, Mamma. Maria Nunziata…the angel!"

Agata raises her eyes to the heavens, a broken smile on her face. "Maria Nunziata, the angel! Maria Nunziata, the angel! At her birth, the bright moon shone, but when the moon grew dark and spotted in the sky, the saints carried her back to paradise."

"Mamma, we got to say a prayer, one last prayer, and it got to be the end of all the sorrow. Ppi piaciri, we got to end the sorrow now."

"She wanted to be with me like a good daughter."

"'A z'a Vincenza says *I* am a good daughter."

"A good daughter that asked 'a Maronna 'a Nunziata if she could stay. 'A Maronna heard her prayers. I felt life in me again. Her eye, her black eye… it never seen the light of day, but it beat in my belly, there, where the truth makes a dwelling, there, where it tells me the right and wrong *you* do."

"'A z'a Vincenza says *I* am a good daughter."

The Mamma lays the beads on the marriage bed. She whispers Alfiu's name and takes the knife from 'neath the pillow and slips it in the girl's hands. "But a good daughter…"

"Papà's knife!"

"A good daughter got to do the one good deed. Then, it ends. With a just eye for eye, the sorrow ends. And, then, you are my good daughter."

"Papà's knife…"

"*Your* knife…"

"Ppi piaciri, the pig's my friend."

"The pig! I ask a greater deed." She sits on the bed and slaps her legs. "This body can't walk the path to the Castle no more. Each day I lose my strength. But before my days end, I got to see the blood flow from the son's heart. I got to hear his cries for mercy. I got to see his Papà rip out his hair and wail u reputu. I got to hear Alfiu's sainted voice shout out from the heavens. 'We live and we die for *our* land!' It's all what I got to hear before I die."

"And that brings the end to your sorrow?"

"Sì."

"But, Mamma, that brings the start to mine."

"Figghia mia?"

The girl rests her head in her Mamma's hands. "I am your daughter, Mamma. Sì, I am your good daughter."

"Figghia mia, the knife is for you and for the son."

"But, Mamma, *he* is not the Papà…*he* done no wrong."

"*Ninna nanna nanna ninna,* a just eye for eye."

"That's not just! 'A z'a Vincenza told me all what's just makes our hearts pure. Such an act makes me not pure. It makes me like the one that killed Papà. Such an act makes me not Papà's child. It makes me the child of the evil one. And *that one* I am not!" The girl flings the knife on the ground. "Here, I learn with my ears. Up there, with the shepherd boy, I learned with my eyes and nose and mouth." She raises her hands to the wood cross. "And, with these, I learned the truth with these. I learned to heal with these. To heal like 'a z'a Vincenza! Not to kill! Mamma…to heal! To heal!"

Where but in her anger does Agata find the strength to rush 'round the cottage, ripping at the woven chairs, pulling out the straw and stabbing her daughter's flesh with the sharp pieces? She squeezes the girl's chin and slaps her mouth. "Who dares to disobey her Mamma? 'A figghia ru diavulu! The daughter of the Devil!"

"No! No! *That one* I am not. 'A z'a Vincenza says…time and again, she says *that one* I am not."

"The coward's wife knows none of it. Who but *his* child got to bring such pain to a Mamma?"

"No, Mamma, no. Don't say the words that fill my heart with sorrow."

"The sorrow's here, and all see and hear it." She slumps in a chair and sobs. "Now, there's none to help me."

"Mamma!"

She grabs the girl's hands. "Help me, figghia mia, help me."

The pig jumps on Agata's lap and squeals out a comfort cry. Agata cradles him in her arms 'til the sun drifts behind the great mountains. "*I* am the one," the girl whispers in the dark cottage and flings the sleeping pig from her Mamma's lap. "*I* am the one to bring Mamma peace. Mamma wanted you dead, that's how she loves you. And, *you*, you think you can bring her peace? You can't! You can't! Only a daughter can bring her Mamma peace!"

The girl picks up the knife and taps Agata's shoulder. "Wake up, Mamma. Sì, I got to help you. You say my sister does your bidding…look at me… look at my hand and all what lies there…now, I, too, stand brave to do your bidding."

The girl holds out her hand, the knife shining there. Agata crosses herself and struggles out of the chair. She grabs the girl's arm and leads her to the bridal chest. She opens the chest and lays quick, hard kisses on Alfiu's bloody shirt. "For you, Alfiu, my ruler, my life." She strokes the blue marriage dress and gathers it in her arms. "Figghia mia, wear this," she whispers to the girl. "Wear all what I got on the day you serve justice."

*

For weeks now, the girl's been a good daughter. "Rest," she whispers to her Mamma each morning before the Mattutinu bells ring out. "Rest, and I'll be back soon." Each day, before the girl sets off, Agata grabs her hand and asks if this is the day the girl serves justice. Each day, she tells her, "Mamma, on the morrow." Agata whimpers and that's when the girl folds back her apron and pats the knife hiding there, and that's when her Mamma smiles.

For weeks now, the girl's been a good daughter, cleaning her Mamma and her bed clothes with the froth from the stems of the dark pink flowers, the way the shepherd boy taught her. She learned where to find them, too, all the plants Vincenza and the shepherd boy found that nourish and calm and heal. In rocks, she finds the ruta, the rue plant that calms her Mamma. In walls, she finds the *erba ri vetu*, the plant that grows where the wind wants to take it. The *herb of the wind* we call it. It helps the blood run smooth. Up all the great mountains she climbs and 'cross burning lava rocks she races, her swift feet scorched, her apron filled with leaves and buds and rootstalks for her Mamma's teas and, hiding 'neath the plants, Alfiu's knife.

For weeks now, she whispers in her hands and closes them tight. When she opens them and spreads her fingers wide to the heavens, her body grows in strength. And that's when she takes off her apron and lays it on the earth to start her work. She piles lava stones one on the other and climbs the stones one on the other 'round and 'round, and, this day, she reaches the top and makes a roof.

For weeks now, she comes 'on dwellings that others built of branches and stones, and, there, she finds abandoned jugs and blankets that she takes back to her own new dwelling. Once, she found a clay lamp and a sack, and she smiled, whispering how such gifts got to please the shepherd boy. For weeks now, on rocky mule tracks, behind this rock and that rock, she lingers, her eyes taking in the landscape like the long lens they say the *hero* Nelson used in sea battles. On rocky mule tracks, behind this rock and that rock, she waits for the boy.

*

*Clippa…cloppa…clippa…cloppa…clippa…cloppa…* On a rocky mule track south of Bronti, Chiazza's hooves quicken to the rhythm of the carter's song, the one he sings in his girlish voice about the little wood dove. The mare's ears fold back. She makes a soft, low sound through her nose, like a cooing, but for what? For a voice that only the horse on all our island loves.

"Gooood Mooooreeen, Mamsella."

The girl brushes the dirt from her hands, folds her apron back to the waist, careful to keep the knife safe 'neath the buds and rootstalks, and runs to the cart. "Si biniric', Mastru Nonziu."

"And may God's blessings be with you, Mamsella. Tell me, is it your Mamma that teaches you to give such fine blessings?"

"No. She's filled with sorrow and gives her blessings to no one no more."

"So, you got to fill her heart with joy."

"Sì, Mastru Nonziu."

"Are you heading back to town?"

"Sì, with buds and rootstalks for Mamma."

"Hop up."

"Mastru Nonziu, you say I got to fill Mamma's heart with joy," she jumps up on the bench beside him, "and that's what she asks of me. But I'm frightened to bring her the joy she craves."

"Frightened? Glorious saints! Joy is the gift the child got to bring the Mamma. This bodes good for the child, too. The child that obeys lives a happy life."

"Sì, and if I obey... Mastru Nonziu, you are a wise man." She tightens the knot 'neath her chin and sobs.

"Who tells you I am wise? Is it Madama what blesses me and sings my praises?"

"*Madama*? You mean 'a z'a Vincenza?" She wipes her cheeks with the fringes of her shawl. "She's a good woman and teaches me all what I got to know."

"How fares the good woman these days?"

"She comes, she goes. She takes me to the edge of the forest where her fingers dig in the earth for rootstalks, the long brown ones to charm *u vermu*."

"Now, why would such a charming woman look for plants to charm the worms? Her mere presence would make the fattest worm scuttle out of a poor peasant's body and worship at her feet." He lets out a laugh. "Mamsella, you don't understand all what I say? Va ben'. What else does the good woman teach you?"

"She brings me to the mountains where she gathers the plants to heal the fever. Her work takes longer now. The heat's not been kind to her. More and more, she looks for the *bburraina*, the blue starflower, and when she finds it, she gathers the dark leaves, the ones pure of stains and insect bites, and, those, she says, to help her heart beat quick and good. Time and again, her face goes pale and her legs go weak 'til she makes the cure. And the dark hair peasant girls, too, they whisper that 'a z'a Vincenza don't fare so good." She hides her face, her voice, trembling, her cheeks, wet with tears. "If anything bad befalls 'a z'a Vincenza…"

The carter whips the reins. "Madama is in good health!" he shouts. "What do such girls know? They gather at fountains, lazy in their chores, and spread gossip. Who are they to speak of health? Of late, their skin is pale and wet, and the life, slow, slow, slips from their eyes. Madama is in good health," the carter kisses his cross. "Don't you know, she got to be? Now, wipe away all your tears, and let us talk of things that bring us joy."

She grabs the edge of her apron and pats her face. Some rootstalks fall on the wood planks. So, too, the knife. "What things?" she asks and spreads her skirt wide over the planks and hides the knife. "What things, Mastru Nonziu?"

"*Jautu*, Chiazza!" he shouts and pulls back on the reins. "Mamsella, what do I see? For if it's what I think it is, it brings you none but sorrow."

"So, tell me, Mastru Nonziu, what brings me joy?"

"For one, the shepherd boy."

The girl lowers her eyes. "The shepherd boy?"

"Oui, Mamsella, the shepherd boy. *Blasiu.*"

"*Blaaazzzeeeuuu…Blasiu…Blasiu.* How the name agrees with him. He is Blasiu that blazes the sky."

"And you search for him?"

"All the days."

"And you wait for him?"

"I wait like Mamma waits for joy."

"To wait…and wait…and wait." He lets out a sigh. "What do the wise words say? To wait for someone that don't come, to sit at a table and wait to eat, to go to bed and wait to sleep, to wait and wait and wait…these are three ways of dying."

"Mastru Nonziu, you eat at the Duca's table, you sleep in the Duca's bed, but still you die each night."

"The girl that sits by my side is not only stubborn but bold."

"I speak the truth. You wait for 'a z'a Vincenza. But I can help you die no more if you take me..."

"If I take you..." He smiles, showing off his long, brown teeth.

She nods and smiles, too. "The child that obeys lives a happy life."

"Now, where do you want to go? To the shepherd boy? I know where to find him, and I can take you there."

She yanks the knife free and jumps in the back of the cart 'neath the fancy dresses and mutters a prayer, quick and cruel, like the prayer the lieutenant whispered on his horse in the neighborhood Santu Vitu before he shouted *Fire!*

"Mamsella, sì or no: do I take you now to the shepherd boy?"

She crosses herself the way Vincenza taught her, three times with three more prayers to 'a Maronna 'a Nunziata. "No, Mastru Nonziu. To the Castle."

# PART II:
# THE CASTLE

*A man shows himself by his word. An ox by his horns.*

A wolf pup—not a man—got eyes the color of the sea. But here it is, the man's left eye, bright and blue, gazing out on the new olive groves. The right eye, he covers with a patch. His cousin, the one he names the *delicate Elizabeth*, she says he got to do it for the island sun causes the right eye much harm. The peasants say one eye's good like the other and that the man wears the patch to look like his long-ago uncle, the *hero*, that gave his Nelson heirs a title and our town.

This Nelson heir marching 'round the Duca's olive groves where peasants dig and plant and hoe, the old ones near collapsing 'neath the scalding sun, this one in his loose grey jacket and vest and his loose grey pants and his black shiny boots, this one sliding his hand 'neath the bright white collar of his shirt, patting away the sweat with his palm and sighing that the heat "grows more intolerant each day," this Nelson heir is no hero. He's the Duca's son, the young Alexander Nelson Hood, that studies documents with raised gold seals locked safe away in the Castle. When his Papà dies, such papers got to make him, the way he says it, *the fifth great Duke of Bronte*. The peasants call him the *Duchinu*, the little Duca. But there's nothing little about him. He's a tall bundle of straw with hair the color of sand…and a clean face. A clean face! A man three past his twenty years and still no beard! A rooster with no crest is what the peasants say of him, the kind slow to take a stand. When his Papà dies, how can the son with such a clean face rule as the *rooster* of Bronti?

The Duchinu scrawls down numbers 'cross his charts for the new plantings in the olive groves all while that conniver of a surgeon, Lucien Gale, kicks the dirt from his worn boots. He fixes his eyes on the Duchinu's patch and scratches the line of scars on his own face and neck, red and fresh like he got the wounds but a day past.

"My lord, you are aware it was pure myth that your great-great uncle wore an eye patch…"

"Dr. Gale," the Duchinu stomps his foot, "that is by no means the reason…"

"However, what is not myth is the brandy cask…"

"Dr. Gale!"

"Yes, my lord, the brandy cask which preserved the great admiral's body and returned him to our England in tiptop shape… And, now, that we have turned our conversation to the talk of spirits…"

"*We?*"

"Very well, *I*. Nonetheless, without a pocket watch, I am a mere peasant relying on bells and nature to tell the hour. And the nature of this conversation suggests to me that a rendezvous with my *green fairy* is fast approaching."

The Duchinu presses the patch to his eye. "Need I remind you of the grievous accusations lodged against you and the manner in which my father…?"

The surgeon throws his shoulders back, a tight smile on his face. "My lord, as I was saying, my *green fairy* shall have to wait."

"Now, shall we continue our study of the groves?"

The surgeon bows, a man old like me, old enough to be the Duchinu's Papà. "Yes, my lord."

The Duchinu waves to a dry clod of earth that an old peasant, leaning on his hoe, turned over but didn't pound. A young peasant eyes the Duchinu, kicks the hoe, and, quick, the old peasant shakes himself free of his tiredness and pounds the earth. "Unsuited to olive growing the administrators said of this land long before I was born. My grandmother agreed. My father, as well."

"The great Duchess of Bronte believed the costs would swallow up the profits. And perhaps she and your father were not wrong."

"I beg to differ, Dr. Gale. I shall make a go of this and prove all past and present administrators of the Duchy wrong. As I am destined to be Duke of Bronte one day, I must see to…that is, I must act…"

"Yes, you must act." The surgeon brushes the knees of his worn brown pants. "Yes, my lord," he pulls at a thread, "and how do you propose to act?"

"Dr. Gale, according to Sicilian tradition, for an olive tree to flourish..."

The surgeon lets out a laugh. "Ah, yes, my lord, the beloved Sicilian tradition."

"Sun, stone, silence, solitude...Dr. Gale, *silence*." The Duchinu jots down a last number on his chart and looks up at the sky. "Sunshine is, indeed, abundant..."

The surgeon takes off his hat and wipes his brow. "And excessive on this island."

"Stone. Unfortunately, the volcano has seen to our having more than our share of stone."

The surgeon presses his tongue to the side of his cheek, "My lord, all we now need is *solitude*."

The Duchinu shakes his head. "Your humor is most appreciated by those who have never been worn down by it."

"I have offended you, my lord."

"Yet I see no repentance in your eyes." The surgeon bows. The Duchinu nods for him to rise, and, quick, like the sun shining through the clouds, a smile brightens his face. "Dr. Gale, although fair play may be a jewel, this is not the moment for... Look! Over there! Deny that jewel of a mare is my Chiazza. You cannot! You cannot!"

"My lord, I fear you've fallen prey to yet another summer mirage."

With one eye covered and one eye narrowing, the Duchinu points to where the old olive groves meet the new. "Perhaps, Dr. Gale," he lets out a sigh, "perhaps you are not wrong. Perhaps my desire to see Chiazza's once-mighty legs crush small green olives at her feet...perhaps I have allowed such reveries..." He throws his hands over his chest. "Oh, my lady! My beautiful lady!" he cries out in our tongue.

"When he was a boy, he wanted to ride a sheep," the peasants snicker. "Now, he's a man, and he wants to ride a worn-out mare." I hold my belly and laugh with them and mock the Duchinu and the affection he got for a horse that's no more good in the fields, that's no more good for nothing. A peasant I am once more, mocking those that stole from us time and again.

"My lord, let us hope it is, indeed, a mirage. If not, then, it is as I have long suspected: the carter is overstepping his peasant boundaries."

From his front vest pocket, the Duchinu takes out a timepiece hanging on a thick gold chain, a gold pocket timepiece with carvings on the back and the front. He flips it open. "Nearing five o'clock. It would, indeed, be earlier than customary. However, I have never encountered the carter anywhere but on…"

"Five o'clock, you say?" The surgeon rubs the thick chain between his fingers. "A most beautiful watch to mark the hour. A gift from your beloved father, I presume. No matter. As I was saying, the Duke would hardly tolerate such impertinence, especially from a carter or whatever he claims to be."

"When dignitaries cease to die, that is when my father shall cease to attend their funerals. When the Queen no longer needs such services in London, my father shall be free to return to Sicily and assume his role as *the fourth great Duke of Bronte*. At that time, he, and, he alone, shall tolerate or not the *impertinence* of his people." He flips the timepiece closed and slips it in his vest pocket. "Until such time, I welcome it."

"As you wish, my lord."

"After all, Dr. Gale, did I not welcome *you*?"

The surgeon's eyes narrow. "And, I, my lord, am eternally grateful for such *benevolence*."

*

There, where the old olive groves meet the new, the reins shake in the carter's hands. "Way over there, see, where the old olive trees…way over there, in the north, at the start of the old olive tree groves, *clicca…clicca…*that's where you'll find me," he tells the girl. "The old olive tree groves." The girl nods. "Whatever you got to do, *clicca…clicca…*and, I swear on my eyes I don't want to know none of it, be quiet and be quick." The girl jumps from the cart. "Wait, Mamsella, don't forget." He pulls at his eye to seal the deal. "If the Excellencia finds out I brought a peasant to the Castle with no permission, my days at the Castle are no more. That'd be a great loss for me. But, see, I share my loyalty to the Excellencia with you. And, you, Mamsella, loyal 'though you be to your z'a Vincenza, now you got to share it with me, too."

In the heart of the old olive tree groves, a roped black dog paces 'round in silence, there, where, each morning, the peasants pile their sacks of bread and cheese and their jugs of wine. These are the treasures the peasants carry when the Star of Dawn shines in the sky and the peasants set off to work on the Duca's land. These are the treasures the dog safeguards. When the sun beats high over Mungibellu, and the Angelus bells ring out through Bronti and all the Duca's land, that's when the men dive in their sacks and devour their noonday meal, always saving a few pieces of wine-soaked bread for the Ave Maria hour.

"For you, Mamma," the girl whispers in the heart of the old olive tree groves far from the carter that kisses his black cross and Chiazza that rests near a broad, gnarled trunk at the north end, the two biding their time. The girl rubs the knife in her apron. She paces 'round the trees. "For Mamma. For Mamma," she whispers. And the words make her brave. She walks. She runs. She races through rows of ancient trees crouching here, there, behind the split-scarred trunks 'til she comes 'on the roped black dog. When the guard dog turns to sniff and pee, he eyes the girl. He howls loud like it's the end of the world. He spins 'round so fast, spinning 'til the rope chafes and sparks and he breaks free. He pounces on the girl. I howl, but he barks with such madness, the peasants in the new olive tree groves got to hear him, too. They throw down their hoes and spades, but the Duchinu raises his hand. They got no way out but to pick up their tools. With their brown teeth clenched, they curse him 'neath their breath and start their work again.

The girl makes a fist, opens her hand and spreads her fingers wide. She opens her mouth, but what comes out, who can make sense of it? The guard dog, he understands. He jumps and rolls on the ground and kicks his feet in the air, his tail slapping 'cross the earth. He licks the girl's hand. She pats his head and sings soft a lullaby, and, with that, he curls on the ground quiet and dreaming.

She leaps over him and stumbles on the sacks of food. A few pieces of brown bread fall from the sacks. The buds and rootstalks fall from her apron. So, too, the knife. She eyes the knife. She eyes the bread, spittle dripping from her mouth. Quick, she gathers the plants back in her apron and hides the knife 'neath them. She kneels on the ground turning over sacks and chewing on bread soaked in wine, no longer sweet, she says, not like the shepherd boy's wine. She reaches for a jug with a big belly and narrow neck and whispers all what the shepherd boy taught her. *This is how a man drinks: Take in a breath with the jug on your lips. Hold it high. The wine got to flow. Your thirst got to be quenched.* She wipes her mouth clean and takes on the ways of a peasant man and drinks all what is *his* right alone to drink.

*

In the new olive tree groves, the Duchinu sighs. "Perhaps it *was* a mirage, Dr. Gale. Perhaps Chiazza shall never return."

The surgeon swipes his hand high 'cross his brow. A few red strands in his thick white hair catch on his fingers. "My lord," he shakes his fingers free, "she shall return, dragging that broken-down cart replete with useless goods for lazy, useless people."

"Useless? The Bronte peasant serves me well." The Duchinu fixes his eye on the surgeon. "Would that I could say the same for all those in my employ." He rips off the corners of his charts. Tiny scraps of paper like the coarse powder of flowers drift in the air and fall to the earth.

"Alec, I see what I see. The manor offers the carter a haven. A glass of fine wine, a warm cake and a soft bed await him through my lord's generosity. Yes, Alec, the mare and her master shall return. Where else shall they go?"

The Duchinu bows his head and cradles the charts, his clean chin brushing the torn corners. "Where, indeed, Dr. Gale, shall any of us go?"

"I suspect our conversation has taken a melancholy turn."

The Duchinu shuffles 'round the surgeon like a man in mourning, his steps slow and sorrowful. "*Merum et mistum imperium.* The highest judicial powers over life and death and banishment. This is the cross the title bears. This is my legacy, the cross which holds me captive on this island." The surgeon presses his hand tight over his mouth, but, still, a laugh breaks free. "Dr. Gale!"

The surgeon lets out a fake cough. "No, no, my lord, you misunderstand the laughter. Such gaiety…"

"Is most irregular."

"In my defense, my lord, it stems from a rather amusing anecdote which suddenly…"

"*Inappropriately…*"

"Yes, my lord, which suddenly and *inappropriately* seized my thoughts."

"Very well." The Duchinu kicks the earth, stirring up the torn corners of his charts. He narrows his eye. The surgeon bows and sweeps up the bits of paper with the edge of his hand. When he drops the last of the scraps in his palm, the Duchinu waves them away.

"My lord," the surgeon clenches his teeth and stuffs the scraps in his pocket, "if I am not incorrect the discourse centered on your highly-esteemed legacy. However, may I remind you the crosses you bear are all of *your* design. This exile from our homeland is nothing if not self-imposed."

"Exile, as my father suspected, proved to be *your* saving grace."

"We are talking of yours, my lord."

"Mine is tantamount to *duty.*"

"Duty." The surgeon fixes his gaze on a titmouse, the long tail swishing on the ground, *petu petu petu petu petu*, the loud song trailing in the wind when the bird flies away and disappears in the grey smoke of Mungibellu's breath.

"Yes, Dr. Gale. Duty. Perhaps you've deemed such a guiding principle superfluous in your life, but I have not." And, there, 'round the surgeon, the Duchinu marches, the titmouse of the Castle, swishing 'cross our land, his tired song of *duty duty duty duty duty*, loud and empty and trailing in the wind.

"And did this sense of duty compel you to cultivate the land and rebuild the manor?"

"You know it did."

"Then, my lord, to paraphrase our great Vice-Admiral Lord Viscount Horatio Nelson, *you have done your duty to the Sicilifying of your conscience.*"

At the sound of the name of his long-ago uncle, the Duchinu presses the patch to his eye and bows his head.

"Come now, Alec, let us rid you of this melancholy. You and I have no choice but to make the best of our circumstances." He slaps the Duchinu's back but, quick, drops his hand. "My lord, as I was saying, your town may not be paradise, but neither is it hell, although, according to your peasants, Etna, indeed, provides a most convenient entranceway to the underworld. It is there, is it not, that Hades abducted Persephone? Ah, would there were still virgins in Bronte!"

"Dr. Gale, must you always divert the conversation to the shortcomings of the fair sex?"

"Their shortcomings, as you say, are my delight. The Bronte peasant girl is a whore, desperate for recompense of her flesh. And the Bronte peasant boy, well, he is a hotchpotch of his environs and history. He is like his *beautiful mountain* which is on the verge of erupting at any moment. What beats in the heart of this Bronte peasant boy? Like his volcano, he is a composite of a thousand elements, elements from his conquerors and their cultures, elements which tangle him in the web of mythologies rather than realities. I am too kind. Simply stated, your Bronte peasant is a volatile, superstitious fool."

"His superstitions have classical roots. Nonetheless, I assure you his soul is not so consumed with the darkness of the underworld as it is with the fertility Persephone embodies. For the peasant, the love of Nature reigns supreme."

The surgeon grabs his belly and lets out a thunder laugh. "Alec, how you dream! The peasant's love of Nature! Ha! The peasant's love of hatred would be more precise."

"*Hatred?*"

"Yes, *hatred*, and, you, Alec, deposited on this island to stir in your share of social justice which falls on deaf ears. Hatred, Alec, and I shall explain. You speak of Nature. For the peasants, Nature is Land, and the peasants have long claimed the land is theirs. The courts have yet to be convinced by their arguments. Thus, the land incites their hatred. And their justice, although not doled out in court, is, nonetheless, executed in the manner for which they are renowned. Thievery. Yes, my lord, thievery. Alec, do not be naïve, your good and loyal peasants steal from you. If not olives, oranges." He pulls a small branch from inside his jacket. "If not oranges, *pistachios*." He waves the branch in the air. "Voilà, the green gold of Bronte. This offers proof, the explanation of which I shall provide at a later date. For the moment, know your greedy peasants steal. And not solely for hunger's sake."

The Duchinu throws his charts in the air. The surgeon leaps for them, his arms flapping up and out, each of the charts safe in his clenched hands before grazing the earth. "Lucien, when shall you realize it is in the web of injustice where hatred resides? Sicily is my home. I must strive to do all in my power to save her."

The surgeon, breathing hard, bowing low, passes him the last of the charts. "Very well, Alec, render your conscience less miserable. Take action in a just fashion." He flicks his head and shines a wide smile in the Duchinu's eye. "Be just, Alec. Be just. Give it away. Give it all away. Rip up that decree our great Vice-Admiral Lord Viscount Nelson prized so much. Make a speech and give the peasants back their land. Let us make the world a kingdom for the common creature and crown all the peasants kings. No, my lord? Not today? Not tomorrow, either, I suspect." He pats the charts in the Duchinu's arms. "The simple act of justice...not so simple after all."

The Duchinu lets out a sigh. "Lucien, please, this is precisely the subject I had hoped to avoid for our delicate Elizabeth's sake. She has ofttimes pleaded for happier moments when we dine. At the very least, let us honor her request this evening."

"I shall, when the evening is upon us. However, here and now, I have still much to state. Let us assume you wish to share that which you own with your peasants...I assure you their feelings for you shall never change."

"Feelings? That is your realm."

"And respect is yours. I assure you, Alec, you are not only hated by your peasants. As an unworthy adversary in their eyes, you are not respected. Yes, I fear you are neither loved nor respected. Come now, Alec, pouting is unbecoming of a Duke's son. As your father's friend, I do not wish to offend you, however, let us be candid: when, pray tell, was the last time a peasant kissed your hand?"

The Duchinu gazes at his hand, the pale back, the smooth palm. "A primitive custom," he strokes it, "which does not enter..."

The surgeon grabs the Duchinu's hand. "And I shall forthwith relieve you of your misery." He brings it to his open mouth and lays a hard kiss on it.

"Dr. Gale!"

"No need for alarm, Alec," and swipes his mouth 'cross the back of his own hand. "A mere pleasantry, a fulfillment of, as the peasants say, *disziu*."

"Disziu?" You have much to learn of *this* nobleman's *desire*." Spittle shines on the Duchinu's hand. He shakes it off with such vigor that his fingers hook on to the thick gold chain in the front pocket of his vest. The gold pocket timepiece breaks free and swings 'cross the surgeon's face.

The surgeon grabs hold of it, flips it open and eyes the needles that cut the plane. "Six o'clock! Dash it all! My *green fairy* awaits me!"

"*Green fairy*, indeed! A most endearing term for a most vile indulgence."

"Absinthe, my dear Alec, makes the heart grow fonder. And many a lady, indeed, has grown fonder in my eyes and I, in hers, simply by imbibing."


*Only those that do nothing never make mistakes.*


The black guard dog wakes from his dreamy sleep and howls for his masters. The peasants throw down their tools again, but the Duchinu, he narrows his eye, and, with that, the peasants take off their caps and bow. "Continue your work, men. I shall go and investigate." He turns to the surgeon. "Be so kind as to pour our delicate Elizabeth a pale sherry in my absence. And, please, convey my apologies to her." He undoes the button on the deep pocket of his jacket and pulls out a pistol with a short barrel and a wood handle and waves it in the air.

"Now, what do we have here?" The surgeon swallows a laugh. "With a longer barrel and a flourish of filigree, we should have the makings of a fine dueling pistol."

"Dr. Gale, enough!"

"Seriously, Alec, why are you brandishing a revolver?"

"A Webley. And would you not be the first to discourse on the savagery of the island?"

"Don't be foolish, Alec."

"Now, I am a fool? Take your leave, Lucien, and be swift. My dear cousin awaits you."

"With pleasure, my lord."

"Dr. Gale?"

"Yes, my lord."

"Be the gentleman I pray you are."

*

The Duchinu lays his charts on the ground and waves to an old peasant to guard them. His cloudy peasant eyes dart, here, to the charts, there, to the other old peasants turning over clods of earth where soon they got to plant new trees. The old peasant rubs his eyes and takes in the new groves where the young peasants dig furrows for streams of pure water flowing from the large mill at the top of the hill to the narrow ripples in the fertile soil. He wets his lips. *Pure water* for the dirt and the trees. *Pure water* and close enough for the old peasant's mouth to taste.

Past the old and young peasants, the Duchinu races, his knees shooting up to his belly. How swift he got to think he runs in his fancy garments and his high polished boots that do none but slow him down. When he nears the guard dog and eyes the girl patting the black dog's snout, he drops the pistol at his side. "Is this yet another summer mirage? If it is not, what manner of creature stands so courageous?" He slips behind a tree, taking in the girl and the sacks she rifles through and the bread and the cheese that she stuffs in her mouth. She holds the jug up high and shakes the last drops of wine on her tongue. "Who are you?" he whispers. "What are you?"

She rips off the heavy brown shawl.

He grabs the tree.

Her long red hair falls 'round her.

He swoons.

She bundles the remains of food in the shawl and ties it up tight. She licks all what's on her hands, the crumbs that stick to her palms and the dirt that coats her fingers. What is this? The Duchinu licks his hands, too. What spell is this? "Duty be damned," he whispers and lays soft kisses on his palms and fingers and sends the kisses off to the girl.

She throws the shawl over her shoulders. He whispers nonsense prayers.

She flings her head back, her hair brushing the knotted trunk 'til it settles on the earth. He throws his head back, too, his hands reaching out, him none but a child that craves the plaything he'll never own.

The Ave Maria bells clang full and loud through the Simetu valley. They shake the girl from her glutton ways and the Duchinu from his spell. "Signurina...land... of...hair!" he cries out, fuller and louder that they near drown out the bells. She flicks her head, and, in a flash, she's gone from view. The Duchinu runs 'round with his hands high to the heavens. "Let this not be the last of her!" He falls on his knees and sobs. "O brilliant sun, with your assistance, I shall find the girl!" He slumps on a knotted trunk, his chin near scraping his chest. With his eyes shut tight, he prays. "O brilliant sun, shine your light upon heaven's chef d'oeuvre. Singe her shawl for all eternity so that I may share in the delight of this angel's fiery hair...this angel, this angel who graces my earth."

The bread gave the girl strength. The wine, courage. She peers from behind her own knotted trunk at the Duchinu shouting out his nonsense prayers in our tongue. She rushes at him, waving the knife in the air. She holds her breath and waits 'til he finishes his prayer before she sends him off to paradise. "Singe her shawl for all eternity," he prays, "so that I may share in the delight of this angel's fiery hair...this angel...this angel..."

She looks 'round, but no angel with fiery hair comes in view. She mouths the word. *Angel.* She taps her bare head. "Me?" The knife quivers in her hand. "Me?" Behind the ancient tree where he prays, she crouches 'til the sky grows dark and her lips near bleed from the holy word. "Angel," he whispers. "Angel," she whispers, too.

When the light of the moon shines bright on her and the Duchinu drifts to sleep, she breaks free of the spell. She empties the bread from the shawl in her apron, piles her hair 'neath the shawl, knots the brown fringes tight 'neath her chin and stumbles back to the cart at the north end of the old olive tree groves. She throws herself 'neath the fancy dresses and wipes clean her lips. The carter turns 'round. "Mamsella," he kisses his black lava cross, "I don't want to know."

*

On the rocky mule track back to Bronti, the carter starts to sing his nonsense tune of the little wood dove. *Tonight I dreamed I was in the Castle,* and like he can't bring no more words to mind, he stops his singing. "No more, Mamsella, no more." He winds the reins 'round his hand and unwinds them. "Enough. We are near to town, and I got to break the silence, or I am the one to break wide open. I said I didn't want to know. I lied. I lied. What were your intentions back there?"

"How close…how close I was…"

The carter turns 'round and rifles through the dresses 'til he finds the girl's hand and grabs the knife. "Then, to these intentions, Mamsella, I say *No!*"

"Va ben', Mastru Nonziu. *No,* to what I do and, *No,* to what I cannot do this day. *No,* to what you see and, *No,* to what blinds your eyes."

"I am a simple man. You speak the cluttered language of dreams."

"Not of dreams. Of secrets."

He waves the knife in the air. "Reveal your secret!"

"No!"

"Mamsella," he takes in a breath, his voice now low and calm, "reveal it, and I'll reveal mine. Then, we'll be servants of each other. A secret from you…a secret from me…and servants of each other. What do you say?"

She peeks out from a fancy blue dress. "I say that long ago you revealed your secret to me. *Avaja!* All the town knows you long to know the hour."

"What hour?"

She jumps up and snatches the knife back and leaps on the bench beside him. "The hour when 'a z'a Vincenza comes to see Mamma. It's after the hour of the Vespri, after all the Vespri prayers. That's the hour. That's all what you want to hear."

"Oui, Mamsella, that's all what I want to hear. And, now, Mamsella, your secret…"

She tucks the knife in the folds of her apron and strokes it. "On my Mamma's life, not you, not none in all the world, got to hear my secret. Bring me back to the Castle the day I am more my Mamma's daughter and the pretty prayers of noblemen change not my deed. That's all what you got to know."

The surgeon profited by the Duchinu's absence. While the Duchinu said his nonsense prayers in the old olive tree groves, the surgeon roamed the Castle, waving his hand 'cross paintings of noblemen, toasting himself "for days that are no more" and cursing "upstarts and titled fools." Now, he comes 'on a room with walls the color of pale roses and a round wood table in the heart of the room with four wood chairs 'round it. He shuffles 'long the open windows in the flickering candlelight to a table in the corner where he picks up a carved bottle with bright red spirits floating inside. "Ah, my elderflower cordial." He pats the flask in his vest. "Do not be envious, my *green fairy*. I have saved you for dessert." He takes a swig of the red spirits right from the bottle, like it's a peasant's jug of wine.

He sets it down and eyes a girl 'cross the room, a girl in a blue dress with a high collar and long, wide sleeves and a wide band at the waist tied and bowed at the side. "Who is this pretty young lady reclining in her favorite chair?" He shuffles to the green chair with a high back and low armrests. "Oh, my," he reaches for a candle and waves it near the girl's face, "at closer look, I do not recognize her. Where is the rosy bloom I have grown to love these years?" He pinches her cheek. "Elizabeth?"

"Where am I?" The Duchinu's cousin struggles to rise, her hands clutched 'round the armrests, but she falls back down.

"Shall I accompany you," the surgeon leans in and whispers, "shall I accompany you to your room?"

She digs her fingers in the sleeves of his jacket. "Close the shutters, I beg of you." She throws her arms up and knocks the surgeon to the ground.

He kneels by her side and lifts her lids. Her green eyes roll 'round in their sockets. That's what Patri Radici says the Devil's eyes do. She wraps her arms 'round her belly, her chin dropping to her chest.

"Close the shutters or let this be the end of me!"

"Elizabeth, the sun has already set. Now, enough of sunlight...or moonlight, as the case may be. Allow your Dr. Gale to assist you to your room. I shall help you disrobe, and you shall confide to me where the pain..."

"In my stomach."

"Yes, Elizabeth, as, always, in your stomach."

"Dr. Gale, this is of a…different…*nature*. I beg of you, help me before I die!"

The cousin keels over, but the surgeon pushes her head back and grabs a glass on a small table near the chair. "My dear, it is always of a different nature," he mutters and takes out the jewel flask from the pocket in his vest. He pours the green drink in the glass. "A liqueur," he whispers and pours a glass for himself. "*Allez*, Elizabeth, a sip for your Dr. Gale."

He wraps her fingers 'round the glass. Quick, she flicks it away.

"No! No! No! No! No! No! No!" How he wails when the green liquid splashes in his face!

"Growing…crawling inside my stomach…Dr. Gaaaa…"

The surgeon flicks his head to one side, then the other. The green liquid drips from the deep scars right in his palms. He licks them clean 'til his chest puffs out. He laughs and slaps it down. He puts his arm on the cousin's knee and opens his mouth and shows off all his teeth. He reels like a drunk peasant, crouching over her the way he does, him, more beast than man. He sweeps her up and takes her to the long chair where he turns her on her side, and, her, moaning through it all, with cheeks and lips whiter than Mungibellu's snow. Her face falls in a rolled green pillow. He strokes her hair and pulls three painted pins from the back of her head. Her hair breaks free, falling in wild red curls past the shoulders of her blue dress. The surgeon breathes hard in her face while his fingers rub the sides of her throat. "Is the pain here, my dear?"

"Dr. Gale…"

"No?"

"Dr. Gale…help…me."

"My dear, I shall help us both in a matter of moments. Lower? Lower?" he asks, his hand falling 'neath the high collar.

"Dr. Gale? Elizabeth?" At the sound of the Duchinu's voice, the surgeon wipes the wet from 'round his lips. He lets out a sigh and pats down the shoulders of the fancy blue dress. He shuffles to the threshold of the room and shouts for the Duchinu, the tight smile back on his lips.

"Alec, come quickly! Elizabeth is not well. I shall see to her recovery. However, I shall need assistance transporting her to her room."

"Immediately!" The Duchinu rushes to his cousin's side. She throws her arms 'round him. He calls to his servants, once peasants that labored in the Duca's fields and now, in blue vests and leather shoes, labor inside the Castle walls. They bow entering the room, their brows near brushing the floor.

"Up! Up!" The Duchinu flaps his arms up and out. "Not me, you fools, Donna Elizabeth!" He slaps the servants' hands from his legs and pats his grey vest down. "Dr. Gale, lead the way upstairs, and, for God's sake, do something!"

*

For three days, the carter stayed away from the Castle. What made him think the Duchinu knew the girl had a plan and that the carter was a part of it? That's what he told himself, and, so, for three days he stayed away from good food and a soft bed. But here he is again, that conniver of a carter, sitting in the room with the round wood table, talking about this and that with the Duchinu and reaching for another piece of warm lemon cake.

"You deliver rousing speeches of loyalty and reciprocity, and, now, the hour approaches when I shall put your speeches to the test."

"Your Excellencia?" The carter shifts on his haunches and munches on a corner piece of cake. A crumb sticks to his fingers. He shakes it in his mouth.

"The peasants refer to you as *Nooonnnzzziiuuu*. However, I should much prefer to call you *Joseph*."

The carter's eyes open wide. His mouth fills with water. "*Joseph*," he whispers and wipes the spittle from the corners of his mouth. "Your Excellencia, I relish it."

"Very well, Joseph. Now, if I take you at your word, I believe you would like to repay me, as you say, for all my kindness."

"The tree that bears no fruit got to be cut at the base."

"Joseph, please, this is not the moment for your people's adages."

"Your Excellencia, I am your tree of gratitude. This tree bears the fruit of favors. And my fruit is ripe for the picking."

"I am desperate. My cousin has fallen ill. For three days, she drifts in and out of sleep, delirious from the "*living creatures*" in her body. Her stomach swells as each day passes, and," he whispers in the carter's ear, "I am hesitant to say, a most unpleasant odor emanates from her mouth."

"But…the surgeon…"

"Dr. Gale, yes, of course. He attempts to bring her comfort. I see no improvement. I see no comfort. I sent for you against his better wishes."

"Your Excellencia, I am not a…"

"*You* are not. However, you have ofttimes spoken of a gifted woman, a healer who dabbles in some sort of *magic*. I believe that was your word."

"She is one of many on our island that heals."

"Bring her to the manor tomorrow."

The carter wipes his brow. He lets out a fake cough, and this to bide him time. He knows Vincenza is the only one to do the healing, but, for all his fancy words, not by truth and not by trickery will my Vincenza ever set foot in the Castle. "My lord, she's not well. For such a journey, better to ask a donkey than an angel."

"Joseph, it is hardly my concern whom you ask. The donkey or the angel. Ask them both, or, better still, ask Chiazza for the little I care." He stands up and leans rigid over the carter. "Do not play me for a fool. Bring someone to heal my cousin tomorrow or do not attempt to set foot in the manor again."

The carter opens his mouth wide, his jaw clicking out a wild tune. "I understand, Your Excellencia, *clicca…clicca*. I understand. Do bad and remember. Do good and forget. 'Til the morrow, Your Excellencia, when I pray all my deeds will be forgotten.


*The dog always chews on the pauper.*


The peasant girl with burnt fingers wears the blue skirt her Mamma sewed in haste last night. Her friends wear the blue skirts, too, the dark hair peasant girls that shouted out their gossip and told their tales at all the fountains in Bronti. Each Papà hangs black ribbons on the cottage door and wraps a black ribbon 'neath his daughter's chin and ties it at the top of her head. Each Papà wears his garments inside out and tears at his eyes now that he got to wrap his daughter in long, rough leaves and carry her to the neighborhood church.

Carpenters began their work early this day. They nailed planks of wood one to the other and brought the boxes to the churches for the girls to rest in. Before the hour of the Vespri prayers, this Patri and that Patri got to bless the girls in all the churches, and all the Papàs got to bury them.

Behind the mournful sounds of a brass band, the Mammas wail u reputu through the roads, their eyes flooded with tears, their feet, leading them off Corsu Umbertu to via Leanza and past the low, round archway to the neighborhood 'a Maronna ri Loretu and the first cottage door. Here, seven Mammas and three old cummari spit on the threshold and shed their tears 'til the sorrow soaks the earth.

"*Untore! Untore!* Spreader of the sickness!"

At the sound of the curses, the girl shoves the table to the door and rushes to her Mamma's side. The strong women push through. An old cummari eyes the wide mouth jug by the hearth. She splashes her hands in the jug and, quick, jumps back, shaking off the cold water. "This is not what we drink!" She spits in the jug. The seven Mammas take their turn, splashing their hands and spitting in the jug 'til the water rises and foams. Like magpies, *maga maga maga maga maga maga maga,* they cry out their song.

"No one weeps in this cottage."

"No one."

"The daughter lives."

"No one weeps."

"Cursed like her Mamma, the daughter lives."

"Cursed and spared…"

"Cursed and spared while the sickness strikes the blessed down."

"Untore! Untore! Spreader of the sickness!" they all shout 'til the girl leaps up and spits in the old cummari's eyes.

A Mamma with burnt fingers of her own rips the heavy brown shawl from the girl's head and throws it on the ground. "Look at her!"

Another Mamma rushes to the marriage bed and spits at Agata. "Curses on a woman that lies with the Devil! And curses on the child they make!"

The girl tries to shout. The Mammas throw her down and kick her while an old cummari cups her mouth. "Untore! Untore!" they cry out.

The girl makes a fist, opens her hand and spreads her fingers wide. The women's hands chafe and spark, and, the girl, she spins 'round and 'round like the black guard dog in the old olive tree groves. She breaks free and rushes to her Mamma. Agata falls on her knees, ripping at her hair, crying out her own mourning wails. "Mamma, no!"

Soft, like a whisper, a blessing drifts 'cross the cottage, the melody of the voice soothing all inside. "Blessings to you."

The Mammas and the cummari bow their heads. The girl grabs her throat, but she's not the one that blesses them. Agata sips from the wide mouth jug. She's not the one, neither, that brings them all to silence.

*Blessings to you…blessings to you.*

"Blessings to you." Vincenza bows at the threshold, two baskets, one big, one small, rocking in her arms. The seven Mammas and the three cummari step to the side and let Vincenza pass. She sets the baskets near the hearth, helps Agata back to bed, takes in a breath and kisses the girl curled at the foot of the bed. "Good women of Bronti, you have no business here. Signa Agata is sick with grief. How can she make her way through the town to spread the sickness? Spreader of the sickness? You name her all what she is not. Now, receive my blessings, and be on your way. May 'a Maronna 'a Nunziata comfort you."

Vincenza blesses the Mammas when they take their leave, but the Mamma with burnt fingers of her own, hunched over and dressed in black from the head to the toes, she runs back in and grabs the drawing of 'a Maronna 'a Nunziata folded in Vincenza's small basket and tears the face in a hundred scraps and pieces 'til all what remains is 'a Maronna's dark, sad eye looking back at her. "How can she comfort us?" the Mamma cries out. "She knows none of what we suffer. The one we pray to, 'a Maronna 'a Nunziata, the great patron of Bronti, she was but a girl when the angel messenger visited her. She had yet to bear a child. This young Maria is the one we pray to, but what does she know of all what we suffer?"

"You know better." Vincenza crosses herself and waits for the Mamma to cross herself, too. "'A Maronna 'a Nunziata keeps our town safe from harm. That is the comfort she brings to you and all of you. I say you know better. All of you know better. How do you cry for daughters that have yet to bear their own children?"

"They came from our flesh."

"But they have yet to make a mark on life. Now, wipe your tears. Go home with my blessings. Your daughters are in peace."

"Sì, Signa Vincenza. They are at peace."

*

The Angelus hour and the Ave Maria hour passed long ago. The Mammas and the cummari took their leave from the Saitta cottage long ago, but Vincenza and the girl still kneel by the hearth near the strong fire, Vincenza, calm, the girl, shuddering. "Calma," Vincenza whispers and holds tight to the girl. She strokes the crown of the girl's head and braids her hair and wraps it back 'neath the heavy brown shawl. "Child?"

"Sì, z'a Vincenza, I know. Calma. I try to be all what you ask of me, but my thoughts fight the calm. Z'a Vincenza, the Mammas called my Mamma…"

"The women spoke from grief."

"But, you, you spoke the truth."

"Turn your thoughts from all what I spoke when the moment called for comforting."

"You told the Mammas their daughters made no mark on life. I am of their age. The peasant girls and me, we done the same chores. We walked the same roads. Me, I can die with no mark made, with no blessed mark made on my Mamma's life, with no path. Z'a Vincenza, with no name!"

Vincenza pulls the girl back in her arms. "Heed my words. The day you issued forth, you made a great mark on life. And your path…it's greater still. For the grieving Mammas, comfort is a greater balm than truth."

*

"Goood daaaay, gooood niiiight, Madama." The door opens, and, there *he* is, his arms filled with a sack of wheat.

"Mastru Nonziu, how you are needed this day! Who works such magic to conjure you here?"

"It nears the hour of the Vespri prayers. 'Though deep in my own prayers to the Savior, Him that battles all the darkness," his eyes to the heavens, "'though deep in my prayers, by an incantation, I know not from where, I put them aside. Now, I find myself here." He clasps his hands. "Madama, let us say our Vespri prayers together."

"It is by 'a Maronna 'a Nunziata's grace that you put aside your prayers. The girl and me, we prayed to her all day. You are what she sent us. I give thankfulness for she knows that now I need your kindness."

"Good fortune smiles on me for the fruit of my tree is ripe with kindness. But is it mere kindness or the fruit of boldness and bravery you seek? Tell me the gift to brighten your face, for if it grows inside me, you can take it now." He nears Vincenza with a face red like Mungibellu's fire. I see now how the blood courses through his body to regions it ought not settle in, and, there, the regions grow. How his heart beats wild! How Vincenza, for her part, grows red! And what is it that shines there? A light in her body, from the head to the toes? I howl like a wild dog and watch with joy when the *brave one* flies 'neath the table, flinging the small black pig out from his hiding place.

"Mastru Nonziu, shake free from the fear of that creature outside. When I first heard his howling, I was frightened, too. But he howls day to night and don't show his face."

"A coward through and through! I don't fear such creatures, Madama. No," he shudders, "I reached for the pig to settle *his* fear." He takes in a breath. "But let us make our way back to more pleasing talk. You seek the ripest fruit, Madama?"

Vincenza curls her finger. The carter crawls out from 'neath the table. "He that leaves his home," she whispers, "got to find himself in a better place."

"A better place?" The carter shuffles 'round her and pulls on his dark beard. "Let my thoughts bring to mind the true meaning of the wise words. Glorious saints! A better place!" The carter bungles a swift tune and kicks out his legs. "I am your servant, Madama. Where am I your servant? In such a *better place*. Glorious saints! At long last, you consent to be my..."

The small black pig races through the open door and dives in Vincenza's small basket. He lets out a squeal when she grabs his legs and throws him back out the door. She shakes her head and sits on the marriage bed where she strokes Agata's hair. "Mastru Nonziu, the cross-eyed lunatic makes more sense than you. Listen to what I say. Signa Agata and her daughter got to leave their home."

"Leave Bronti?"

"Sì. Before the morning prayers."

"What happened here?"

"All what you got to know is that we need to find a safe place."

"Madama," he sits on a stool and slides it to the marriage bed, "I know of many places, Rannazzu, for one."

"Mastru Nonziu, better death than life in Rannazzu!"

He kisses the cross 'round his neck and sighs. "So, not Rannazzu."

"So, where? The two now risk their lives in Bronti."

"I know where we got to go." The girl taps Vincenza's knee, her eyes on her fingers, tapping, tapping, tapping 'til Vincenza jerks her knee to the side and the girl's hand falls on the hard dirt floor.

"But I know. I know." At the sound of the words, Vincenza scratches her ears and sticks her fingers deep in them 'til they turn bright red, but the words still buzz like mosquitoes in the night 'round and 'round her head. "I know. I know. Z'a Vincenza, I know where we got to go."

"*You?*" Vincenza opens her eyes wide and jabs her finger at the girl's brow. "*You* know where?"

"Z'a Vincenza, don't look at me with such eyes. I know many places. And I can take us to a secret place."

"A secret place?"

"A place where pots and beddings wait for us. And a clay lamp and a sack. We can be safe, all of us. When the shepherd boy comes back…"

Vincenza grabs the girl's face and slaps it. "But I can help Mamma," she whimpers and rubs the red mark on her cheek. "I can help but first you got to heed my words."

"Heed the words of a child so bold?"

"Sì, heed my words. When you hear all what I got to say, if you want to strike me more, strike me! If you want to kill me…"

"Child!"

"Kill me! Your blows can't kill the shepherd boy in my heart!"

Vincenza lets out a cry and grabs the girl's shawl and whips her arms and legs. "No more of him! No more of him!"

The girl curls on the hard dirt floor, her body heaving.

"Madama," the carter leans in, "let us hear all what the girl got to say."

The girl swallows hard and pulls at her throat. "Ma...Ma...Maaastruuu Non..."

"Slow, slow, Mamsella. *Chianu, chianu.*"

"Mastru Nonziu, it got no hearth. You got to make it from the rocks. You got to empty your cart of beddings and clothings and give us all what we need."

"Bold, bold, and more bold!" Vincenza throws out her hand, but she near slaps the carter's cheek. He smiles and leans back on his stool. A smile. That's all what he gives to my Vincenza. Soon that he smiles, her hand drops. Like it got no more life in it, it falls heavy on her lap. I swear on my eyes, he casts a spell on her. He smiles. And my Vincenza's calm. I howl to shake her from his spell. She pays no mind to the howling, and, him, now, too, he pays me no mind.

"Child, we were there on the first of May..."

"No, z'a Vincenza. This is a secret place. It's a new dwelling. It's made from a longing for all what's good."

"Who lives there?"

"No one."

"No one? So, where *is* this dwelling?"

The girl runs outside and points to the mountains south of the town. "Far from Bronti." She runs back in and falls at Vincenza's feet. "O, how empty of life and forsaken of hope it is 'til the shepherd boy makes it a home!"

Vincenza leaps from the bed, swatting the air with an open hand. The carter pushes the girl to the side, bows and begs Vincenza's forgiveness for his own boldness. He grabs her waist and swings her 'round, nose to nose, mouth to mouth.

"Madama, basta! The beatings do no good."

"They protect her." She turns this way and that and breaks free of his hold.

"From what, Madama? They only cause her sorrow."

"You don't know all what I know. There's a greater sorrow…"

Vincenza whispers, but the carter, he pulls his ear and fakes a deafness 'til she breathes in his big ear. "Madama, did you say a *greater sorrow?*"

"Sì…the boy is cursed."

"He's a fine boy."

"A fine boy, Mastru Nonziu, with a curse in him!"

"How a curse?"

"The animal lives inside him and gnaws at his soul. All the world knows what beats 'neath the flesh of that shepherd boy. Does the girl know? It's there on his face for all to see. Does the girl see? If she stays with him, the curse falls on her, too. Then, who got to protect her?"

"Sì, Madama, you're right. The girl's wrong. The girl's a fool." A smile flickers on his lips. "But I am not. A thought comes to me. What if I journey with the girl and look at her secret place? Mamsella," he whispers to the girl, "is it where I seen you but a few days past?" The girl nods.

Vincenza throws a look at Agata, now fast to sleep. "Mastru Nonziu," she whispers, "you want to go and see if it's safe for my cousin?"

"Sì, sì, to go and see it's safe."

"How long will you be away from us, Mastru Nonziu?"

He waves his hand. "I had a fine little wood dove," and sings out his nonsense tune. "*Bacenza,* Madama, patience. Before the stars light the sky, I'll find my way back to you." He takes off the lava cross and kisses it. "Take this. What I wear 'round my neck my Papà worn and his Papà before him. Take this, ppi piaciri, take it now and give it back to me when I return." He keeps his head down and holds out his hand. "But, Madama, if it pleases you, for this what you call my kindness, if it gives you joy, I'll take from you a small token. Your basket, that's all what I desire for my *perilous* journey. Foolishness, I know. No, Madama, ppi piaciri, please, *not the small one.*"

*

The girl leaps in the cart, the knife in her folded apron, the big basket rocking on her arm. The carter, he lights three lanterns, hangs two on the sides of the cart and one near the bench. He whispers to Chiazza that she got to journey far this night. The three of them set off on the trazzera north of Corsu Umbertu, the girl, lost in her own web of thoughts, rocking like a mourner, her hands cupping her eyes, the carter, smiling, and Chiazza, blowing out her hard breath, the only sound in the quiet of early night 'til the girl breaks the silence. "Mastru Nonziu, the secret in my heart…"

"Sì, Mamsella, sì, you got to tell me all the secrets in your heart that Madama keeps in her basket."

"O, Mastru Nonziu," she cries out, "it hurts! Untore, untore, that's what they called my Mamma!"

"This is good. This is good."

"Mastru Nonziu!"

"No, no, Mamsella, the basket…the basket's good. The basket and all Madama's secrets."

"Untore is what they called my Mamma. Spreader of the sickness. My Mamma!"

"Mamsella, look inside."

She shakes her fists at the darkening sky. "I got to kill them all!"

"Sì. Sì. I got to kill them, too. But, first, look inside Madama's basket, quick!" The carter pulls on the reins, the mare slowing her pace at the end of the rough road. He points to the new carriage road that comes in view. "Mamsella…before it's too late, ppi piaciri, look inside and tell me all what you see there."

"What? 'A z'a Vincenza's basket?" She lowers her face in the basket and strokes the plants, the greens, the browns, the yellows, all what Vincenza gathered. She breathes them in. "They're all the plants 'a z'a Vincenza honors."

"Glorious saints! What kinds?"

"All the kinds."

"What parts?"

"All the parts. The leaves, the buds, the rootstalks."

"You know all these?"

"They're all the parts of the plants that heal."

"Good. Keep them apart. Or gather them up. Say a prayer. Or be silent. What Madama does, now, you got to do. Take my knife. Take this rope. Put them in bundles for the cures."

"No, Mastru Nonziu, this is not the deed I set out to do." She raises her eyes to the heavens. "Wait, Mastru Nonziu!" She turns 'round. "There, near where 'a bacca fades from view, that's where you seen me!" She tries to stand. She falls back down. "'A bacca! 'A bacca!" she cries out for that weakling of a mountain. "To the south! My dwelling's not in the *north*…the Castle, Mastru Nonziu…the Castle's in the north!"

He flicks the reins. Chiazza's pace quickens, the girl jostling the carter on the narrow bench. "Listen to me. There's no greater deed and no greater road."

"Mastru Nonziu, there *is* a greater deed…but I'm not yet bold enough for the task."

"Mamsella, the Excellencia's cousin, she suffers in her bed. Can you make a tea for her?"

"This is not the deed," she whispers, "not the deed."

"*Not the deed. Not the deed.* Don't you see, not you, not me, got a say in this?" He reaches for her hand and holds tight to it. "*Child*," he whispers, "*can you make for her the cure?*"

At the sound of the words, she shudders from the head to the toes. The carter grabs a blanket and throws it 'round her shoulders. "What happens here? In the month of August, you're chilled to the bone."

"Mastru Nonziu, the way you ask…you ask the way 'a z'a Vincenza always asks." She holds her heart, crosses herself and takes in a breath. "*Can I make for her the cure?* Va ben'. I'll answer with the first question I ask 'a z'a Vincenza. So, Mastru Nonziu, is it in her belly?"

"How do I know?"

"If it's in her belly, and there's evil inside, and, more, if it grows…'a z'a Vincenza makes the tea from the rootstalk of the *filici* but only the boy plant…"

"Is it in Madama's basket?"

"Sì. I see it."

"Heal her!"

"Mastru Nonziu, this is not the deed…"

"Mamsella, *it is*. Are your eyes so blind you don't see it is for Madama that you do this? She wants you to heal the sick girl…Mamsella," he drops his head and lets out a fake moan, "in dreams, she told me so."

She throws her fingers over her mouth. "In dreams, she told you so?"

"Sì, *clicca…clicca…*in dreams."

"'A z'a Vincenza comes to me, too, in dreams."

His mouth shapes to a grin, so wide a grin it is that it reaches from one ear to the other and squeezes his eyes shut tight. "Mamsella, I got eager ears. Sì, eager ears, and you got to tell them each and all of your dreams."

She closes her eyes and tells him this dream of the plants and that dream of the teas and all of a healing nature while Chiazza's hooves brush 'long the new carriage road. "And when I was on the mountain with the shepherd boy," she brings the last dream to mind, "'a z'a Vincenza come to me and told me of the girl like me but not me that got the affliction. Is *this* the girl I got to heal?"

He shrugs his shoulders. "If so, what's her affliction?"

"If she cries and moans and talks no sense and holds her belly…"

"Oui, Mamsella, oui to all of that."

"Avaja! Her affliction is the fright."

The cousin talked her nonsense from the day she pushed her way through the Castle with all her cases and trunks. I seen it all in Alfiu's ball of light. I heard her, too, opening up her bag of wind to make her high and mighty speeches that blew in the ears of any poor creature that gave her the time of day. A chattering magpie with a hundred different songs, some of fear, some of illness, some real, some faked, and some to give her the fright.

The carter grabs the girl's shoulders. "Swear on your eyes, Mamsella, swear you'll not breathe one word I tell you."

The girl takes in a breath and nods.

"Good. Now, it all makes sense. I seen Donna Elizabeth. I seen her on a day the Excellencia invited me to *dinner* one late afternoon. I watched her nibble on some bread and take in a spoon of minestra. That's all what she ate. She set a cloth over her dish and wiped her mouth clean, but I seen a longing in her eyes, a near evil longing, and it made me ill at ease. The Excellencia protested, "Elizabeth, this is hardly sustenance for a bird." She smiled when he called her his *delicate Elizabeth*, and, soon after, when he had his fill of food, he went back to the groves with the surgeon. That's when the cousin ordered all the servants to work upstairs, and she bid me farewell, too. I seen the signs, and they wasn't good. Evil lurked in the Castle, and no plot was too big for me to unmask. A conniver I am when I want to be, so I stayed behind and hid myself good.

"She sneaked inside the kitchen and crouched 'neath the cutting tables where she stuffed her mouth with meats and cakes that were bare cooked 'til sleep got the best of her. When the Ave Maria bells woke her, she rushed out and kicked this dog and that dog and shouted out this blame and that blame to the poor yelping creatures for the empty bowls and trays her own self took to licking clean. I followed her. She made her way to her room and unlocked a door to a big cupboard. I peeked inside. 'Neath all the fancy dresses on the floor of the cupboard, that's where she pulled out a small jug of vinegar and splashed but a little in a smaller jug of water. I near choked on the sharp smell, but I stayed to see what evil she plotted and planned. Quick, she gulped the liquid down, and this to make her throw out the cakes and meats that found their way deep in her belly. What a sight she was, heaving and crying and ridding her belly the best she knew how of all what she eaten! But there was no plot. No evil. No plan. Only a girl what feared…for if the Excellencia ever come in 'on her and seen all what she stuffed in her belly and all what she done to rid herself of it…glorious saints, that could give even the bravest one the fright! Mamsella," he puts his finger to his mouth, "there's more. One night, all in the Castle thought I was fast to sleep, but I wasn't. I woke to see…Mamsella, give me your word. This is a secret from me to you."

She takes in a breath and nods.

"Donna Elizabeth called it an *invisible demon*. He come to her late and held out a glass filled with green liquid and made her drink it all in her sleep. But it wasn't in her sleep. In the morning, I seen Donna Elizabeth's wet clumps of hair and her torn bed clothes. I seen it, and I seen *him*. No ghost, Mamsella. The surgeon, it was. And that could give even the bravest one the fright!"

"Mastru Nonziu," the girl yanks the reins from his hands, "you watched a poor girl in peril, and you said and you done *nothing*?"

He yanks them back. "That I been a coward at the Castle is all true. Cure Donna Elizabeth, and I'll tell the Excellencia all what I seen. I'll tell Donna Elizabeth, too, and, if I'm punished…if I can never no more go back to the Castle…" He snivels and wipes clean his cheeks of the phantom tears. "I won't be a coward no more, Mamsella. But, first, for all our sakes, you got to rid her of the fright."

"In my dreams, 'a z'a Vincenza showed me how to make the fright leave the girl."

"So she can rest?"

"Sì, she'll rest from the fright, but…Mastru Nonziu, you know what comes with…"

He shakes his head like a fly's buzzing 'round it. "You're wrong! Donna Elizabeth don't got the…"

The girl puts her hand on the carter's shoulder. "Mastru Nonziu, you know what comes with the fright. *U vermu.* And that never brings no rest, not to the rich and not to the poor. You told me what you seen. You told me she ate meats and cakes and none cooked through and through. You told me the sorrows and fears she holds inside. She got the fright, and, Mastru Nonziu, she got u vermu, too."

"She can't be afflicted with the *worms*! What do I tell the Excellencia? 'Your cousin isn't a delicate creature with the appetite of a bird. And I know for I seen it all, the way she drinks vinegar and water to throw out all what she stuffs in her mouth. And I know she's no more delicate than a peasant's dirty child what steals food and stops at nothing to satisfy her longings.' He'll kill me for my boldness!"

"Mastru Nonziu, twist and turn your tongue if it pleases you. But *I* tell you all what's true. With the fright comes u vermu."

The carter jumps off the cart. He throws himself on the ground. "This is the worst calamity to befall me. "She can't have the worms…"

The girl pats the carter's seat. "Mastru Nonziu, brush yourself off and hop up."

"Va ben'…va ben'… He jumps back up and clasps his hands in prayer. "But can you make for her the cure?"

"'A z'a Vincenza fights u vermu. How many times I watched the slimy thing jump out of a peasant's body."

"But can you make the cure if Madama's not by your side?"

"She's always by my side. That's the power of the gift."

"What gift?"

"She put u vermu in my hand. On 'a bacca, she told me so."

"Mamsella, she put the worm in your hand on 'a bacca?"

"No, but on the small mountain, she told me. My thoughts were busy that day. But, now, I bring it all to mind. She told me when I was but a baby, she breathed in my mouth and said the sacred prayers and passed the healing powers…" She throws her head back and slaps her brow. "Mastru Nonziu, she passed the healing powers to *me*!"

"Mamsella, she put a worm in your hand when you were a baby?"

"Maronna mia, she put it there! She told me so."

"A worm in your hand? Do you know all what that means?"

"And she said the prayers. Mastru Nonziu, things been happening to me. Things more than 'a z'a Vincenza knows. What she wanted for me, this healing I can do. I can fight u vermu and heal all the sickness in the town and all the sickness in the Castle."

"Glorious saints! How calamity turns to fortune! This is greater fortune than I ever dreamed."

"Greater fortune than I dreamed, too, for now I grow bold to the task." She pats the knife in the folds of her apron. "I can bring Mamma joy, and, then, who can say, I can heal her, I can heal my Mamma, and, then, she got to…"

"Make the cure first, Mamsella…for Madama. The deed for your Mamma, the good or the bad of it, it got to wait."

*With a doctor comes pain.*

When the cart made its way on the new carriage road, I hid on the trazzera behind a heap of rocks, far from the carter, but, still, I seen and heard more than I could bear of him, his yapping mouth shaping tall tales to suit himself. Now, behind a heap of cypress trees, I hide. Behind a forest of vines, the sandstone walls of the Castle hide, too. All hide behind the closed gates. The doors and windows closed, too, save for the window of the cousin's room, the shutters opened wide, but I got to turn away. To look inside could give even the bravest one the fright.

The cousin lies in a bed near the window, a shiny metal bed with knobs that top the four posts and curled leaves wrought in the high head and foot boards. What a sight she is! Her small green eyes dart, now, at the angels on the ceiling in long white garb, their wings spread wide, now, at the thick red flower rug, now, at the rose color walls lined with paintings of pale women in stiff clothing, the cousin, paler than the lot of them.

What an ugly sight she is, ripping at the stitchings of her collar with her thick fingers, moaning in her white bed clothes 'neath the lace bed covers! And her hair! It heaves about the pillow like a seasick boy, the wet curls stuck to the embroidered letters, *CMN*, for the third *great* Duchessa of Bronti, the niece of the admiral Nelson, Carlotta Maria Nelson, Charlotte Mary Nelson, the Duchinu's *Nanna*, his Papà's Mamma, a hateful woman that called us *savages* and visited our land but once near forty years ago, and, that, for only three days, but three days was all our land could bear of her.

*

Who don't still bring to mind the Duchinu's *Nanna* and her journey to Bronti? She broke our donkeys' backs when the guards strapped them with litters for *Her Royalty's* comfort and treasures, and the donkeys lost their footing and slid down the mud of the low lava road. Didn't she know the small, grey creatures belonged to a sacred breed? Didn't she know the crosses that marked their necks and backs were gifts the Savior gave them when *He* rode one of their ancients through *Girusalemmi*, and the people lay palms 'cross the road? What evil coursed through her blood when she weighed the poor beasts down with those stretchers filled with cases of jewels and gold? She was the one that gave the orders when the jewels tipped over. In her yellow bonnet and her yellow dress splattered with mud, with her finger crooked at the donkeys, she made the guards shoot the suffering creatures, more precious to the Bruntiszi than gold.

I watched with my Papà. There I was but a young boy sick with fury, and there was my Papà wailing u reputu when the litters dipped and scraped the mud road. The shots rang out. The donkeys fell one by one. They lay silent 'cross the rocks, their sacred vapors and their sacred blood pouring from their bellies. I spit on her memory, she that vowed the journey to be her last and, new road or not, never to set foot on Bronti soil no more "unless there is a revolution in England, and even then I should probably go elsewhere."

*

The cousin lets out a wild moan. The surgeon pats the cloth on her brow and wipes the spittle from her mouth, her big hands fighting him off. How many times Alfiu showed me in his ball of light the cousin taking great pains to hide her thick fingers and making this plea or that plea not to play the *pianu* when the Duchinu begged for a *gentle piece of music.* Now, she throws off the bed covers, lifts her bed clothes and, with her big hands and thick fingers, scratches her belly with the vigor of a scabbing dog.

The surgeon tugs at the cousin's bed clothes. The Duchinu nods to the servant girls 'round the bed, five girls from Bronti, all with dark hair and sad faces that, quick, pull the bed clothes down and tuck them 'neath the lace bed covers.

"Come in, Signurina." The Duchinu waves the girl in. The carter pushes her and bows. The Duchinu slides his hand 'long the rose color walls. The carter bows again and pinches the girl's arm when the Duchinu's hand slides to the door and drops 'neath the girl's tight lips.

"Kiss his hand," the carter whispers, his chin to his chest. He presses the girl's head down. She shakes him off and raises her eyes. Quick, the Duchinu turns away from her gaze. But what is this? I see it. A shudder snaking through his body from the head to the toes.

The girl takes in the room. Cupboard, lamps, tables, rugs, bed covers, all in a room bigger than any cottage in Bronti. Furniture and decorations all that shine their bright jewel colors right in the girl's gold eyes. She fixes her eyes back on the Duchinu and his loose shirt and pearl buttons. "White shining jewels near the heart," she breathes out in bare a whisper, "for the deed I got to do for Mamma."

The carter looks 'round at the faces staring back at him. He lets out a fake cough, clasps his hands and starts his tale. "A perilous journey I undertook on rough roads with outlaws skulking behind rocks and aiming their ill-hidden rifles at me. Who could protect me? My sole companion was the angel of death, and he taunted me at each crossroad. Why make such a perilous journey?" He grabs the rose color wall. "To find the one true girl to do the healing."

I hold my belly to keep the laughter in, but the others, they take his tale for truth. The surgeon, he puts the cloth to the side. The Duchinu, he lowers his hand. The servant girls that long know the carter's ways, they stand still like holy statues. I swear on my eyes, even the cousin stops her moanings and listens to his nonsense words. But the girl, she profits by the carter's babbling and roams the room with no eyes on her.

When Vincenza heals in a peasant's cottage, where are her eyes? Not on the peasant's small treasures. Where are her hands? Not reaching for them. The girl's eyes and hands learned none of this. With all eyes fixed on the carter, none sees the girl creeping slow, slow, 'long the wall on the thick red flower rug. When she nears the cousin's bed, she stretches out her thin fingers to the spindles of the rocking chair. With all eyes fixed on the carter, none sees the girl sliding her fingers to the white seat where five small women sit in their bright ruffled skirts, the smallest woman, wearing the brightest color and the biggest ruffles.

"Si biniric'," the girl bows to the small woman in the bright yellow dress with ruffles edged in red. The woman shines her eyes at her. "What is this?" she whispers. "No blessings do I get from you? But 'a z'a Vincenza says I got to bless all our betters and wait for them to give back the blessings."

She blesses her again and waves her hand at the woman, near touching her face. The woman shines her eyes at her. The girl bows. "Signura, 'a z'a

Vincenza tells me not to look at the Bruntiszi for they say I give the evil eye. The lot of them in Bronti, they turn from me and crook their fingers. They say this keeps them safe from me, safe from the one with the pale eyes, safe from the one that gives the evil eye. But who can turn a gaze from you? You're beautiful. I give you blessings, not the evil eye." She reaches out and touches the woman's white shiny face. "Signura?" She touches her round red lips. The woman shines her eyes at her. The girl touches her yellow hair, curled at the back of her neck and left uncovered in a shameless way. And, then, she gazes long in her eyes. Eyes that shine at her and never close. Eyes like the Duchinu's eyes. Eyes the color of the sea.

The girl tugs at the ruffles of the yellow dress. "You, with the beautiful face…you don't move? Signura, are you an angel come down to keep me safe from harm?"

How long the carter babbles of his tale of peril, who can say? At long last, the Duchinu presses his lips tight and stomps his foot. All in the room start up again. The cousin moans. The servant girls pat the bed covers. The surgeon, kneeling by the cousin's side, he wrings out the cloth on her brow. A hundred times and more he dips the cloth in a bowl of water and wrings it out and lays it on her brow, swaying on his knees. "A bit of stiffness," he slaps his leg and stretches it out long, but his foot kicks out when he tries to stand. He throws his hands 'cross the seat of the rocking chair to steady himself. This makes the small women tumble to the floor.

"*Ahi*!" The girl cries out, her, more hurt than the small women, for in their eyes, they show no signs of pain. The one in the bright yellow dress lies on the rug near the surgeon's chest. He picks her up and dangles her by her soft white slipper. He whips his arm 'round and throws her 'cross the room.

"No!" The girl makes a fist, opens her hand and spreads her fingers wide. Where does the strength come from? She pushes the surgeon with the back of her hand. He flies 'cross the room, belly down on the thick red flower rug, the small woman, her face nuzzled at his ankles, the yellow ruffles edged in red brushing his leg. The girl rushes to her. She tugs the dress down over the ruffled undergarments and the wool stockings and pats the woman's slipper with her foot. "Animal!" She spits at the surgeon's feet.

He leaps up and lunges at the girl. Quick, the carter opens his arms wide and throws himself in the thick of it. He pushes the surgeon to the side, all the while bowing like a drunk peasant. "Your Majestia... Your Surgeon Sir..." He sounds like a drunk peasant, too. But, what is this? With each low bow, he sweeps the girl behind him. "Mamsella," he whispers, "be not the cause of trouble."

"The woman," she says, breathing hard, "she don't move."

He slaps his brow. "Mamsella, she don't move for she is a..."

She points to the surgeon that the Duchinu holds back. "That one, that Devil, he killed her!"

"*Sst.* He's the doctor. Bow to him before you make trouble. Bow! Good. Now, listen to me. The woman, Mamsella, she don't move...can't you see she don't move for she is a *doll?*"

"*Daaalllaaa?*"

"*Sì*, a doll...a plaything."

"A plaything? A plaything like my plaything? No! Their bodies are not of binding twigs. Their heads are not of lemons. Look at them. They are of flesh. They are of blood."

"*Sst.* They are the playthings that give joy to the cousin. They cannot breathe. They cannot speak. Now, wipe your eyes and kiss the Excellencia's hand."

The Duchinu taps his foot. "What is your name?" he asks, his eye darting from one doll to the other.

"Your Excellencia, she is a shy one, indeed." The carter pulls at her chin, her face nearing the Duchinu's hand.

"Joseph, is she not capable of simple conversation?"

"Your Excellencia, she is...with time, she can speak of a great many things." The carter squeezes her lips. "Mamsella, say your name." He pushes her head down 'til her lips brush the Duchinu's hand. "And kiss his hand. Kiss it or..."

Her mouth opens wide. Spittle scatters 'cross the Duchinu's boots. She raises her head and points to the patch. "What shame do you hide behind the patch?"

The carter pinches the girl. "Are you mad? It's the Excellencia what asks the questions. Now, tell him your name."

"If your eye is sick, I got to heal you. Mamma says when the one that heals is the one that betrays, then…"

"I am in the best of health," his gaze now fixed on the small yellow dress with ruffles edged in red, "but this insolence…"

The carter slaps his jaw and presses the back of his hand to his chin and hums a nonsense tune. "For both our sakes, *clicca…clicca…*Mamsella, tell the Excellencia your name *clicca…clicca…*and, ppi piaciri, kiss his hand."

"My Papà was here. My Mamma, too."

"Heal my cousin, and they shall come again," the Duchinu says, raising his hand.

"My Papà's dead. My Mamma's sick. I'm here to do their deed."

His hand drops in the high slit pocket of his pants. "And I am here to do *mine.*" He stomps his foot, a brightness in his eye when the tables and lamps shake. At the sound of such thunder, and for no good reason, the carter begs forgiveness for his sins.

"Joseph, my good man, ease your nerves. We are all somewhat ill-disposed… Now, girl, what is your name?"

The carter grabs the girl's shoulders. "Basta! Enough and enough and enough! I made no promise to be silent. I'm not good to no one, not like Madama's good and kind. Such a promise she made at your baptism, *sì,* at your baptism, but this is the Excellencia what stands before us. For both our sakes, he got to hear an answer to his question…and, *me,* I made no promise." He bows to the Duchinu. "Her name is Saitta." He wipes his brow and looks up to the heavens with the sorrow of a sinner. "Gratia Maria Saitta."

Joy spreads 'cross the girl's face now that her ears take in the sound of the words. In all her life, it's the second time she hears her name. The second time…but what does she know of the first?

*

There, at her baptism, I seen it in Alfiu's ball of light, the carter hiding in the sanctuary, gazing at my Vincenza. She spoke the girl's name in her own soothing way, and the girl, but a baby, fixed her eyes on her godmother. Patri Radici poured the holy water 'cross the baby's brow, and Vincenza wiped it with the crisp white cloth that she, one day, would sew and drape over the girl's plaything.

Vincenza lit the candle, kissed and blessed the baby in her arms while Agata crouched at the back of the church. "The Devil got to her," she muttered. "The Devil got to her. The Devil got to her."

What does the girl know of Agata's Mamma, her good Nanna, and the way she pleaded with her daughter to take the girl to church? "Agatuzza, figghia mia, two months the baby is with no sacrament, two months I scatter salt on the floor to keep the Devil at bay and keep her soul pure. How many rosaries, how much salt, how many candles to chase away the Devil before he comes for her? No more, Agata, no more. This is the child that lives, Alfiu's blessed child, and *she* got to be blessed in baptism. Give me your word. Give me your word."

Agata gave her word. I seen it all. The girl's Nanna, filled with joy to be the baby's cummari and filled with joy that the baby bore her own name, the girl's Nanna, when the Mattutinu bells rang out on the morning of the baptism, she took her last breath, and the saints brought her to paradise.

What does the girl know of the carryings on that day in the sanctuary when Patri Radici could take no more of Agata's rantings and shouted for Vincenza to leave with the baby and her Mamma? Agata rushed out through the bronze doors and stood 'neath the sandstone portal, 'neath the chiseled angels and demons that bless and curse and fight for souls. "Listen to me, Vincenza," she whispered with a calm and quiet not in her nature, "I got to mourn for my own Mamma now. Soon that my Mamma left this world, I made you the cummari. I done this for my Mamma's sake for she held you in high regard. My Mamma was a saint. She seen all and forgave all. The one in your arms bears my Mamma's name, but she's not blessed. Shout out my Mamma's name, Vincenza, 'til all the saints in paradise hear it and bow in reverence. That is good. That is holy. The one in your arms, she's not good, she's not holy, and she got but one path in life, the path I'll put her on. Dare to speak her name and show her another. Dare to speak the name that gives blessings, a name she got no right to bear, a path she got no right to go on. ..."

"Agata!"

"Vincenza, dare to whisper her name," she grabbed Vincenza's arm and shook the baby awake, "and I swear on my eyes, the day you say it is the day she takes her last breath. Now, swear on your eyes."

"Cousin…cousin…"

"Swear on them!"

Vincenza bowed her head. With each word she whispered, she kissed the baby's brow. "I…swear…on…my…eyes."

"Now, you are welcomed in my home."

*

The girl knows none of this.

*

She opens her mouth wide. "Gggrrraaa…Gggrrraaa…tttiiiaaa… Gggrrraaattttiiiaaa…Gra…tia…Gratia…Gratia Maria…Gratia Maria…"

"*Gratia Maria* like your Nanna," the carter whispers, "and this stays our secret, for the good and the bad of it."

"Gratia…Gratia…" Like the carter that sings out his nonsense tune of the little wood dove, the girl got it in her to sing out her name again and again. "Gratia…Gratia Maria Saitta. Gratia…Gratia Maria Saitta." In all her days did she ever sing a sweeter song?

"Excellent," the Duchinu says. "However, I prefer Grace."

"Mamsella," the carter whispers, "thank the Excellencia. Say 'Voscenza, thank you for this honor.'"

"No, Mastru Nonziu. Gratia Maria Saitta is my name, and a path shines bright before me." Tears fall from her cheeks, soaking her apron and the knife. She flicks her head, and the tears fall in Vincenza's basket and waken the smells of spices and earth.

"Saitta?" The surgeon passes the wet cloth 'cross the cousin's brow. "Gratia Maria Saitta…hmmm…" The surgeon strokes the scars on his face and neck. "I know the name. If memory serves me, you are not the first Saitta to trespass these grounds."

The Duchinu flashes his sea-eye at the surgeon's tight smile. "Dr. Gale, your musings have no merit here. Please do me the honor of assisting our guest."

"*Assisting?*" The surgeon narrows his eyes, his face flushed.

The carter smiles at the girl and shows off his long, brown teeth. "Do this for Madama's sake."

"For my path..." The girl nears the cousin's bed, tapping 'round and 'neath it. "Where is it?" she whispers to the carter.

The carter swallows, his neck stretching long. "The chamber pot, Your Excellencia," in bare a whisper, "the girl needs to see..."

The Duchinu waves his small finger at the door of a wood cabinet in the corner of the room. The carter waves the same small finger at the girl. She shakes her head. "Sì," he nods, "it's there." She pulls the knob and opens the door. There, on an iron stool, sits a white pot with a cover and a green handle and painted roses on the front side. She lifts the cover and plunges her face inside. The Duchinu grabs his throat. The surgeon gasps.

"*Agghiu,*" the girl whispers, eyeing the wastes with its tiny eggs floating on top.

"The girl needs garlic," the carter says.

"*Ogghiu.*"

"Wait! And oil, too."

"Ah," the surgeon says gaining back his breath, "she comes to prepare a salad. What else can the Saitta girl do?"

"Lucien!"

"I apologize, Alec. I shall put hurt feelings aside and *assist* the peasant girl." He orders a servant girl to the kitchen and bows to the Duchinu. "At your service, my lord, and always at Elizabeth's."

The girl points to the cousin's hair splayed on the pillow. She taps her heavy brown shawl and pulls the knot tight. "The girl like me, but not me, the way 'a z'a Vincenza told me in my dreams." She strokes the wet strands of the cousin's hair. "Like the fox," she sighs, "like me." She eyes the Duchinu standing tall at the threshold. "What breed of men roams this Castle," she whispers in the silent room, "where none cower in fear at the sight of such red hair?"

The cousin moans. The girl takes in a breath, the surgeon breathing over her. The girl closes her eyes and folds back the lace bed covers. With eyes shut, she sees none of the cousin's fancy bed clothes, the long white dress of fine linen with its high lace collar and cuffs and its small white pearls for buttons, a fancier dress for bed than my Vincenza worn on our marriage day. She rubs the cousin's belly and sings a prayer in her ear, the prayer I heard Vincenza sing long ago. "Calma. Calma. Calma. Faith to make you strong. Faith to make you strong. Faith to take away the fright. Faith to make you strong."

At the sound of the words, the cousin opens her eyes and holds tight to the girl's hand, tighter when she eyes the surgeon leaning over her, the stubborn red strands in his white hair brushing her face. The cousin screams. The girl waves the surgeon away. He clenches his teeth and grabs the pitcher of oil and the small plate of garlic from the servant girl that rushed back in, her apron blotted with spilled oil. "Turn your backs," she tells the men. The girl takes a cup from the bed table, rubs it with the garlic and the oil, lifts up the cousin's bed clothes and places the rim of the cup on the cousin's belly.

"It sticks," she tells the carter. "*U vermu tagghiarinu.* That's what it is. That's what it is." Quick, the carter turns 'round, shakes his head and lets out a loud cough so that none can hear the girl or the Duchinu when he asks the nature of the illness.

"Here." The cousin brings the girl's hand to the heart of her belly. The girl rubs small circles on it. The surgeon rushes over to help, but the Duchinu grabs his arm. They whisper, and the surgeon bows again, shuffling to the threshold.

"Here, in the belly? That's where we keep our truth." She nods and three times makes a cross on the cousin's belly. "Water on the fire," she says to the Duchinu. He waves the servant girls out the door. No sooner they rush out, they rush back in, running 'round the cousin's room with fancy cups and plates, all with a painted boy and girl embracing 'neath a flowering tree, and all on trays clinking in their hands.

"Who called for cups and saucers? This is not an afternoon tea. Grace needs boiling water in a pot, perhaps two. Hurry! Do this before I lose my patience!" The servant girls rush out. *Water* they got to understand. The rest he speaks in a boastful way and all in our tongue, mashing all the words, and for what? For who? The girl don't even raise her eyes.

When they come back in and set the pot near the bed, the servant girls, arms rigid at their sides, wait for more orders. The young one with the round face tightens her lips. "The fox," the young one whispers to the others, "does best to stay in the forest and not make her home in the Castle with us."

The girl rummages through Vincenza's basket and passes the servant girls a thick brown rootstalk like a small stick but for the root threads that sheathe it from end to end, once the anchor of the bush with green feather leaves, the bush that thrives in secret places. "Put this in a pot." The Duchinu nods for them to do so. The servant girls grab it and scowl.

"Mastru Nonziu, 'a z'a Vincenza does right to gather the boy filici in the summer when the rootstalk gives the most good."

The carter bows to the Duchinu. "Your Excellencia, the girl is ready. I know she's ready now to do her work."

"And, these," she says and hands the long forked leaves of *'a canfuridda* to the servant girls, "wrap them in a soft cloth and place them 'neath the sufferer's pillow. U vermu hates the smell of 'a canfuridda. They turn and move the other way. That's when we catch them. The plant, it calms us, but it makes u vermu crazy." The servant girls understand, but she waits for the carter to tell the Duchinu in his tongue.

"Chamomile," he says through a fake cough. "It calms us but traps the…" The girl's gold eyes shine in the carter's, and, quick, the cough ceases. "It traps the *worm*." He holds his head and leaps 'round the room.

"Joseph, what in the world are you doing?"

"What the girl wants me to," he says and bows to the Duchinu. "*Bazu, bazu*," and mimics the jumping worm. "She puts chamomile 'neath Donna Elizabeth's pillow to make the worm *crazy, crazy*, and make it move the other way. She wants Your Excellencia to know."

With a slight smile on his lips, the Duchinu nods to the surgeon. "I suppose we must do whatever Grace wishes."

I smile, too, now that the girl pays no more mind to the side of her apron and the knife hiding there. Like a true gifted one, she keeps her eyes closed and waits for the rootstalk of the boy filici to darken the water. She takes it out and presses two slices of i limuni in the water.

"Lemon," the carter says, "to cut the bitter taste."

Such a foul smell, but the girl pays it no mind, praying to 'a Maronna 'a Nunziata the way she does and telling the cousin she got to pray, too.

"Only the *male fern*, only the *boy filici*," the carter whispers to the Duchinu, "the girl knows this alone will cure Donna Elizabeth. The girl wants you to know your dear and delicate cousin got to drink all the tea, too, no matter the smell, no matter the taste, 'til there's no more."

The Duchinu nods. The surgeon leans on the door frame with no hint of joy on his face. The Duchinu towers over him and sighs. The surgeon looks up and presses his lips tight like he got to keep back all what he wants to say now that the girl starts her healing.

"Cut one, cut two, cut three. Cut u vermu that takes the hold of you. Three times cut u vermu, here and here and here." The servant girls drop to their knees.

"The words…she speaks the words." When was the last time the servant girls heard Vincenza say such words to heal their Mammas or their Nannas or their own selves in Bronti before they settled in the Castle? Like a fervent prayer heard long ago and now brought back to mind, they close their eyes and savor each word. The young one with the round face sobs. She begs forgiveness for her sharp tongue. They kneel 'long the curled metal leaves of the foot board, tiny blue birds, the lot of them, with Ave Maria prayers on their lips.

From the pot, the girl scoops the cure in a cup and lays the cup on a small plate.

The cure is hard to look at, dark and of the earth. The young ones that eat all what they find near cottage doors and on the road, and for such ways, got to drink the cure, they know it's hard to look at and hard to swallow. But with no sour look on her face, the cousin swallows it quick. The servant girls bow their heads. They're the helpers, not the surgeon that orders agghiu and ogghiu from the kitchen. The servant girls know: Vincenza of Bronti is the worm charmer and the healer, the gifted one. Now, they know, so, too, is the girl.

"It's moving! Make it stop! Make it stop!" The cousin grabs the lace bed covers and throws them over her face.

"Good. Good." The young one with the round face laughs. "U vermu jumps when it got no place to go. It won't go up now, not when 'a canfuridda is 'neath the pillow. It got no place to go but out."

All night the girl been praying at the cousin's side. All night the cousin been moaning and holding her belly. Now, she drops her hands low. The girl smiles, reaches for u pisciaturi and tells the carter it's time for the men to leave.

"You may leave now, as well," the cousin whispers to the girl. "This is a private matter." The girl shakes her head and passes her u pisciaturi.

When the cousin does all what she got to do, the girl scoops out the head of u vermu with its hooks and suckers and waves the worm's head past the cousin's eyes. She faints straight away. The girl shakes her. She comes 'round. She looks up and smiles, then falls back on the pillow and crosses to a deep sleep.

"Z'a Vincenza, you teach me well," the girl whispers and wipes the cousin's brow. She takes some mint leaves from the basket and passes them to the blue apron servant girls. "Put more water on the fire. Seep these leaves in the water. When the sick one wakens, she…what? The mint leaves? No, not for the cure. They're but for the belly and to make the mouth fresh."

The four servant girls grab hold of the young one with the round face that asked of the leaves and ply her fleshy arm with hard pinches. They bow and leave the room. That's when the girl tugs 'neath the pillow at the soft cloth and wraps the head of the worm with its hooks and suckers inside the leaves of 'a canfuridda. She holds the cloth tight in her hands. "'A z'a Vincenza knows you don't like the smell of this plant, you evil worm, and, Maronna mia, good for the sick one that you crawled away from it and all the way back down and right in u pisciaturi."

The girl's hands smell of the innards of the cousin's body, a smell that spreads through the room and out the window and behind the cypress trees and right 'neath my nose, but who got to be sickened by the smell of healing? She opens the door and lets the Duchinu and the surgeon back in. Who got to be sickened by the smell of healing? The one that jumps back and, through his fine cloth handkerchief, chokes. When, at long last, the Duchinu gains back his breath, he asks the carter a flood of questions.

"Donna Elizabeth's good," the carter tells him. "Chamomile to calm Donna Elizabeth and trap the worm. Mint to refresh her breath." The girl nears the carter with the head of the worm. He waves her away. "Your Excellencia, the sickness won't come back. The girl wants you to know, it won't come back now that...now that Donna Elizabeth... passed...the head...of the...worm."

The surgeon rubs the scars on his face and neck. "Alec, are you blind to that which surrounds you? This is sorcery and superstition, pure and simple."

"Grace, Joseph, please wait outside." The Duchinu closes the door behind them. "If he lives, it is the work of the worm charmer and her herbs; if he dies, it is the work of the doctor and his medicine. Is that not what the peasants say regarding illness and recovery? Apparently, all their superstitions have merit."

"You find this amusing?"

"Come now, Dr. Gale. The girl is not a sorcerer. She has healed with the knowledge of the earth and with a pure heart."

"A pure heart?"

"She *is* pure, Dr. Gale," he stares down at the surgeon, "and she shall remain so."

"Pure? Her kind has not grasped the meaning of the word." He throws his hands through his hair and lets out a laugh. "Grant her a favor or lead her to believe there is a favor in the making and let us see how quickly the apron is undone and the bodice unbuttoned."

"I shall not hear another word."

"My lord, with your permission, you shall, indeed. Elizabeth had taken a turn for the better when that Saitta girl skulked into her room, a fox with a bag of tricks."

"My dear Doctor Gale, you talk with the spitefulness of a rival. Yet you insist you have not made the girl's acquaintance."

"She is not the one I know."

"Then you talk as though you fear her."

"I fear only those who bring you harm with their cunning. Have you looked into her eyes? The eyes of a fox...and so are her ways."

The Duchinu pats the surgeon's back and lets out a small laugh. "The peasants speak of the fox as the pet of the Devil, do they not? I should think after all your transgressions you would fear more an angel from heaven than a *pet* from hell."

"Alec, it is your prerogative to make light of the situation. Nonetheless, bear in mind our great Vice-Admiral Lord Viscount Nelson's immortal words: *No captain can do very wrong if he places his ship alongside that of an enemy.* The Saitta girl is trouble. Keep her close as you would an enemy ship but profit from her proximity."

"Enough, Lucien. Whether she is trouble or not does not affect my gratitude. A worm is a worm. A dead worm is a dead worm. And the simple fact remains: Grace is the one who has cured Elizabeth of a most unsavory condition."

*What you despise today, you may desire tomorrow.*

The carter taps his fingers 'long the blue walls and rocks side to side 'til he can't hold back his joy no more. "The Excellencia don't want us in Donna Elizabeth's room," he whispers to the girl. "See? He's preparing a great surprise for us." The girl shrugs, but the carter, he's filled with a young boy's fire, and he drags the girl down the long, blue hallway, past paintings of battle scenes and seamen, past rooms with books edged in gold and carved bottles of color glass on round tables. His face beams. His chest puffs out. What makes him so proud? What did he heal? What did he pray? "Mamsella, where is your joy? You healed Donna Elizabeth, and your z'a Vincenza got to bless you this day."

"Sì, Mastru Nonziu." She pulls out a sprig of finucchina from Vincenza's basket. But before she rubs her hands clean of the cousin's body stench, the carter snatches it away and spreads it all over himself. He lets out a great sigh, the kind he makes when he dips himself in a warm tub of water to let all the island know he's clean. "But, Mastru Nonziu, what brings 'a z'a Vincenza joy brings pain to Mamma, and, you, you told me that a child's joy is to obey her Mamma, so, this day, I bring pain to my own self, too."

He pats the heavy brown shawl on her head. "*Bella. Bella.* That's what we called your Mamma. Agata, with the long, black curls and the round, dark eyes. Beautiful. Beautiful. That's what your Papà called her, too, the first time he seen her. He ran home and asked his Mamma for her blessings.

She went to your Nanna's cottage, and, Mamma to Mamma, they arranged the courtship. Your Papà carved the marriage chest. Your Mamma and your Nanna sat at the loom day to night and weaved the linens for her dowry. Hard work brought your Mamma joy. Hard work, sì, but your Papà …he brought your Mamma her greatest joy."

"Mastru Nonziu, all what you say is the joy of the past."

"Mamsella, to see your Mamma the way we seen her! A worker like none other, leaving her bed when the moon still lit the sky to labor side by side with your Papà before he worked the Duca's fields. Up the rocky lands they climbed 'til they came 'on trees, the trees in lava rocks. They cleared the land and planted more trees and named the land their own. 'A frastucara, that's what we call the trees. They grow out of rocks. For your Mamma, what ought not to grow, grew. What ought not to be, thrived. That was what brought your Mamma joy."

"More of the past. I speak of what brings her joy this day. And I got to obey her and bring my own self joy. You told me so."

"What you got in mind to do don't bring joy. It only fills the world with sorrow."

"You talk of joy. Now, you talk of sorrow. You talk of this and that and nothing. 'A z'a Vincenza says when you die, and you are none but bones in a grave, your mouth still got to flap your nonsense to the worms. To the worms!"

The carter shakes her. "When you learn to speak your own words, talk to me!" He throws his hands in the air and races back down the long, blue hallway, the girl not far behind. When he nears the cousin's door, he hurls the finucchina at the wall where the *hero's* painting hangs. "And if you don't never learn your own words, then, learn to listen with your own ears."

"Listen with these ears?" She strikes them again and again 'til the carter yanks her hand away. "These ears been burning all their lives with tales of a Mamma's sorrow!" She flings Vincenza's basket at the cousin's door. "No more! No more!" The buds and leaves and rootstalks fly out the basket and perch on the fringes of her heavy brown shawl. "No more!" She shakes off the plants. They drop on the rug like small dead birds. "Fool that I been to want to know my path. This is my path! To bring my Mamma joy! And when she's filled with joy, she got to…at long last, she got to…"

She falls in his arms, her, sobbing like a hungry child, him, his own eyes filled with tears. "Mamsella, calma, you think I don't know your Mamma's sorrow…or your Papà's? Before you seen the light of day, a shadow of a bird flew in his eyes. Some say it was a magpie with a withered heart. Whatever it was, that was the day he cursed his small patch of lava land and looked to take back *all* the land from the Duca. And that was the day he grew mad."

"Mad…mad like the brave Orlannu?"

"Sì, mad and brave like Orlannu. And he died brave, too, in the neighborhood Santu Vitu. Mamsella, don't look at me with such eyes. I speak the truth. Your Mamma spun her tales of the Castle and its crimes for so long, now, you believe them, too, but your Papà, he was shot in the square, and that's where his sorrows ended. But, for your Mamma, that was the start of hers."

"I can make her sorrows end!" She pushes him away and crushes the buds on the rug and breaks the stalks and tears at the leaves. "A z'a Vincenza breathed in me all the healing," she throws the broken plants at him, "but Mamma breathed in me all the justice! The healing got to stop! The justice got to start! That is how the sorrows end!"

He kneels and pulls her back in his arms. "You healed the Excellencia's cousin, but it wasn't for Madama. Look in your heart. Did you suffer from the healing or did it bring you joy?"

"Basta! Mastru Nonziu, leave me be!" She jumps up, spitting at the plants. "Kindness got no place here. I know all what brings the suffering joy. I know Mamma got to suffer no more. All what I got to do now, I got to do for Mamma."

The carter puts the broken plants back in the basket, save for a dark stem rich with strong-smelling leaves, the shape of small eggs. He holds the stem out to the girl. She swats the spicy leaves away. "Va ben', pay no mind to all what Madama teaches you and do the deed for your Mamma. But, then, what befalls you? Soon, you'll find yourself in a world of demons. Do the deed, Mamsella…"

She pulls the knife out and waves it at the carter. "Sì, I'll do the deed with Papà's knife!"

"Do the deed with that cursed knife of yours and live out the rest of your days alone. Alone," he whispers, crossing himself, "*alone*, I say, for you'll never find your way back from such darkness."

The Duchinu opens the cousin's door and stumbles on the basket. "Give it to me, Joseph." He holds out his hand and pats the surgeon's shoulder. "Dr. Gale, be so kind as to set Grace's basket next to Elizabeth's night table. Grace may need additional herbs when our delicate Elizabeth awakens." He eyes the carter and the girl, their eyes fixed on each other like a beast and his prey. "Joseph, Grace…whatever furor may have transpired between you, do not taint this joyous moment. Elizabeth is healed! She is healed! How shall I ever repay…yes, of course, and it shall be a true delight. Do not tarry, follow me."

"Very well, Your Excellencia." The carter bows. "Here it comes," he whispers to the girl, "a reward like no other," and makes his way behind the Duchinu. "As you wish, Your Excellencia."

"Not you, Joseph…Grace."

*

The Duchinu takes the girl to a dark room where chairs crowd 'round three steps leading up to a wood platform. He waves to a servant that, quick, lights long, thin candles in their holders. He waves, again, and, quick, a second servant jumps to light the lamps hanging on the walls, shining metal lamps with white shades that the servant got to first fill with oil. He fastens the wick in place and rubs it. Oil drips on his palms. He swipes his hands 'cross his pants with no fear of punishment for the Duchinu sees none of it, fixing his gaze the way he does at the door and at the girl, her hands wrapped 'round the frame.

The Duchinu taps the high back of a chair. "Sit."

She sinks in its soft flower cushions. "*Ahi!*" she cries out, and this makes the Duchinu laugh. He waves to the first servant that bows and lights more candles. The girl shadows her eyes from the glow. The Duchinu pats her shoulder and rushes to the wood platform and behind a thick red curtain.

"I could not help but notice how awestricken you appeared upon viewing Elizabeth's dolls." He peeks out. She shakes her head. "Now, Grace, do not deny that which I have already witnessed. They are the very few of hundreds which my cousin insisted upon transporting from London."

"*Daaalllaaa.*"

"Yes, Grace. Although there is no way to compensate you for Elizabeth's restored health, please allow me to show you my gratitude and demonstrate how dolls can, indeed, come to life."

"Life?" The girl grabs the knife in her apron. "Come to life? Come to life? Who comes to bring my Papà back to life? None of you that took him from Mamma!"

The Duchinu pushes back the curtain with his boot, his hands wrapped 'round an iron bar. He stabs at a large crate and pries the lid open, the wood screeching out a long, suffering song.

"Who comes to bring my Mamma back to life?"

The lid crashes on the floor. "Grace, louder!" He stabs at a second crate. "Granted I may be the instigator of such cacophony, nonetheless…"

"Me, I bring my Mamma back to life…and, you, you bring her back to life when I do the deed. I know my path…I know my path…justice I got to serve to bring Mamma joy, and, then…and, then…at long last, she got to…*love* me."

The girl rushes to the wood platform and pushes the curtain back, her fist clenched 'round the handle of the knife. The Duchinu, his back to her, he pries open the lid of the second crate. He leans over the third and battles with the lid.

"Grace, if that is you skulking on the stage, I command you to return to your chair." He waves his hand, his fingers tangled in the laces of thick strings. "I intended this to be a surprise for our delicate Elizabeth. There shall be many more surprises for my cousin. May this be my special gift to you."

He pulls out the last of the stubborn nails and with such force that the lid of the third crate flies open and out of his hand. It spirals over the girl's head. It crashes on the platform, the narrow wood slats of the lid now a pile of long splinters. The Duchinu grips the box the best he can, but it tumbles to the side. Out from a swell of straw, a leg sheathed in armor issues forth.

"You send your warriors to kill me?" She stabs at the straw. "But not if they die first! I'll kill them all, and, then, I'll kill…"

"Grace, are you mad? Put that knife away! Calm yourself and watch closely." He lifts a warrior from the box and cradles it. She throws her fingers 'cross her mouth, the knife falling to her side. "The artwork never ceases to impress me. These are carved by the most talented artisan in Catania, who, may I add, was kind enough to lend his wonderful apprentices to me for one week. Grace, see those young boys in the wings? George and Charles shall aid me. However, with no further ado, may I present the guests of honor."

The Duchinu stands the warrior up, a warrior with a dazzling shield and a helmet with bright red plumes springing from the crest. The Duchinu raises the visor. There, they stare back at her, the eyes of the warrior dark and crossed.

"Orlannu!" She cowers behind the Duchinu.

"Yes, Grace, Charlemagne's prized paladin is, indeed, an impressive warrior. However, he lacks one or two *accoutrements*." The Duchinu flings the straw in the air and rifles through the box. "Here is the most important. Who is Orlando without it?"

She reaches out to a long, shining blade and a gold and jewel hilt that the Duchinu locks in the warrior's hand. "*Durindana!*"

"Voilà, Durendal, Orlando's magic sword. What is a hero without his sword?"

She grips the knife tight in her hand. "Durindana," she whispers.

"Now everything stands in place." He gazes down at his jacket, brushing a few pieces of straw from the pockets.

She lunges from behind. "All but the enemy!" She wields the knife in the air but stumbles over the pile of long splinters and falls in a box eye to eye with a painted face and a sharp black beard that scrapes her cheek.

"Grace, the enemy *is* here." He pushes her to the side and lifts the warrior in black armor. "May I present Medoro, the Saracen enemy. And in the last crate, this young lady is, as you well know, Orlando's beautiful Angelica who shall fall into the Saracen's arms, although not today. Medoro, Angelica, Orlando, may I present Grace."

*Ppù! Ppù!* She spits at the Saracen.

"Come now, Grace. They are not real. They are marionettes and here for your pleasure. I promise that Orlando shall win every battle. Moreover, he shall win the affections of Angelica. Now, please, return to the seat of honor so that I may begin the narration."

The girl lowers her eyes and makes her way back to the chair. "Orlannu is brave."

"Yes, Grace, Orlando is brave, but he is also *babbasuni.*"

The girl turns 'round and lets out a laugh. "You speak in our tongue, but…"

He stomps his foot. "No, I did not mean *stupid*…he is…impulsive."

She slips the knife back in the folds of her apron and presses the smile from her mouth. "How do you know of our heroes?"

"I have many passions, one being your epic heroes. However, had they bored me, I should still concern myself with them. The Duke of Bronte must comprehend the interests of his peasants. Only, then, might he truly comprehend their desires. In comprehending their desires, might he, then, truly anticipate their actions."

"You are but the son. And you know none of what a peasant desires."

"I know his heart and soul better than he. And I know the Bronte peasant would be wise not to play me for a fool." He stomps his foot and sends the lids and crates and straw flying high to the ceiling. "Grace, take your seat or the entertainment shall not commence."

*

There are three of them behind the curtain, two that work the strings and the Duchinu that tells the tale in a deep and solemn voice:

*"Orlando wields his sword and cuts through a thousand Saracens on the battlefield. Before our eyes, there remain only two warriors, Orlando, our hero, and Medoro, the Saracen, who fights with all his strength. He thrusts his sword into Orlando's armor and thrusts it into his shoulder and leg. The hero falls to the ground. Orlando is brave and holds his sword against his heart. Durendal's power courses through the hero's body and gives him strength. He labors to his feet and shouts* Infidel *to the warrior who all but claims victory. Orlando wields his sword in the air, slashing Medoro's pride and limbs until the Saracen falls, his shield and sword crashing to the ground. The hero lords over him. With one powerful thrust to Medoro's heart, the Saracen is dead."*

Quick, it starts. Quick, it ends. The young boys carry the warriors back behind the curtain, the thick strings swishing 'cross the wood platform. The Duchinu smiles and talks of this and that with them. He eases back the curtain and eyes the girl through the soft glow of the candles. "Brave Orlannu, good Orlannu, like my Papà," she whispers and raises her eyes to the heavens.

"Beautiful. Beautiful. Beautiful. Beautiful. Beautiful." He says the word 'til his throat goes dry and his face goes pale. The young boys scramble to fetch him water. His legs quiver. He holds tight to the bunching of the thick red curtain, but, still, he near falls. He lets out a sigh, a powerful sigh like the foreign wind, a mighty gust that rips the girl's heavy brown shawl from her head. She flicks her head, her red hair sweeping down her back and 'round her feet. He falls to his knees. "Signurina…land…of… hair… Signurina, land of…it is you, my angel of the olive groves… Grace, how could it *not* be you?"

There, behind the curtain, he lifts his eye patch and wipes the tears from his sea blue eyes. There, in the soft flower cushions of the high back chair, the girl wipes away her own rush of tears. "Brave Orlannu," she sobs, "like my Papà." The Duchinu grabs his heart. "Heaven's angel," he whispers, "this must remain our secret."

What does the carter care where the Duchinu took the girl and what she seen? He got a belly full of food and a warm bed to sleep in at the Castle, and, this, with no twists and turns of his tongue. The Duchinu already said his farewells to the carter and the girl but, still, he waves to the cart in the distance. "Good-bye," he shouts out, "and take with you my undying gratitude for Elizabeth's…*Elizabeth*!" He throws his hand over his heart. "Elizabeth, my dear cousin, how I've neglected you!" He races up the great stairway, slaps his brow, "Grace!" and races back down and out the door. In his high leather boots, he splashes through the puddles 'round the new bushes in the rose garden. This isn't a short way to the new carriage road, what makes him think it is, but the carter, sniffling back his tears now that he got to leave the Castle, he fumbles long with the reins, Chiazza drags her hooves, and, quick, the Duchinu catches up.

"Seh...ven...o...cl...o...cl..."

"Your Excellencia?"

The Duchinu wipes his neck, loosens his collar and tightens the patch over his eye. "Seven o'clock," he says, taking in a breath. "Seven o'clock. Forgive me, Joseph, a mere shortness of breath. Seven o'clock. Day after tomorrow," he looks out to the east, to Mungibellu now hidden in her own smoke, "unless Etna's vapours have other designs for us."

"Thank you, Your Excellencia."

"No, thank *you*, Joseph. You have more than paid your debt. And I am a man of my word."

"Yes, Your Excellencia."

"The day after tomorrow we shall celebrate not only our delicate Elizabeth's eighteenth year but, with gratitude to Grace, her restored health as well. Be so kind as to relay my invitation to...Joseph, where is...?" He looks 'round and throws his face in the cart, pushing the fancy dresses aside and smiles. "I shall relay the joyous news myself." He shakes the girl from her sleep and holds out his hand. "Grace..." The girl raises her hand in kind, but higher, right 'neath the Duchinu's nose. The stench of the cousin's innards comes alive in the morning air. "Grace, I...you..." He pulls his hand back and presses his fine cloth handkerchief over his mouth. "As I was saying, Grace, you shall be the envy of all the peasant girls."

"Your Excellencia, the girl...she don't understand the ways of the Castle...not like we do. See how she dresses, with rags for a skirt and rags for a shawl. The girl is not of *our* nature. She don't understand *our* ways."

"Very well, Joseph. As this appears to be of great concern to you, bring her to the manor by six."

# PART III: THE DWELLING

*Death is not the worst thing.*

They honor her for seven days, the patron saint of Bronti, the young Maria and her angel messenger that make their home above the altar in the sanctuary 'a Maronna 'a Nunziata that wanderers built when they founded Bronti. Once a year in the early days of August, the Bruntiszi take 'a Maronna 'a Nunziata from her dwelling and hoist her on a platform that weighs down the shoulders of their strongest men. There, they parade her from church to church for seven days, Bronti's one-saint army that lords her power over Man and Nature.

The horns rehearse a solemn march for the procession this last day. Chiazza rocks her head side to side. The carter swings the reins in the air, the two marking the rhythms of the march while the cart rumbles back to town.

"Wake up, Mamsella, and come sit by my side." He fixes his eyes on the bench and shines a big smile. If he fixed his eyes on Mungibellu's smoke, the grey now black, there'd be none but fear in his eyes, but the Castle clouds his thoughts and reason. "For a good day's work, you got your own self an invitation to the Castle. And at a celebration! Glorious saints! Who says our great desires go unfulfilled?"

The girl pats her apron, the line of Alfiu's knife pressing through. "What do I care for such desires? They're like *ceci* beans in the hands of those that don't cook. These are your desires, not mine. Stuff your belly full of them. I want no part. Don't you see, I missed a second time?"

"Mamsella, these are not my desires. My desires..."

"Sì, Mastru Nonziu, sì. Your desires all got to do with 'a z'a Vincenza."

"She's but a part of my desire." He stands in the cart, his hands clasped, and sings out his nonsense tune of the little wood dove. "But when I tell you all of my desire," him, puffing, near out of breath, "then..."

"*Then*…and then…nothing! I missed a second time!"

"Mamsella, I seen the knife." He sits back down and presses her hand in his. "I seen your desires. What I don't know, the rest I surmise. But let us move our talk to…to me and my desires that you never surmised." The carter pushes the heavy brown shawl back and whispers in the girl's ear for the mare and the road and the air not to hear. "You know there are men that sing the tales of the brave Orlannu and his kind and…"

"Sì. They go from town to town."

He folds the shawl back over her ear and smiles. "That is my desire."

"What?"

"To sing out these tales in all the squares in all the towns on our island."

She shakes her head. "Mastru Nonziu, better to live a hero's life than to sing of one."

"Mamsella, better to sing of heroes than cowards."

"Va ben'. Va ben'. But, Mastru Nonziu, there are many tales. You got to learn them all."

"I know them."

"You know *all* the tales that such men sing?"

He nods.

"And this is your desire?"

"With Madama by my side. Sì, this is my great desire. Mamsella…now, tell me, what is yours?"

The girl jumps from the cart. "Mine?" she laughs. "It's to go on foot."

The carter flicks the reins. "Va ben', Mamsella, see where it gets you!"

Chiazza quickens her pace. The girl runs by her side, but soon that the girl makes a fist and opens her hand and spreads her fingers wide, the mare slows to a trot and lowers her head. "Chiazza," the girl whispers, "Mastru Nonziu wants to know the desire that makes my heart beat. How my heart got to beat when I tell Mamma all what happened at the Castle. All of my name. All of my path. And, then, she got to give me blessings, and, then…and, then…she got to *love* me." She waves to the carter. "Do you hear my desires, Mastru Nonziu?"

"Mamsella?"

"No? You don't hear them? Va ben', I got to shout them out. When I tell Mamma all what happened at the Castle…"

"*Jautu*, Chiazza, *jautu*!" The carter yanks the reins. The mare squeals and comes to a halt. "What did you say, Mamsella?"

"All what happened at the Castle, Mastru Nonziu, I got to tell Mamma."

"Mamsella, listen to me. This day we speak of desires. Desires that are our secrets. The secrets of the Castle we dare not tell Madama or your Mamma. Now, give me your word. Not *one* word to your Mamma."

The girl throws her arms up and twirls 'round and 'round. "I give you my word. Not *one* word. No, no, Mastru Nonziu, not *one* word. Not *one* for I got to say them all, all the words on the island I got to say to Mamma. I got to walk up and down like the Duca's men with my hands behind my back and make my speech. 'Mamma, I been to the Castle!' I got to shout out. 'Figghia mia,' she got to sob, and, then, she got to give me blessings, and, then, she got to..." She taps the knife 'neath the apron folds. "Mamma got to smile when I tell her all what I know. And she got to smile more when I tell her the third time got to bring good fortune."

The carter flicks his fingers 'neath his chin. "Mamsella, put an end to such foolishness!"

"What foolishness? At the feast, when the Duchinu and his kind dress in their finest, that's when Mamma says blood spilled for justice sake always shines the brightest. Bright, bright, bright like the Angelus sun this day."

What does the girl know of the sun? Where does she look to find it? Not at the sky, for if she looked up, she'd know, the Angelus bells ring out, but the Angelus sun don't shine, now that the dark smoke from Mungibellu hides the sky and the beautiful mountain and all the land from view. I look 'round. All is dark. Gone are the horn players. All is quiet. But for the cart high on Corsu Umbertu, Bronti is a town forsaken 'til a man comes in view, more a shadow than a man. He limps down from the narrow bends of via Grisley to make his way to Corsu Umbertu where he bangs his drum.

It's the crier, old and weak in body, but still strong in voice. His crippled legs hobble up Corsu Umbertu. He shouts out his warnings like the cross-eyed lunatic that limps behind him, waving his sword of binding twigs at the empty road. "*Fora, fora, fora!*" the crier shouts out and, quick, finds himself eye to eye with Chiazza. "Fora, fora, fora!" The mare's ears pin back.

She stares at the crier with a hard eye and stomps her hooves. The crier got his own fears and worries and hobbles right past her.

"Fora, fora, fora! Out of your houses!" Small black pigs rush from the cottages and squeal back the orders. "*Fora, fora, fora, Mungibellu si scassò!* Out of your houses, the beautiful mountain breaks wide open! The beautiful mountain breaks wide open!" Mammas pull babies from hammocks and rush with them outside. "Fora, fora, fora, Mungibellu si scassò!" Young girls drag old cummari past walls that creak and shake, the old cummari cursing when their needlework flies out of their hands and 'cross the moving earth. "Fora, fora, fora!" Rosary beads click like a thousand summer insects. Peasants drop to their knees, and, in the roads, they tremble and pray.

"Look, Mastru Nonziu, 'a z'a Vincenza told me this is how 'a Maronna 'a Nunziata goes to paradise, in clouds."

The carter raises his eyes to the sky and jumps from the cart. "Clouds? Mamsella, can't you see the signs? These aren't the clouds the Savior sends down to take 'a Maronna to paradise. These clouds are thick with smoke. They bode no good." He pulls the girl down Corsu Umbertu. "Quicken your step. By God's good graces, may your Mamma and Madama be safe as safe can be."

The girl looks up at the dark sky. She claps her hands, but her fingers fade in the smoke. "You're right, Mastru Nonziu, these aren't the Savior's clouds. These are the Duca's clouds, and they're all 'round us now, and they bode much good. On such clouds, the Duca and his son will go back to their demon dwelling. Mungibellu will swallow them up, and the one-eyed monster will lead them down the path where the Devil been waiting to welcome them home. Mamma told me of this day. It's on this day Mamma and me rejoice."

"Mamsella, basta! You talk with two hearts, your Mamma's heart and Madama's heart." His hands on his knees, he lets out a hard breath when they near via Leanza. "But ask yourself this: what does your own heart say?"

"*My* heart?"

"You talk of paths. I talk of hearts, for when the tongue wants to speak, it got to first ask the heart. Ask your heart what it wants of you. When you know, then, speak the words. Speak the words, but not this day. Hurry! Hurry to your Mamma's cottage! Glorious saints, now is not the time…"

"*Sst...sst...*" The girl pulls him back. She puts her finger to her mouth and crouches on the ground. "Mastru Nonziu...listen."

"Mungibellu?"

All what the girl hears, I hear, too, sounds deep to the ground that grow loud with each breath I take. I cup my ears. The pounding of hoof beats, I hear a thousand of them...

"What, Mamsella?"

The girl looks to the south, up to a jagged slope, where, out from Mungibellu's smoke, a lamb races down, her soft wool strands flying in the air. When she reaches Bronti, she flies to the open arms of the girl.

"It's you..." I can bare hear her whispers, lost the way they are in the noises of the earth. She cradles the shaking lamb, but, still, the lamb bleats, and, still, Chiazza squeals, and, still, the crier and the carter shout, but who can hear them? The cracking of the earth drowns out the cries of man and beast, now that the one-eyed monster shows no mercy and tramples through Mungibellu, and now that Mungibellu...

"Mamsella!" the carter shouts out, deep rumbles from the earth rising through his body, shaking him 'til he near falls down. He wails a mourner's cry and grabs hold of the girl and turns her 'round. "Mamsella, Mungibellu breaks wide open. She shows us all the fire she holds from hell. By God's good graces, leave your foolishness behind. Your Mamma and Madama need our help."

"This isn't foolishness, Mastru Nonziu." She wipes her cheek of the lamb's lickings. "The lamb's a gift from the Savior. And the greater gift can't be far behind."

"Mamsella, where is the Savior to help us now!"

"We're not frightened," she whispers, covering the lamb's sad eyes when the beautiful mountain throws out her hot lava rocks. "The one-eyed monster don't roam 'round for long. When he tires, he got to snatch Mungibellu's fire back to her belly."

"Don't be frightened, my precious little lamb," whispers a voice behind them. "The girl got to keep you safe."

The girl cups her mouth. Slow, slow, she turns 'round. She fixes her eyes on the dark, wet eyes of the shepherd boy, his thin fingers pressing the long tail of the stocking cap to his cheek. She falls to the ground, her body trembling on the rocking earth. "It's you. Shepherd boy, it's *you*. How my heart breaks from joy!"

He kneels by her side. "My heart, too, how it breaks from joy!"

"I waited, shepherd boy...Blasiu...Blasiu that blazes the sky, I waited and made a dwelling for you."

"The lamb, she always wants the liberty. Now, she comes to Bronti. But to take my own self back here when I am cursed..." He waves his hand at small dark shapes huddling near churches, their eyes to the earth, their lips in prayer. "My Bruntiszi! I got to spare you!" He reaches for the girl's hand. "I got to take the lamb and leave before an innocent one looks 'on me, and I curse him 'til his dying day."

"I look 'on you, and, cursed, I am not. Blessed, I am. Blessed, I'll stay 'til my dying day."

The carter sweeps his hands through the dark smoke and tries to take hold of the girl. He shouts. He curses. He falls on the ground and moans, "I'll not leave the girl!"

The boy kisses the girl's hand and holds it up to his face. "I, too, am blessed...'til my dying day."

Four black pigs squeal 'round the boy and girl. She holds out her arms to sweep up the lot of them, but, quick, they slip from her hands. "Where are you, little ones? I hear you, but where are you?" She waves her arms in the air 'til she touches the boy's face. "Blasiu, Blasiu, I gazed in your eyes but a moment past, and, now, where are *you*?" She opens her eyes. She closes them. "Maronna mia, what happens here?"

"Darkness from Mungibellu!" the shepherd boy shouts.

"No, I am blind. Blind to the pigs and blind to *you*."

"Hide from my sight, girl! It's the curse!"

"No, shepherd boy! It's by your side I got to stay."

The carter throws his head back, his legs, still and steady on the quieting earth. He raises his hand to his face and counts his five thick fingers.

The shepherd boy waves his hands in the air, tapping his way to the girl's scarf and brow and cheeks. "But, wait...what happens here? I, too, am blind to the pigs. And, I, too, am blind to you."

"Blasiu, I hear your voice, but…" She buries her face in her hands. She taps her small, thin fingers on her brow and lets out a laugh. "They're warm, Blasiu. My hands are warm. And I can see them, too!" She rubs her eyes. She opens them wide. "Blasiu, all is bright and warm 'round me. Sì, I am blind, but I am blind for all is light." She touches his face. "All is light and bright 'round me. Your face, your face is sheathed in light. And, look, there's Chiazza, bright and calm and nearing sleep. And, there, the peasants, bright and dancing." She wraps her arms 'round the boy. "O, Blasiu, you're not cursed. Feel how the earth quiets down. Blasiu that blazes the sky, see how you make the sun shine!"

The carter swings them 'round and pulls them in a spider dance. "Listen! Not a sound! Look!"

In the sky, bright summer rays cut through the black smoke. Streams of fire headed straight to the town find their way back inside Mungibellu's precious flank. The smoke and ash all but fade from view. The hot rocks torn from the flank, what are they now but small, bright playthings that tumble harmless to the town? Shiny horns blast their tunes once more. Peasants make their way back home, slapping each other for good fortune while their wives cross themselves and give thanks to 'a Maronna 'a Nunziata. The girl's not wrong. The one-eyed monster don't roam 'round for long. When he tires, that's when he snatches Mungibellu's fire back to her belly.

The crier unlatches the drum strap. Arm-in-arm with the cross-eyed lunatic, he hobbles to the sanctuary where the holy statues of 'a Maronna 'a Nunziata and her angel messenger dwell. The carter blocks their passage with a song and a dance. The lunatic waves his sword of binding twigs at him and finds his madness once more.

"My gooood man," the carter sings out to the cross-eyed lunatic, "in spite of your curses that burst with grief, may God's graces shine on you for we live another day. And," he turns to the shepherd boy, "may God's graces shine on you. Stay near to us and bathe in His blessings."

"Mastru Nonziu, thank you for your blessings, but I got to leave before the innocent ones look 'on me, and they take on my nature."

"Only the spoon that stirs knows the troubles of the pot. Only you know the troubles your life takes on. Be brave, Blasiu. Now is the time to be brave. Don't act the coward like…like the one that holds my Vincenza's heart captive. Lay down the spoon. Let your troubles sink to the bottom of the pot. Signa Agata and Signa Vincenza need our courage now."

The shepherd boy throws a look at the girl, her eyes to the earth, her lips shining such a bright smile. He shakes his fist at her. "You can't make me brave with a smile. Nothing can make me brave. I am cursed! Cursed!"

"Blasiu, leave the girl be. We are all cursed…'til we find our blessings. But now's not the time to speak of blessings or curses." The carter waves his hand at the low, round archway that opens to the neighborhood 'a Maronna ri Loretu. "Look 'round. See where your feet brought you."

'Neath the ancient archway, at the small shrine carved in stone, the boy bows his head. Slow, slow, he taps his way 'long the stone wall to the first cottage and the small wood door. "Open," he says. "Still open for me. Opened when I was but a child, and it welcomed me. The good man that lived here brought me food when my Mamma was sick. His young wife took pity on me and knitted me this cap." He slaps his face and stops a tear at the hollow of his cheek. "I know where we are."

"Now that you know, you got to step inside and show Signa Agata your thankfulness."

*

Inside the cottage, Vincenza pushes the marriage chest back to the foot of the marriage bed and sets a wood chair back on its legs. She wipes up the water that splashed on the dirt floor when the pot flew like a big, black bird 'cross the cottage. She drags the pot to the hearth and hoists it back on its iron stool. 'Neath the broken loom, she comes 'on all what remains of the cross. She picks up two thick splinters and crosses them and ties them with straw and hangs them back over the marriage bed. Agata sits up in the bed, laughing and clapping her palms quick and loud each time Vincenza throws out her hip to move the bed and, slow, slow, push it back near the hearth. "It's by the grace of 'a Maronna 'a Nunziata that we live another day," Vincenza pats her brow and takes in a breath, "and to give thankfulness, we…"

Agata throws a look at Vincenza. The laughing and clapping fall to silence. She throws the sheet over her face, hiding all but her narrowing eyes. Slow, slow, Vincenza nears the side of the bed and tugs at the sheet. "Thankfulness? Leave me be," comes the rasping voice 'neath it.

"I can't, cousin. We got to dress you. Mastru Nonziu got to be here soon."

Agata's head drops back on the pillow.

"Don't lie back down, Agata. Help me."

"Help you?" Agata's hands rise up like claws. "Help you the way your mountain of a vigliaccu helped my Alfiu? With his knife, I'll slit my throat before I ever help the wife of a coward."

How many times she got to blame Vincenza for the past that others carved? How many times my Vincenza got to take on the sorrows and guilts of others? In the face of such insults, how many times does she got to forgive?

She pats the sick woman's brow and slips her fingers 'neath the pillow. She rummages through the marriage chest. And, what is this? She throws her face 'neath the bed and in the brown clay pot the girl left full this day. "Cousin," Vincenza whispers, "I can take no more. It is the cause of all your sorrows. Rid yourself of it, and grief won't find a home in your heart no more. By the grace of all what's good and holy, Agata, tell me where you hide the knife."

Agata sits up, a sick woman healed by the balm of anger and rants of desires and deeds and all what the girl got to do, there, in the Castle.

"Cousin, I'll find the knife, and, when I do, I'll hurl it straight down Mungibellu's throat to put an end to all of this!"

"Find it? Never! It's safe and grows in strength like Orlannu's sword."

"*Orlannu*! Mad and senseless to the bone!" Vincenza throws her hands in the air and busies herself with the chores of the cupboard, setting right the small jug of olive oil, the small bowl of salt, the tin plate, the tin cup, the wood fork, the wood spoon. She scoops the oil that drips from the rim of the small jug of olive oil and taps it back in the jug. "Cousin," she cradles the jug and lets out a sigh, "let us move our talk from heroes…"

"And their swords."

"Sì, Agata, and their swords."

"And…their knives."

Vincenza sets the small jug of olive oil back on the shelf and nods. "Sì, Agata, and their knives."

"Swear on your eyes."

"I swear on my eyes. No more talk of knives and where they hide and what they got to do. Now, quick, we got to dress you. Mastru Nonziu got to be here soon."

Vincenza knows full well the moon long past faded in the sky and so, too, the carter's promises.

*The Mattutinu bells long ago rang out. So, too, the Angelus bells. A night come and gone. A morning and a noon. Where is your carter, Vincenza? Where are his promises? He knows the starving heart feeds on broken promises. He knows no word spoken fares better than his feasts of words that do none but feed your starving heart with hope. Still he gave his promise. Still, Vincenza, you believed him, and, now, you starve the more.* I ready myself to say all this, to show myself to Vincenza, to meet her eye to eye and say all what's in my heart, but she raises her eyes to the splintered cross and whispers a prayer. Like an old cummari in church, I fall silent, my throat too thick for words.

She kneels at the marriage chest and puts all what she can in Agata's basket, a woven sheet, two small cases for pillows, a rosary and a picture of 'a Maronna 'a Nunziata. She presses Agata's blue marriage dress to her chest. "My dear cousin," she whispers, "may you wear this dress on the day you suffer no more on the earth." She folds it in the basket, and, on top, Vincenza lays Alfiu's blood-stained shirt and his marriage vest.

Agata throws kisses to the marriage vest. She blesses it and bows to it the way the faithful throw kisses and bless and bow to the sacred scraps of clothing once worn by martyred saints. In a flash, her dark, mad ways crawl out of her like maggots from a carcass. "Cousin, help me get dressed," she whispers quiet and calm.

"Sì, cousin, sì." Vincenza lifts Agata from the pillow and raises the sick woman's arms, but my Vincenza slumps back down, her own body limp, her own strength lost in sorrow. She curls in Agata's arms and sobs.

"Vincenza, dear cousin, what's the cause of all this sadness?"

"Agata, all what we lose, we lose great."

"Vincenza…Vincenza…"

"All what we lose, Agata…"

From out of nowhere, the nonsense tune of the little wood dove fills the cottage. Vincenza turns 'round. There, at the threshold, the carter shows off his long, brown teeth in a grin that reaches ear to ear.

Vincenza kisses the black lava cross 'round her neck and wipes the wet from her cheeks. "Dear cousin," she stands straight and strong, her eyes fixed on the carter, "let us dress you and be on our way. This day 'a Maronna 'a Nunziata hears our prayers."

*

The shepherd boy waits outside behind Alfiu's pile of stones 'til the carter waves for him to hoist Agata in the back of the cart. The girl's the last to leave the cottage. She gives the small black pig blessings and sends him on his way to a new cottage. She pulls the door closed with her foot, her arms weighed down by Alfiu's thick green cloak and Alfiu's goat skin *scappitti* that she passes to the shepherd boy. "For the cold months," she whispers, "when you got to keep your body and your feet warm." The girl scoops up a handful of dirt and puts it in a small brown sack. "For good fortune. When we come back to town, I'll throw it near the cottage. Bronti earth to Bronti earth." She hands the sack to the boy. He ties it on the red sash knotted at his waist and wipes his brow, suffering the way he does 'neath the hot summer sun in heavy cloak and shoes.

The carter takes Vincenza's arm and helps her on the bench beside him. He hangs two lanterns on the side of the cart and one near the bench. He flicks the reins. "The girl's dwelling's a good one," he sings out loud and high, "I seen it, and it's good!" He turns to the girl. "Where I seen you but a few days past, sì?" he whispers. "When we spoke of a Mamma's joy, in the south, sì?" The girl nods.

The boy races 'long the cart. Vincenza says not one word, but, time and again, she throws a look at him. Good to keep him far from her. The sheep graze at the bottom of the hill 'til the boy taps the long cane 'cross his thigh. Their hunch backs race up to him like quick-rising stars in Mungibellu's sky. When night falls, the carter lights the lanterns. They clink 'long the sides of the cart. *A good setting,* he got to think, *the quiet and the dark.*

He drives Chiazza too hard, him, in such a hurry, paying no mind to the road, tapping his head that got to be filled with a hundred twists and turns of lies and flatteries, and all to spill out, I fear, in the trusting ears of my Vincenza. The poor mare can't take no more. Who don't hear the panting? Who don't see Chiazza's hooves digging in the rocky earth, the legs near bent in prayer for the carter to ease on the reins and give her rest?

Vincenza sees. Vincenza hears. She smiles and waves her hand. Does the carter think it's all his doing, that, from out of nowhere, he's the one what conjures up the new, smooth road? Her gait, slow and steady now, her breath calm and gentle now, Chiazza pulls the cart through a narrow path of oak trees where birds nestle on low limbs for the night. The carter eyes the smooth road and flicks the reins, his chest puffed out in pride. Brave the carter. Brave, too, the birds that line the limbs 'til the night hunters sneak up with their sticks and sacks.

Brave, the birds. Brave, the night hunters. Brave, the carter and his nonsense tunes. Me? I could be the great night hunter feared by all. And I could kill the lot of them with my bare hands, the thrush and blackbird, the linnet and wren. Me, the strong and swift and cunning one, I could kill the lot of them, the birds and that nonsense beast 'neath the oak trees now singing out his nonsense tunes, now whispering in ears he got no right to close in on. I could kill him, but Alfiu holds me back. *For good,* he whispers 'cross my heart, *and only for the girl.*

*For good.* I shake myself free of the carter the best I can and fix my eyes on the girl in the back of the cart. Agata's head rests on her lap. Agata's cheek, pressing on the knife in the folds of the girl's apron, bears the print of the blade. "Good news, Mamma."

"Watch what you say. Your sister sees you."

"I know my sister sees me. And I know she tells you all the news I bring."

"She's weak now and can't see so keen."

"So, I got to tell you all what she can't. Mamma, I got to be the guest at a feast the Duchinu makes for his cousin… Mamma, at the Castle!"

"The Castle?"

"Sì, Mamma, for I saved the girl like me but not me."

Vincenza turns 'round and puts her finger to her mouth. "Your Mamma's sick with grief. You raise her demon hopes when you speak with such foolishness."

"Foolishness? Mastru Nonziu got to tell you all what I done and all what I seen."

The carter sinks down in his bench, his eyes darting from Vincenza's pressed lips to the steep incline of the road.

"No, Mastru Nonziu? Va ben', I got to tell it all myself. Z'a Vincenza, I helped the girl like me that suffered from the affliction. I saved her with all what you taught me in my dreams."

"Saved her? Who are you to speak with such pride?"

"Z'a Vincenza, it's true. The first deed at the Castle, I done for you. This one, I got to do for Mamma and my path." The girl lifts her Mamma's head. "See, Mamma?" she whispers and folds back her apron.

"Orlannu's sword."

"Sì, Mamma. Durindana."

"Durindana?"

"Sì, Mamma. What is a hero without his sword?"

"Figghia mia."

"Sì, Mamma. I am your daughter. I am your good daughter." The girl rubs the blade 'long Agata's round, red knuckles.

*"Nanna ninna ninna…"* She kisses her daughter's hand. "Harden your heart to kill the big."

*

High above the mountains, the moon's soft glow cools the air the best it can. The peasant's labor ends. None but his fears and superstitions linger in the night. What can the peasant do but thank the Savior for one more day that he lives with no curse on his own head? A prayer to the patron saint, a crook of the finger, a curing tea, that's all what it takes for the curse and all the sufferings to pass on to others. Who does the peasant curse? Who does he fear? The ones not like him, the ones living in their own sorrowful world like the girl and her Mamma that got to leave the small treasures of their home, they're as good a well for fear and curses as any in Bronti.

In the wild, the girl and her Mamma can be safe.

The dwelling the girl made, it was, in truth, a good one. The carter jumps off the cart. He takes a lantern, hands one to the shepherd boy, another to the girl, and the three run up the mountain. But what is there to see? Rubble…rocks scattered on the ground, rocks crushed one on the other… The girl lets out a cry. "Mungibellu done this! Mungibellu and her one-eyed monster! They spread their anger far and wide all the way to this forgotten mountain and my dwelling!"

The carter lets out a sigh. "Mamsella, we got lots of work to do."

While Chiazza snores, while the hunchback sheep gather 'round her, while Agata sleeps in the cart buried in her fitful dreams, while Vincenza's lids droop and her head rocks and she whispers out regrets for a simple life like the mare's, the shepherd boy and the carter huff and wipe their brows and take up the stones and heave them one on the other to make what they can of the shelter and the hearth. "*Uffa! Uffa! Uffa!*"

The girl races down to the cart and empties it of pots and jugs, pillows and beddings, a distaff and a spinning wheel, bringing all the carter's treasures back up. Careful she is not to wake her Mamma that lies 'neath the fancy dresses, fine blankets they prove to be, finer than the thick green blanket the carter boasts of, the one he says comes from Rannazzu. The carter carries up the mattress and lays it near the small stones of the new arched hearth. With the shepherd boy, he carries the sick woman up the hill and rests her on the soft bedding. "*Uffa!*" He bends and grabs his knees. "*Uffa!*" The carter moans so loud he shakes Vincenza from her sleep. She rubs her eyes and climbs off the bench, face to face with the carter and urges him to take a breath. "*Uffa!*" He throws a sad, weak look at her, and tries, he says, to gain back his breath, but, still, he got strength enough to take her arm and lead her to the dwelling. He starts a fire, and when he finds his voice again, he waves to the boy and the girl and my Vincenza to gather near the hearth, now that he readies himself to tell a tale.

It's a tale ripe with lies, a tale of a new mattress that a young orphan girl stuffed with soft cloth on her marriage day, happy and ignorant of the thick white water that would soon spill out of her. "When it done that," the carter whispers, "her new maritu, an orphan, too, he seen the signs of the sickness, and, frightened that she was the spreader of such sickness, he brought her to the black church where they prayed for healing. There, they stayed with no food or sleep, the young boy's lips swollen in prayer to Santu Giuseppi,

Rannazzu's patron saint and protector of the poor. There, they lay, the two of them at the altar table where I found them.

"'What can I do for you?' I asked and put to the side my prayers. "You'll always find me in this church or that church praying for the sick and the poor." Vincenza's eyes dart from the carter to Agata, fitful in her sleep. Her thick brows meet. The carter lowers his head, a child scolded for talking too loud.

"'Say a prayer for us! Bless us the way a Papà would!' the young ones cried out." He throws his finger over his mouth and nods to Agata sleeping quiet now. "Madama, they cried out the words, but hear how soft I whisper them for your cousin's sake. 'We have no family!' they cried out. 'If you pray with us, for such kindness, for we both know how kind you are, you got to have all our world goods.'"

The carter goes on and tells of the hours he kept vigil. "'My suffering children,' I prayed, 'may our Savior and our saints have mercy on you.' When the Savior called them to paradise, her, of the sickness, him, of the broken heart, I buried them."

The carter ends his tale waving his hands at the pots and jugs, the clay pisciaturi, the dowry goods, the linens and beddings and the small spinning wheel, all what got to make him a fine profit. Vincenza looks 'round at the treasures and lets out a quivering sigh. The carter sways like a lovesick girl. He opens his mouth wide, the click of his jaw loud and wild. "And… and…and…if Signa Agata keeps all my treasures? *Clicca…clicca…*this… this, Madama, will make you happy?"

She kisses the carter's cross 'round her neck and nods.

"So, take it all to the last portion of my wealth. Take all what the neighbors Saitta need."

The tears rush from Vincenza's eyes. She vows to pray for the carter and help him the best she can. She can praise and promise all what she likes 'til she takes her last breath, but she never seen the carter's true nature. One meal at the Castle, and the Duchinu got to shower more gifts on the carter's thick head than any poor ones ever showered on him in Rannazzu. Don't Vincenza know by now? The carter never seals a deal if a better one's not soon in the making. If she don't know, I fear this truth will come to her too late.

*Good times and bad times never last.*

The boy leans on a low lava rock and plays the tune of the lonely life of a shepherd. The sad, long tones of his flute bring the girl to tears. In the dwelling, the carter sings out the words but changes them to suit his own desires. "On your breast, embraced, I'd stay a thousand years." Vincenza lowers her eyes and bows her head. What is this? I swear on my eyes, I see a redness on her cheek. He sees it, too, and his body grows in strength. He rushes out, grinning like the cross-eyed lunatic, that conniver of a carter showing off his new-found strength and heaping more stones on the dwelling to make the walls and the roof.

All this carrying on, and none pays mind to the dog that yelps and whines in the distance. A dog that yelps and whines…in the dark…in the distance. It bodes no good. I howl to wake them from their foolish ways, but it all comes too late. Agata grabs u pisciaturi. I watch the *zzilla* spill out of her. I howl to shake off their spell, but none pays me mind. Soon that she drops the pot, and what a noise she makes, Vincenza turns 'round and eyes the thick white water on the sheet and shouts for the girl.

"Child, your Mamma, she's sick with the sickness of the town!"

The girl rushes to Agata and falls on her chest. "No!"

"Child, fetch my basket."

"Ppi piaciri, z'a Vincenza, help Mamma!"

"Child, my basket, quick, in Mastru Nonziu's cart!"

Like a bolt of lightning, she's back at Vincenza's side, the small, dark basket swinging in her arms. "Take it, z'a Vincenza! Take it and help Mamma!"

"Sì, sì, child, soon that you bring me the big…"

The girl drops the small basket filled with young plants and brown bread and torn holy pictures. She falls to her knees and sobs.

"Calma, child," Vincenza grabs the girl's face, "calma."

"Tell me, z'a Vincenza, tell me…that all the cures are in the basket."

"Calma…calma. Sì, child, all the cures are in the basket Mastru Nonziu took from me. Go to the cart and bring it to me."

"But, *here*, there are cures in this one, too."

Vincenza slips the carter's cross from her neck. "Who are you to say you know? Now, take Mastru Nonziu's cross, give it back to him and bring me my basket."

The girl bows her head. "It's not here," she whispers. "Z'a Vincenza, it's in the Castle."

"The Castle?"

"Sì, z'a Vincenza. I seen the brave Orlannu come to life, and he battled the enemy and…and…I didn't go no more to the cousin's room. And I didn't give her blessings. And I didn't take back the basket. Who can say what they done with it in the Castle. But I can run, swift like a fox I can run, to the big room where the girl like me…"

"Again, the girl. Basta with your foolishness of the Castle!"

"I speak the truth."

"So do I!" Vincenza spreads her fingers. She presses them at her chin like a peasant that gets ready for a fight. "If you hope to care for your Mamma one more day, go to the cart and bring me my basket…*now!*"

The girl kisses Vincenza's fingers and hides her face in Vincenza's lap. "It's not there. That's what I been trying to tell you. But I swear on my eyes, I'll bring you back the plant to heal Mamma."

"With my help," the shepherd boy whispers, him taking in all the talk, there, at the mouth of the dwelling.

"*You?* You can't find it." She pushes a stool near the mattress where Agata moans. "It's nowhere to be found. The last few leaves are in the basket I gave to Mastru Nonziu. We can't bide our time 'til another spring for the plant to thrive."

"There got to be others, z'a Vincenza. I know of many plants." She nods to the shepherd boy that nears her. "Blasiu taught me all of…"

"You know nothing of the plants and nothing of their secrets." Vincenza waves her hand at the boy's cheek. "You say you do, so, how does the mark still stain you? I see what I see. I know what I know. What feeds your nature still marks your flesh. You are cursed! Cursed!"

"And the girl?" He points to the mouth of the dwelling. The girl shuffles there, her low lip pushed out. Tapping her foot on this stone and that stone, there, alone, she bides her time. "The girl, is she, too, cursed? No, Signa

Vincenza, she is not. And…I am not. We are both blessed for we found each other."

"You speak the wisdom of the cross-eyed lunatic."

"Mock my words if it pleases you, but, Signa Vincenza, we have no more time to spare. Sì or no…are there other plants to heal the girl's Mamma? For if there are, I got to find them."

"Who are you, shepherd boy, to speak so bold? You know nothing of such ways. They are passed down. Who passes the teachings down to you, the Duca's sheep?"

"Signa Vincenza, say what you got to say, but from my nature and from my loneliness, I learned such ways. And, I, too, taught the girl."

"Va ben'. There *is* a plant with strong-smelling leaves in the shape of small eggs. Let your nature tell me where you got to find *u basirico*."

"*Basil?* It's everywhere…in a rich man's garden and a poor peasant's hearth."

"Where are these gardens and hearths, shepherd boy?"

"Avaja! Everyone knows they're in Bronti!"

"And this is what your nature knows? Go back to Bronti and poison all of us! The water is unclean. All what grows near the town is unclean. You know so much but not that this is how the sickness takes hold."

Vincenza's right to tell the boy not to go back to Bronti where water and waste flow outside cottage doors, a crashing river of stench and filth that chokes the town. And what do the Bruntiszi do? What can they do? They lap up the water wherever they can find it with no thought of the sickness that spreads time and again through the town.

"So, I'll climb the beautiful mountain far up where no one climbs. I'll bring back the pure water before…"

"It's too late…too late for u basirico to thrive and too late to fetch the pure water. We spent the night in joy and pride, and now we pay. Soon, the Duca's men will be there, at the foot of Mungibellu's precious flank, ready with their papers." She leans over and wipes the sick woman's brow. "What they ask is more than we can pay."

The boy pulls a jug out from 'neath the carter's goods and waves it at Vincenza. "Pay? For water that Mungibellu gives us? No! They got to fight me for God's riches that we Bruntiszi…"

"Bruntiszi?"

"Sì." He holds the jug high over his head. "Bruntiszi! That is what the girl shows me I always been."

Vincenza pulls on his red sash, the sack of Bronti earth swinging at his waist. "Va ben', you say you are one of us. So, learn all what we know. Learn of the field guards and their ways. If you are rash, they are cruel. What good are you, then, to your sheep in a prison? And, to us? Look at the girl's Mamma. The girl and I cared for her the best we knew how. But the grieving Mammas turned up at her door and shouted *untore* and done who knows what to the water in the cottage that we tried to keep pure. This much I know. Signa Agata's afflicted with their sickness, the sickness of the town. We need your help, not your rage… Maronna mia, Agata!" She grabs u pisciaturi and lifts Agata the best she can, straddling her frail, wet limbs over it. "Shepherd boy, go to the girl and turn your back on us. Some things a boy ought not to see." The boy rushes to the mouth of the dwelling, the jug, swinging at his side.

He grabs the girl's hand. "Signa Vincenza," he shouts, "is this true? You need my help?"

She presses her lips tight. "Sì."

He cradles the jug. "Ppi piaciri, please, let me help you. Signa Agata was kind to me. It's my duty never to forget such kindness."

Vincenza puts the last of the dry bed clothes on Agata and waves to the girl. She kisses the boy's hand and pushes him back in. "Listen to me," Vincenza whispers to the shepherd boy, "Mastru Nonziu brought pure water. I can make the cure with it. But there's only enough for the cure. None more. My cousin's throat is parched. I got to…"

He lays the jug at her feet and smiles. "I know of a plant that can quench Signa Agata's thirst."

Vincenza leans back and holds her fingers 'cross a growing smile. "You know of such a plant?"

"Sì, Signa Vincenza, that I do. I tasted it but one time 'though I no longer bring to mind where to find it."

"Listen to one that knows. Go to the rocks that look out on the lava sand. There, harbored in the crevices of these rocks, 'a ocitura waits for you to find it."

"Sorrel? The leaves look like warrior shields, sì?"

She leans in. "Sì, and the flowers are red and blossom like grapes."

"I picked it when sleep tempted me. I chewed on the stems to keep awake, but the stems made my mouth dry."

"For you chewed on the old stems." She fixes her eyes on the hearth. "They're dry and make a good fire."

"Some made my mouth wet."

She wipes the spittle from Agata's mouth. "The new stems. The water from the new stems feed and quench the plant. It quenched you that day... Blasiu, heed all what I tell you..."

"Sì, Signa Vincenza, sì. I listen to all what you got to say."

"Cut none but the top of the new stems."

He nods and smiles. "None but the top of the new stems."

"Dig deep in the crevice of the rock for the new stems and cut the tops. They're red and juicy and tender to chew...they can quench a thirst."

"So, you tell me, and, so, I got to do."

"Now, for u basirico. It's the *sacred* one, that's the one what cures the sickness. Where u basirico thrives is not where the sacred one grows."

"Then, where?"

The girl runs to Agata's side and strokes her hand. "I know, z'a Vincenza," she whispers, her eyes to the earth, "I know. Z'a Vincenza, sì, in truth, I know. There's a garden where all the plants grow."

"No, child. The secret of the plant was handed down from my Mamma and from her Mamma before her. The sacred basirico is not from our island. It was a gift from a foreign healer of the East that sailed off before the Duca's men could get their hands on him." Vincenza lets out a sigh. "In my Mamma's day and her Mamma's day before her, there always been a Duca and always his men to do the bidding. In secret, my Nanna planted the gift. In secret, the gift thrived."

"Z'a Vincenza, I know..."

"The child talks when the teacher teaches?"

The girl paces 'round Vincenza 'til the shepherd boy grabs her shoulders. "Listen to your z'a Vincenza."

Vincenza clasps her hands. "'Warm is warm, sun is sun, a prayer is a prayer. Little does it matter where u basirico grows when it knows it got to heal.' That's what the holy man from the East said to my Mamma's Mamma when he took her hand and poured the seedlings in it. She cupped her hands. She was young like you. A stem appeared, the color dark like violet, and small leaves, soft and hairy to the touch, tickled her palm."

"Z'a Vincenza," the girl holds out her hands, "when I cup my hands, like this, there happens to me..."

"For the good or the bad of it, I know, child. You were none but an innocent one when you showed me all the gifts you held in your hands 'though you understood none of them."

"And, you, z'a Vincenza...? You guarded the sacred plant to cure the sickness of the town. It was in your basket all the while, but you done none to help the young peasant girls, the girls like me."

"What do you know of all what I do? Your Mamma, even when the madness takes hold of her," she reaches over and kisses Agata's brow, "your Mamma knows all what I do. In all her grief, deep in her heart, she knows. She's my cousin."

"She's my Mamma!"

"All what I had, I kept in the basket." She beats her chest, rocking low to the earth. "Now, there's no more sacred basirico 'til the spring, and, for your Mamma, that's too late."

The girl throws herself at Vincenza's feet. "The teacher teaches, but I can no more stay silent. You're wrong, z'a Vincenza. You're wrong. There's more, and it's in a garden east of the Castle, a garden that's filled with the sacred basirico and all the plants from our island and all the plants from foreign lands. I seen them from Dunna Eeelisabettu's window. I seen the garden and all the island from there. How many windows in the Castle, I couldn't count so high, but I looked out of that one. I threw my face out. I smelled all what was outside. From a baby, I learned from you the sacred plant, the leaves and the smell and the cure. I know what it looks like. I seen it. I smelled it. I know where to find it."

"I'm too tired...too tired..." Vincenza struggles up from the stool and shuffles to the mouth of the dwelling. She points to the east. "The Star of Dawn already lights the sky. Go where you got to go. May 'a Maronna 'a

Nunziata keep you safe from harm."

The girl rushes to her and throws her arms 'round her waist. "Z'a Vincenza, Blasiu got to come with me."

"No! He got to find 'a ocitura. You, you got to find u basirico."

She squeezes her waist tight 'til Vincenza lets out a soft cry. "We got to help each other."

Vincenza crosses herself three times and whispers three prayers to 'a Maronna 'a Nunziata. "U basirico is but part of the cure. You got to bring back three limuni."

The girl waves the shepherd boy to her side. "There were lemons in the girl's room, big and yellow like the sun. My mouth fills with water when I bring them to mind. The Duca's groves are far. We can't bring limuni back from there. But if we take the new carriage road… Don't look at me with such eyes. Who dares to hinder us? On the road, we got to pass a small orchard where fruit grows for the wishing. I swear on my eyes, our hands got to fill with limuni soon enough."

"Signa Vincenza, the girl knows we got to help each other. She knows where to find all what we need."

Vincenza pushes them out in the cold mountain air. "So, it's all what the girl says. You got to help each other. So, hurry! Hurry before it's too late!"

*

The moon still hides behind dark clouds. The sun still struggles to light the day. In the early morning light, past plants that grow on mountains, on the sides of roads near Bronti, in stony walls and hidden places, the boy and the girl journey to reach the plants that grow in rocks that look out on the lava sand.

"Sick I am…sick I am with the name the cummari called my Mamma."

"Hurry!" The boy grabs the girl's hand and races up the rocky slope.

"How the women shouted their curses! 'Untore! Untore!' they cried."

"That is…bad…to be called the spreader of the sickness, and, now, your Mamma…wait…" The boy kneels near a small rock. "Maronna mia! Look! Look! Here in the rock, look!"

"What, Blasiu?"

He pulls the girl down. "Here! Are these not the shields of warriors?"

"If there are no new stems, they do us no good." The girl pushes her small fingers in the crevice and snaps a piece of a young stem and chews on it. She wipes the wet from her lips. "A ocitura, Blasiu. You found it!" She sits on the ground and clasps her hands. "Blasiu that blazes the sky, you found it!"

"Take the stems. All of them. It got to quench your Mamma's thirst."

"When Mamma's healed, all in Bronti got to beg her forgiveness. Blasiu, come. I got to tell Mamma."

"Don't be so quick on your journey. There's still u basirico to find."

"Sì, u basirico, the sacred one." She slaps her brow. "Where are my thoughts?" She buries her face in his chest. "Blasiu, a woman that spreads the sickness like a sower spreads his seeds... 'Untore, untore, spreader of the sickness!' they shouted at my Mamma. That is where my thoughts take me."

He grabs her hand and drags the girl down the slope. "See that hill, over there, in the north? I know it well. Many times, I brought the sheep to graze there. Down that hill is a trazzera that can take us to the new carriage road and the garden at the Castle." He kisses her hand and smiles. "Your Mamma don't spread the sickness. Amuninn'! Let's go! When I gain back my breath, I'll tell you a tale of a true untore."

"Blasiu, a true untore?"

"Sì, my Papà knew a man that come from Rannazzu but left the town when he was but a boy. It's good that we live in Bronti and not Rannazzu. It's a bad town with black churches and chambers 'neath the ground where they seal the guilty up while still breathing. No wonder he left such a town. This man they called *Nascarussa* for his nose was always red. The peasants said the redness come from drinking all their wine. When the sickness spread through the town, they knew a man that drank their wine and come from Rannazzu was none but a true untore. 'Ppi piaciri, lock me up 'til the sickness takes the last poor soul,' he begged the jail keeper. When the sickness took the last poor soul, the jail keeper let Nascarussa go."

"And when the sickness takes the last poor soul in town, Mamma got to go back to Bronti."

"No...no...there's more."

The girl throws her arms out and swings herself 'round. "Here, Blasiu, here is the *more*. We run too swift up the new carriage road. We near pass the orchard. See. Look 'round. These trees are poor of fruit. They wait for us and, now, they'll blossom all what we desire. She crosses herself three times the way Vincenza taught her and says the prayer that none can understand. She makes a fist, opens her hand and spreads her fingers wide. She takes a leaf and folds it in her palm. She breathes 'cross her knuckles. She opens her hand. Three ripe limuni fall at the boy's feet.

He jumps back. "What demon magic is this?"

The girl picks up the fruits and throws them in the folds of her apron. "All this you can't understand. Me, too, I can't understand. 'A z'a Vincenza says such gifts got to be for others. This is for Mamma and not to satisfy our longings. So, this is good and right. And this much more I know. The Devil got none to do with the healing of my Mamma. There's no demon magic here. Only good. Now…tell me, what is the more of *your* tale?"

The boy pounds his head. "No demon magic?"

"Blasiu, the tale."

"The tale?"

"The tale of Nascarussa. He went back to Rannazzu, sì?" And, with that, she grabs his hand and pulls him up the new carriage road past the orchard where the solemn cypress trees come in view.

"No, he couldn't go back. No road welcomed Nascarussa. He journeyed nowhere. Wherever he walked, wherever he slept, all the town threw stones at him."

"All the town?"

"Sì, all the town."

"His wife?"

"Sì, his wife."

"His children?"

"Sì, his children. All threw stones at him. This is how he lived his days."

"Was there none to help him?"

"No. He helped himself…or so he thought. One day he was so tired of stones cast at him that he crumbled up the last scraps of bread he had in his sack and spread it 'round him. 'Here's the sickness. And here's how I'll spread it!' he shouted to the peasants that gained fast on him. With that, the peasants ran away. He thought he was safe once more 'til he slept one night at the mouth of a cave high on a rocky slope. The peasants found him there. All the town hurled stones at him 'til he took his last breath. They burned his lifeless body. And they cursed him, too, a true untore from Rannazzu."

The girl eyes the sack of earth swinging on the boy's red sash. "Give it to me." She opens the sack and shakes the last of Bronti soil out on the ground. "I gave this to you when we left Bronti for I thought we'd go back soon. Now that I know what a town can do to an untore, or to the one they name untore, can Mamma ever go back?"

"Can *you,* the offspring of the one they say spreads the sickness? What is there in Bronti for you now, not when I…"

"Blasiu, quick!" The girl runs past the last of the cypress trees, all the way 'round the Castle to the north and to the east where they come 'on the Duca's garden. She waves her hand 'cross the low bushes. She throws her nose in the small, full leaves of u basirico and breathes them all in. "Here! I told you! Run, Blasiu, run," she calls out, "come and see how the Duca grows such fine plants with such strong smells! I got to ask the son how he makes them grow when I sit at his table, there, when he takes his last breath."

The boy catches up. Through quick, hard breaths, he lets out a laugh. "My precious lamb got to sit at his table before you do."

The girl rips a stem of u basirico from the bush. "You know none of where I been, and none of what I got to do."

"*Sst…sst…*now is not the time for foolishness." He points to the east to three field guards on donkeys in the distance, riding back from Mungibellu to the Castle. "We're targets in the bright sunlight. Take all what you need of the sacred plant before the Duca's men come 'on us."

*One nut in a sack makes no noise.*

One full day the boy and the girl journeyed from the dwelling to find plants that heal. One full day Agata moaned on the mattress, and the carter, with sorrow in his eyes, poured her pure water in a tin cup. One full day,

Vincenza's heart broke each time she snatched the water away to wet but her cousin's lips. "For the cure, Mastru Nonziu, we need all the water for the cure."

Now, the moon shines bright, and the carter hunches to light the lanterns, his eyes filled with joy, his shadow jumping 'cross the rocky wall. I cup my ears when his voice climbs to a high, girlish pitch. "By day I go and toil, by night I use the oil." Singing his nonsense tunes, he scoops a ladle of water for a cup of u basirico leaves. With his thick fingers, he slices the limuni and presses the juice in the already green water.

"Mastru Nonziu, you do the fine work of a woman." Vincenza laughs, but, quick, she lowers her head and presses her lips tight and wipes the joy from her face. She picks through the stems of 'a ocitura on her lap and throws to the side but a single short one. "The boy speaks the truth of his nature. He knows the secrets of the land." She leans over Agata and waves a stem 'cross her mouth. It puckers open like a baby bird's. "Blessings to the boy and the girl. They do fine work this day."

"They're like our children. We teach them the ways of the world."

"Your ways, Mastru Nonziu, are but filled with songs and desires."

"One song, Madama. One desire."

"And…this is what you teach the boy and the girl?"

"They're their own teachers. And, for Signa Agata…"

"What, Nonziellu, what do you hope to teach my cousin?"

The carter's shadow jumps in a spider dance. "*Nonziellu… Nonziellu*, is that what you name me now? My ears are thick with dirt, but this I hear: you say my name with affection."

"No! No!" She throws the shawl 'cross her shoulders and clasps it tight at her chest. "A vow is a vow. My word is my word. One heart for one man… I cannot, Mastru Nonziu. I cannot."

"Your words say one thing. Your heart says the other. *Nonziellu* your heart names me. And it names me with affection!" He reaches for her hand and twists the marriage ring up past the bend of her finger and the nail. He snatches the ring. With his head thrown back, he opens his mouth wide and sings out a foolish tune. "A maritu to my Vincenza I got to be!"

"Nonziellu!" She grabs for the ring. He holds it up high.

When he finishes his tune, he drops the ring in his mouth. I howl. I howl louder than all the wild beasts in all of 'a Sicilia. He pays me no mind, him, so brave now, swallowing the ring like a small, sweet cake. He pats his belly, licks his fingers and smiles. "Now, what do I hope to teach your cousin," he belches out the words, "all what I hope to teach you, my dear Vincenzina...to *forget*."

*

With a lantern in his hand, the boy bowed to Vincenza when she said the first of the healing prayers. "Let Signa Vincenza do her work," he whispered to the girl and grabbed her hand and led her out the dwelling. There, he sits on a small rock, takes up his flute and plays a tender song. When the song ends, he taps the rock, and the girl sits by his side.

"Blasiu," the girl whispers, "you done so much for me. You taught me all the lessons of the wild...but when can I do for you?"

"I still got more to teach you..."

"But our time nears the end. I got to stay with Mamma...and, you, you got to go back..."

"Not if I take you...not if you'll take me..." The boy takes out a small wood box from his pocket. "Take this," he says, his eyes to the earth, "it's not a marriage chest. But it's all what I got. I carved it for you this morning."

This is how it got to be, with no boy's Mamma to start the courtship, with no dowry list or carved marriage chest or blessings on the couple. What can the boy do but carve a small wood box to seal their fate?

"I seen what you done in the Duca's orchard. You can make all what I give you a better gift."

The girl holds out her hand and cradles the box in her palm. "It's all what I desire." She raises her eyes. "I accept."

He kisses the back of her hand. "It's our secret 'til the moment's right. First, I got to bring back clean water from Mungibellu before the light of day. Then, I got to ask for blessings from your Mamma."

"And from 'a z'a Vincenza?"

"Sì, from Signa Vincenza, too."

"This is your word?"

"This is my word, but, first, it's time to ask you…what do I call the girl that soon makes me her maritu?"

"It's right and good that you know. Saitta. Saitta, through and through, for my Papà's Papà and my Mamma's Papà were cousins."

"That is the name I know. But what is the name a maritu longs to call his wife?"

She throws a look to the dwelling where her Mamma drifts to sleep. She closes her eyes and takes in a breath. "Sì, Blasiu, it's time for you to ask me… and time for me to tell. Gratia…Gratia Maria is my name, the name of my Nanna. Gratia Maria, that is the name a maritu longs to call his wife."

"Now, it's no more a whisper in your heart."

"No more."

"Gratia…Gratia that graces the earth."

She throws her arms 'round him. "Blasiu…Blasiu that blazes the sky."

The boy folds the girl in his arms and wraps Alfiu's thick wool cloak 'round them. That is how they pass the night outside the dwelling. The boy wakes with a start and gazes at the heavens where the Star of Dawn now flickers in the dark sky. He runs inside, his hard breath waking Vincenza. He bows and grabs two wide mouth jugs near the hearth.

"Blasiu, none but pure water."

"None but pure water, Signa Vincenza."

"It's good you leave early. That can only bring us good fortune," Vincenza whispers and lays her hand on Agata's brow.

"Signa Vincenza, I'll bring you more good fortune this day," he says with a bright smile and takes his leave.

She crosses herself three times. When she raises her eyes, he's gone from view. "May 'a Maronna 'a Nunziata keep you safe from harm," she calls out after him.

*

'Though the sun heats the early morning sky, waves of clouds hide Mungibellu from view. This is the hour Bruntiszi women start their chores, but Vincenza rests by her cousin's side, the stem of 'a ocitura in her hand, her chin dropping to her chest, her lids fluttering. The carter keeps his eyes on her. When she is fast to sleep, soft, soft, he taps his foot and whispers out a tale…

"On the west of the island near the sea, there once lived a very wise man. Word spread of this man's wisdom, and people came from near and distant towns to hear his good counsel. But he was old and soon was called to paradise.

"What do you surmise took place at the hour he died? Here, in Bronti, an old peasant woman working at her loom grabbed her chest when the wise man took his last breath. She opened her mouth and out poured the beautiful words that the wise man spoke to calm and heal.

"The old woman left her cottage. She happened 'on a young woman crying in the road for she could bear no children. She happened 'on a peasant that lost his wife but a day past. She happened 'on a midwife that reached in and took out none but the unborn from the Mammas that put their faith in her. The old woman cried with all of them and gave them good counsel. One by one the Bruntiszi sought her out. Day to night, they waited outside her cottage door to listen to the wisdom of the poor, simple woman, a wisdom that wiped clean their pains and sorrows."

The stem of 'a ocitura drops from Vincenza's hand. "Rest, Vincenzina," the carter whispers, "and know you wipe clean my pain and sorrow. See how you heal even the ones that can't be healed?" Vincenza stirs but hears none of his speech, lost the way she is in sleep and dreams. "What makes a man happy?" he asks and pulls on his dark beard. "His beard, his money, and his Vincenzina." How Vincenza smiles in her dreams, and how she raises not one finger to brush away the hand that strokes her face.

\*

How much time passes? Beasts in the wild know the sun and the moon, the heat of the day and the cool of the night. They know when to sleep, when to look for food, but not when the land is safe from the Duca's field guards. Only a peasant knows. The boy set off for Mungibellu when the Star of Dawn flickered in the dark sky. Now, the Mattutinu bells ring out in Bronti, and the sun already started its journey 'cross the sky.

"He's gone too long," the girl curls at Vincenza's feet and tugs at her

thick fingers. "I hear the bells in Bronti. Z'a Vincenza, he's gone too long."
She hears the morning bells? We that got the gifts of animals hear all the
sounds of the forest and the town, the mountains and the wild, but the girl?
All what they say of her got to be true. The girl crosses two natures.

Vincenza pats Agata's face and brushes a stem of 'a ocitura 'cross her lips.
"*Mbu...mbu...mbu...*" Agata sucks on it like a baby, calm and comforted.
The carter sings his nonsense tunes soon that Agata stirs. He gives her bread.
She shakes her head, the crumbs falling on the girl's apron. "Mamma does
right not to eat," the girl whispers. "And I do right not to eat. Not one
crumb got to pass my lips. Not 'til Blasiu comes back to me."

Vincenza pushes herself up and passes the stem to the carter for Agata to
suck on. "Child, you said you heard the morning bells?"

The girl nods.

Vincenza shudders and breathes out a cloud of cold air. "Something
happened to the boy. I feel it."

"He's gone too long, sì, but nothing happened." The girl leaps up and
buries her head in Vincenza's chest. "Nothing happened! Z'a Vincenza,
nothing happened for the shepherd boy is blessed."

Vincenza pushes her away. "Sì, child, with each breath I take, I breathe
the danger in the air. I sent him. Now, it's my duty to find him."

"No!" the carter leaps up, too, and, like a baby, can't hold back his tears.
"We're safe here. Vincenza, if you climb Mungibellu when the field guards
take their posts... No, I won't let you, the climb's too steep!"

Vincenza brushes her skirt and pats her hair down. "And my blood is
weak and old..."

He grabs her shoulders and shakes her. "You're not weak! You give the
weak strength! You're not old! A woman with bones of forty years..."

"...and more...many, many more..."

"Readying herself for a new life and a new *maritu*."

"Nonziellu!"

His hands drop to his sides. "Vincenza," he whispers, "you're not weak.
You're not old. And this isn't *duty* what you got in your mind to do." He
clenches his long, brown teeth. "This is foolishness. Foolishness!"

"Nonziellu, it *is* duty. I got mine. Now, you got yours." She holds out her hand. He grabs it and lays hard kisses on it. "For my sake, stay with my cousin and the girl. Signa Agata got to rest and dream her calming dreams now that the Bronti sickness leaves her body. The grief sickness, none can shake her free of it. But it's not for healing that you got to stay here. You got to protect her. What if a thief happens on the dwelling? There got to be a man here, a man brave and good like you, Nonziellu. Ppi piaciri, give me your word."

The carter throws the last branches and twigs in the fire and kneels by it and prays, loud, he says, for the Savior to hear…but it's not for the Savior. It's for Vincenza, *my* Vincenza. He prays like a holy man, but with poison prayers on his lips that all but kill the vows in my Vincenza's heart. I howl like a mad dog. He jumps 'round and cowers behind the girl. I howl, loud and wild, and watch him shake in his laughing boots, his face pale, his eyes wet and wide. Vincenza jumps, too. What is this? She takes hold of his hand. What is this? What is this? She buries her face in his chest. I grab my throat, but where are the sounds to frighten them the more?

Soon that the carter wraps his arms 'round her, Vincenza breaks free. "I'll be back soon," she whispers. He holds tight to the black lava cross and brings it to his lips. She takes it in her hands and kisses it, too. He shuffles with her to the mouth of the dwelling. There, he throws kisses. She turns 'round one last time. She smiles. He smiles, too. Slow, slow, she digs her feet in the rocky path. Past the slopes, she fades far from view.

"Mastru Nonziu," the girl kneels at her Mamma's side and cradles the boy's small, wood box, "'a z'a Vincenza got to bring the shepherd boy back to me."

"Mamsella, the sun's now high in the sky. The Duca's guards wait at the foot of Mungibellu. Does Madama think of the danger? Does she think of her weak legs or her poor health? No, all she thinks of is her duty and her promises." With that, he laces up his low boots and presses down his vest.

"Mastru Nonziu, what are you doing?"

"What am I doing? I'm taking my leave. That is what *I* have in mind to do."

"You gave your word to 'a z'a Vincenza, but, here you are, the one that takes his leave of us."

"I didn't give no word. And, Mamsella, I take no leave of you. *You* got to come with me. Where are your thoughts? The Duchinu invited us to a celebration but two days past. You and me, the two of us…"

"And to *him* you gave your word?"

"Sì, I gave my word."

The girl jumps up. *Ppù! Ppù!* She spits 'til the earth is wet and kicks it 'round the carter's boots. "You and the coward you despise are of the same clay. You say the pretty words, but you do all what suits you. Mamma needs me. I got to stay. This is my word, and I give it to her."

There's peace in the sick woman's face when the daughter speaks. She lies still. It's but her tongue what moves 'round her mouth, licking at her lips. How moist her mouth stays now that 'a ocitura does the work.

"Madama got to understand. See how your Mamma sleeps? She wants no food or drink 'til sleep tires of her. I gave my word to a gentleman. Chiazza waits for us. Amuninn'! Come on, we'll be late!"

The girl nestles 'neath her Mamma's arm. At such a tender touch, Agata's lids flutter like the wings of a small baby bird, her breath quick and gaining strength. She grabs the girl's heavy brown shawl and shouts out a nest of curses and nonsense in her sleep. "Figghia ru diavulu! Figghia ru diavulu! Figghia ru diavulu!"

"Mamma! *Figghia*, that's who I am. Figghia, figghia, figghia, your daughter, your good daughter, not the Devil's…"

Agata swats the air. "*Zzu…zzu…zzu…zzu…zzu…* I chase away the Devil and all his pretty words!"

"Figghia…figghia…figghia…figghia…that is…who…I…" The girl falls on the ground, and, quick, the carter rushes to her and carries her out the dwelling.

"Basta, Mamsella! You cry too many tears for your short life. Amuninn'! Chiazza waits for us. And your Mamma needs her rest."

"But I am the one to bring her rest! And not you, not 'a z'a Vincenza, not even my shepherd boy can stop me now!" She leaps from the carter's arms and runs back to the dwelling. "There's no need for fancy dresses." She forages through Agata's dowry and pulls out her blue marriage dress. "Here's what I got to wear this night. Mamma wants me to wear it on the day I serve justice."

The carter grabs the dress and throws it behind him. "Mamsella, there are many dresses for you in the cart. But, this one, you cannot wear."

"It's *her* dress."

"I know. When your Mamma worn it, that was a day of celebration. When she wears it once more, it got to be on the day of her...."

"If not *her* death, then the death of..."

"Mamsella!"

"Mastru Nonziu, give it to me."

"I'm sick of all what you plot and plan." He slaps his brow. "Now, I know the cause of all my worry. It's the feeling of a Papà what courses through me."

"Give it to me!"

He hands her the dress and kisses her hand. "This much I know. From this hour, no matter what the danger, I got to keep you safe from harm."

She fixes her eyes on him 'til a shudder rises in his body. "Mastru Nonziu, I near lost Mamma last night, and the pain was more than I could bear. I know what I got to do to bring her joy. You, go sing your tales to Chiazza." He stares back, his mouth open wide. "I got to ready myself."

No sooner she turns her back on him that the foreign wind blows the carter out the dwelling and all the way to Chiazza where, for no good cause, he sings his love song. The mare's ears tilt back when she hears his voice, her lip hangs in calm. She knickers with delight, the carter and the mare lost in a nonsense song.

The carter gave his word to keep the girl safe from harm, but, how, when he don't see her? He don't see the girl slip on her Mamma's blue marriage dress and a white apron, and, in the apron folded at the waist, he don't see the girl hide a knife. And he don't hear the girl sob or see her wipe away her tears when she whispers, "Mamma, bon riposu, this day I bring you joy." The carter don't see and he don't hear none of this.

She rushes down the slope, a basket in her arms and the boy's small wood box rocking on top. She rips the shawl from her head and throws it at the mouth of the dwelling. She leaps in the cart on the bench by the carter, her red hair, thick and shining. She shakes her head, throws her fingers through her hair and lets out a dark laugh when it sweeps over the fancy dresses. "Sì," she shouts at the carter, his hand slapped over his mouth, his wide eyes fixed on her hair, "sì, Mastru Nonziu, now you know. This is who I am!" He clutches the reins. She grabs them and whips them 'til Chiazza grunts and groans racing the way she does over sharp, low rocks down this trazzera and that trazzera on the way to the new carriage road.

"Slow, slow," the carter stammers, at long last gaining back his voice, but the mare don't pay him no mind, whipped the way she is, veering side to side and quickening her pace 'til I no more see her hooves touch the earth.

"Faster! Faster!" the girl cries out. "But what's the good? I can no more dodge all what I am and all what I got to do!"

*

The Angelus bells ring out. On a rocky mule track below the dwelling, a foreign cart slows to a halt. On one red panel of the cart, Orlannu, the cross-eyed hero, throws his mighty sword, Durindana, in a poison river to spare it from falling in the hands of the enemies. On another red panel, Orlannu goes mad at the sight of his beloved Angelica in the arms of the Saracen. 'Long the panels, lanterns clink and shine. Two strangers leap from the cart that's stuffed with color rolls and thick sheets of paper.

"This is a place forsaken as any," the tall one says, a dark man with a thick, black fortress of muscle that juts 'cross his bare chest. The two strangers slap each other's backs and rush 'round the rocks like boys in mischief. They heave a barrel over their heads and throw it 'cross the rocky landscape. Their eyes bulge in their sockets with the desperate look of a man condemned. Dark, desperate men, they got to be from that dark, desperate town that breeds *untori*.

All on our island know the strangers' barrel and live in fear and pride of the power it holds. Yellow powder from our sulphur mines, charcoal from our pine cones, and stone salt from the dung heaps of our men and beasts, all mixed one to the other to make the black powder that fills our guns. But the strangers have no guns. They scoop the black powder from the barrel and pour it on a thick sheet of paper. They drop their pants and piss on the powder, for good fortune and bright light, they say. This puts such a wide grin on their dark, desperate faces.

They roll the thick sheet in a large shell. It's the short stranger that adds the red salt and carries the shell up a hill. "You're right," he shouts to the tall stranger, "this is a place forsaken as any!" He sets the tail of the shell on fire and rolls down the hill. He crouches behind a rock 'til a thousand streams of red light burst in the sky, there, where the booming sound of a thousand canons meets them. What weapon is this, loud like the one-eyed monster, bright like Mungibellu's fire?

"What now?"

"Now," the tall one says, "now, we know the Duchinu got to be pleased with his *royal illuminations*. And, now, we got to roll the other shells."

The short stranger pulls sheet after sheet from the cart while the tall one stuffs them with black powder. Some he sprinkles with yellow and blue and red salts and rolls them the way Vincenza rolls the maccarruni. It takes two of them to load the rolls back in the cart. "*Uffa!*" They stop to rest, leaning on a lava rock, guzzling wine from their jug, laughing when they tell their untrue tales, that the Bronti peasant sleeps with his neighbors' wives, two, three at a time to stay warm in winter; that the peasant wife cuts her hair to weave it on the loom for her maritu's clothing; that the Bronti peasant can't leave his town for no other town wants him. Choking on their laughter, they rip out pages from a book and turn them over and stroke the words and numbers like they make sense of all what they can't read. "The contract and the fees," the tall one says, "and all in order." They eye the rolls they still got to load and guzzle more wine and tell more untrue tales of Bronti.

*

Who is deaf to the booming sounds or blind to the bright lights the strangers set off? Not Alfiu's widow. Agata wakes from her deep sleep with a pink glow on her cheeks and eyes wet and shining. Agata, a woman healed of Bronti sickness but not of grief. She rips off her bed clothes, sips the last of the cure and rifles through all what remains of Alfiu's life. She grabs his clothes, holds them up to the small bones of her body and slips them on.

The buttons of his bloody shirt dig in her skin. She tightens his marriage vest over it. She ties her hair back with a red ribbon the way Alfiu's Mamma tied it on the day she called Agata her figghia. I want to say she looks like a bride once more, but near twenty years come and gone. When she pledged her faith to Alfiu, her hair was dark, her blood filled with passion. Now, her hair is white. Her blood runs cold.

She gazes down at her body and reaches for the bed clothes, the clean and the stained, and tears the stitchings open to make a skirt, one on the other that she ties with a sash 'round her waist. She stands straight and strong and shifts her shoulders like the Duchinu's cousin when I seen her in Alfiu's ball of light, looking at herself in the long glass in the corner of her room and stroking her finger and a phantom ring. Agata strokes her finger, too, and the small gold marriage band 'til it burrows down in what's left of her flesh. Her finger chaffs to the bone, the gold band, lost in blood. I jump back. Like on the strangers' dark, desperate faces, there, it spreads. I howl to frighten it away. But it spreads, it thrives…the wide grin near swallowing her face.

She races out the dwelling and down the slope and happens 'on the strangers' cart. She hides behind a rock and eyes them slapping each other and laughing out their tales of Bronti. How 'a ocitura nourished Agata's body! How her sharp bones grown in strength! Now, I see, it was all for this hour. She leaps in the cart like a mountain cat and slips in a corner 'neath the shells. The tall one acts brave and strong. Over his shoulders, he throws the last of the shells in the cart.

Where are the cries of pain when the shell pummels her body? She's the one that's brave and strong and silent. Her face rises from 'neath the shells. The grin fades. Specks of light spatter from the wet and the dark of her eyes, two black jewel eyes that shine in a cart that makes its way through the land of black lava rocks, two black jewel eyes in a foreign cart that rattles down this trazzera and that trazzera with the hope, the strangers say, to bring their cargo to the Castle before dark.

*When fortune turns her back, so do the friends.*

What mystery did the boy unmask when he stared up in the sky 'til grey morning light gave way to blue? He climbed Mungibellu's precious flank, but, in a spell, he gazed at the sky like a lovesick girl, all while holding tight to a pointed knife and a long piece of wood and, there, in the wood, carving the rough beads of a rosary. Time and again, he wiped his brow as the sun beat down on him and melted the snow 'neath his feet. The boy traveled far, I'll give him that, but when he blew the last wood shaving to the wind and seen his feet sinking in the wet earth, he shook himself free of the spell and whispered Vincenza's words. "The end of the journey for our neighbor is but a resting place for us." At long last, he grabbed the two wide mouth jugs and climbed farther, still. But the foreign wind threw him down and whirled 'round his body like the spirit of the Devil and made the boy's journey up the beautiful mountain a battle to the end.

At long last, he fills the jugs with snow, all the pure water Vincenza desires. He crosses himself and names himself blessed so loud and bold that he don't hear the *clippa cloppa* of donkey's hooves at Mungibellu's feet. Three field guards, two brothers and a son, they laugh and wave old documents with raised gold seals and prattle of a good day's meal and the turning tides of fortune. Their mouths fill with water and their bellies rise when they corner the lamb that waits for the shepherd boy. "Good fortune shines on us," the brother with a Garibbaldi beard says, "and a good day's meal." He pulls out a knife and shines it in the lamb's eyes. The lamb bleats out a slaughter cry. "Help me hold her down," he tells his brother that pulls out his own knife. The young guard turns away, his hands shaking over his ears. The two old guards slit the lamb's throat. The young guard sobs and scrapes his boot on a rock, the lamb's blood dripping from its leather stitchings.

The shepherd boy, high on Mungibellu's precious flank, sees none of this. But Vincenza, searching for the boy, she happens 'on the crime. So quick she runs! So loud she wails! She leaps 'cross rocks pressing her hands tight at her chest. She rushes at the Duca's men and spits at their feet and on the documents now soaked in blood. She pushes them to the ground, all three of them, each one laughing at the other 'til he, too, lands face down in the dirt.

"This day of all days you slaughter the innocent! Animals! Animals, the lot of you! The tenth day of August…and you kill!" She leans on a rock, her body curled 'til she gains back her breath.

*The tenth day of August…* My dear Vincenza, am I no better than the

Duca's men? Me, I live like an animal and dodge such memories when long ago I made my pact for food and shelter in the wild. Me, I gave up all what Man knows and feels and desires 'til you bring it back to me, my dear Vincenza, and grief comes rushing through my body, and my stone heart beats like a peasant's heart once more. This is the day stone turns to flesh. This tenth day of August, this is the day the blood of Bronti courses through my veins, Bronti and all the neighborhoods and the churches and the squares, Bronti and the neighborhood Santu Vitu where, long ago, the firing squad stood rigid and aimed at our brave men, Alfiu, the bravest of all.

How proud he stood with the others when Garibbaldi's lieutenant gave the order. "Fire!" he cried high on his horse. Quick, like a summer storm, bullets and smoke filled the square. How quick they slumped to the ground, our brave men, Alfiu, the bravest of all. How quick the women rushed to them with heart-breaking wails, mourning for the men that died, mourning 'til the hour of the Vespri prayers when the lieutenant seen fit for them to take the bodies away, all mourning save Agata and me.

I didn't mourn with the others. Agata and me, the two of us, desperate in our own way…a widow rushing to the Castle, a coward rushing to his cottage. I hid safe in my bed 'til the peasants pounded at my door. "Coward!" they shouted 'til I could take no more. I fled Bronti that night and lived out my days like an animal. But this day, my heart beats like a man's once more. I am brave this day and join my Bruntiszi in sorrow and memory. And, like a man, like a good maritu, this day I'll stop at nothing to keep my wife safe from harm.

The two brothers push her and laugh. They kick her and laugh, my Vincenza, clutching her chest, bare a breath in her body. She crawls to the lamb, rips her apron and presses the torn cloth on the lamb's wound. The lamb, still like a holy statue, drops her head, her eyes shining out on the land.

The creatures smell the killing. From forests and caves, they come and make a circle 'round the lamb. The brothers wave their blood-soaked knives. I howl all what's in me, but the sound is weak. I try to run. My legs are slow. Alfiu that gave me these gifts, now that I need them most, he takes them away. I beg him. "Alfiu," I pray, "let me pounce on the lot of them and tear them limb from limb." The donkeys roll in the dirt, the crosses on their backs clean as clean can be. The creatures circle them. Quick, the donkeys kick up their hind legs. The weak creatures run back to caves and forests, but the strong ones, they watch and wait.

"I'll take the woman back to town," the young guard whispers. He crosses himself and takes hold of Vincenza's arm.

"Let her go, son! Don't you know she came for something?" the brother with the Garibbaldi beard shouts back.

"Snow from the mountain, Papà."

He waves his arms 'round. "Where's her jug?"

The young guard slaps a tear from his cheek. "So, she came for the lamb."

"Does she look like a shepherd? No. She's here to warn someone."

"Papà, the lamb wasn't ours to kill. It belongs to the Duca."

The two brothers laugh. "Did he give birth to it? Did he suckle it?" They throw a look at the young guard 'til he lowers his eyes and shakes his head.

What do you say now, Duchinu, of the loyalty of your Papà's men? Strip away their warm lemon cakes and their embroidered vests stuffed with papers and raised gold seals. What you got, Duchinu, is a peasant that knows he got the right to more than he owns and does his best to claim it back. Field guards…peasants…and none of them loyal to you or the Duca!

"Papà," the young guard swallows hard, "we'll be punished."

"Listen, son," the old guard says, "this is a lesson you must take to your grave: none of the Duca's men will ever be punished. On the contrary, today we'll all be rewarded. This woman came to warn the one hiding in the mountains. If she and the lamb are in his care, he'll want to save them both. When he appears, we'll be ready for him."

"But the Duca's son…"

The old guard flings the documents with raised gold seals in the air. "When are you going to learn? The son! *He* is not the father! The good doctor will relay all that transpires to the Duca. And he'll reward us handsomely… that's all you need to know."

The young guard points up to Mungibellu's flank. "But whoever is out there is still in hiding."

"Because he's a coward. And there are plenty of them in that town." The old guard throws a look at his brother. The two nod and laugh.

Quick, Alfiu takes away the gifts. Quick, he gives them back to me. *Coward* is what the old guard calls the Bruntiszi. "Coward!" I howl back at him and leap from behind the rock, the biggest beast they ever seen, with long white fur that once was hair and beard, with limbs, quick to pounce, and hands and feet, sharp and clawed. The creatures rush back to their forest homes. The donkeys gallop away. The three field guards, they fight to hide one behind the other, and, with pushes and shoves, they chase the donkeys down the road. *Ve*'! *Ve*'! they cry out. My howling turns to laughter. The donkeys turn 'round. And, what is this? They laugh, too. Sì, the donkeys laugh at such orders and gallop on their way.

I look 'round. All is silent save for Vincenza that moans on the ground. I rush to her. She gazes up at me. "What creature is this with the black eyes of my maritu?" She wipes the flood of tears from my eyes and pats the white fur on my chest. "Can you be…?"

"Vincenza," I look down at her face. Deep lines cross her brow. But when I say her name, and I say it clear and good, that's when they fade from view.

She takes in a breath, her voice, bare a whisper. "I gave you my word, child. This day, I shout out your name for all the world to hear. Gratia Maria Saitta! Here is your name. Now, choose your path and make your mark on life! Gratia! My Gra…"

"Vincenza, rest…" I kiss her hand, her cheek, her mouth.

Her eyes to the heavens, a broken smile crosses her lips. "My maritu come back to me…my maritu…I…kept…I…kept…my…vow…I…"

I close my eyes. My heart hears Vincenza's song, the song she sang when she worked her flax on the loom, the song she sang in search of plants, the song she sings in my dreams each night to comfort me. But, my ears, they hear no such song. I slap them to make them hear the sweet sound, the sound my heart hears, the sound that quiets my dreams, but all they hear is Vincenza moaning.

"Vincenza, forgive me." She holds her heart. I take her hands and fold them in prayer. With the little strength left in them, they shake themselves free and brush the lamb's head, but all too soon, they fall to the earth.

"Vincenza…"

"Go," she whispers, "go…before…I…"

"Vigliaccu, they called me, but a coward I won't be no more. I got to stay with you."

"If you stay, I'll fight to stay, too."

"Fight, Vincenza, fight!"

"Fight and never go in peace? No, it's time…"

"Vincenza," I throw my head back, "I won't let it be time!" I look 'round at the joys and sorrows of Bronti that fill my heart and break my heart, the island sun burning in the sky, Mungibellu's jagged slopes, the shepherd boy rushing down…and my Vincenza lying on the ground.

"Go, my maritu…"

"No!"

"So much I already forgiven. So little I ask now…go, my maritu…go…"

"*Ahi!*" I kiss her mouth, a hard and bitter kiss, and give her all what she desires. Alone, she lies on the warm earth 'til the shepherd boy… Let him soothe her 'til she takes her last… Let *him* be brave. Now is the time for me to grieve.

# PART IV:
# THE PARTY

*A man born round cannot die square.*

The creatures of the forest don't mourn. They don't hang black ribbons on their caves or wear their skins inside out. They wail no mourning cries when stronger beasts move in and kill their young. All what they do is roam to higher grounds to seek fresh food and deeper caves and leave all what they know behind them.

The forest called to me. There, I grieved…there, alone, I said a prayer for my Vincenza 'til *his* voice called to me. I ran and hid, but, Alfiu, he found me.

Alfiu found me when I killed the weak creatures of the forest and feasted on them 'til stronger creatures tore at my flesh and death closed in. I welcomed it, but the strong creatures turned coward, and they fled, frightened by my cousin's spirit. "I owe you nothing, and nothing is what I give you!" I shouted and ripped at my body to rid it of him for good, but he held fast in me. Shackled with no chains, bound with no ropes, fight as I might, I couldn't break free 'til I gave my word to find the girl once more and keep her safe from harm.

*

Here, on the new carriage road, I come 'on her slumped on the carter's bench, all the fight drained out of her, quiet and still now, a deaf ear turned on all the carter's nonsense talk of the Castle and its glories. And the carter, what a sight he is, the reins flicking in his hands once more, gulping the green spices of the air that he tells the girl make his throat clean and cold. He leaps from the cart and stretches out his hands to touch the tall, solemn cypress trees, waving his fingers up at the thick green sprays like this is the first time he happens on the road. "I am home, I am home," he whispers and wipes the wet from his cheeks and beard. He jumps back up and flicks the reins when the Castle comes in view.

The Castle is of sandstone, built low and square with two courtyards and a forest of bright green vines creeping up the windows. Two tall iron gates, the letter **N** wrought in a circle on one gate, the letter **B**, on the other, stand at the entryway of the South portico, a shaded passageway that opens to the first courtyard. There are no high walls like a real castle, only two small towers, remains of long ago, a poor show for guard towers to stave off intruders. No one and nothing intrudes on the Castle no more, not Man, the Bronti peasant waging his desperate battles for the land, not Nature, the river Simetu rolling 'cross a stone bed and heeding boundaries beyond garden walls.

The carter pulls back on the reins. Chiazza stops at the iron gates. He waves his hand, breathing out the words *granary, winery, chapel.* "And all in the Castle, Mamsella, to eat and drink and feed our souls. See how beautiful it is here? Oui? Mamsella, you heard me say that word before. It is a foreign word. Oui. You say it when you agree with someone. In the Castle, you always got to agree with someone. And, you, too, you'll learn all the foreign words if you desire to be a guest like me. It's my joy to teach you these words and all the Castle manners, much the way the Excellencia teaches me."

The girl shrugs her shoulders and sighs.

The carter points to a cross in the courtyard that stonecutters chiseled from lava rock. "A Celtic cross" is what the Duchinu called it when he sent for Patri Radici to make a blessing.

"A circle of the Savior's eternal love" is what the priest sighed when he looked up at the cross and pointed to the carved ring.

The carter tells the girl all this, but she shrugs her shoulders and sighs.

The carter bows his head and crosses himself. "Immortal Hero of the Nile," he whispers and points to the foot of the lava cross where such chiseled words honor the Duchinu's long-ago uncle, the *hero*, if *hero* we got to call him.

At the iron gates of the South portico, he digs 'neath the fancy dresses for the blue shawl the bride from Rannazzu wore. "This is beautiful, too, oui? It's yours. Now that you're calm, Mamsella, put it on. Tuck all your hair 'neath it like you done so good when you worn your brown shawl. Glorious saints, the Duchinu means to reward you, but looking like this…with such wild hair…"

She throws her hands over her eyes and sobs.

"No, no, don't cry, Mamsella. It's not so wild."

"Blasiu…Mamma… I was brave when we started on our journey, but now I'm weak…"

He grabs the fringes of the blue shawl and wipes her eyes. "Mamsella, the boy is safe. Your Mamma is safe. And, Madama, I got to pray that she's safe, too."

"Mastru Nonziu, how can you know who is safe?"

He tucks a strand of hair in the blue shawl and pats her cheek. "Mamsella, *this* I know for sure: *we* are safe in the Castle."

*

The cousin's yellow dress sweeps 'cross the smooth stones 'round the lava cross. The brim of the cousin's yellow hat brushes the lace ruffles of her white umbrella. She walks past the cross and through the courtyard. Slow, slow, she makes her way to the iron gates of the South portico. There, she holds out her gloved hand and waits for the carter to jump off the bench and kiss it. "I am better now," she sighs, "and all due to the kindness of our dear Grace. I pray you both fare as well." She pats her cheeks and mouth with a small lace handkerchief. "Ah, the summers on this island. Forgive me, but they are simply not for the faint of heart."

"Donna Elizabeth, the heat of our island but serves to complement your beauty," the carter says and kisses her hand.

"Let this prove to be the last summer I must endure here. Taormina by the sea would be a pleasant change and a welcomed respite from this God-forsaken plot of earth."

"This God-forsaken plot of earth, as you say, would be all the more forsaken if you leave us."

"The words of a gentleman. And while we are on the subject of courtly manners, I should be most remiss if I did not seek your pardon."

"*Our* pardon?"

"Yes, Joseph, in not conversing with either of you during my illness. I seem to have been in a veritable hypnotic state."

The carter helps the girl down from the bench and pinches her arm. "Mamsella, take note of Donna Elizabeth's shining words. She speaks such beautiful words and all in our tongue." *How* the carter wonders and stands still with the girl 'til the cousin waves them on and she opens her bag of wind to start her tale, the carter and the girl walking slow, slow, with the cousin through the courtyard to the entryway of the Castle.

*

"I met a peasant from Bronte when Lady Bridport welcomed me to her London estate. No," she lets out a laugh, "I did not actually meet the peasant when I first arrived, I, being a mere baby, orphaned and alone. However, when Lady Bridport deemed it appropriate, I believe I was ten years of age at the time, Lady Bridport arranged the first of many lessons for me which would not terminate until the day I set sail for Sicily. Many would say the peasant was quite old, in her sixtieth year at the very least, I should venture. In spite of her years, she still maintained her loveliness. Her dark, round eyes struck me first…and, she informed me, that was what struck the boy, as well. You see, she loved a boy who was quite outside her peasant class, an artisan, with talents in metallurgy. He loved her, too, she said, but the love was doomed from the beginning although she spurred every effort her parents endeavored for a marriage in her class. I suspected she still harbored a devotion for him. I perceived it in her eyes, especially when she prattled about the sword. It seems this swordsmith forged a sword for her, a most dazzling one which he took great pains to sharpen and polish and which he professed he should brandish in battle against those who dared tear them apart. She spoke of his having the blood of a hero as he was brave and honorable, and, like the hero, Orlando, yes, Orlando I believe she said, he, too, had eyes which crossed, a sign, she maintained, of his great courage and the great madness of his love.

"However, Lord Viscount Nelson's niece, the grandmother of, as you say, your *Voscenza*…well, Lady Bridport had a plan of her own. On her singular visit to Bronte, Lady Bridport, you may know her as the Duchess of Bronte, in any case, Lady Bridport envisioned in the young savage… Oh, does the word *savage* offend you? I mean no harm. As I was saying, Lady Bridport envisioned a way to assure that all her heirs might know the language of the people they ruled, and, thus, might learn of revolutionary plots before they transpired. She offered to take the girl back to England. The girl's parents were nicely compensated. I believe they purchased two donkeys and built a small cottage through Lady Bridport's generosity. The girl, now an elderly peasant, still sang a tune she said all the peasants sang in the fields: 'I have a child, and only, now, this little ass. Leave me, then, the beast that wins me my day's bread, and take in trade my little child, and I vow for three days a lamp shall burn at thy shrine.'

"It little mattered when you passed her room, the song drifted from beneath her door through the hallways of the private apartments day and night as though a specter with a most charming voice took residence there."

The foreign wind picks up strength and blows the cousin's umbrella this way and that. "My parasol!" She holds tight to the wood handle and staves off the dusty earth that whirls 'round her. "My gracious! When shall we see an end to this sirocco?" Quick, she says the words like an incantation. Quick, the wind dies down. The cousin grabs her belly and takes in a breath, and, in the breath, she takes in all the spirits of the dying wind.

"To return to my story…the boy was not so fortunate. The day the girl sailed off for London, he told her his heart had broken. He vowed not to rest until she returned to him. He vowed to roam the town and declare his love and, if need be, to assemble an army to fight across land and sea and bring his *Lady of the Castle* back to him. That is the last she heard of him. However, she was certain he presently lives a happy life, married and blessed with many children and grandchildren."

The carter tugs at the girl's arm. "I heard of such a tale," he whispers, "when I first come to Bronti. I heard of a girl ripped from her Mamma's arms and of a boy gone mad for love. But can it be more than a tale? Can it be true? Can…"

The cousin throws a look at the carter. Quick, he slaps his mouth and falls to silence. She bows at the lava cross in the courtyard. The carter bows, too, so low his brow near scrapes the foot of the cross. When they reach the entryway of the Castle, she closes her umbrella, holds it out and waits 'til the carter slaps the dust off his hands. Fumbling with the lace ruffles and folding them the best he can, he takes the white umbrella in his charge.

"Lady Bridport was a wonderful woman. She and my dear grandmother (whom, I should reveal, was deceased one month before my birth, my parents shortly after) were cousins, but my devotion to Lady Bridport was nothing less than that of a granddaughter for her grandmother, and, I am moved to say, lovingly reciprocated.

"However, to return to my story, Lady Bridport was a wonderful benefactor. She kept the girl in a small corner room on her estate where the once peasant girl transformed into a demure woman, her thin peasant form draped in fine satin and silk brocade and her dark peasant skin lightened with the finest crèmes and powders from Paris. She sat in a lovely low floral chair and spoke words, words which related to the sketches Lady Bridport's artists provided of daily life in the Duchy, sketches depicting at once the animate and inanimate. The peasant held every sketch and named every depiction. That is how all those in Lady Bridport's trusted employ who were soon to depart for Sicily learned the peasant's language, that is to say *your* language. However, your *Voscenza*, stubborn at nineteen years of age when he set off for Sicily to reside at the manor, refused to adhere to his late grandmother's wishes, bellowing something about the nature of man and the nature of animals and that he would rather learn the language from his peasants than a pet.

"That is where your *Voscenza* and I differ. Since I was a child, I studied Italian, that is to say, the fine Tuscan dialect. Lady Bridport was quite pleased with the progress I made, she, having provided me with the most knowledgeable Tuscan tutors. However, she also rejoiced in my spending time with the peasant from Bronte and being schooled in *her*, that is to say, *your* language. *En fin de compte*, Lady Bridport's dying wish was for me to take permanent residence at the manor and for the Duke of Bronte's son to ask me…that is, for me one day to be his…that is, for me to be addressed by the peasants as…as…*Your Grace*."

She stands at the foot of the great stairway. "None of this is verily your concern. The hour of my party is fast approaching. Your *Voscenza* has asked me to be of some assistance to you. Come with me, Grace. We shall prepare ourselves for the evening's festivities. As for you, Joseph..." She turns to the carter and holds out her hand, but he shuffles 'round her, his eyes to the floor. "Joseph, I am speaking to you. Please tend to your horse. Your *Voscenza* should be quite distressed if you were not solicitous of her needs. When you return, the servants shall show you upstairs."

"Donna Elizabeth..." The carter looks up, his thick brows raised, his lips pressed tight. He holds his hand at his jaw, but, try as he might, he can't stop the wild clicking. "Donna Elizabeth, *clicca...clicca...*can it be? Was that loving boy, that talented smithy, was he *clicca...clicca...*is he now but a sorrowful lunatic wielding a sword of binding twigs through the roads of Bronti? Donna Elizabeth, *clicca...clicca...*please, tell me the old woman's name. Please, tell me this is the lunatic's peasant girl, his *Lady of the Castle*. Tell me she is safe and well. If, true, this is not a tale, I can now bring... *clicca...clicca...*some shard of hope...*clicca...clicca...*to a mad man."

"Her name?" The cousin lets out a soft laugh. "I never thought to enquire."

*

The cousin leads the girl up the great stairway to the long hallway where paintings and ribbons and medals decorate the blue walls. She stops before this sea fight and that dying scene and all to talk of the *hero* and what she says was "his bravery in defeating the French partisans and restoring the monarchy in Naples." The cousin pinches the girl's shoulder and smiles. "Grace, I see in those strange eyes of yours how impressed you are."

She swings the girl 'round. "How much more impressed you shall be!" She points to all the small hallways that wind 'round and make their way back to the long, blue hallway. "It is, indeed, a veritable labyrinth leading us to rooms and galleries of still more paintings and sculptures. Oh, Grace, I am afraid these delights must be reserved for another visit. Nonetheless, for the moment...shall I confide in you that which the Duke's personal physician, or, to be more precise, his former personal physician, once expressed regarding these paintings? Last month, Dr. Gale was alone in the drawing room inspecting another portrait of the Duke of Bronte which your *Voscenza* had commissioned. He toasted the portrait while commenting that if one had only amassed the *decency* to sell a single portrait, Dr. Gale should have sufficient funds to purchase a large estate." She lets out a laugh that trails behind them. "I am sure he knew I overheard him. When I laughed, his eyes met mine, and, suddenly, he dropped his glass so that I should laugh the more. Dr. Gale possesses a most keen wit, would you not agree?"

The girl looks 'round at the paintings and the sculptures in the hallway, shrugs her shoulders and sighs. She brushes her hand 'cross the painting of a man with white hair and a fat nose, but the cousin pulls it back and waves it over a document locked in a glass case, the document the king signed when he gave away a title and our town. "This is a copy of the royal document, which, along with the original will of our beloved Lord Viscount Nelson, the first great Duke of Bronte, is safe and secured in the salon, the last room to the left of the gallery. However, I regret to inform you that you may not gaze upon these archival splendors. They are under lock and key and admittance is reserved for the *fifth great Duke of Bronte,* our future Duke, and, *he,* alone.

"In perpetual property," she reads from the copy, "the land and the same town of Bronte, the revenue stamps, the incomes of the vassals, the servitudes, the rents… Shall I continue?"

The girl shakes her head.

"Why ever not?"

"When you speak," the girl fixes her eyes on the painting of the man with the white hair and the fat nose, "I make no sense…"

"I shall continue. I must! This is how it all began…in a sense, for you and for me. I have been informed that the manor was once an abbey, abandoned and in total disrepair. Nonetheless, on the tenth day of the tenth month in the year 1799, King Ferdinand I, ruler of your Naples and Sicily, granted that the abbey and the town, indeed, the Duchy of Bronte, should officially become an inheritable property, and, although neither of us had been born at the time, on the tenth day of the tenth month in the year 1799, both our lives changed irrevocably."

The girl's nostrils flare, and her jaw stretches out to stop a yawn. "Oh, my, Grace, you are, no doubt, fatigued. Conserve your strength for the final jewel. Regard this copy of the Admiral's will." She takes in a breath. "Regard how the hero signed his name, *Nelson and Bronte*. And, here, here is a decanter with two glasses. Aboard *The Victory* the night before he was shot, the great Vice-Admiral Lord Viscount Horatio Nelson drank from this very glass. Look, on the wood base, you shall never believe what is carved there. Oh, you cannot read. I shall read it to you.

## N 1805 B

"Now, do you understand, Grace? As scrolled on gates, **N** and **B**. As engraved beneath treasures, **N** and **B**. Oh, Grace, he knew! And I know, as well! The great name of Nelson and the Duchy of Bronte shall always be united!"

The girl shrugs her shoulders and sighs.

"The Admiral would be very proud to know how we have all honored his legacy and taken up the gauntlet of bravery in his manor. And the Duke's son…your *Voscenza*, well, he is the bravest of all, waging battle after battle in court for the land which shall be his one day and treating those attempting to seize it with…kindness, with utmost kindness. A gentleman, indeed, and a hero, in his own right. As we speak, he is delivering his very own provisions to his townspeople. As we speak, that is exactly what he is doing. A hero…a veritable hero!"

She takes in a breath.

"Dr. Gale tells us there is a cholera epidemic, *'a quarara*, as you say, or some such illness, stemming from the most flagrant abuse of hygiene. Dr. Gale is indisposed, otherwise, he, no doubt, would have joined your *Voscenza*. Early this morning, he rode with his men to makeshift hospital quarters to deposit his wheat for the ones who survive the illness so that they may be nourished and regain their strength to work the land. If I were one of his peasants, I should be so grateful to the future fifth great Duke of Bronte, I should work the fields for the rest of my days and ask for nothing in return. Grace, whatever is the matter?"

"I make no sense of all what you say. You speak in our tongue, but I…"

"You speak our language, *Donna Elizabeth*…"

The girl bows her head and digs her feet in the long red rug. "You speak in our tongue, *Dunna Eeelisabetta*, but I make no sense of what you say."

"Then, I must teach you. I must teach you the way Lady Bridport taught her young savage. Do you enjoy music? That is the first project we shall undertake, to play the pianoforte in the music room, there, to the right of the gallery past the drawing room. The pianoforte was a most generous gift from Lady Rolle of Bicton on the occasion of your *Voscenza's* birthday, and, in the music room which he created in my honor, you shall see a Bechstein. A Bechstein! And producing the most beautiful sound. In the music room, I shall teach you to play beautiful pieces. Do all peasants sing as sweetly as Lady Bridport's savage? You and I shall sing our very own compositions."

The cousin fixes her eyes on the girl's thin fingers and how they spread and how they curl and none by force. She throws her own thick hands behind her. "No, no, this shall never do. On second thought," she nibbles on her lip, "some talents take a lifetime to learn. And I feel it is much too late for you to cultivate any of them."

\*

No matter what Patri Radici preached of the Savior's heavenly home, the girl says the cousin's room is paradise and waves to the white angels floating 'cross the ceiling with wings spread wide. And when the angels are tired, she says, they slip 'neath the lace bed cover and rest their heads on the soft pillows and fall to sleep on the mattress that her own fingers near sank in when she helped the cousin drink the cure. And they got to do some things in private, too. That's when they reach for the pretty white pisciaturi. And when the young angels want to play, that's when, the girl says, each cradles her own *daaalllaaa*.

"Grace, how charming and fanciful you are! Now, enough of angels and dolls." She points to a large cupboard of dark wood with carvings on the two thick doors and the two round arches. "That upon which you are about to gaze in the armoire...dear girl, why are you looking at the ceiling? You have no idea what an armoire is, do you? It is a French word. It is like a cupboard but, as you see, abundantly more beautiful. *Armoire* can you say it?"

"*Ammuarru*."

"No, you cannot. Very well, I shall teach you French. Round your lips as though you were on the verge of kissing…well, whoever it is you desire to kiss, although, I, for one, cannot fathom a peasant boy being desirable. Yes, that's it…yes…my, you are a bright girl or I…yes, that's it…*I* am an excellent teacher.

"In my reveries, I've ofttimes imagined King Ferdinand I offering the armoire to your *Voscenza's* great-great-uncle, Vice-Admiral Lord Viscount Horatio Nelson, upon the signing of the royal document. The document, Grace. Pray tell me, you recall my lesson in the gallery."

The girl stretches out her jaw again, and, through a yawn, she whispers, "No."

"Oh, very well, I shall repeat it later. However, that which I am about to divulge is not reverie. It was, indeed, a true and noble token of gratitude bestowed upon our beloved Vice-Admiral Lord Viscount Nelson when the document was signed. Oh, you cannot imagine what it was! A diamond encrusted sword which belonged to King Ferdinand's great-great grandfather, the great Louis XIV. Imagine that! A sword from the Sun King!"

A tight smile crosses the girl's lips. "A sword? A peasant don't waste his earnings on a sword, not when a knife's good to do the deed."

The cousin slaps her hand 'cross her chest. "Grace, you simply refuse to comprehend the significance. It was a gift, not to utilize, but to admire. You must not think in little ways any longer. You must think in grandiose and significant ways. Pray tell me, what do you imagine the Admiral answered when he received such a gift?"

"Grazii. That's what 'a z'a Vincenza says I got to say when a kindness comes to me."

The cousin lets out a laugh, a high laugh, a loud laugh, that shakes the dark wood doors of the cupboard and the runners and the seat of the rocking chair and the cousin's dolls that tumble to the floor. "Thank-you? I'm afraid the Admiral was a bit more eloquent. 'The bounty of your Majesty has so overwhelmed me that I am unable to find words adequate to express my gratitude.' Are you capable of remembering his words?" She throws a look at the dolls and waves her hand. At the cousin's bidding, the girl picks up the dolls, kisses their small, webbed fingers and sets them back on the rocking chair. "If you are not capable, I shall help you, but you must say these words to your *Voscenza* at dinner: '*Voscenza*, this bounty has so overwhelmed me that I am unable to find words adequate to express my gratitude.' Oh, do try, Grace."

"Voscenza, this bounty…no…Dunna Eeelisabettu," she turns away from the dolls, and, eye to eye with the cousin, she whispers, "I got to say all what's in my heart this night."

"Very well." The cousin turns the key and opens the thick carved doors of the cupboard. There, 'neath the two round arches is a wood bar, and, on the bar on cloth covered frames with hooks, hang the cousin's dresses, red, yellow, white, blue, green, and purple dresses, and all with ruffles and high collars.

"Grace, oh, what you must be thinking! As my dressers may never arrive from England, and, as I may never lay my beautiful dresses in a drawer again, you must be thinking, *Donna Elizabeth is relegated to hanging her beautiful dresses as a peasant would on branches in her cottage.* No, perhaps you are thinking, *I should so love to touch Donna Elizabeth's beautiful dresses.* Very well, I give you permission, although, by the look in your eyes, I imagine you feel they are quite a struggle to wear. Come now, Grace, as ladies, we must bow to the dictates of fashion. This is my favorite, in the style of the young Sarah Bernhardt. Take note it is made of crinoline, much softer than the wire cages our mothers wore. See how the silk pulls in the back to form a bustle? See how it moves in the air? It can make the most unattractive girl beautiful. Would you like to try it on? Why ever not? Lilac is my favorite color, so reminiscent of eternal spring. Persephone at her finest. This is the dress I shall wear tonight."

The cousin slides the dress off the small cloth frame and lays it 'cross her arms. "I simply refuse to dress '*a la sicilienne.* That is to say, the way certain young titled Sicilians dress for formal dinners in their short sleeves and décolleté gowns. No matter how repressive the heat may prove to be, I am English and, nothing, if not modest." She locks the cupboard and points to a high corner table where a large blue and white pitcher sits in a bowl. "While I am finishing with the preliminaries, please do me the courtesy of cleansing yourself. I'll need your assistance with the corset."

No wonder the cousin finds fault with the heat on our island. It's all what she wears what makes her so hot all the time. She stands before the girl in white stockings and cotton drawers and a thin cotton blouse with no sleeves. She holds out a stiff white garment in the shape of an hourglass and rocks back and forth 'til the narrow part is just at her waist. She fastens the front and tells the girl to pull the ties in the back.

"Do you see the laces?" She takes in a breath. "Pull them, Grace, tighter. Tighter. I am able to endure a great amount of discomfort. After all, with great pain comes great beauty."

She puts on another thin blouse over the hourglass garment and then slips on the dress. She pushes the sleeves up, stops, and pushes them up more. "You see, Grace, here is yet another challenge. The sleeves are cut too narrowly at the shoulders. Do you see all which I must endure? I shall, indeed, have a word with that charlatan of a seamstress the very next time I am in London…sooner rather than later if a certain gentleman would only rid himself of his shyness and ask for my hand… Oh, help me, Grace. Your arms, I suppose, would slip into the sleeves quite easily, but you are not the one to wear it. Look at the ruffled collar. Is it not the most beautiful in the world? Button me, Grace. Do not miss a single button. Voilà! Here it is. Here I am. And, you, *you* remain silent."

The girl shakes her head and lets out a laugh. "If a peasant woman had to take so much time to put on so much clothes, when would she do her chores?"

The cousin pinches the lace ruffles near her waist. "We are not talking of a peasant woman and her dirty clothes." She looks at herself in the long glass in the corner of the room and smiles, shifting her shoulders side to side. "Look at my dress. Have you ever seen anything quite so beautiful?"

The girl throws a look to the rocking chair. "Sì."

"A comparable dress? Very well, Grace, pray tell me, where does a peasant girl gaze upon such dresses?"

"Here." She pats the slipper of the smallest doll in the yellow dress with ruffles edged in red. "The dress that your daaalllaaa wears. I had a daaalllaaa, too, with binding twigs for a body and a head of limuni. I was her Mamma. She was my good daughter. She wore a beautiful dress that 'a z'a Vincenza made."

"Yes," the cousin presses her fingers to her mouth and lets out a small laugh, "with a lemon for a head. I am sure she was quite beautiful and the dress, as well…but, use your common sense." She twirls 'round the girl, the weight and girth of the lilac skirt and its ruffles near pushing the girl down. "Grace, was it more beautiful than *my dress?*"

"More beautiful? There was a dress…I seen it in a big box. It was the one Angelica wore when the Duchinu made her come alive with Orlannu and the Saracen."

"Orlando?" The cousin jumps back and grabs the glass knob on the door. "No…no," she turns the knob 'round and 'round 'til it near flies off. "Grace…"

"Sì?"

"Grace, if nothing else, learn to address me properly. 'Sì, Donna Elizabeth,' you must say. Very well, I see this shall take time and practice. And patience on my part." She gives the glass knob one last mighty turn. "However, of a more pressing nature is that which you imply. Am I to infer that your *Voscenza* displayed *my* marionettes to *you?* Before you answer, know that I shall see in those strange eyes of yours a truth or a lie."

"Sì, they came alive. I cried. He thinks I seen none of it, but he cried, too."

"How your imagination labors on! First, the angels, now, the marionettes." Her fingers flutter on her cheeks like big, white wings. "It is a mistake. And you are mistaken about the beauty of my dress. No…now, it all comes to light. It is no mistake. There is envy in those creature eyes of yours. You must speak the truth. Only then, shall I be your benefactress. Answer me, Grace. Look at my dress and answer me. Have you ever seen anything quite so beautiful?"

The girl nods and looks down at her blue dress and white apron.

"Grace," the cousin sighs, "how dreadful! Now, I comprehend why you cannot discern the truth. You are troubled. Indeed, you are a troubled girl. You cannot possibly mean to compare *that* dress…dear girl, say you do not mean that *sack* you are wearing… Grace, I am nothing if not candid. It is simply dreadful. Without a doubt, it shall be the ruination of our dinner party. Bring me the glass on the night table. Water, Lady Bridport was wont to say, is the singular remedy to calm the nerves."

Her lips pucker 'round the rim of the glass. Like a fish, she draws the water in. "Ça va mieux. Perhaps I was too harsh. Allow me to explain. Mrs. John Sherwood in her *Manners and Social Usages* speaks of the appropriate dress for the appropriate time of day and the appropriate silks and satins for the appropriate occasion. Now, do you understand? I shall be your benefactress, Grace, as Lady Bridport was to her young savage. As your benefactress, I shall straight away confide to you one rule of etiquette which, I believe, Mrs. John Sherwood never thought necessary to proffer: any type of headwear at the table indicates a lack of breeding. Undo your shawl." The cousin clutches her chest. "My heavens, what a monstrosity! Have you never in your life heard of shears? Or a *knife*? My heavens, this is not amusing. Why are you grinning like a fool? I speak of shears and knives, and this amuses you. Very well. Does the distress in my voice amuse you, as well? It is too late. It is simply too late. Now, how shall we ever set a curl to that hair?" She points to a small cushioned chair in the corner of the room. "Sit down. At the very least, braid your hair." She holds out her arms and crosses them. "Like this. Must I teach you everything?" She points to her own head of hair, the curls falling on her brow and pinned up at the neck. "Look," she pats the top of her head, "my curls cover the part, but your part must be in the center; now, you must parcel the hair in small divisions. Don't pile it! Wrap it...neatly... My heavens, we have no more time! Oh, do what you must. It is a disaster in the making. A *dis...as...terrrr...*" She eyes the floor and the girl's black feet digging in the red flowers of the rug.

"Disaster!" She fumbles for the key, unlocks the cupboard and flings the doors wide open. On the floor next to the jug of vinegar, she grabs two blue slippers. She pokes her finger through a small hole on the side of one slipper and rubs a dark stain on the side of the other. "I intended to discard these, but I see their usage is requisite this evening. I'm certain you've never worn a finer pair of slippers. Even if the ulcers on those swollen feet of yours could slip inside a fitted shoe," she gasps, "I should have no recourse but to throw the diseased pair out by night's end. Very well, let us see how you walk."

The cousin slides two white cotton stockings, both with holes in the heel, to the chair where the girl still braids her hair. "Enough! Just put the hose on." The girl snivels and struggles with the toes. She looks up, her low lip quivering. "Put these on, too." The cousin slides the slippers to the chair. They're light with thin soles, but the girl can bare lift her feet, weighing her down the way they do. And they burn and tear at her flesh. That's what she cries out when she rips them off. The cousin, she waves her hand and makes her put them back on again and laughs when the girl stumbles 'round the room in the white cotton stockings and the blue silk slippers that make her cry and cut her from the earth.

"Don't you dare remove them! Now, on your toes, Grace. One would think you had never walked before. On your toes. You are not crushing grapes in the pressing room. Gently…gently… Oh, this shall never do. My only consolation," she lets out a loud sigh, "is that our beloved Mrs. Sherwood is not here to witness a guest so impudent as to arrive for dinner in the barest and most sullied of feet."

*

The door to the cousin's room swings open and sweeps the girl behind it. "A man in my room!" the cousin cries out and wraps her hands 'round the curled metal leaves of the foot board. "My Goodness! Alec! You frightened me to death!"

The Duchinu holds tight to the door frame. "Elizabeth!" he cries out and stumbles to the bed, the wet clumps of hair sticking to his brow, the wet shirt sticking to his skin. With the little strength he got left in him, he taps for the eye patch that falls to the side of his face and brushes it back over his eye.

"Alec…where…where is your waistcoat? My God, Alec…where is your coat?" The cousin asks a hundred questions and answers all of them herself. "Mrs. John Sherwood always says a gentleman arrives at a lady's door in complete and proper attire, does she not? She does! She does!" That is how she asks and answers, for how long, who can say, and, her, near out of breath 'til she reaches for the glass of water, but the Duchinu grabs it first.

She takes in a breath and throws out more questions like Mungibellu when she throws out her fire and ash. "How have your hands gotten so soiled? How has your shirt…? My God… How have the tails…? Alec, how have you been so remiss as to leave the tails…*untucked?* Alec…Alec…what has happened to you?"

He rolls the glass of water 'cross his brow. "May God be merciful and heal them or take them all to paradise. This purgatory of life and death shall be the ruination of each and every one of us."

"My goodness, Alec, look at yourself! I hardly recognize you."

"There was dying everywhere, not the death scenes one admires so in oil paintings. Today, real men battered about on cots, a violent vomiting seizing not only the men, but their delirious wives and children, as well. Soon after the vomiting, a liquid, white yet of a murky nature, oozed from their bodies as though they were shedding a part of themselves as the snake does its skin. The liquid lay there until their germ-infested sheets sopped it up. And the cries in the ward," he throws his hands over his eyes, "how they shall haunt me for the rest of my days!"

He falls in the cousin's arms, but, quick, she shakes herself free. "Alec, please," she brushes the dirt from the skirt of her dress, "a different circumstance and I should more than welcome your embrace. However, Alec…you are not *clean.*"

"Clean?" He pounds at his chest. "There is blackness all about me. I have seen too much. This illness kills at once the patient and the healer."

"My dear Alec, you are the bravest man I know." The Duchinu stumbles back to the door and grabs hold of the glass knob. The cousin eyes the blue shawl in the corner and, quick, throws it behind the door. "Please, Alec, I appreciate your wish for privacy. However, with all this talk of bravery, we need a bit of air. Be so kind as to leave the door open. A little more. A little more."

He staggers to the curled metal leaves of the foot board and shakes his hand in the air. "I am not the one who stands brave. A brave man shares the little he has. 'Drink, *Voscenza,* drink all what we have and all what we drink.' This was a dying peasant's plea today."

"Did you?"

"The most curious aspect was the brave fellow's smile which accompanied such a noble gesture. How brightly he smiled, as though I were one of them, as though I suffered as one of them and would cry out as one of them." He shakes his head and sighs. "All this generosity from a peasant, in spite of witnessing his loved ones taking their last breath."

"Did you, Alec?"

"Pardon?"

The cousin throws her hand over her mouth and swallows hard. "Alec, did you drink that which the peasant offered you?"

"Elizabeth, I have never offended my peasants."

She shakes her head, her hand tight over her mouth. "How could you?"

"Such brave men."

"Then, Alec, I beg to differ with your definition of bravery. In spite of such enormous peril, you fulfilled what you believed to be your duty. That is bravery. You showed yourself one with your peasants. And, that, too, is bravery. Yet, now, I must ask at what cost to you? You are pale and fatigued."

"It shall pass."

A foot juts out from behind the door, the white cotton stocking rolled 'round the ankle, the blue slipper, dangling on the toes. The cousin holds in a breath 'til the foot fades from view. "Alec," she says, letting out a sigh, "your fatigue shall not pass until I have the servants prepare your bath. Pail upon pail they shall pour for your comfort, the steaming hot, the cooling water, until your bath reaches the perfect temperature."

"My delicate Elizabeth…"

"The image of your peasants' sufferings shall soon diminish from your memory."

"Elizabeth…"

"Come now, Alec, this is the first of many kindnesses I shall execute on your behalf. Now, off with you. You shall return to your former self long before Dr. Gale pours the first apéritif."

"You are not only delicate, but kind."

The cousin bows and holds out the lilac skirt and twirls 'round him. "Delicate and kind…and…"

"And?"

"I see we must bide our time for the occasion when you are more disposed to free the sentiments locked inside your heart. For the moment, the little I request is your word. Promise me, Alec, promise me you shall never venture to that God-forsaken town again."

He tightens his hand 'round the glass and shakes the last drops of water in his mouth. "My dear cousin, my delicate Elizabeth, I shall not give my word. Duty may compel me to dishonor it."

The cousin throws her shoulders back and bows. "Duty." She shuts her eyes and grabs hold of her throat like what crossed her lips was poison. "Duty." At the threshold, she pinches the girl behind the door. "Stay," her lips shaping the word. She closes the door and leads the Duchinu down the long, blue hallway, the empty glass swinging at his side.

The cousin holds tight to the Duchinu's arm 'til she reaches his room near the great stairway at the far end of the long, blue hallway. "Sì," at long last, the girl whispers, *sì*, she'll stay and wait in the cousin's room. What a small, quiet word it is, small and soft and fading in the air but to the one what yearns to hear it. It reaches the Duchinu's ears. He shudders.

Like in a spell, he breaks free of the cousin's arm and stumbles past a hundred rooms, the cousin not far behind, whispering that he's none but *delirious*. In and out of a hundred small hallways he stumbles, nearing the room where he keeps the secret documents at the west of the long, blue hallway, the glass still shaking in his hand. A table is all what he needs for it, and he comes 'on one, at the east of the long, blue hallway, near the door of the cousin's room, a long table where a pitcher and two glasses sit on top of a wood base carved with the year **1805** and the letters **N** and **B**.

The Duchinu pushes the door open. The girl stands before him, her hair sweeping the rug, a beam of light shining on her face. "My God, it *was* your voice I heard." He trembles and loses his grip on the glass. It falls behind him and hits a glass on the top of the wood base. The two clink and twirl the way glasses do when Castle folk make toasts. The cousin lunges for the glasses. "No!" she cries out.

They shatter.

They fall.

On her knees, she scoops up shards of glass. She takes great pains to put them in their own piles. In the end, they're all the same, the Duchinu's glass and the *hero's* glass. What makes the cousin think she knows shard from shard? Glass from glass? In the end, they're all the same.

"Alec!"

He kicks the door frame and shakes a few stubborn specks of glass from the stitchings of his boots. He pushes his hair back. "Grace, forgive me. A short while ago…I did not see you…I did not offer you…my greetings." The cousin looks up from her piles of glass and fixes her eyes on the Duchinu, how he bows to the girl and closes the door behind him. "Grace, you look *lovely*," his words, like small flames, curl from 'neath the door. The cousin throws the shards at the blue walls. "*Lovely*," he whispers. Alone in the long, blue hallway, the cousin cups her ears. She moans. She wails. "Yes, Grace, absolutely *lovely*, this evening."

*

On three squat legs, the pianu rests. They say an artisan from the Hapsburg land carved it, but what carpenter in Bronti that makes the cabinets and the coffins, can't work his own wonders in that wood? The pianu is of a foreign wood, foreign, too, the pale carvings and the thick keys. The Duchinu calls it his *chef d'oeuvre*, a masterpiece he never touches. That, he says, is his cousin's duty.

Before the Duchinu filled the long, blue hallway with the last of his flatteries to the girl, the cousin rushed to the pianu, but not to play a tune. She draped herself over the instrument and tapped the keys from one end of the board to the other. She taps them still, the last note ringing loud and deep like a mourning knell.

"Elizabeth, lilac is, indeed, your color." The surgeon stands at the threshold of the music room, dressed all in grey, much like the Duchinu when he studied his charts in the new olive tree groves. He wears grey pants, a grey vest buttoned high on his chest, a grey jacket, a white shirt, a long, full grey tie and a high black hat. This is what the rich and titled ones wear, but, at close look, the hat is spotted, the buttons on his vest hang loose and his pants fray at the knees. Like a peasant, he wears his *one good suit*, time and again, 'til it rips to shreds.

He takes off his high black hat and lays it on a small table. Alfiu showed me this room in his ball of light and all what goes on there. The surgeon shuffles past the carved bottles of red and green and yellow spirits and the small round glasses, past the high back chairs where the surgeon and the Duchinu sit at night to play the game of cards they call *piquet* all while the cousin makes this excuse or that before she sings out a nonsense tune. "A lieder? A pastoral?" she asks, but the Duchinu near always begs for a hymn, the one hymn she sings time and again, her mouth, tight and round from start to end, and, him, joining in, "Things that once were wild alarms cannot now disturb my rest."

The surgeon sits in a green high back chair and smiles. "Lilac, I repeat, is, indeed, your color. Elizabeth, when a gentleman compliments, although, due to misfortune, he dons no evening attire, he is, nonetheless a gentleman, and it is customary for the lady…"

She pounds her hands on the keys. The surgeon rubs his ears. "Elizabeth, if such is your idea of a joyful song, well, I should hardly dance to that."

She presses the back of her hand to her mouth. "I shall not bring you joy today, Dr. Gale, nor do I wish anyone to dance at my expense."

"No singing. No dancing. Now, this *is* a serious matter. Who dampens the spirit of our delicate Elizabeth?"

"The peasants say that jealousy is a barking dog attracting thieves."

"Elizabeth…"

"Forgive me. I am a fool today."

"You are no fool. And I am no thief. I take that which is my right," he fills a small, round glass with red spirits, "and I suspect you do the same. As for any and all barking dogs, allow me to share a poorly-guarded secret. My dear, the constellations howl with envy upon such visions of comeliness."

"Oh, Dr. Gale…thank you."

"Now, recount to me the events and the name of the wretched coward whom I must challenge to a duel so that your beautiful green eyes may shine brightly once more."

The cousin moves to a yellow high back chair and curls her finger, and, in a flash, the surgeon slides to her side, the tight smile back on his face. "Dr. Gale, you cannot challenge a girl to a duel."

"Elizabeth, has one of the servants caused you this grief?"

"No, Dr. Gale." She nibbles on her lip, her head down. "I am ashamed to say the one who caused this grief is the very one who saved my life."

He leans in. "The Saitta girl?"

"You remember her name?"

He rubs the scars 'long his face and neck. "Some people, you shall learn, leave their imprint on you."

She digs her elbows in her sides, her head in her hands, her fingers pressing on her puffed cheeks. "So, you, too, believe she is without fault?"

"On the contrary, Elizabeth, she is very much at fault."

"How can you be certain?"

"All her people are very much at fault." He shuffles to the carved bottle of red spirits, pours himself another drink and raises a small, round glass to her. She shakes her head. "Yet, why such concern over a peasant girl?"

"My concern is that Alec…"

"Yes, that Alec…"

"Dr. Gale, I shall state it directly. Alec has taken an interest in Grace."

He throws his head back and gulps down the red spirits. "Ha! That is absurd!"

"It may be absurd, but I believe it is true."

He sits back down. "Dry your eyes, Elizabeth," he whispers, "and take a cue from me at dinner. If that is, indeed, the case, before our beloved Alec takes his first sip of wine, a seed shall be planted in his heart. Shortly thereafter, he shall learn of all the deceptions which beat inside that peasant girl. And, then, my dear Elizabeth, his singular interest shall be to bring her to justice." He takes out a small branch from the pocket in his vest and waves it in the air. "After all, I know of matters to which only God and his peasants are privy."

"What is that?"

"In time, my dear."

"I have no more time. What if Alec refuses to believe you?"

"Have I ever spoken to you of my dear departed mother? Maman, I should rather say, as she was French and named me after St. Luke, the patron of physicians. She destined me for the profession which I…"

"Dr. Gale…please…"

"Ah, yes, Alec. As I was saying, dear Maman was fond of the old adage that a lie could travel halfway around the world before the truth ever slipped its boots on."

"Lucien…"

"*Lucien?*" He licks his mouth all over like he just bit into a juicy cut of meat.

The cousin's finger moves to the back of his hand and falls in the furrows of his knuckles. "Lucien, would you do this for me?"

"I would," he says and waves the branch in the air. "As a man of medicine, I have a duty to keep Alec and the manor safe from infection of any kind."

"You make me very happy."

"And I rejoice in your happiness. Now, this shall make you ever more content. Listen well. Alec, no doubt, has spoken to you of *Ferdinandea?*"

She pinches the ruffles at her collar and sighs. "Yes, he's spoken of the island, ofttimes, and with a fantastic longing to inhabit it someday. Pray tell me, how does one inhabit a mythic island?"

"Elizabeth, it is not mythic, not by any means. It is very much an island, a volcanic one at that, although, at the present, very much submerged in the Mediterranean."

"Now why on earth would he wish to live there?"

He throws his head back and laughs. "Because he is a dreamer. Need I remind you the son is not the father? Nonetheless, that is not my point. Listen well. Ferdinandea made its last appearance years before you were born, and, briefly, at that, as it was soon swallowed up by waves. At the present, there is no trace of the island."

"Interesting although that may be… Lucien, what does such an island have to do with…?"

He brings her hand to his lips and kisses it with an open mouth. She pulls it back and lets out a cry. "Elizabeth, I should advise you to be more receptive to my revelations."

"Oh." She lays her hand soft on her lap.

"As I was saying, the girl may leave her mark on Alec today. However, in the very near future, her peasant ways shall swallow her up whole. And…*I* shall see to that. Let her stir up all the turmoil she desires. It shall always take place beneath the sea, so to speak, on deaf ears and blind eyes."

Her lids flutter. "And she shall disappear forever from his eyes and his heart?"

"Much the way Ferdinandea disappeared."

The cousin jumps up and twirls 'round. The surgeon laughs. With one hand, he waves the branch. With the other, he snatches the ruffles of her skirt. "You are not wrong, Dr. Gale, I am ever more content." She takes in a breath and sits back down. "And, now, a favor in kind. Be assured of this: when Alec and I marry," she lowers her eyes and draws small circles with the tip of her finger on each of the surgeon's knuckles, "you shall be our most intimate friend, and we shall, naturally, do everything in our power to protect you."

He swipes his hand over his wet mouth. "If that be the case, I shall impart *all* my knowledge."

"There is more?"

"Before I make my point, a bit of judicial history regarding Alec's *beloved* Sicily. I believe it was in the thirteenth century...if a crime were committed on the island, the transgression would be written on a tablet and the tablet placed in a vat of water. If the tablet floated, the accused would be set free."

"And if it sank..."

"And this is precisely the reason you must learn from me. My tablet would sink, wholly and irretrievably, and I would be condemned to a rapid execution. However, on the way to my death, I would ply the accusers, the judges, and all the spectators with my *green fairy*, and all would begin to doubt their eyes. A tablet sinking to the bottom of the sea? On the contrary, they would see ten tablets floating in the sky. *Crimes*, although I prefer to think of them as *slight imperfections of the truth,* may be committed this evening." He pats the small branch and puts it back in the pocket of his vest. "Nonetheless, the tablet shall float."

"Yes, Lucien, I believe you. The tablet shall float."

The surgeon leans in. His hand brushes the cousin's cheek, the small finger catching in the ruffles of her collar. When it breaks free, it flies 'cross her chest, and, him, taking it all in, his tight smile widens to a big, haunting grin. "A good surgeon has an eagle's eye, a lion's heart and a lady's hand. Another of Maman's adages, and the one I take great pride in shamelessly misinterpreting. Remember, *a lady's hand*...delicate, soft, knowledgeable of regions...ah, the regions into which we shall delve...at a more propitious time." He takes her hand and lays hard kisses on each finger. "Elizabeth, I offer you a great service, and, in return…"

"In return?" She pulls her hand back and wipes the wet from her fingers. "Dr. Gale, I believe I have given you the wrong…"

He shakes his head. "No, not the wrong impression, not by any means. You have designs to marry Alec. I shall be of great service in that regard. However, there is always the matter of recompense. Elizabeth, my beauty, you look confused. En fin de compte, it's quite simple. Alec shall no longer be the singular source of all your amusements." She lets out a cry. He leans in close 'til the hot vapor of his breath near scalds her face. "Tut, tut," he strokes the dark red marks rising on her cheeks and gazes in her widening eyes, "yes, my delicate Elizabeth, I believe you comprehend our transaction and its fees."

Her head drops. She opened her bag of wind, and, now, she got to pay. With her mouth open like she wants to take back all the wind, sobbing, shuddering, she nods.

"Good," he whispers and pats her cheek dry. "Now, dab some cold water on those pretty cheeks. And leave the *tablet* in my hands. Your Dr. Gale shall be the bearer of many surprises this evening."


*The door only opens from the inside.*

"Lucien, you've done well, today," the surgeon whispers to himself and slaps his back. "A conscious mistress shall prove infinitely more entertaining than an unconscious one." He leans on the door of the music room and tips his hat to the back of the lilac dress that swishes down the long, blue hallway and rises and falls with each heaving breath the cousin takes. When she reaches her room overlooking the North courtyard, the cousin turns the glass knob and, without a word, throws the blue shawl at the girl and shoves her in the hallway.

"Hello? Hello?" The surgeon waves to the girl from the threshold of the music room. "Come here, Grace, perhaps I may be of some assistance."

The girl hops down the hallway, pushing her fingers in the blue slippers, stretching the length and breadth of the toes and the heels and the sides.

"Dunna Eeelisabetta ordered me to wait in her room. Voscenza, he came back, but he come and gone long ago. I waited. But, now, she..."

"Donna Elizabeth needs some time alone, and your *Voscenza* is dressing. As for the carter, he, no doubt, is lurking in the kitchen enjoying a prelude to his dinner. That leaves the two of us. Why should we not adjourn to more comfortable surroundings? You and I shall talk of many things, of herbs and medicine and, as the walrus said, 'of cabbages and kings.' Lewis Carroll, my dear...a reference to a poem in his recent book. Ah, the knowledge you shall learn tonight, knowledge you never dreamed existed in our universe."

The surgeon leads the girl down the great stairway and west past the kitchen to a small room in the north. "For centuries, the monastic residents used it as their granary," he tells her. Her eyes take in the room, the bare walls and floor, the chairs with their cloth coverings ripped wide open, the tables with their chipped and broken legs. His eyes follow hers. "No, my dear, if you are thinking this is how the Duke of Bronte's son sees fit to have me live... no, this is neither my room nor my furniture, which, although on the verge of being discarded, still serves a purpose: my great purpose, my sole purpose." He throws a kiss to a pitcher of water and two glasses on a small wood cabinet of drawers with chipped glass knobs, and throws another kiss to the worn brown leather bag near the cabinet, the kind of bag doctors carry to connive the sick.

"Your *Voscenza* is planning a massive renovation in the North wing. And as you see in this most forsaken corner of the manor, an extension, as well. In any case, a small fortune I should say for such an undertaking." He points to the sky and lets out a laugh. "We shall have to make due *sans* ceiling, *sans* roof. My apologies. And my apologies for the squalor to which you are not...no, I do believe you are *quite* accustomed. The servants neglect this room," he swipes his hand 'cross the top of the square table, his fingers blackened with candle soot, "and I could not be more pleased. I enjoy its privacy. One day, it may be nothing more than a sitting room. If that be the case, what do you suppose you and I shall do here?"

She points to a small chair with white silk covering ripped from its low back, there, in the corner of the room.

"Very good. My, you are an intelligent creature. That is precisely what we shall do. We shall *sit*. However, before sitting..." He takes out the jewel flask from his vest. "As this is customary at the manor, and, I, for one, would be most offended if you did not deign to..." He passes her the flask. She leaps behind the small white chair. "Now, Grace, listen carefully. I act on the Duke of Bronte's behalf and on behalf of his son. You do not wish me to discharge you from the manor for your insolence, do you?"

She jumps up and pats the knife in her apron. "I got to stay."

"Yes, indeed, Grace, you *got to stay*. Now, come here."

She shuffles to the surgeon. "I got to do my deed."

"And, I, mine. There, like this, now hold it to your lips."

She puts her nose to the flask and smiles.

"Yes, Grace, it's sweet, and to savor it, you must throw your head back and swallow quickly. Do not be shy. There is more. There is always more to satisfy us."

She presses her lips tight and takes a sip. "Finucchina." She shudders.

He pushes his tongue in his cheek and pats the blue shawl. "Oh, my, you *are* an herbalist." He holds the bottom of the flask and tips it up. "Now, don't be clumsy. Hold it securely. Yes, you do, indeed, taste fennel...but there are other components to the *liqueur* of which you and all your fellow magicians know nothing."

"Finucchina, 'a z'a Vincenza says, washes clean the body smells, but I don't like..."

"And wormwood shall wash clean all a peasant's inhibitions. Drink, Grace. Remember, this is our custom. You do not wish to be unpleasant at the manor...do you?"

She shakes her head. The surgeon presses the flask to her lips. With each swig he makes her take, he whispers tale 'on tale of his life, a happy life in Lundra 'til *they* filed charges, 'til the battles waged in court to clear his name, 'til the *savings and stipends* faded, 'til, "most painful of all," he cries out, "the title bestowed by Her Royal Majesty confiscated like a debtor's goods!"

The flask drops from the girl's hand. The surgeon smiles when she pulls at her throat and the flesh on her cheeks.

"I suspect you are quite done. Ladies are accustomed to drinking this liqueur with a silver spoon. Watch and learn." He empties the flask in the glass on the small wood cabinet of drawers. He tugs at two chipped glass knobs, rattling the first drawer 'til it opens. He grabs for a spoon, the shape of a leaf, with holes cut in it. "One must not forgo the sugar." He rattles the last drawer and reaches inside for a small white cone. "One of the many small sugar loaves Cook has yet to miss." He unlocks the worn brown leather bag and rummages through the dull metal instruments 'til he pulls out a small tool with a handle and a blade, more a chisel than a knife. With it, he struggles to break off a piece of sugar from the small white cone. "Are you watching? Are you learning?" he asks the girl, her mouth open, her eyes shut tight. "The sugar, neatly cubed or, as the case may be, crudely chiseled, is placed on the spoon, thusly. And the spoon is balanced on the rim of the glass." Slow, slow, he drips water on the sugar. Slow, slow, the water and the sugar drip through the holes in the spoon. Like magic, what is green in the glass turns white, a thick white liquid like what pours out of the sick in Bronti. "Voilà." He takes a swig. "No need for you to indulge in this manner. You are a peasant, of hardy stock, not delicate, by any means. You do not need such intermediaries, so to speak. You drink like a man, an addicted man, a man who knows no hope for tomorrow."

She falls to the ground. She holds out her hands and tries to make a fist. Her fingers fall open and graze the floor.

"Now, what is this?"

She pushes herself back up and swats the air.

"Are we about to engage in battle? For if we are, you shall lose. No, peasant girl. No battles this evening, that is, not on your part. I do believe you need to sit down." He pushes her back down. "Here, on the floor, where you belong. Sit. Good. Good. Like a good peasant girl. Now, let us see how good you are. Raise your skirt." He kicks her skirt up and kicks her hands that grab to pull it back down. "Good. Good. Your *Voscenza* believes you are a healer with a pure heart. He does not know you. I know you. Spread your legs. This is who you are."

I howl. At the sound of my mad cries, the girl shakes off the spell the best she can. She grabs hold of the white chair and pulls herself up. The surgeon kicks her ankles. She falls back down.

"Does that infernal howling frighten you?" He lets out a laugh through his nose, a snorting sound horses make when danger nears, but the surgeon, he howls, too, and he don't seem scared of nothing. "We are quite safe here. Be assured that wretched howling is the very least of your concerns." He looks down at the girl. "Yes, safe from all that is wild…except you. Now, be a good peasant girl and spread your legs. It is in your eyes, *peasant girl*. You are eager and most willing to perform tricks for us, tricks, some might deem, of an animal nature. However, such performances must wait until your *Voscenza* discovers you here, for he shall witness with his own eyes how brazen you were to wander through the manor and drink yourself into a stupor and, upon my shocking discovery, put *me* in compromise… You shall be disgraced, the one he holds in high regard. This, the first of many bitter disappointments, shall contribute to the unraveling of the fifth *great* Duke of Bronte. What say you now, Alec, *my little Duke*? Treat me like a common servant, will you? Dole me out a pittance of a stipend and even less respect? We shall see who is compromised in the end. First, peasant girl, we must begin with you. I shall call for your *Voscenza*, and he shall learn the truth about you and all your magic ways." He throws the glass, the thick white liquid splattering the wall. "Charlatan! Whore!"

*

The Devil's gone. I leap on the window's ledge and howl, but the girl, she hears none of my pleas, curled on the floor the way she is, spittle beading at her mouth. With no thought of traps or danger, I slip in the room and crouch by her side. I look at her, so still and silent, her tongue hanging, a green froth rising from her nails. Curses to the poison that makes a home in one so pure! I hold her fingers to my mouth and suck out the poison coursing through her and spit it out. Her fingers curl. A good sign. I bless her, and, quick, I am gone. Slow, slow, her hands make a fist. She opens them and throws them in the air and spreads her fingers wide. She crawls to the door. But what is this? A drop of poison, bright like a king's green jewel, shines in the corner of her lips. She licks it clean, and, in a flash, leaps up, tearing at the blue shawl like it's on fire, her eyes, wild, shining like a demon's.

Wild, the girl races through nearby rooms, wielding Alfiu's knife, turning over tables, slashing chairs, smashing oil lamps. The crashes and booms could frighten anyone, but the surgeon's feet galloping up the great stairway and the surgeon's fists pounding at the Duchinu's door, now that could stir the dead.

*

The Duchinu tugs at his dark grey vest buttoned high on the chest and pats the gold and pearl pin on his grey tie. Like his shirt, his cheeks are white. So, too, his lips. Slumping at the door, eye to eye with the surgeon, he shouts in a weak voice, "Dr. Gale, if I hadn't opened the door…in another minute, you might have knocked it down! You should be aware by now that we strive for decorum at the manor. Obviously, your headache has subsided…"

"My deepest regrets," the surgeon near sings out, "that I could not labor shoulder to shoulder with you this morning…"

"That which needed to be accomplished for my peasants was, indeed, accomplished…with or without your services…and, now…"

"As the day progressed, my headache…no, I shall not burden you with tedious details. Let us say it was a miracle wrought by the peasants' Madonna of the Annunciation or some such saint." He holds out his hands, turns 'round, and bows. "My lord, gaze upon your rejuvenated gentleman." He kicks up his legs and lets out a shout.

"Dr. Gale! Decorum!"

"My lord, come with me," he bites away a smile, "and you shall see which of your guests exhibits decorum and which does not. But, first, a bit of legend to set the mood."

"Perhaps another evening…"

"Your father, the fourth great Duke of Bronte, would proffer me the courtesy."

"Very well."

"Very well, indeed." The surgeon takes his arm and leads him down the first step. "I assure you. It shall not disappoint. You, no doubt, are familiar with the legend of the bridge over the Simeto River."

The Duchinu holds on to the wall and takes in a breath. "I am not quite…"

"I shall refresh your memory. It is a favorite among your peasants. An Arab…"

"An *Arab?*"

"Yes, a giant of an Arab straddling the Simeto."

The Duchinu sits on the step, his head in his hands. "The Simeto?"

"Alec, whatever is the matter? Yes, of course, the Simeto River…the Arab who shows the hapless Bronte peasants where to build the bridge…"

The Duchinu reaches for the surgeon's arm and tugs at his sleeve. "Dr. Gale…"

"Oh, Alec, the bridge!" He hoists the Duchinu up and leads him down the stairway. "Come, we're wasting time…"

"Dr. Gale, I am not feeling well…"

"You shall feel much better when you see how legends come to life… replete with legs astride."

The Duchinu stops, holding tight to the wall. "I am sure the source of my discomfort is this unrelenting heat. I suspect it shall pass when the evening is upon us."

"Alec, one would never believe you a suffering man. You, the picture of health. Now, quickly, come with me before our very own *legend…*" The surgeon looks up, but, quick, pulls back. "Well, now, what do we have here?" He throws his face in the Duchinu's chest and fixes his eyes on the gold and pearl pin. "What a charming cravat pin…a gift from Your Royal Highness, I presume?"

The Duchinu slips his hand over the jewel. "A memento of our dear Prince Albert."

"The Queen must think very highly of you."

He shakes his head. "Of my father."

"And you have seen to borrow it this evening. Look at you." The surgeon eyes the Duchinu up from the bright white wings of his collar down to his shiny black shoes. "A veritable Prince of Wales. Perhaps your tailor can spare a few hours next week to sew a pair of pinstriped pants for me, as well."

"Dr. Gale…"

"No, perhaps not. Nonetheless, in regard to the Prince, the Duke informs me Her Majesty's son may soon be a guest at the manor, and, then, you must urge your tailor to sew not merely a pair of pinstriped pants for me, but a waistcoat, as well. Of a bright color, if it pleases my lord."

The Duchinu reaches for a fine linen handkerchief in his pocket, wipes his brow and makes his way back to his room. "Lucien," he holds out his arms and waits for the surgeon to help him with his long black jacket, "you and my father correspond on many subjects of which I am not privy."

"I may be your companion," the surgeon pinches the fine cloth of the Duchinu's jacket, "but I remain the Duke's *confidant*. Now, enough of fashion. Come with me, Alec. You shall be astonished at the legend which awaits you."

The Duchinu breaks free of the surgeon's hold. "Your legend shall have to wait, Dr. Gale."

"Alec, it cannot wait much longer."

"Then, another legend at another date. Come, Lucien, let us adjourn to the drawing room."

"Yes, in the North wing!" The surgeon races down the great stairway.

The Duchinu holds his belly and presses out the air, but what comes out is none but a whisper. "I should hardly expect to entertain my guests in a room which has not as yet been fully constructed." He waves his hand at a nearby room, east of the great stairway. "I've been informed Joseph has been waiting for some time."

"But, Alec, the *legend*..."

"Please, Lucien. No more talk of legends. I must greet my guests."

*

Cushioned chairs crowd what the Duchinu calls his *drawing room*. In red and yellow and green cloth with high and low backs, cushioned chairs crowd the corners and the heart of the room, and, alone in the drawing room, the carter takes his turn sitting in all of them. At the threshold, the Duchinu lets out a fake cough. The carter jumps up and bows, and, quick, when the surgeon pours him a drink of a pale yellow liquid, the carter stomps his foot and sings out a tale of a Bruntiszi peasant and his neighbor's wife. The Duchinu drops his head, but the surgeon lets out a loud laugh, so loud that who can hear the noise the girl makes down the stairs? Not the cousin in her room. The girl, she's in the north, too, and the cousin got to hear all her ruckus, but, the cousin, her own loud sorrows in her heart, she's deaf to all the noise down the stairs. She sits on her bed, her hands clasped in prayer, her cheeks wet with tears.

'Neath the cousin's room, the girl throws over chairs and rips down paintings of mountains and seas and slashes wall coverings with fancy designs, the color of wine. In the drawing room up the stairs in the south, the carter, in his high girlish voice, sings out another tale, this one of a Bruntiszi wife and a priest. The surgeon laughs louder. 'Neath the cousin's room, the girl slumps in a soft green chair and clutches at her throat. In the drawing room, the carter says he got one more tale to tell. The Duchinu, he slumps, too, in a red high back chair, but the surgeon standing over him, he laughs louder still, and his laugh, like Mungibellu's fiery lava, snakes down the long, blue hallway and down the great stairway, burning in the ears of the cousin and the girl. They slap their ears and cry out, "Leave me be!" 'Neath the cousin's room in the north, the girl jumps up and yanks a thick gold frame from the wall and slashes the painting of a plump woman with a lace veil and a small crown on top. Up the great stairway in the drawing room in the south, men toast each other and tell tales 'til the carter tells the last, of a foreigner that found the Bruntiszi so dull and stupid... The surgeon don't wait for the end of the tale. He slaps the carter's back and lets out such a thundering laugh that, in the north and the south and up and down the great stairway, all the tables and lamps and chairs shake.

At the sound of the surgeon's laugh, the cousin grabs the small doll in the bright yellow dress with ruffles edged in red and flings it 'cross the room. At the sound of the surgeon's laugh, the girl spits 'til her mouth goes dry, ridding her small body, I pray, of the last of the poison. She throws the knife back in her apron, slams the door behind her and runs. She slaps her ears and races past rooms in the north and rooms in the west, all with candles flickering. She races past the great stairway and races to the east. When the surgeon's laugh trails away, she grabs her chest and crouches at the threshold of a dark and solemn room. The room got more chairs than I ever seen 'round a table longer than I ever seen, a room with walls of dark wood and windows with curtains drawn, a dark room with candles that branch from long stems, and, hanging on the wall, oil lamps waiting to be lit.

On the table in the dark, four servant girls pile dishes up high. Small dishes, round dishes, dishes on the side of dishes, in blue and red and all with the Nelson coat of arms. They set down the glasses…too many of them to count and for what? Signori 'nglisi, the English Gentlemen, they got to be dry a lot to drink from all their glasses before they ever quench a thirst.

The girl crawls to a red velvet chair with a high back and carvings on the armrests. She slumps in it and lets out a sigh. Two servant boys light the candles and the lamps, and that's when the blue apron servant girls eye the girl. "The healer," they whisper and bow and, quick, grab her 'neath the arms and hoist her back up. They drag her behind a chair just like the one she sat in, but not, they say, at the head of the table. "Wait. Wait." They hoist her up again and point to the threshold each time she tries to sit back down. "Not 'til Voscenza comes," they whisper. Where are the girl's thoughts? She got to know. No matter how we hate them, it's always in our blood: we got to wait for our *betters* to sit.

The girl shakes her head, her red hair flying, and struggles to sit back down. The two servant boys, their mouths open wide, they run out shouting prayers and cursing demons. But the four servant girls, they gulp and gulp, their eyes fixed on the red hair that snakes over their leather shoes 'til they can't gulp no more, and the shouts break free.

"*Ahi!*"

"*Ahi!*"

"*Ahi!*"

"*Ahi!*"

In the drawing room, the surgeon toasts the carter and begs for one more tale. They laugh and toast and pay no mind to the Duchinu that stumbles out the room and down the great stairway and happens on the servant girls, kicking out their legs, shouting and crying. He holds tight to the high back of a red velvet chair. "How dare you conduct yourselves in such a manner!"

"Voscenza…Voscenza…" The round face servant girl cups her mouth and points to the red hair 'round her shoes.

With the back of his hand, he wipes his brow and cheeks. "Grace… Signurina, land of hair," he whispers and throws a look at the servant girls. They bow and run 'round like chickens in and out the room.

In the drawing room, the surgeon looks 'round. "Hmmmm," and rubs the scars on his cheek. "Perhaps, Joseph, our host's absence indicates that dinner is served." He slaps the carter's back for "tales well told" and slaps it a hundred times and more all the way down the great stairway and all the way to the room in the east with the red velvet chairs. When he eyes the Duchinu and the girl, his hand drops from the carter's back. He rushes to their side. "Grace," he whispers in her ear, "we meet again." He curls his fingers like he's holding a glass and throws his head back like he's taking a swig from it. She cups her nose and mouth.

"Lucien," the Duchinu says in a weak laugh, "I believe you dabbed on too much cologne this evening."

"Next time," the surgeon says in an even weaker laugh, "I shall dole out the right amount of liquid. Would you like that, Grace?"

She clutches her throat and whimpers.

"I believe what Grace would like is to sit. Let us dispense with rank and order this evening. Allow me to show you to your chair, here, to my right."

The cousin stands at the door, pale and silent, the lilac ruffles of her dress crowding the threshold. "Ah, Elizabeth, please come in," the Duchinu waves his hand, "and sit to my left. Dr. Gale next to our delicate Elizabeth and Joseph next to Grace. I suppose by her early arrival, Grace has indicated to us that it is time to dine. The sun is setting, and, as neither my father nor Mrs. John Sherwood is present to tell us otherwise, let us further ignore protocol and dine at an earlier hour."

The cousin stretches out her jaw and shows all her teeth like all what she aches to do is smile, but there's no joy in her eyes. Through her teeth, she breathes out all what she got to say. "Alec, it is not quite seven."

"My delicate Elizabeth, an hour earlier or later is hardly of any consequence. We shall have our soup and wait for the other courses. Or shall we begin at the end and have our dessert first?" he asks with a tired laugh. "Grace shall, no doubt, enjoy 'a mustardda. At their celebrations, all the peasants clamor for it."

"'A mustardda? Alec, please do not tell me Cook has prepared that vile concoction. If she has, I shall scold her until the end of her days."

"Elizabeth, you shall do nothing of the kind. It is a sweet…"

"Of *prickly pears*! And you know the difficulty I've always experienced," she presses her fingers to her mouth, "the difficulty in digesting that dreadful fruit. Why the very thought of it renders my stomach queasy. And I...*I* do not clamor for it."

"It is for Grace," he whispers, breathing hard. "There are other sweets for you."

She shakes her head. With her eyes shut tight, she lets out a quivering sigh. "Alec, I am at a loss for words."

"Elizabeth, it may be true that we celebrate your birthday this evening, nonetheless, we *do* have guests. Come now, there is no reason to look so forlorn. I assure you the evening shall be replete with surprises."

The cousin leans in and whispers in the surgeon's ear. "If you are true to your word, Dr. Gale, some surprises, I suspect, shall unnerve even the lord of the manor."

The Duchinu smiles at the girl. "Elizabeth, may I remind you that you might still be suffering if not for Grace."

"Never! Dr. Gale would have tended to all my needs." She waves her hand so broad in the air that she near slaps the Duchinu's face.

He grabs her hand and presses it on the table near a small dish. "Calm yourself," he whispers, but nothing he does or says can hold it down. It springs back up like a fat frog and springs back down on the fine woven cloth covering the table. "Elizabeth, this behavior...is hardly..."

He sits and swipes his hand 'cross his brow. "Please, everyone, take your seat. Now, Elizabeth, no more of this. I implore your assistance in showing our Sicilian guests an Englishman's hospitality. Elizabeth, the visitor's book."

She puffs out her cheeks and pushes herself back up and reaches for a brown leather book in a drawer in a small cupboard. She hands it to the Duchinu and holds out a small well of ink. He dips the pen and presses it on a white page edged with gold. "Like this, Grace, here, as a place of honor," and passes her the book.

The cousin yanks the pen away. "Now, this is too much! She is not an invited guest. She is merely *admitted* to our dinner."

The Duchinu holds out his hand. The cousin drops the pen in his palm. "She *is* a guest. And she shall be my guest at *Villa Falconara*, as well."

"Our villa in Taormina?"

"Her services shall be indispensable."

"She shall, indeed, be of service as your servant, but she shall never be your guest. My people shall see to that."

"*Your* people? Not another word, Elizabeth. As for you, Grace, here, on this line, at the very least, make an *X*. Joseph, be of some assistance. Excellent. Thus, all shall know…"

The girl looks up with a tight smile on her face. "And Mamma, too, got to know that I come to the Castle to do the deed."

"Yes, Grace, all shall know that you are a wonderful healer." He grabs hold of a glass, sips the water, chokes and near throws it out. "How I wish I could enjoy the meal with you, Grace, and show you my proper gratitude. However, my appetite has somewhat waned and…"

"By contrast," the surgeon says with a booming laugh, "mine is insatiable." And, with that, he talks of top hats and Lundra and the Queen's son, the young Prince of Wales, all while he wets his lips when a servant girl fills his top dish with a minestra, a water more than a soup, with a few thin slices of greens floating on top.

The girl's dish is the last one they fill. She raises it to her mouth, but, quick, the carter snatches it. "What are you doing?" he whispers through his long, brown teeth.

"*Zafattiari*," the cousin says with a wide smile. "Joseph, is this not the word for ill-bred creatures in your language?"

The Duchinu looks up, the girl's dish still shaking in the carter's hands. Quick, he mutters how the girl dropped her spoon, and, quick, he forces out a long laugh now that the surgeon comes to the end of his own tale of *a tenor and his protégée*.

Two servant girls take away the top dishes. Two others bring in what the cousin says is "the fish course." There, on the serving dish, a cut of baked fish sprawls on a bed of curled greens. The cousin says the greens are garnish. "Zafattiari!" she calls the girl and slaps her hand when the girl scoops the greens up in her palms and throws them in her dish. The Duchinu pays no mind to nothing but a small round bread on a tray of breads and cheeses that the round face servant girl, still kicking her legs free of the phantom hair, dropped on the table in haste.

"Cheese, bread and butter are usually served with the salad course. However, by the likes of tonight's confusion, Grace, we are dining 'a la bohemienne.'" He spreads the round bread with what he calls a sweet cream butter and puts it on a small dish for the girl.

"It's not like Blasiu's bread," she breaks it in small pieces, jabbing at the inside. "It's not brown and blessed by the sun."

"She would like the bread brown," the cousin whispers to the surgeon. "Let her spread her dirty feet across it. It shall, thus, be rendered more black than brown and, verily, to her liking."

"Elizabeth, guard yourself," the surgeon whispers back, "and allow me to direct the discourse."

She shuts her eyes and takes in a breath.

"Now, Joseph," the surgeon says, "what do you think of the swordfish this evening? Fresh from the Ionian Sea. I would have preferred a thick piece of tuna from the Mediterranean, but it is, nonetheless, quite delicious, do you not agree?"

The carter nods. That's all what he needs to push himself up, take in a breath, stomp his foot and mark his own rhythm like he got it in him to sing out a tale of an epic hero.

"Long ago, there lived a boy named *Colapesci* that loved the sea. He spent his days swimming and paying no mind to his chores on the land. One day, he woke up and what did he find? His fingers all webbed and his sides sprouting fins. A happier boy you never seen. He said good-bye to his tearful Mamma and plunged in the water to live in the sea. But, soon, he took it 'on himself to find the end of the sea. He swam, but the end of the sea was far, and he grew tired. That's when he seen a big and angry fish. He swam 'round the fish 'til the fish gone mad and swallowed him whole. And the fish swam with Colapesci in his belly, and Colapesci swam inside the fish to the end of the sea. That's when Colapesci cut the belly of the fish wide open and climbed out. A happier soul you never seen, ready to start his life at the end of the sea."

The carter bows and sits back down. The Duchinu raises his head and smiles. "A fine rendition, Joseph, although the tale takes on a more colorful permutation in Naples, *Napuli*, as you say. A king figures prominently as does a treasure chest at the bottom of the sea. All which makes for a somewhat more interesting folktale."

"This is better," the girl says. "Colapesci was smart when he got the fish to do all the swimming for him. That way he saved his strength for when he used the knife." She grabs a knife from near her dish and holds it high. The carter slaps it away. She grabs it, again. He slaps it away, again. Quick, he lets out a fake cough, but all for nothing, for none paid mind to the knife or the girl or the carter. Through all the carryings on, the Duchinu, his head down, he been wiping his brow. The cousin, her head down, she been wiping her eyes. And the surgeon, his head down, he been gorging on his fish. He's still gorging 'til there's none left in his dish.

"Mastru Nonziu," the girl whispers, "eat 'til your belly moans. I got a real good knife to use when the time's right." With that, she grabs the Duchinu's knife and scoops out the sweet cream butter from the warm bread. "The cream Blasiu makes," she licks the blade, "is better."

The cousin lets out a soft cry. "Elizabeth," the Duchinu whispers, "she is a bright girl, although, I agree, lacking in social graces. Nonetheless, under your tutelage, she shall learn our ways." He turns to the girl and smiles. "Grace, I intended to ask you before," the Duchinu pats his wet neck and the wet wings on the collar of his shirt, "when did you make your acquaintance with the shepherd boy?"

The carter blows out a breath and leans back in his chair. "Answer Voscenza, Mamsella."

"He nourished me and gave me shelter when I was lost."

"He is a good boy," the Duchinu says, "although quite unusual. The other shepherds play their bagpipes and seek each other's company for music and conversation. Yet Blaise has taken it upon himself to withdraw from the others to live a solitary life. Nonetheless, I have heard him play his own charming instrument. It is quite moving in its simplicity. Yes, Blaise...Blaise plays the flute much like a lone and melancholic shepherd of the classics would in an ideal bucolic setting...a..."

The surgeon raises his glass of wine. "A *Bacchus* or a *Pan*?"

"Dr. Gale," the Duchinu grabs the cloth from his lap and wipes the beads of water 'neath his chin, "Blaise has none of the attributes of your god of wine or of his son. He is a good boy. He helps all God's creatures find their way in life."

The cousin mashes a thick piece of fish. "Some of God's creatures would be better off lost," and throws a look 'cross the table at the girl.

"Elizabeth, I beg to differ. His sheep cross natures, that, I grant you. Their appearance may frighten you, but their milk is quite delicious, and Blaise has been known to make a wonderful ricotta from it."

"But that hideous one…" her eyes still fixed on the girl.

"The ewe died last year. According to Blaise, she left us a most perfect lamb and quite an intelligent creature at that."

"Delicious, too," the surgeon says.

"That shall be determined tomorrow evening, Dr. Gale."

The surgeon pats his belly. "Tomorrow, indeed, when the Vice Consul and his wife are the manor's guests."

"Precisely. Let us pray, by tomorrow evening, my appetite returns."

The girl pulls at the carter's sleeve. "Mastru Nonziu, what are they planning?"

"*Sst…sst.* It's nothing, Mamsella. There's always great confusion when Castle folk speak our tongue. Now, eat. You'll never get a better meal."

The servant girls race from the kitchen and carry large silver trays with round covers. They line them 'long the table by the wall. When they throw off the covers, the smell of crisp brown meat makes my mouth water. I want to howl and scare them all away. I want to leap on the long table and rip at the plump bodies of birds and animals. I want to gnaw on each last piece of flesh and bone and muscle. But I got to howl for good, and only for good, and only for the girl. That's what Alfiu whispers 'cross my heart. And, so, I watch the trays come and go. I don't howl. I don't scare them all away.

"Ah, the main course," the surgeon wets his lips. "What do we have here? Some mutton cutlets, braised beef, and, no doubt, the shepherd boy's lamb, roasted to perfection. My mistake…lamb is tomorrow's fare."

The girl throws a look at the surgeon. He smiles and pats the cousin's hand.

"Grace, have you ever tasted lamb? It is positively succulent. We shall dine on it tomorrow."

The girl leans in, her hands on the table, and pushes herself up. "Lamb? Blasiu's lamb?"

"You have to cook it first."

"I know meat got to be cooked." She stomps her foot. "I don't want no worms from raw meat, not like your kind gets. But if I get the worms, *I* can cure them!"

The cousin jumps up and slaps her face. "Zafattiari! You come to the manor in your bare feet! You come and… Apologize immediately to both of us!"

The girl slumps in her chair. "Blasiu's lamb?"

The surgeon fixes his eyes on the girl. She fixes her eyes on him, too, like the two of them got caught in a spell, and the cousin, she's caught in the spell, too, for her eyes shine bright when the surgeon whispers to the girl, "Grace, shall I save a leg for you?"

The girl jumps up and kicks her feet. The blue slippers fly on the table and right in the cousin's dish. "Animal! Animals, the lot of you, to kill Blasiu's lamb!"

The cousin throws her face in the surgeon's chest. He opens his arms wide, and, quick, like the jaws of a mountain cat, they trap the cousin in. "Alec, lock up this wretched beast," the cousin whimpers. "Lock her in a cage with starving wolves so that they may…yes, may they tear her to shreds!"

The Duchinu lifts his eye patch, his wet, sorrowful eyes pleading for the girl the cousin curses. "Elizabeth, she is our guest. And it is our duty…"

The cousin breaks free of the surgeon's hold and pounds her fist on the table. "Duty!" She turns over her dish, pouring the slippers and cuts of meat in a big, round tray. "You disgusting peasant girl," she cries out, "put those slippers back on your dirty feet before, duty or not, I throw you in that cage myself!"

"Grace, Elizabeth, calm yourselves."

"Voscenza," the girl whispers, "don't kill the lamb. Blasiu's like her Papà…he *loves* her." She presses her lips in a big *O* and lowers her face 'til her mouth near brushes the back of the Duchinu's hand. "Voscenza," she kisses his hand, "don't kill Blasiu's lamb…I beg you…"

The surgeon throws his lap cloth down. "At long last, Alec!" He kisses his own hand and waves it in the air. "Behold your glorious victory!"

The Duchinu pulls his hand away. "Grace, please, put your slippers on. You see I am not myself this evening. All this excitement…you must excuse me but I must rest before the pyrotechnic display."

"Voscenza, I beg you."

"Calm yourself, Grace." He points to the slippers. She picks them up and throws them back on her feet. "As for the lamb, you have my word."

"Dear Alec," the cousin whispers, "and should *duty* compel you to dishonor it…"

"Elizabeth, please." He stands, grabbing the table and breathing out each word. "I…am…not…well."

The surgeon shuffles behind the Duchinu's chair. With bare a tap on his shoulders, the surgeon pushes him back down. "A moment, Alec, before you take leave of us. I have news regarding your beloved peasants."

He raises his eyes and smiles. "Good news?"

"Old news. And, yes, good news if you are not a peasant which, certainly, you are not, although, at times…"

"Dr. Gale!"

"Very well…to the point. Do you recall when your peasants killed your father's men?"

"You scavenge too deeply into the past."

"A moment, please. As I was saying, when they killed your father's men in…1865…"

"Eighteen hundred sixty."

"Bravo, Alec. 1860. Bravo."

"Lucien, the point…"

"You prove a point, although an ancillary one: there are certain events in life one must never forget. However, there is a greater purpose to my speech. In June of the following year, an agreement was drafted…"

"The Transaction."

The surgeon's teeth dig in his lip and bite away a smile. "Bravissimo. The Transaction of 1861," and bows his head, "which called for half of the Duchy's forest and a large portion of its lava lands to be returned to the Commune. *Success* the peasants might have thought," the surgeon leans over, his lips near brushing the Duchinu's ear, "but your father's Notaries were clever and arranged for the peasants to have all the land they *rightfully* deserved, that which was hardly suitable for cultivation."

The Duchinu pushes the surgeon back the best he can. "Old news, indeed, which only serves to irritate my patience."

"Then, I shall be brief. It has come to my attention that seventeen years ago, a man and his wife planted on a portion of the lava land they did not possess at the time." He takes out the small branch from his vest and waves it in the air. "Their crops have been thriving, and, good news—disastrous, if you are the peasant couple—the trees should bloom this year which should make for a plentiful harvest."

The Duchinu holds tight to the armrests and leans in. "Joseph, have you heard any news of this in Bronte?" The carter points to his throat and lets out a fake cough. "Never mind, Joseph. Dr. Gale, what can possibly grow there?"

"Now, I suspect, they worked very hard. Indeed, I shall give them that. The crop which flourishes is none other than the *green gold* the Queen finds so tasty in her cakes and which you so obligingly send her on an annual basis."

"Pistachios?"

"Pistachios, indeed."

"There has always been a small grove of pistachio trees…"

"And you receive revenue from them, small though it may be. My point is you have received nothing from this man and his wife who have worked your land. They cheated you all these years."

"But the land…"

"Alec, the land was not theirs at the time of the Transaction. Now that their crop is ready to harvest, they shall cheat you from your profit. The field guards are close to determining their identity." The surgeon taps the branch on the table 'til the girl looks up. "If Joseph has no idea what is transpiring in the town, perhaps Grace knows something about this crime."

"You talk of crimes?" She jumps up and points to the table by the wall where the serving trays burst with meat. "I know the crimes of the ones gorging themselves day to night while the poor and the good starve. I know what I seen on my Mamma's bare table. I know what she ate! And I know how thankful I always been to the man what brought us wheat and a paper cone filled with green…"

The carter, red like Mungibellu's fire, he pushes her back down. "The girl knows nothing. She rants of this and that, but she knows nothing."

The cousin's head jerks back. A broad smile stretches 'cross her mouth like this is all what she been waiting for. "By the look in her eyes, Alec, I suspect Grace knows a great deal. However, at the moment, I am more troubled by Dr. Gale's revelations. A peasant confiscating your land…that is, indeed, a *crime*, is it not? Alec, is it not?"

"I…I…" The Duchinu slumps in his chair. "Lucien, please, I need your assistance."

"You shall have it…immediately. I shall inform the Notaries. An arrest shall be forthcoming…"

"Lucien, please, I need your assistance to my room…"

"At once, Alec. Elizabeth, your cousin is fatigued. Although a grave disappointment, we must postpone the after-dinner delights until tomorrow."

The cousin shakes her finger. "No need for further festivities, Dr. Gale. This has proven to be a most memorable celebration…and a most memorable judgment day. Dr. Gale, I do believe the tablet floats!"

The Duchinu grips the armrests of the chair. He falls back down. "Elizabeth, I shall not hear of such amendments to our plans. As hostess this evening, please see to it that the conversations remain light, the courses remain constant, and our guests remain content until I return. Lucien, your arm."

*

On the new carriage road, a foreign cart with its painted panels and its cargo of shells travels past the solemn cypress trees 'til it comes 'on the iron gates and the South portico of the Castle. A wreath of flowers on her head and red feathers 'long her mane, the proud speckled mare pulling the cart stops at the lava cross soon that the tall stranger yanks on the reins and shouts *Jautu!* A few red feathers fall to the ground. The mare throws her ears back and grunts up a storm. The short stranger got no way out but to leap from the bench and stick the feathers back in.

"Someone got to help us unload," the tall one says. "Go find servants," he leaps from the cart, "or the Duchinu himself for all I care." The tall one, he lets out a yawn and leans back on the wheels. The weight of his body shakes the cart. This makes the rolled sheets of paper crackle…and rise…

Agata's face peeks out from 'neath a shell in the corner of the cart. The stranger drops to his knees. "Specter of the Castle, have mercy on me!"

I grab my belly and laugh. Is this the God-fearing prayer of the men from Rannazzu, the prayer they shout out through sealed walls and in black cathedrals? No wonder the Savior and Santu Giuseppi ignore the lot of them.

Agata shakes off the black powder and stands. She opens her mouth and breathes in the warm night air, her black jewel eyes darting 'round, taking in the Castle the way Colapesci took in all his new surroundings at the end of the sea.

*

In the room with the long table and the red velvet chairs, the servant girls pour more wine in the carter's glass and dish out green peas and more roasted meat. Their large spoons and forks clink a happy tune. That's what the carter tells them each time they fill his dish. And this nonsense tune of forks and spoons, it plays on 'til the girl stands up and yanks the forks and spoons away.

"*Sst…sst…*listen…you hear his cries?"

"Who cries?" the carter asks, his mouth stuffed with dark meat.

"Mastru Nonziu, outside the Castle, he cries in pain."

The cousin wipes the corners of her mouth. "Perhaps the girl hears her own stomach crying for sustenance other than bread and sweet cream butter."

"It's not the girl's belly," the carter says. "Look at her. She hears something. She knows something."

"She knows nothing. Your *Voscenza* should want us to finish our meal. As hostess this evening, I must insist you do so. If, indeed, someone calls in distress, Dr. Gale shall attend to him shortly."

"The man needs us!" The girl jumps up and races out the door, knocking over her chair and the cakes in fancy plates on the table by the wall. She rushes past the great stairway to the South courtyard, the carter, a piece of warm lemon cake hidden in his lap cloth, and the cousin, pinching her lilac collar, trailing far behind.

*

There, at the foot of the lava cross, the tall stranger cradles his own body and sobs that the Devil's hand's in this one. The girl pries his arms open and whispers a comfort prayer.

The cousin points to the carter's lap cloth and holds out her hand. He stuffs the cake in his mouth and passes the cloth to the cousin. She shakes it at the tall stranger. "Now, wipe away your tears and tell us of what madness you speak."

"The eyes…the bloody shirt!" He grabs the cloth and throws it over his face. "The specter heralds the end of my days!" He holds the girl tight. "Stay and pray with me!"

The cousin narrows her eyes and nears the cart. "My God, what form of being is this with hair and eyes so wild?"

The carter raises his eyes and spits out his warm lemon cake. "Glorious saints! Donna Elizabeth, that's no creature! A woman she is, a troubled Bruntiszi, but she means no harm."

The cousin slaps her chest. "No harm? Joseph, look at her!" She pulls the girl from the tall stranger's clutches. "Look at her, Grace! A filthy, horrid peasant like you! Look at her!"

The girl looks up and gasps at the sight of Agata in her torn bed clothes and Alfiu's bloody shirt, her cheeks smudged with black powder. "Nooooo!" She rushes to her Mamma. Agata pushes her down and throws out a nest of curses.

The carter pulls the girl back up and takes her in his arms.

"Grace!" The cousin yanks the girl away. "Once again, I suspect you know a great deal." She smiles and tightens her hold on the girl's shoulders. "Who is this peasant? A relative, perhaps? That should not surprise me."

The carter pulls the girl back in and hides her face 'neath his brown velvet jacket. "Donna Elizabeth, the girl is frightened of this woman. See how she hides. So, I got to speak for her…the girl knows nothing."

"My God! Joseph, look!" The cousin shakes her finger at Agata, Alfiu's once beautiful Agatuzza, rolling on the cobble stones, none but a donkey cleaning herself in the dirt. "What…in…heaven's…" The cousin grabs hold of the foreign cart and near faints straight away at the sight of Agata scratching her way to the carter's feet and suckling the laces of his boots.

*When the Devil flatters you, he wants your soul.*

There, in his worn grey vest, his worn grey pants and his spotted high black hat, the surgeon shuffles to the South courtyard and bows at the lava cross. "Imagine my surprise, Elizabeth. Upon my return to the dining room, the servant girls, in unusual frenzy, pled with me to rush outside and heal the wounded. Now that I am here, please enlighten me as to this fine Greek tragedy."

"Dr. Gale, pray tell, how fares my Alec?"

"He is resting."

"You saved his life."

He pinches the ruffles on her collar. "And is there yet another life which I must save?"

"Dr. Gale, please." The cousin points to the body curled at the carter's boots. "Look at that stowaway creature. The man who brought the pyrotechnics is distressed and, rightfully, so. And look at Grace, the way she wrings her hands and sobs. By her comportment, I believe Grace knows who the woman is."

The surgeon nears Agata, falls back and scuttles behind the lava cross. "If, verily, this creature is a woman. Stand your distance, Elizabeth. I must take a closer look." He kneels and peers in Agata's black eyes, the scars on his face, red flares of fire.

"Diavulu! Diavulu! Diavulu!" Agata throws up her hands and digs her nails in the surgeon's wounds.

"Good God!" He jumps back, patting the blood on his cheeks. "The peasant girl may claim not to know this woman, but I do and a more disturbed one you shall never find. The peasants give themselves license to be mad at *Carnivale*. This one has taken up the gauntlet and enjoys such madness throughout the year."

The cousin presses her hand on the surgeon's shoulder. "Dr. Gale, explain yourself, please."

"Her name is Saitta." He shakes off the last beads of blood from his face. "And I had hoped never to cross her mad soul again."

"Saitta? But that is Grace's name, Dr. Gale."

The girl breaks free from the carter's hold. "*She* is my…"

"She is…*clicca…clicca…*that is, it is…*clicca…clicca…*a most common name in Bronti. Donna Elizabeth, I know the girl never met *clicca…clicca…* another Saitta." He snatches the girl back and tightens his grasp. "*Sst…sst…* Stay silent, Mamsella, or you bring more sorrow to your Mamma. All what happens now, be good and silent."

"Joseph, when I first arrived in Sicily, I journeyed to Bronte. It is not so grand a village that one might not encounter another with the same last name."

"I apologize, Donna Elizabeth. My English…"

"We are speaking Sicilian."

"Sì, but I am not from the girl's town. Now and again, I suffer confusion of the words. I intended to say that she is a distant relation, but her Mamma, a great woman, has kept the girl sheltered from such elements as you see before you."

"Is this true, Grace?"

The girl looks up at the sky, at the islands of grey and pink clouds and the soft red glow behind the great mountains. She pulls on the carter's ear. "The heavens give me no sign. Mastru Nonziu, what do I say?"

"Bite the truth, Mamsella," he whispers back, "and speak the little that brings no harm to your Mamma. I see it in her eyes. Donna Elizabeth's ready to open her bag of wind. Let her talk. Let the surgeon talk, too. You and me, we got to stay silent." He throws a look at Agata, back at his feet, a suckling lamb finding calm and peace once more in the laces of his boots. "Silent, Mamsella, like your Mamma."

The girl sinks in the carter's arms. "It's all the truth what Mastru Nonziu tells you. My Mamma is a *great* woman."

"Very well. Let us excavate the truth. Dr. Gale, what did this woman do?"

"Where shall I begin? During that wretched 1860 revolt, the woman's husband killed a most indispensable man in the Duke's employ. A Notary, if I am not mistaken. Well, when the Italian general heard of this, the woman's husband, after a hasty trial, was shot. Either she was not aware of the outcome or merely refused to accept the truth.

"In those days, the Duke enjoyed the services of a doorkeeper. One evening, when this doorkeeper had taken ill, Alec's father urged me to come to his aid. As you may or may not know, I owed the Duke of Bronte my life and would have done anything for him. I still would. And, so, I stayed with the doorkeeper at his post and listened to his murmuring nonsense through the night and morning (a bit of nausea from one too many drinks, I'm afraid, and nothing more serious) 'til a frantic knock on the door disturbed his rantings. I unlocked it. Before my eyes, a rather beautiful peasant girl held out a basket of eggs. 'Please, I got to see my maritu. He got to be hungry now.' The doorkeeper awoke from his stupor. 'He got no use for eggs,' he shouted, 'not with two holes in his head!' 'No! No! No!' she cried. 'Don't kill him! If you take away my maritu, you take away my ruler!'"

"Ruler?" The cousin lets out a small laugh. "Was he heir to the Duchy?"

"Elizabeth, she was an ignorant peasant. Nonetheless, I took pity on the girl. I told her to return the following day, and I would do all in my power..."

"To help her, Dr. Gale?"

With the back of his hand, he strokes the cousin's cheek. "To help myself, my dear. True, I took pity on the girl but I also perceived an opportunity for myself. I convinced her that I could restore her *ruler* to his proper throne. I instructed her to return each day at the allotted hour, when the morning bells tolled. There was such desperation in her eyes..."

"She must have been mad."

"Desperate. And desperation breeds passion. Each day I sent the doorkeeper on a mission at the very hour she appeared with that small basket of eggs and her breasts heaving beneath her clasped shawl. She insisted upon seeing her husband in prison, begging in her desperate, passionate way, as though Alec's father had constructed a prison cell in the depths of the manor properly for him. *Go to the gallows if you are looking for a dead man,* I so wanted to shout, *or, better still, to that San Vito square, although that madman you call a husband has long since been carted away.* No, I did not shout such condemnations. On the contrary, I whispered my instructions for her to return. And, for my part, I waited…"

The cousin swallows hard. "Waited?"

"Yes, Elizabeth, until she spoke the words."

"I do not understand."

He waves his fingers near her face like he's tapping the keys of a pianu. "Pray tell me, you have not forgotten our tender moments in the music room? My dear Elizabeth," he wets his lips, "I suspect you understand my motives perfectly, yes, quite perfectly. Nonetheless, I shall elucidate. Each day, I told the girl her husband was not on the premises until the day she reached for my hand and spoke the words…yes, the words which I had long been anticipating. 'I got to do anything to see him…anything.' This she whispered and in such a fragile voice."

The cousin's eyes dart, here, at the girl curled in the carter's arms, there, at Agata curled at his feet. "She was grief-stricken, Dr. Gale."

He nods and rubs the scars on his face and neck. "And desperate. You do understand *desperate,* my dear. Nonetheless, the peasants say the wind can stop a man dead in his tracks, but if a woman takes on the ways of the wind, she can take a man's breath away. What recourse did I have? I am, after all, a man of flesh and blood."

She lowers her head, shuddering from the head to the toes. "Yes, Dr. Gale."

"That peasant girl could take away any man's breath."

Agata pulls the laces from the carter's boots. She holds them up and swings them in the air. "No, Signa Agata," the carter whispers, but she throws her head back and dangles them on her tongue. He holds tight to the girl. "Still and silent, Mamsella," he whispers. "For your Mamma's sake, still and silent."

The cousin waves her finger at Agata. "I shall never believe that creature could take away a man's breath."

"Elizabeth, she was *beautiful.* She was your age, perhaps a year or two younger, at the peak of her beauty. Her hair was dark with curls that cascaded about her face. And, her eyes…shining black…although, with time, they became quite lifeless. The rest is inconsequential."

"Anything you reveal shall not surprise me."

"No, I suspect it shall not. Very well. It is no secret women provide me with great pleasure." He nods to the cousin, his tongue licking his low lip. "She, I am reluctant to admit, was no exception. She came to the manor for weeks. Oh, how many Ave Marias or some such prayers she uttered before she lay by my side. Yet, shortly after saying two or three rosaries, and with the assistance of my *green fairy* which she guzzled like, well, a peasant, she was more than compliant with my desires and needs. Unavoidably, the question arose when she could see her husband. *Tomorrow, if I deem you a good little peasant girl* was always my response.

"After several weeks, when she could no longer tolerate my *green fairy*, I suspected she was with child. I intensified the charade and *confided* to her that no proud Sicilian man would ever raise another's child. Shortly after, she said she would somehow find a way to resolve the problem."

When he tells his tale, the surgeon stands straight and still. But, Agata, she grabs her belly and lets out a cry, like she knows his tongue and the vile truth it spills, the truth that her own madness hid from her for years. She throws the laces on the ground and pushes herself up, grabbing on to the carter's pants and the girl's blue dress 'til she stands eye to eye with the girl. She points to the girl's red hair and spits on the ground. She looks down at the dress, her dark eyes narrowing. "What's this?" With her round, red knuckles, she strokes the white apron and the laces of the bodice. She pulls the girl's chin and brings it to her face. "Who are you to wear my marriage dress?" She jumps back. "Figghia ru diavulu! That's who you are!" She throws herself on the girl. The carter pulls her off. "No Devil's child got to wear my marriage dress!" She claws at the sleeves. She claws at the apron 'til it's in tatters and the knife shines through and falls to the ground, clinking 'long the stones.

The carter pushes her down. There, with all eyes on Agata, the girl grabs the knife and slides it in her white cotton stocking. "Hold this woman down before she brings more harm!" the carter shouts. With the help of the short stranger, the tall one seizes her from behind and hoists her back in their cart.

"Let her be!" the girl cries.

"*Sst...sst.* She got to be safe with the foreigners," the carter whispers. "Mamsella, look away if you got to, but for all our sakes, be still and silent."

The cousin waves the back of her hand at Agata, crouched in the cart. "The poor woman."

"As I was saying before the *dramatic interlude*, the young widow wished to resolve the problem."

"Resolve?"

"And she did so in a most unspeakable way."

"Nooooo!"

"Yes, Elizabeth. She spoke to me of knitting or some such needles she lodged in private parts and herbal concoctions she drank like wine. I told her I did not deign to learn the rest. Truthfully, the farce had become too tiresome. And, so, my revelation was forthcoming: her husband had been dead for weeks, and I was done with her. 'Diavulu! Diavulu!' she cried and ripped strands of hair from her scalp."

Agata leans over the sides of the foreign cart and strokes the painted panels. "Good Orlannu. Brave Orlannu," she whispers.

"*Luu...ccii...eenn,*" the cousin's voice trembles, "she called you the Devil. Lucien, the Devil!"

"That is not the worst of it. She dug her nails into my skin and scratched my face from eye to chin. Not being satisfied, she dug those sharp weapons into my neck and deeply into my chest."

"Lucien, the Devil!"

"A wilder creature you could not imagine, a creature spouting curses and obscenities and claiming vengeance on the manor. Nonetheless, through all my discomfort, I must admit, I found that mad peasant girl quite enticing."

"Dr. Gale," she nibbles on the corner of her low lip, "you are certain this is the woman?"

"I am."

"Then, I have no choice. On behalf of the future Duke of Bronte, and as his future wife, the Duchess of Bronte..."

The surgeon bows. "You were saying, my Grace?"

"I shall punish her. Yes, I shall punish her. *Merum et mistum imperium.* And all such manner of *duty.* That is what distracts Alec so. The power of life and death and banishment. Why shall I not act...?"

"Perhaps a lady acting in her lord's behalf would not fare so well in England. However, we are far from that civilized society. It is your right, Elizabeth. Now, when shall she be shot?"

"No...she shall be banished from the manor before she does more harm to any of the Duke's guests."

"Naturally. However, if there is to be no firing squad, I should be more pleased if she were banished from the Duchy and, therefore, from my sight for all eternity."

"Dr. Gale, I must ponder the consequences of such a decision."

"And what might they involve?"

"Not what...but whom. I must consider Alec and his father and do my utmost to keep these small matters from their knowledge."

"You do well to keep *all* matters from their knowledge." He pinches her cheek. A pink mark rises there. She rubs it 'til the flesh is raw. "Tut, tut." He lets out a laugh. She narrows her eyes. He flicks his head this way and that and grabs her chin. "Elizabeth, a thought. By chance, are you contemplating banishment for me, as well? If you are, I should have no recourse but to divulge your schemes, your deceits, your ..."

"Shhhh...please, Dr. Gale."

"Your *manipulations...*"

"Please...please..."

"No, dear Elizabeth, I am not banished. And *you* have learned a valuable lesson. A peasant or her noble complement," he takes off his spotted hat and bows, "is always aware of a man's intentions and if she should gain some advantage from them, more than willing to satisfy."

*

"Diavulu! Diavulu!" Agata cries out in the cart. The carter, he heard all what the surgeon and the cousin said in their tongue and ours, too. His wide eyes and his open mouth tell me he made sense of all what they said, but what can he do? He takes the girl's hands and sobs in them.

"*Sst…sst*, Mastru Nonziu," the girl whispers at his chest. "You said, 'still and silent,' and I been good, but look at you. Your body shakes, and you sob so loud."

Who can fault him? Bella, bella, we called Agata all those years ago, her, in the blue marriage dress with the dark hair combed and shining. Our beautiful Agatuzza. What is she now but a creature tearing at Alfiu's blood-stained shirt and ripping out her wild hair? Who wouldn't sob at such a sight?

Agata thrashes 'round the cart, her hands clasped in prayer. Who does she pray to? What does she pray for? She thrashes 'round with such a force that the cart tips low to the ground. What does she pray for? For strength, it got to be. Whoever hears her prayers, they answer them. She breaks free of the strangers' hold and leaps out of the cart. 'Round and 'round she marches with her mouth open wide 'til she holds her head and falls.

"O, how you suffered! Signa Agata…O, how you suffer still!" The carter rips at his beard. "Mamsella," he pushes her away, "you understood none of what they said." He holds his belly and tries to gain back his breath. "Look at them! They speak in their foreign tongue and laugh at our ways. Bring to mind the wise words, and you'll understand the lot of them. When the Devil flatters you, he wants your soul. The Devil flattered your Mamma with lies and vows and stole her soul. Now, he masks repentance. Look at the surgeon, the way he turns his back on us and leads Donna Elizabeth through the passageway and back to the iron gates. Look how he whispers in her ear. More flattery, in more ways, and, now, to gain another soul."

"A word or two she said in our tongue. Those, I made sense of. Mastru Nonziu…is this the Devil in his fine clothes and flattering ways? For if it is, I swear on my eyes that he is cornered and caught." The girl grips the knife in her white cotton stocking. "And I can put an end to him right now."

The carter grabs the knife and plunges the blade deep at the foot of the lava cross. "Battle like the mad Orlannu, Mamsella, and see how you lose your head."

"And if I battle like my Papà…"

"Better to battle with words and live to see a new morning. Suspicions of your Mamma whirl like the foreign wind. Glorious saints! You got to know it was your Mamma what planted those trees with her Alfiu to make the grove their own. Were you deaf to the surgeon's rants at dinner? He knows *the what* and *the where*. All he waits for is *the who*. And once the Duchinu takes on these suspicions, it got to be no time before they find us guilty."

"So, I got to find a way…"

"Mamsella…the pear's already ripe. It falls on its own."

"So, I got to cut down the tree before it bears more fruit."

"Where are the talents of the town crier now that I need them most? The twists and turns my tongue knew so well fail to reach my lips now that I got to speak the truth. Mamsella, the fruit is there for all to see."

"The truth?" She waves her hand to the cart and throws kisses to her Mamma. "There is but *one* truth: Agata Saitta is my Mamma, and I got to keep her safe."

"*Sst…sst.* Mamsella, say one more word, and you got to kill her."

She spits at his boots. "Speak in such a way," she shouts, "and I got to kill *you*!"

"Mamsella, if you say one more word with such a loud voice, you got to kill the lot of us." He grabs her shoulders. "I beg you to heed my words. Mamsella, look at me. On my honor, your Mamma comes to no harm."

She tugs at the carter's sleeve. "Tell me true, this is your word?"

"To bring no more harm to your Mamma? Sì, this is my word. Mamsella, your Mamma locked herself in her own sorrow for too long. That is the cause of her rage, but I can make it right."

"You, vigliaccu, too frightened to stay and fight…"

"Coward you call me? Coward? Call me all what you want. But put your faith in me. Donna Elizabeth sends your Mamma far from the Castle. A finer bit of fortune we couldn't hope for. She'll go back to the dwelling with me, and my Vincenza will care for her 'til you come back. That is my word. That is what I got to do."

She grabs the collar of his brown velvet jacket. "I want to go!"

"Mamsella, ppi piaciri, they grow suspicious. You're not the one Donna Elizabeth sends away. So, they got to wonder what the girl gains from leaving with a troubled woman. *The woman and the girl,* they got to whisper. So, they soon got to think *the Mamma and the daughter.* So, they got to think the two of them take all what belongs to the Duca. *The two of them side by side. Side by side, the two of them punished. And the carter that brings the girl to us, him, the worst of the lot.* No, you got to stay at the Castle. Turn your face from your Mamma. Deny all what she is to you. Do this 'til I come back. Look at me. Look at me. Listen...listen... There is *more.*"

She throws her arms to the sky. Quick, the carter slaps them down. "What more can there be? You take my Mamma from me!"

He turns his gaze to the iron gates and bows. "Bow, Mamsella. Look, Donna Elizabeth breaks free of the surgeon's hold. She makes her way back to us. Bring to mind that she speaks and understands our tongue."

"So, she got to listen, too. What is the *more?*"

"*Sst.* This is the *more.* Your Mamma never been a bad woman."

"I know. I know."

"No one surmised her great secret."

"Out with it!"

"She was beside herself with sorrow. How she loved her *maritu!* Alfiu was good, we knew that 'til the day he died, a hero gone mad like our brave Orlannu. When they ripped him from your Mamma's side, she gone mad, too. She didn't reason when the surgeon took her to his bed. She done all what he asked. She hoped...she believed all what he told her. Then, she felt a beating inside her. That's when she knew she could never keep another man's...that's when she tried to rid herself of..."

She pounds the carter's chest. "Your tongue moves, then it stays silent! Out with it! Out with it all before you have no more tongue to move!"

He grabs her hands and kisses them. "Child," he whispers, "Alfiu was shot hours before your Mamma showed herself at the Castle gates with a basket of eggs in her arms. And when she heard all what the surgeon told her of how a *maritu* could never raise another's man's child, she tried to rid herself of..."

"Mastru Nonziu, ppi piaciri, end what you started, *she tried to rid herself of...*"

He shuts his eyes and grabs tight to her, breathing out each word like they was the first he ever spoke. "Child...*you...you...*were...the...angel..."

"The angel?"

"Sì, the angel…*spared*. Mamsella, there were two of you. But what ought not to be, thrived. And you, *you*, were spared."

"Spared of what?" She pulls her hand back, makes a fist and shakes it at the carter. "Of what a Mamma got to give her daughter?"

"No," he whispers, slapping the tears from his face, "of the poison and the tools your Mamma took to her own self when you lay quiet in her belly. Now, everything's clear. I seen her on the road, how many times I seen her on the road to the Castle, and always the same prayer on her lips. 'You see my heart, Sant'Agata. You know my desire. Make me worthy to overcome the Devil.' I understood none of this and believed she was mere praying to her namesake. I greeted her with blessings, but, soon, there came a time when she wandered right past me with no nod and no small blessings. Now, everything's clear. Your sister, she wasn't spared. Your Mamma, she wasn't spared. But you…*you* are spared."

The girl holds her head. She holds it like she got to keep all the carter's words tight in it 'til she makes sense of it all. "If I am spared, and Mamma went to the Castle each morning, and Papà was already gone, then… Maronna mia! It's the way Mamma always said it was! The Devil is my… and *I* am his…"

"*You* are spared…*you* are spared…that was the miracle. That's all what you got to know. Say no more. I can't bear for you to speak no more of this. The surgeon bit like the spider. Your Mamma danced his mad dance. But *you* are spared. And, none, not the Duca, not his son, and not the Devil in his fancy garments got to bring you harm now that I'm here."

The girl falls back in the carter's arms. "Mamma's hatred for the Duca and his son…her hatred for all in the Castle, this is what she taught me. How it burned in me all the years of my life. Mamma wanted vengeance for Alfiu Saitta, sì, but, she wanted vengeance for her own self, too, 'though, in time, she buried the sorrowful truth deep inside her. Mastru Nonziu, now, I understand. The one Mamma wanted dead, he's not the one that caused her sorrow!"

"My brave Mamsella, no more sorrow. No more sorrow for your Mamma or for you. But you got to heed my words. Make my words your own no matter how foul the taste in your mouth, and, glorious saints, keep your anger down in your belly. Gratia Maria…Gratia Maria Saitta, my brave little one, do all what I do."

*Gratia Maria.* How he whispers the name in her ear, soft like a lullaby. She whispers it, too. "Gratia Maria Saitta I am, the daughter of Alfiu Saitta. But if my blood is of this Devil Papà, then, I got to be sure to stop his ways."

"Gratia…Gratia…"

"Speak my name a hundred times and more, Mastru Nonziu." She throws her head back, breathing in all the air 'round her. "Each time, you speak it, it's like a prayer that gives me strength. With no Mamma and no 'a z'a Vincenza and no dear Blasiu to guide me, this day, alone, Gratia Maria got to find her true path." She looks up at the carter, and I jump back. So far away I am, but I see it, there, in her eyes, the shadow that I seen in Alfiu's eyes and Agata's eyes, the magpie with a withered heart. "Leave me be, Mastru Nonziu." She throws her shoulders back and stands rigid like a soldier. "This hour my heart beats strong. This hour I hold in my heart all the truth 'round me. Sì, Mastru Nonziu, I got to do all what you ask of me. And, then, I got to do the *more.*"

How long the cousin been at the carter's side, who can say? But, there she is, lost and pitiful, wringing her hands and looking back at the surgeon and his long, curled finger that strokes the loops and lines of the **N** and the **B** on the iron gates. The carter bows to the cousin and narrows his eyes when his lips brush her hand. "A troubled woman banished from the manor with no further punishment. A nobler act of mercy I never witnessed. Donna Elizabeth, if you allow me, I got to accompany this Saitta woman far from the Castle with gratitude for her liberty. With your permission, the girl got to stay in your keep 'til my return."

"Joseph, your courtesy is duly noted. As for the girl, Grace and I have much to discuss before your *Voscenza* returns to us."

"Before I take my leave, Mamsella," he pushes the girl eye to eye with the cousin, "Donna Elizabeth waits for a kind word from you."

The girl nods to the carter and bows low. When she looks up, there it is like on the surgeon, a tight smile shining on her face. "I beg your forgiveness, Dunna Eeelisabetta. I got to be slapped a hundred times and more for all my sinful deeds at your celebration."

Soon that the surgeon shuffles near, the cousin pushes the girl's head down. "Grace, for your *Voscenza's* sake, you are forgiven," she throws a look at the surgeon, "unless Dr. Gale deems otherwise."

He flicks his hand in the air. "Magnanimity is a virtue Alec holds in high regard. You do well to master it."

The cousin pushes the girl's head 'til it near scrapes the cobble stones. "Yes, Grace, you are forgiven."

"Grazii, Dunna Eeelisabetta. Grazii, Duttori. 'Til the day I die," the girl whispers through her teeth, "I got to bring to mind all what you and your kind do for us."

*

A cut of meat falls from the apron of the round face servant girl when she charges 'round the lava cross, her mouth and hands still brown and bloody from all what she snatched from the table by the wall.

"He's near death! Come quick, Duttori! Voscenza's near death!"

"Another Greek tragedy unfolds before our eyes." The surgeon waves his finger at the round face servant girl's hands and mouth. "Please enlighten me as to the hour this tragedy occurred. Pray tell, was it *ante* or *post cibum?*"

The cousin grabs the servant girl's hands and slaps them. "How dare a peasant steal food or for that matter *anything* or for that matter *anyone…*"

The servant girl wipes her hands clean on her apron and clasps her hands in prayer. "I beg your forgiveness for my boldness, Donna Elizabeth. But, Duttori, I got to make you understand. Look, here come the others. They got to tell you all what I seen."

Three servant girls in blue aprons all with thin faces and black curls pulled back at their neck, rush through the courtyard and 'round the lava cross to the cousin and the surgeon.

"Voscenza's like a mad dog and spews his venom from all sides 'cross the room," says the round face servant girl.

"It was white," says the first of the three.

"More brown than white," the second.

"And thick," the third.

"It spewed forth like the raging Simetu," says the first.

"I heard his cries," the second.

"I knocked. There was no call to come in," the third.

The round face servant girl shields her eyes and whispers, "I entered."

"And, me, behind her," says the first.

"And, me, behind her," the second.

"And me, behind her," the third.

The cousin pulls the servant girls' dark curls and gives them all slaps 'cross their cheeks. "What insolent creatures you are! How dare you enter your *Voscenza's* quarters!"

"Mastru Nonziu," the girl whispers, "when the servant girls talk of the Duchinu, there's such sorrow in their eyes. Is he sick? For all the harm I had in my heart to do to him, now, I got to make it right. I got to help him."

"And I got to help you." The carter leads the girl to the foreign cart. "Still and silent, Mamsella, still and silent, but, if you got to say your farewells to your Mamma, do so with your eyes and in your heart."

The round face servant girl rubs her cheek and sobs. "Donna Elizabeth, you got to come and see. Punish us for your delight on the morrow, but, ppi piaciri, come now!"

"Dr. Gale, before I beat these girls to a pulp, do you believe such ranting merits our disturbing Alec?"

The surgeon puffs out his chest. With his hands behind his back, he makes a speech like the Notaries do in court. "It is fatigue. Alec works tirelessly for his peasants, the consequence being, this evening, he suffered for it. However, I left him a short while ago, resting quite comfortably, may I note. That is my singular prescription. Rest for the evening. However, if you insist upon lending credence to the rantings of your servants, I fear I may disturb his sleep."

"I shall not insist."

"Elizabeth, Alec will recover by the morning. However, to remove such troublesome thoughts from your mind, may I suggest," the surgeon looks up at the darkening sky, "a pyrotechnic display of our own devices. And, for a chaperon, may I call upon our *green fairy*." He pulls the jewel flask from the pocket in his vest. "For a more intense visual pleasure."

The cousin heaves a sigh, such a mighty sigh it is that I swear it's the foreign wind gaining strength. "Dr. Gale, please…"

He waves his fingers in the air like he's at the pianu and playing a happy tune. "And what music shall you play for me on the platform when we set up the pyrotechnics? Do not forget our transaction in the music room. Oh, come now, Elizabeth, I am not a heartless beast. Our time away shall afford us further opportunity to discuss the next ingredient for our stew."

Tears rush from her eyes. "I…do…not…follow."

"The first ingredient, the peasant and his wife; the second, the pistachio grove; the third, my *love* for law and justice, all finely prepared at the dinner table. The question at hand is when shall we add the fourth?"

"Lucien," with the back of her hands, she pats her cheeks dry, "at dinner…was it all a fabrication on your part? A mere tale of a peasant and a pistachio grove which you devised at Alec's expense?"

"Elizabeth, Bronte is a town of peasants and thieves. For our purposes, the peasant and thief must be the girl's father. Naturally, we must ascertain who the father is, and, then, with utmost outrage, I shall assert that he plotted with his wife to plant crops and profit from their harvest, all while laboring on lands he unlawfully seized." He pulls the branch from his pocket. "It is not only in the theatre that one relies on props."

"No, no, I do not understand. How should Grace be found culpable for her father's actions?"

"She, too, worked the land, at least that is what I shall say, and when she was afforded the opportunity to reveal the crime and make amends at your celebration, she guarded her silence."

"And Alec shall believe you?"

"He shall not. However, his father… Ah, the Duke of Bronte, so far from us in our beloved England, yet still very much involved with the finances of his Duchy. He shall hear from a Notary who owes me a favor. This Notary shall inform the Duke that the Saitta girl is the offspring of the very peasants who must be imprisoned for revenue transgressions, tax evasions, trespassing, and still more heinous charges which the Notary shall, no doubt, delineate." He takes in a breath and kisses her hand. "Elizabeth, you have not told me what you think of my plan."

"Grace punished for all eternity, and, I, innocent of the intrigue… Dr. Gale, I have not quite caught my breath."

"When your breath returns, I trust you shall concur with my prescription for Alec's rest and quietude while you and I set the pyrotechnics in motion and allow ourselves the time and intimacy to add a few more ingredients to an already most delicious stew."

She lowers her eyes. "I desire to be rid of Grace," she whispers, "and I desire that Alec…"

"And I desire, as well." The surgeon takes her arm and leads her to the foreign cart, the carter and the girl walking 'round it arm in arm with Agata. "Go find your broken-down cart and your broken-down mare," he whispers to the carter, waving his hand at the South portico, "and get that horrid peasant woman out of here."

*

The carter and the girl struggle through the South portico to the iron gates, Agata tight in the carter's arms, the girl ready, time and again, to snatch her Mamma back when she breaks free of his hold. He kisses the girl's hand, and the girl, her Mamma's. "Go back, Gratia Maria Saitta, go back, and do all what you got to do." Agata gazes up at the darkening sky. The girl falls to the ground and kisses her feet. "That's enough, Mamsella. Go back." With her eyes to the earth, slow, slow the girl shuffles back through the South portico to the courtyard and the lava cross.

Chiazza waits at the stable, her head down, her eyes closing, her hind leg soft, the hoof resting up on the toe. When the carter comes near, he pats Chiazza's flank and lifts Agata on the bench and jumps up beside her. The mare shakes her head and raises her hooves. I swear on my eyes, she nods. She knows it's time for them to leave.

The girl's eyes shine with tears. She kneels at the lava cross and kneads the grooves 'round it, paying no mind to the cousin's rantings. "Pray that upon my return, peasant girl," she shouts, "my mercy shall not diminish!"

The surgeon throws a look at the tall stranger. Quick, he helps the cousin and the surgeon up on the bench in the foreign cart. The ruffles of the cousin's lilac dress spill on the surgeon's lap. She tries to pile them back on her own, but he takes hold of her trembling hand and pats the ruffles 'cross his legs. He struggles with the reins while the tall stranger and the short stranger steady the shells and light the lanterns 'long its sides. He takes off his hat and waves a farewell to the strangers. They bow, but when the surgeon flicks the reins, they curse him through their clenched teeth now that they got to bid their own farewells to the proud speckled mare that trots 'round the Castle to the north.

Alone in the courtyard 'neath a near full moon, the girl pulls the knife from the foot of the lava cross. She runs to the entryway of the Castle. "Mercy, mercy from you?" she shouts back to the cousin in the distance. "No! But you and the Devil got to soon pray for mine!"


*God protect me from my friends.*


The girl rushes up the great stairway and throws open the door to the Duchinu's room. A small brown dog lunges at her and yaps a warning to his master. No sooner she kneels and whispers to the dog that he tears at the girl's slippers and the white cotton stockings and rips them to none but long blue and white threads. She shakes her feet free, makes a fist, opens her hand and spreads her fingers wide. That's all it takes for the dog to jump on the table near the bed, the black tip of his tongue lapping up the berries in a small dish near the Duchinu's eye patch.

The Duchinu, he lies on his bed, his eyes shut tight, flinging this pillow and that bed cover 'cross the room 'til the bed is near bare and he cries out for the world to end the pain.

The girl crouches at the foot of the bed near the leaf carvings of the thick wood posts. The dog jumps in her lap, opens his mouth and drops the berries in her hand. He presses them with his paws and squeezes out the juice 'til it flows in her palms. "Grazii," she whispers and kisses the brown head and licks her palms clean.

At the sound of her voice, the Duchinu opens his eyes.

And when he opens them, there she is, standing over him, the knife clenched in her hand. "Voscenza, look at me and what I hold in my hand.

Here is the blade what dripped with the blood of a man Alfiu Saitta killed." She presses the knife at the Duchinu's wet throat. "With this knife, he killed for the land. Now, all what Agata Saitta dreams is here before my eyes. Mamma! Mammita! I can end all the sorrow in your heart!"

"Saitta?"

"Saitta. You know the name I bear. You heard it when I cured Dunna Eeelisabetta. Now, know its vengeance."

"Saitta? My God, why hadn't I recalled? There was a Saitta, a man who killed my father's Notary during the revolution… Can you be his daughter? You are! I see it in your eyes! Grace, has this all been a charade on your part?" He yanks the last of the pillows from 'neath his head and throws it over his eyes. "And now you come for vengeance?"

"I can all but hear how the blade cracks your bones. In my mind's eye, I can all but see how the blood pours out the wound and how the brown dog laps up the blood like water. This is all what Mamma told me to see and told me to hear from the moment I seen and heard the world 'round me."

"Hear? Did you not *hear* how you berated Elizabeth at dinner and called us animals? I defended you, but it is *you* who are the animal, an animal out for vengeance!"

"Sì, I taste the justice of an animal. The marrow of Mamma's vengeance nourished my own vengeance from the time my fingers first curled 'round Alfiu Saitta's knife."

He throws the pillow at the pale green walls. "Then, *animal,* do your deed! I am too weak to fight. And I shall never beg for mercy."

"No," she tucks the knife back in the tattered folds of her apron, "I do none of what Mamma dreams. My belly no longer hungers for *her* vengeance. What it hungers for don't lurk in this room. On my Mamma's sorrow, I swear to you the dog licks none of his master's blood this day."

"Then, save me, Signurina, land of hair, as I saved you tonight. You and I shall save each other, come what may. And we shall live here, and I shall protect you…"

"*Sst…sst…*rest." The girl throws her hands in her hair. It falls 'cross the Duchinu's body, cooling it, he says, *as silk cools a fevered man.*

He grabs the girl's hand. "Stay."

"Voscenza, I…I need to see all what's in u pisciaturi."

"No. I command you."

She kneels on the green flower rug by his bed, quiet and still in a room in the south, her hair spread 'cross his body, 'til he falls to sleep to the booms and flashes of red and green illuminations set off on a platform in the north.

And when he falls to sleep, she creeps to a wood cabinet in the corner of his room and pulls the knob. She reaches in for u pisciaturi, a dark gold pot with designs of green and red jewels. What a price his pisciaturi got to fetch, a donkey, or ten, and here it is a prized vessel hidden in a cabinet full of the waste of his royal organs! The girl murmurs a prayer and looks inside at the thick white liquid.

"Voscenza," she whispers, shaking him awake, "you got the sickness of the town, but I can make the cure. Ppi piaciri, let no one in 'til I come back."

The Duchinu wipes his mouth on the sleeve of his bright white bed clothes and lets out a cry when spittle runs down his chest. "Send for Dr. Gale and my delicate Elizabeth!"

"Voscenza, the sickness shows you more loyalty than the ones you name for friends."

"How dare you!" No sooner he lifts his head that it drops back on the pillow. "Grace, I command you."

"Voscenza, we make our eyes see the tale our fool hearts whisper to us. But there are times our hearts trick us. You know this, too, for doubts long made their dwelling in you. Listen to these doubts. I beg of you, don't let the surgeon and Dunna Eeelisabetta inside this room. They are no friends to you, Voscenza. But, me, raised to be your enemy, me, I am…"

His dull, lifeless eyes gaze up at her. There's no strength left in him. With a dry, open mouth, he lets out a hard breath, and, slow, slow, he lifts his hands. "You speak of tales," his thumbs stroke her face, "then…what tales must I see in *your* eyes? My God, they are beautiful, strange and wondrous. They render my heart weak." He throws his hands over his eyes. "Signurina, land of hair, I lose my common sense. Do what you must. Take the key, all the keys which hold me prisoner. Lock me inside these walls until you see fit to set me free."

"Up, Chiazza, up," the carter whispers, "you take too long this time." The fault is his, none other. On narrow dirt roads, 'cross lava rocks, through empty lands, he rifled through his bag of tricks, a tale here, a song there, 'til he undone Chiazza's harness to show off her own tricks, the way she kneels and rises, and all for Agata and the calming of her madness. Now, the carter flicks the reins and tries to gain back all the hours. He lights the last lantern, the lot of them swinging 'long the sides of the cart. They shine their light the best they can, but in the dark, Chiazza still stumbles like a new foal and slows him down.

"No!" Agata cries out when the cart comes to a clearing. The carter looks 'round. He kisses his black lava cross now that he eyes two lava rocks, and, growing out of them, two trees, their small grey bending trunks and their long twisted branches crawling 'long the earth. "Signa Agata," he grabs hold of her hand and kisses it, "forgive me…forgive me…" He throws his hands over her eyes, but she pushes them away and raises her own hands to the heavens and murmurs a prayer to the good and the pure Sant'Agata.

"Forgive me," he whispers. "A lifetime ago, I passed you here…how many days and weeks, I passed you here… Signa Agata, how could I know all what the Castle plotted? Signa Agata, quick, let us leave this cursed place."

The carter gazes back at the rocky trazzera they journeyed on. "Signa Agata," he smiles, "you're a good woman with a weak body. This road got to be better for your journey." He whips the reins and looks out in the distance where a lone rock rises in the landscape, the great rock we call *u Ruccazzu*, a jagged rock with a smooth table top, so pale some say it been washed clean by the sun, a lone rock, but not lonely. Our ancients seen to that. Long ago, they dug out chambers in u Ruccazzu and buried their dead, chambers hollowed at the foot of the rock and higher up, too, where the dead squatted with hands on their knees, to wait and watch, and, now, where outlaws find refuge and watch and wait.

Who are these outlaws? What is their justice? They hide in the chambers and huddle in silence 'til a carter and his goods or a peasant and his donkey or a young girl and her jug of pure water cross their path, and they show themselves with worn clothes and rifles, and before a soul can beg for mercy, they leave the rich poor and the poor poorer still…or, so the carter says. But who ever seen or heard these outlaws…that is, 'til now?

The foreign wind whirls the earth up 'round u Ruccazzu and up 'round the cart. It seizes in its path a cry, shrill and desperate in its tone. The carter's eyes dart here, there. He holds his head and sobs. Of all the tales he ever told, the outlaw tale this day rings true.

The carter whips the reins again. Chiazza trots and jerks in and out of a steady pace. Agata's body rocks 'cross the bench. The carter pulls her up by her shoulders to sit her back upright, but she flops back down from side to side like there's nothing in her no more to keep her strong.

He shouts at Chiazza, he shouts at Agata, and, this, to drown out the shrill, desperate cry that grows louder still. He yanks on the reins and stands straight up on his bench, shaking in his laughing boots, his jaw clicking loud and wild. "Stay back! We are armed! We are armed!" He reaches for the thick branch in his cart that holds the leather boots in place. "See? We are armed! Stay back! Stay back I tell you or we got to kill the lot of you!"

Agata pushes herself back up. "Stay," she whispers and takes hold of the reins. She raises her eyes to the dark sky and points at the red and green flashes of light in the north. "It's a sign."

"Sì, Signa Agata, a sign to leave this demon place." He grabs the reins, whipping them, working Chiazza the best he can, fleeing the cry the best he can on a narrow dirt road all the way past Bronti 'til the lava rocks jut out before them, the rocks that bear their own shape and story.

Young ones we were that seen adventures in all of them. Here, ripples in the desert sand. There, a storm cloud. There, a demon to fight. Demons of the sea. Cords and weapons. Faces. Limbs. Shapes and stories far that the eye could see…and, us, the young ones, we wasn't afraid. We conquered each one of them with all we had of phantom swords and warrior minds…save one…the *beast*. "You there, Muntagna, conquer the beast," the boys shouted at me, "and we'll take you for one of our own!"

Still now, their taunts crowd my thoughts, but a young one I'm no more. Not me and not the carter. And this is none but lava rock what crosses our land. Still, the reins shake in the carter's hands when he rides past the black beast where the shrill, desperate cry grows louder. The carter whips the reins, but Chiazza stops dead in her tracks. The carter grabs a lantern and waves it at the black beast. There, behind the lava beast, a hunched shadow figure issues forth.

*

"Demon! Devil! the carter shouts. "Whatever you are, spirit of the dead or a thief, wherever you come from, you got no place with the good. Go back to u Ruccazzu and hide and leave the good alone."

"Take the evil, not the good. Take the evil, not the good," the shadow figure cries out.

Agata claps her hands and mimics the shadow figure's cries. "Take the evil…take the evil…" Her black jewel eyes got joy in them once more now that she sings a song of madness.

"Signa Agata, you got to kill us both if you make one more sound." With that, he cups her mouth.

"Take the evil, not the good," the shadow figure pleads.

Agata bites her way through the carter's hands. "Take the evil, not the good!" Agata shouts back.

The carter opens his eyes. He narrows them. "But wait," he rubs his eyes with the heel of his hand, "does the dark play tricks on my eyes or is this demon none but a boy? You there, thief, ladened with the booty of your shameful deeds, we'll heap no more treasures in your brimming arms."

A boy takes on the skin of a man not by years, but grief. This shadow figure, none but a boy, once a happy shepherd boy, staggers to the cart a sorrowful man that can do none but stumble 'long the road, the limp body of the lamb 'cross his shoulders like the collar of a royal cape and my precious Vincenza, her limp body cradled in his arms. Behind him, the hunchback sheep trail in mourning, their white tufts near scraping the earth.

"No! No!" the carter cries. He jumps from the cart and throws his body at the shepherd boy's feet. "Vincenza! Vincenzina! Vincenzina! My life! My heart!" He throws his arms up and shakes Vincenza's toes. He shakes her legs. He shakes her fingers and swings her arms in the air. He shakes her body 'til the boy loses his steadiness and falls to his knees.

"Too late. Too late," the boy sobs. "To undo the past cannot be done."

The carter grabs Vincenza and rocks her in his arms. He kisses her face, her eyes, her mouth, kissing what's the right of a maritu, alone. I howl like a mad dog. He shakes his fist at the heavens and shrieks and wails louder than any creature in the wild. He kisses her palms, and the smell of sacred basirico fills the air. He breathes it in and cradles Vincenza's body, his cheek brushing her cheek. He strokes it and kisses it, again, again, again, 'til his lips bleed. He spits out the blood and pounds his head on the narrow dirt road.

"Mastru Nonziu, ppi piaciri…"

"With my bare hands I got to kill them all 'til the last outlaw begs for mercy. Then, I got to kill that one, too."

"So peaceful they lay at the beautiful mountain's feet," the shepherd boy whispers and strokes the lamb's limp legs. "I make no sense of all what happened, but this much I know. The outlaws took no part in their massacre."

"No part? If this be truth, that the outlaws took no part in it, then, I make sense of it all. At Mungibellu's feet, you say. It was the field guards. Sì, the Duca's men. They killed the lamb and when Vincenza came 'on them… the rest I dare not imagine…" He narrows his eyes. "Blasiu, where were *you?*"

"I…"

"Blasiu, where were you! Sì, you heard her cries for help. You heard them! And none came to mind but to flee?"

"No…no…"

"A massacre takes place and you, *you* are spared? Only a coward what makes pacts with the Devil got to be spared."

"I…"

"Better to save your own worthless skin, is that how it goes? A coward, vigliaccu, he that stands before my eyes that once called himself a shepherd boy. You were cursed the day you were born. Now, you got to die cursed!"

The boy lays the lamb on the ground and jumps up. He rips the cap from his head. He scratches at his face and digs his fist in the hollow of his cheek. "I *am* cursed! Cursed, the day I was born! Now, I got to die cursed! This I know! This I know!"

"Blasiu…"

"*The end of the journey for our neighbor is but a resting place for us.* That's what Signa Vincenza told the girl and what the girl told me. Up, far up, far past the end of our neighbor's journey that's where I gone. That's where I found the pure snow. When I climbed back down, there was Signa Vincenza cradling the lamb, the both of them quiet like thieves. She opened her eyes. Sì, she opened her eyes. I pressed my ear to her mouth. What did she want of me? To bring the pure snow to Signa Agata. I shouted at my legs to run. The jugs were heavy. My legs grew tired. I struck them with my cane. 'Quick! Quick!' I cried, but they brought me to the dwelling too late." He throws a look at Agata, clapping her hands and laughing. "Signa Agata was gone. I struck my legs again and hit them here, here, here, 'til the blood poured down. They raced back to Mungibellu, quick quick…but too late. There, Signa Vincenza lay quiet and good with the lamb still in her arms, and, then, she spoke no more to me. And, then, she breathed no more for me."

The carter kisses Vincenza's head and pulls the boy back down. "Blasiu, forgive a grieving man. I spoke too soon and chewed none of my words."

"Look at what I done! My precious lamb! Your precious Signa Vincenza! No, Mastru Nonziu, you spoke all what's true. This is the end of my days. I got to bring the sheep back to the Castle and ask none for gain. I crave no more the life I lived now that sorrow weighs on it. Where the wind tosses me, here, there, like a shipwrecked sailor, that's where it'll take me, that's where I'll go. Beside the cross-eyed lunatic I'll take my place and wander the land and seek forgiveness where forgiveness turns her back on me."

"Blasiu, my Vincenza seen what a fine boy you are."

"No more!" The shepherd boy struggles to stand, Vincenza rocking in his arms. "It's time. Mastru Nonziu, get up and hold out your arms for the treasure I give you."

The carter rips a small piece of brown velvet from the pocket of his jacket. He ties it 'round Vincenza's marriage finger. "She is now and forever in my care."

"A good woman like Signa Vincenza…"

"Blasiu," the carter shakes his face free of the tears, "I got to take care of her now in a good and proper way. Help me, slow, slow, to the back. Lay her on the dresses, a bedding soft and worthy of a queen." The carter dips his finger in a small jug of oil and rubs her brow and lips. "Blessed is the blessed. Holy is the holy."

The shepherd boy kisses Vincenza's hand and sweeps the lamb in his arms, Vincenza's cloth, a precious collar, still wrapped 'round the lamb's neck. He bows to Agata. She tugs at the fancy dresses and wraps them 'round Vincenza and sings out the shepherd boy's sorrowful song. "Take the evil, not the good...take the evil, not the good...take the evil, not the good..."

*

"Quick! Quick!" The girl rushes out the Duchinu's room and down the great stairway, shouting orders to the blue apron servant girls. They greet her at the kitchen door and slice three limuni at her bidding. They place a pot filled with water on the wood-burning stove and nod when the girl tells them to wait by the Duchinu's door 'til she unlocks it.

The girl hurries out, hurries back in and pulls the round face servant to her side. She lays her hand on the small mound 'neath the blue apron and tells her that before the celebration of the birth of the baby Savior in December, her own baby got to enter the world, his hungry mouth crying for food.

"Crying?"

"Sì, crying," says the girl, "not quiet like his Papà, and making such a noise that the one-eyed monster cups his ears in fear."

"Crying," the servant girl whispers and licks away her tears and kisses the girl's hand.

"No." The girl reaches for a basket, the shape of a hammock where babies sleep. "Now is not the time for joy," she races out the door. "We got work to do. Now is not the time for joy."

When she first came to the Castle, the young servant with the round face and dark full eyes cried of the journey she took each morning to far-off hills where she picked fresh plants for the day's meals. She breathed her desires to the young gardener that, from the time the orphaned boy came to live with the master gardener and his wife, uttered not one sound. But the young gardener makes the round face smile now that he grows the plants the servant girl needs, past the South portico and the lava cross, to the east, where trees bear pink star flowers, there, where the smell of bushy leaves fills the air with mint and spices. And when darkness spreads 'cross the sky, the young silent gardener sneaks in the round face servant's room and lies 'cross her bed 'til she, too, puts a smile on his face.

Past the South portico and the lava cross, to the east, where trees bear pink star flowers, here, in the young gardener's fertile green garden, the girl fills her basket with the sacred basirico for the Duchinu's cure. The moon casts a soft glow in the garden. All is calm. But what is this? She trembles in the warm night air. All is silent but, still, she cups her ears. I hear it now, too, a heartsick pounding 'cross the earth. She looks up. There, in the darkness, the shadow figure issues forth, his footsteps solemn and heavy, the lamb in his arms, the hunchback sheep trailing behind, bleating out their own grief and sorrow.

The girl lets out a cry. "Blasiu, it's you! And...*you*, little lamb!" The girl cups her eyes. "But, wait. Our precious lamb, silent and still in Blasiu's arms? No. The moon plays tricks on me." She spreads her fingers and peers through them. "No!" She sobs and claws at her hair. She throws the basket up to the boughs and thrashes in the falling leaves. The hunchback sheep rush to her. They circle her and rub their white tufts 'cross her face. And when they're done wiping it clean of tears, they nudge her to the shepherd boy.

"Blind yourself to what my deeds done wrought! Blind yourself to what I bring 'on the innocent! I drown in the blood of angels!"

"Blasiu, the blood of angels?"

"Stand back!"

"No! There's none to fear when I'm near you, for you are blessed." She strokes the mark on his cheek. "Here, I bless you all the more."

The boy shakes her off and races back to the South portico. In the courtyard, he lays the lamb's body at the foot of the lava cross. "Hero of the Nile! *You*, the great Nelson, *you* are no hero. *This* is a true hero, a hero sacrificed for none but the sorrow the deed aroused."

The girl rushes to his side. "Blasiu that blazes the sky..."

"Stand back!"

She kneels and reaches for his hand. "Blasiu, speak to me. Who dared to do this evil deed?"

"I saw none of it. I lingered and made a marriage gift. Up, far up, I climbed the beautiful mountain. I lingered and made a marriage gift. A marriage gift!" He throws the carved beads at her feet. "A marriage gift..."

"A marriage gift? So, the fault got to be on my head, too."

"They got to pay. All of them...and all of us."

She taps the knife in her apron. "'Til there's none left in the world?"

"Sì, 'til the world empties of evil and..."

"And the world empties of good? Va ben', no more evil like the Duca and his kind, but, Blasiu, no more good like 'a z'a Vincenza and her kind? No more 'a z'a Vincenza? No, I can't live in such a world."

"You live in it!"

She shakes her head. "Blasiu," she sighs, "how did hatred find such a home in your heart?"

"My heart?" He kisses the lamb's head. "My heart! My life! They got to pay," he sobs, "the Devils that slit your Mamma's throat; the Devils that slit *your*... Where was I to protect you? They got to pay! *I* got to pay!"

'Round the lamb's wound, Vincenza's precious cloth holds tight. Soon that the shepherd boy peels it away, the dried blood runs fresh and bright. He wipes his tears with the bloody cloth, the tears and blood steaming his face, the tears and blood dripping, slow, slow, in the hollow of his cheek.

In the north sky, a bright funnel bursts in shards of red and green light. Far from the girl and the shepherd boy, far from their grief and sorrow, the surgeon sets off the last illuminations, the lights and booms and cheers of celebration.

"All what lights the sky now fills my spirit with darkness... Gratia, Gratia that graces the earth..."

She wraps her arms 'round him. "How you say my name with sorrow! If this is what it means to bear such a name, I want none of it."

"Gratia, the name you bear is not the cause of your sorrow." He buries his face in her lap. "You're blind to the greatest sorrow. Mastru Nonziu, he seen the sorrow. Now, his heart's blind with grief."

"You seen Mastru Nonziu? No, Blasiu, no! Mamma? Mammita! Mastru Nonziu gave his word Mamma got to stay safe."

"She *is* safe, but the sorrow I spare you..."

"What greater sorrow is there but to gaze in your eyes now that your precious lamb is gone?"

"Gratia…"

The servant girl with the round face and dark full eyes rushes to the lava cross, the basket of basirico leaves swinging in her arm. "I looked everywhere for you. You got work to do. Wipe your hands! Take the basket! Come quick! Now is not the time for sorrow."

"Blasiu, they wait for me at the Duchinu's door. He reels with the sickness of the town."

"Let him die!"

She holds tight to his hand. "Blasiu, he gave his word to spare the lamb. This is not his doing. How can I hold back the cure? This is not what 'a z'a Vincenza teaches me."

He shakes free of her hold and spits to the heavens. "For her sake, let him die!"

"Blasiu, how sorrow clouds your reason! Sì, evil's at play in the Castle, but the Duchinu, he's a good boy and blind to all of it."

"*He* got to pay."

"Not him. He's but a boy."

He pounds at his chest. "Look at me! A man past twenty years is long past a boy! Not me no more…not him! Such kindness now, and all for a man you spat 'on, time and again!"

She shakes her head. "You're blind to all what I know."

"I know the Devil got to pay."

"Sì, Blasiu, the Devil got to pay."

"He *is* the Devil!"

"No," she whispers, "he's not the one…if I could but tell you all what I learned this day…"

"And, me, all what I…Gratia," he sobs, "Gratia, I can take no more. In the name of your z'a Vincenza…can you cure the Duca's son?"

"With 'a z'a Vincenza's plants and 'a z'a Vincenza's prayers, sì, I can cure him."

"Then, go. Heal the evil and the good. But heed my words: there's none more you can learn from your z'a Vincenza."

"It turns the water, u basirico does. But only the sacred one," the girl holds out the cup for the Duchinu. "When it's ready, see how i limuni join it, i limuni that 'a z'a Vincenza says waken the blood to fight." She stirs the lemon in the water. "Sì, sì, Voscenza, there are more cures. 'A z'a Vincenza has many. For one, she favors onions for the peasant men. But the smell's too strong for me."

She fills a spoon with the cure and nods. "When I was but a child, we visited the man they called *u luppinaru* for he sold the broad beans in all the towns. 'A z'a Vincenza knew from the start he was the first with the sickness. Him, from Rannazzu, the town that brings bad fortune. I cut the onions for her. She set the pot on the iron stool in the hearth 'til the water boiled. She whispered the prayer in u luppinaru's ear. I told her I hated the smell of onions. They sting my eyes like the foreign wind when it throws the earth up in my face. 'A z'a Vincenza said all what grows is different, and all what grows is good. Then, she waved her hand over my cheek like this, but I got none of her beatings. If 'a z'a Vincenza hears the way I chatter now *maga, maga, maga, maga, maga, maga, maga,* me, none but a magpie, she got to hit me hard. All what I say now are the stories and the speeches of others, the gossip she loathes. Who am I but *Dunna Eeelisabetta*? What words issue forth from my mouth but her nonsense words?"

A weak smile crosses the Duchinu's lips. His elbows try to hoist him up, but he falls back down on the wet sheets. "The walls of duty crumble when you are here. With Elizabeth by my side, the fortress stands impenetrable."

"I make no sense of what you say," the girl whispers smoothing out the sheets. "But this much I know. I speak now when the moment calls for silence."

"No silence!" The Duchinu taps his finger on his tongue. "I savor each word as the starving man savors the crumbs on his tongue." He holds out his arms. "Recount to me everything. Say all the words in your heart. Reveal your desires as I shall reveal all mine to you."

"'A z'a Vincenza says not one word when she makes the tea, and the one she cures says not one word. But you and me...*sst*...*sst*...the tea's ready." She crosses herself. "Maronna 'a Nunziata..."

"Grace, I first saw you in my lemon groves, *i limuni*, as you say. You undid your shawl. Your hair fell across the earth like Jacob's ladder. And it rose up to the sky. I climbed the ladder, but I have yet to reach paradise. A lock of your hair, this is all I desire for the last rung to my paradise."

"If that's all what it takes to keep you calm and quiet…" She takes her knife and cuts off a strand of hair. He kisses it and slips it 'neath his pillow. "Patri Radici says paradise is very far from here, but we can reach it when we die if we are good."

The Duchinu grabs the pillow 'neath his head, a big square one with thick borders of lace that weigh his weak arms down. He throws it at the sleeping brown dog that growls with little heart and falls back to sleep. "Gaze upon all I am. Signurina, land of hair, even with the sacrament of your blessed hair, I am not good."

"'A z'a Vincenza's prayers got to make you good."

"That I may enter paradise tonight?"

"Avaja! There's no paradise this night, not when I hold the cure for you." She holds the cup to his mouth. "Chianu…chianu. Slow, slow…sip a little at a time. A little at a time."

"Tonight I enter paradise."

"No, you have my word."

"The word of an angel…"

"Voscenza, there's no paradise for you this night."

He takes a last sip and closes his eyes. "What do the peasants say? The poor marry and make little poor ones. And should a poor one marry a rich one…a rich one marry a poor one…one time…then, all changes for all time…the world order is broken …for that one time…it can happen…the smithy marries a peasant girl…the lunatic takes a wife…we can…Signurina, land of hair," he lets out a yawn, his head falling back, "the lemon groves… the first time my heart…no…it was where the *olives* grow."

\*

"The Duchinu of Bronti had more gold than any titled one in the west or the south or the north, for his Papà owned all the land in the east. In spite of all his riches, the Duchinu was the poorest man alive for he didn't have a wife. And, so, he searched the island for one.

"He stopped at the landowners' homes first. To each landowner he asked the question: 'Have you a beautiful daughter whom I may take for my bride?' To his surprise, each landowner, indeed, had one beautiful daughter. But the Duchinu heard the girls whispering that if he married one of them, she would keep all the gold for herself. The Duchinu loved his gold, and, so, he left the landowners' homes sure to find a wife where fortunes weren't so great.

"He went to all the tenants' homes. To each tenant he asked the same question, 'Have you a beautiful daughter whom I may take for my bride?' To his surprise, each tenant, indeed, had a very beautiful daughter. The Duchinu was a conniver. Day to night, he tried to trick the tenants, but they knew the twists and turns of his questions. They bit their tongues and said all what the Duchinu wanted to hear for each one knew he would live a most comfortable life if his daughter married the son of the Duca of Bronti. But, then, the Duchinu heard the tenants' beautiful daughters whispering that if one of them married the Duchinu, she would keep all the gold for herself. And, so, he left the tenants' homes, fated to marry a poor peasant girl that would be happy with the smallest portion of his wealth.

"He walked past the homes on his estate to the low lava road that leads to the peasants' cottages. He came 'on a peasant. The peasants believed, and the Duchinu came to believe it, too, that Santu Giuseppi disguised himself from time to time to test the Bruntiszi. Eyeing such a poor, dirty soul, he knew this peasant could be none other than the saint himself. If the Duchinu showed how humble he always been, then, Santu Giuseppi, protector of the poor and their households, would reward him, for Santu Giuseppi was a kind saint and the maritu of 'a Maronna 'a Nunziata. And, so, the Duchinu would take himself a beautiful bride and still be a very rich man.

"'My good man,' the Duchinu said, and, quick, the peasant fell to his knees. 'Arise, good man. I am waiting for your blessings.'

"'Si biniric', Voscenza.'

"'And blessings to you. Now, if you please, have you a beautiful daughter whom I may take for my bride?'

"The Duchinu asked a hundred times and more, but the peasant shook his head, his hand wrapped tight 'round his throat. At long last, the peasant cried out, 'Voscenza, it's true! I got a daughter! But by God's will, she's rude and ugly and got to make your life miserable. To none I give her in marriage.' That was all what the Duchinu hoped to hear. He ordered the peasant to bring his daughter to the Castle, draped in her finest garb.

"'Voscenza…'

"'Not another word. On the morrow, with or without your consent, your daughter bears my name.'

"The Duca of Bronti invited the King and Queen to the Castle to attend the marriage of his son. All the guests waited for the ugly and rude peasant girl to arrive. All the guests knew the peasants' tale, too, and they waited to see the girl blessed by Santu Giuseppi change into the beautiful Duchessa.

"The Duca of Bronti hushed his guests. In the marble hall, 'neath a hundred clinking swords, the girl held her breath. The soldiers held their laughter the best they knew how, but when her Papà pushed her plump flesh 'neath the canopy of swords, their laughter burst wide open and shook the marble halls like the one-eyed monster that tramples through Mungibellu.

"The door to the grand *salottu* flung open. A girl wearing a frayed and faded sack hunched at the threshold. Her round nose, the size of a melon, spread 'cross her face. Her chin was dirty and covered with open sores. 'Where's my Duchinu? Where's my gold?' She turned to her Papà. 'Old fool,' she cackled, 'tell me now, or I got to break you in two.'

"The Duchinu fell to his knees. 'Santu Giuseppi, I beg of you, do not hesitate with your grace, for a moment is now much too long to wait. Bestow on me your heavenly gifts. Santu Giuseppi, why so long in coming? Make this creature my beautiful bride.'

"The poor peasant slapped his brow and smiled. Bare a smile it was, but it soon burst wide from ear to ear. He kicked out his legs and twirled 'round in a spider dance. 'Voscenza,' he sang out, 'I am no Santu Giuseppi, but by God's will, a miracle happened this day. Free, I am now. Free! I give you blessings, Voscenza. May you have a long and happy life with this, my daughter, soon to be your wife.'

"And, so, it always is when truth is told, the Duchinu grew sad, the Duchinu grew old, and the peasant's daughter took all his gold."

*

In his sickness, the Duchinu's a bad-tempered child that rips at sheets and screams at demons, not able to quiet his nerves 'til the girl tells a tale. She told the tale of the Duchinu and his bride the way the dark hair peasant girls told the tale near the fountains in all the squares of Bronti. She laughed the way the peasant girls laughed. "*A pacchiana*," she said, "that's all what his bride was, fat and ugly, 'a pacchiana, we call such women. That's all what the Duchinu deserved." The Duchinu laughed, too. What does he know of the name we call him or the twists and turns of our tongue?

"More," he asks when he hears the insults and makes no sense of them. "More stories to soothe my illness." The girl pats the pillows 'neath his head and readies herself for another tale. What a pair they are, stripped of fine clothing, equals in the room, power and power lost in the stew. Before anyone knows anything, God help us all, that's how love starts, not the quick and foolish love what struck him in the olive groves, but the good love. I howl to shake the girl from the spell the Duchinu's casting on her. He looks at her with tenderness and smiles. What fills the room makes me howl all the more. That's how the good love starts, how it started with Vincenza and me, with a smile and a need.

His lids tremble for sleep. He looks like a child on the first of May, fighting to keep his eyes wide open and not cheat himself of the celebration. He dreams of this and that, muttering dreams that take him to the island of Ferdinandea where he lives a long and happy life with his love, the one with the long, red hair, and all 'neath the sea like Colapesci where none can find them, and none can harm them.

"*Sst...sst.*" The girl kneels by his side and quiets him of such dreams and continues her prayers. When she finishes them, she unlocks the door and tells the round face servant girl waiting in the long, blue hallway to fill two jugs with the pure water "for the thirst Voscenza now got to satisfy."

How much water he drinks through the night! The girl pours the last of it in a dark blue glass and lays it on the table near the bed. She lies down in the corner where the brown dog curls in her arms and keeps vigil still and quiet. The Duchinu's still and quiet, too, 'til he dreams of his Papà and the animal flesh. He cries out that it's all 'round him, the flesh and the blood and all the meat inside. The girl lets out a cry and rushes to his side, shaking him 'til he swats himself awake.

"Don't be afraid, Voscenza. I had to get the dream out of you."

"Are you mad, girl?"

"You dreamed of flesh and blood and all the innards of an animal…you cradled the rawness…"

"You *are* mad! You cannot possibly know that which another dreams."

"I do. I do. Voscenza, it was *raw*…it can only mean someone got to die."

"Very well, Grace. You know my dreams…and should I have dreamt of a cooked leg of lamb?" He holds his belly and lets out a weak laugh. "Now, admit this is foolishness on your part. Very well, refuse to admit it." He pounds the pillows and curls back on his side. "Go to sleep, Grace. We both need our rest."

For all what remains of the night, the Duchinu dreams no more. But the girl, her dreams carry her to dwellings and graves. She dreams from night to morning and, in such a low voice, I can bare hear them all. The first dream carries her to the north of the Castle and to the east, where Blasiu digs a grave and marks the sacred space with carved beads. She cries out, but, quick, the second dream takes hold in her and carries her to the hearth in the dwelling where Mastru Nonziu stirs the yellow flower buds to silence her Mamma's own mad dreams. "Good," she whispers, but, all too soon, the last of the dreams floods her heart. Her legs and arms try to fight it off, but the dream stays strong. It carries her to Mastru Nonziu outside the dwelling where his hands bleed 'round the handle of a hoe, and his blood drips on a fresh dug grave. On the grave, he throws long leaves, thick like hides, and, this, to ward off the insects that eat the flesh of the dead. "No! No! No!" the girl cries out when he hits the hoe on his shovel, three times, like church bells that toll for the dead. "No! No! No!" she cries out when he throws himself on the grave and wails u reputu loud and long. The girl wails, too, grabbing her chest, her eyes open wide. And, there, in the pale eyes they say that give the evil eye, I see my holy Vincenza.

The girl jumps up. She runs to the shutters and throws them open and curses the land that couldn't keep Vincenza safe and curses the saints that took her to paradise. The light of the Angelus hour shines all 'round her. She curses the Mattutinu, the Angelus, the Ave Maria, the Vespri prayers, and all the prayers Vincenza prayed that couldn't keep her on the earth.

The Duchinu stretches out his arms and yawns. He rubs the stubbles on his chin, a rooster he came to be in his sickness, a rooster with a small crest. He laces his fingers behind his head and smiles like this is always the way it got to be, him and the girl, the two of them, come from their own two worlds to be together. He reaches for the dark blue glass. He gulps down the water and excuses himself for the sounds he makes. He gets up and steadies himself, leaning on the wide leaf carvings of the post of the bed. "I am better," he says and closes the shutters.

"*Better?* Did you not hear the dreams that filled my soul last night? Nothing's *better* no more."

"Now, Grace, be sensible. If they are *your* dreams, how should I possibly hear them?"

"Me, a peasant, I hear. I know. But, you, the Duchinu of the peasants…"

The Duchinu taps his fingers on his knee. "*Duchinu?* I forbid you to use that…" He takes in a breath and lets out a long sigh. "Very well, Grace, tell me your dreams."

The girl tells him the dream of the lamb. His eyes fill with water. The sickness done him good and made him kind. He falls back on the bed, sobbing, all while the girl stands straight and still with stones for eyes. He belches and wipes the dried green cure from the corners of his mouth. He excuses himself and excuses himself a hundred times and more for the deeds he done and the deeds he still got to do at his Papà's bidding.

"This is my word, Grace. Any man who laid a hand on that poor creature's head shall endure a harsh punishment."

The girl throws the shutters back open. A boy's wailing fills the air. North of the Castle and to the east, 'neath a tree that bears pink star flowers, Blasiu throws himself on a mound of earth. "How he wails! Look at him! He buries the innocent. This is his punishment. Your men got to pay. Your men got to pay like Blasiu that no more blazes the sky. Look at him! He spared me from all what my dreams could not."

The Duchinu sits back down on the bed. "Grace, I am not looking anywhere as there is nothing to see. However, if someone in my charge broke the law, he shall pay."

"Murderers, the lot of them!"

"Grace, be reasonable. A slaughtered lamb? Murder?"

"Murder of all what's good! Murder of the lamb! Murder of my...O, blessed Savior, of...my z'a Vincenza! I seen it! I seen it all in my dreams! They got to pay for all what they done to 'a z'a Vincenza. They got to pay now and be a just eye for eye."

"Grace," he throws his hands over his ears, "your speech is incomprehensible to me. Or perhaps it is that infernal sound which distracts me so."

"It's Blasiu! Ahi! How he wails!"

"No, a tapping, a scraping, a shuffling. It's a sound I cannot quite..." He nods to the girl and shakes his finger at the door. "The carter claims you hear that which we mere mortals do not. Identify the culprit who makes these sounds, Grace."

"But, you, too, you got to know."

He fixes his eyes on her. "Prove to me the powers residing in you."

"Voscenza, they're not far off. You got to hear the man that gasps for breath. You got to hear the girl and how she tries to knock. They want to come in. I beg you, Voscenza, keep the traitors out."

"Traitors? I recognize the voices. Lucien! Elizabeth! Grace, unlock the door. No, wait! I must appear a sight." He reaches for his robe, a silk robe of a two-piece thickness stuffed with cloth and one thickness stitched to the other with lines and designs of small snakes, a robe the color of blood, with a wide collar like a mantle. He tells the girl to turn 'round and slides his pistol in the pocket of his robe. He combs down his hair, takes a last sip of water, and taps for the patch near the dark blue glass. He fixes it over the right eye, "for the sun," he tells the girl. When he orders the girl to open the door, there he stands for the surgeon and the cousin to see, a *hero* like his long-ago uncle.

The cousin stumbles in the room and holds tight to the door, the back of her lilac dress spotted with grass and mud. The surgeon swallows hard and pays no mind to the high black hat crumbling in his hands. The girl eyes them and lets out a small laugh. She calls for the round face servant girl that laughed all night when her young gardener climbed a tree and shook the boughs to fill the servant girl's room with pink star flowers. But, now, the round face servant girl sobs for, now, the girl tells her she got to pick the thorny yellow fruit of the ficarindia, and no matter how her fingers hurt and no matter how they bleed, she got to pick out all the spines and squeeze out all the juice for a cure.

"You got to," the girl spins the servant 'round and points to the surgeon and the cousin, their bodies wrapped 'round the wide leaf carvings at the foot of the bed. They pull their lashes down and plead with the Duchinu to close the shutters. "They got to get the cure soon…their bodies can't take no more. But that won't be the end of it. Look at them. The juice of the ficarindia…it washes clean the pain in the head and the eyes. But for all what they drunk," and this makes the round face servant girl laugh, "it's but time and a barrel of spices that'll wash the stink from their flesh."

"*Ficarindia*? *Prickly pears*? No…no…" The cousin cups her mouth. "Why the very thought…"

The Duchinu throws a look at the cousin's dress. He presses his mouth in a small *o* and nods. "And which thought might that be, my delicate Elizabeth? The thought that, perhaps, though lovely as your dress is, this is not the hour of day to wear such formal attire? Would not your beloved Mrs. John Sherwood agree?"

"Alec!"

"A mere pleasantry, my delicate Elizabeth. Your appearance reveals the entire story, and I am deeply moved, truly I am. You roamed about the gardens all night rife with worry regarding my illness. Did you not? And, I suspect, you indulged in one too many glasses of sherry to calm yourself. Dr. Gale should have deemed it necessary to chaperone." He throws a look at the surgeon, his head low and nodding. "However, all is forgiven on this occasion. Our Dr. Gale most likely kept vigil, as he is wont to do, in his own fashion." With that, the Duchinu lets out a laugh, and the small brown dog lets out a yelp. The Duchinu slaps his thigh and calls the dog near, but the dog stays put. Like the big black guard dog in the olive groves, he paces 'round the surgeon and growls at the slightest flinch.

"My lord," the surgeon whispers, "the rest I prescribed did you a world of good. I am so pleased that now you are able to move about."

The Duchinu waves his hand and laughs at the surgeon, his arms wrapped 'round the post of the bed, the dog tugging at his pants. "More so than you, Dr. Gale."

The surgeon throws out his leg and tries to shake the brown dog off, but the dog holds tight. "Alec, be the trusted friend I know you are. Call off your beast."

"He, too, is a trusted friend. Perspicacious and loyal."

The surgeon throws out his leg, one last mighty kick, and the brown dog flies to the corner of the room, yelping up a storm. The girl rushes to him and takes him in her arms, her pale eyes filled with rage. "Loyal or not, Alec, if that bloody dog makes one more sound, I'll slit his throat!"

"Lucien!"

The cousin holds her head and sighs. "Alec, it would be most considerate to remove your animal."

"Dear cousin, I shall, on condition you provide me with every detail of last night's dinner."

The surgeon pats the Duchinu's shoulder. "Alec, in due time. For the moment, our imminent concern is… Dash it all!" He slaps his brow and reels back from the force of his blow. "My instruments! I seem to have misplaced my medical bag. However, with no body thermometer at my disposal, by your countenance, I ascertain your fever has subsided."

"Lucien, I experienced no fever."

"Alec, do not be difficult. These hands are the hands of a lady, delicate, perceptive, as every physician's should be." He taps for the Duchinu's brow, his hand shaking. "And these hands tell me…that is, if your forehead is any indication…your fever has subsided."

"And I maintain…"

"Rest is a basic yet potent prescription. The rest I prescribed has done you a world of good."

The Duchinu kicks up his legs. "Decorum be damned!" He sings at the top of his voice the hymn, he says, the cousin and the surgeon know well. "Things that once were wild alarms cannot now disturb my rest!" He asks them to join in the song. They cup their ears and sigh.

"Lucien, Elizabeth, gaze upon the miracle before your eyes. What Grace had prescribed has done me a world of good. I suspect the juice she prescribes for you shall do the same."

"Prescribe? A *peasant girl* prescribe for me? Never!" The surgeon throws his hands over his eyes, but it does him no good. The girl fixes her eyes on him, the pale eyes that give the evil eye. "God, my God, my God!" he cries out and rubs his eyes and drops to the floor.

"Voscenza speaks the truth," the girl says, nodding to the surgeon with a tight smile on her face. "If you drink what I give you, it got to cure your sickness. But…what you hide in your pocket got to make your sickness worse."

"Ha! Very well said, Grace," the Duchinu sings out. "You are an intelligent girl, a good girl. Yes, a good girl, indeed, yet one of mystery whom I ofttimes cannot comprehend." He points to the door. "Grace, that infernal knocking is no longer infernal to my ears. You may enter," he calls out to the round face servant girl. She shuffles in, steadying a tray with two glasses and a large round glass pot filled with a yellow liquid.

There, at the top of the great stairway, in the first room to the west of the long, blue hallway, they drink in silence. By his bed, the Duchinu sips from his jug of water, the way he says his peasants do. The surgeon, he leans on one post at the foot of the bed and sips his ficarindia juice from a glass trembling in his hand. The cousin, she leans on the other post and cradles the glass in her palms, holding steady to it the best she can each time she tries to bring it to her lips. With no good fortune, her hand jerks back, and the yellow juice splashes out the glass, dripping down her fingers. The girl, she drinks nothing. There, in the corner near the small brown dog, she fixes her eyes on the lot of them.

Chiazza races up the dirt road. "Quick!" the carter cries and whips the reins. Not the Ave Maria sun beating down on her flying mane and not the small lava stones digging in her hooves can slow her down. She shakes her head. She shows her teeth. She races up the new carriage road. At the South portico, she breaks free and heads through the iron gates. "No, Chiazza," the carter sobs. "Stay, my friend, my..." He takes in a strong breath. "No, Chiazza, I got to do this all on my own." He runs through the portico to the courtyard, kicks the base of the lava cross and races to the entryway of the Castle. He flies up the great stairway, taking in two, three steps, and throws the Duchinu's door wide open.

"My God! Has a peasant ever shown such rudeness!" That's what the Duchinu cries out when the carter barrels in.

The carter grabs hold of the surgeon. "She's gone! She's gone!"

The surgeon frees himself from the carter's hold and shakes his head. "Has a peasant ever shown such rudeness, my lord? Yes, when he has yet to learn his place."

The carter eyes the girl in the corner and throws himself at her feet. "She's gone!"

"Calmu, Mastru Nonziu," she whispers. "I know about the dead. Now, tell me of the living."

"Your...Mamma...safe," him, gasping through a rush of tears.

"Come here!" the Duchinu shouts. "Joseph, what possesses you?"

He looks up and throws his hands to the heavens. "She's gone! She's gone!"

"Who is gone?" The surgeon holds his throat and looks 'round for the one asking in such a strong and steady voice. What gives him such surprise? The girl knows. She knows the juice from the ficarindia makes right the whirling in the head and the shaking in the voice. Now, the surgeon knows, too. He nears the carter and shouts in his ear, "Carter, let us hope it is the Saitta woman who is gone and out of our lives for good!"

The carter slaps the surgeon's hand from his shoulder. Who can say if it's the sound of the blow or the force of the blow or the fear of more blows what makes the surgeon throw himself in the arms of the Duchinu, the two signori 'nglisi huddling in their show of strength.

"The Saitta woman's a good woman!" the carter shouts back. "But your sin spread deep inside her. That's what still drives her mad. Mad and thirsty in the desert…"

"Alec, the carter talks of madness, but he is the one who is clearly mad."

"Yes, Lucien, I suspect the same."

"Mad? What drives a good woman mad? A man with no regard for a woman's pain drives her mad. It happened to Agata Saitta. My Vincenza took to caring for her the best she knew how, and, then, she took to caring for me and made me a good man. And, me, I never drove her mad. *I* had regard for her pain!"

The surgeon brushes down his grey vest, specks of black and red powder falling on the green rug. "Who in heaven's name is your Vincenza?"

"A healer like one you'll never be!"

The surgeon taps his foot so quick that his whole body starts to shake. "Carter, your *Voscenza*, is that not how you peasants refer to the Duke's son? Be that as it may, he has heard more than his share of dribble and madness for the day. Now, leave this room immediately, or I shall be forced to throw you out."

"You have no right to throw out Mastru Nonziu!" the girl cries out. "He's a good man, and you're not! If you try to harm him, I got to kill you. Mamma wants me to kill you…you, the one…" The girl falls to her knees and sobs. "And, me…I want to kill you, too, even though you are my…"

"Grace," the Duchinu whispers, "this is not the talk of one who heals."

"Alec," the surgeon bows, "I say nothing more. You now bear witness to the venom and ignorance of your peasants."

"Lucien, Grace is good. She has done more good for me during one night than you shall ever realize. Grace, be of good judgment. You are not *killing* anyone today."

"Sì, Voscenza."

"Very well. Do you wish to speak on the carter's behalf?"

"Sì, Voscenza. Mastru Nonziu made 'a z'a Vincenza smile and forget her sorrows. He's a good man. But I see in his eyes all what his heart wants to do. It's an evil thing. I look in his eyes. I look in all your eyes…"

She rushes to the carter's side and says the prayers Vincenza taught her to keep the evil at bay. She pulls the knife from the tattered apron and holds tight to it in one hand. She makes a fist with the other and opens it wide. In one hand, Alfiu's knife; in the other, a worm sleeping in her palm. "How it stays in my blood, the longing to take a life. But we got to change our ways. Mastru Nonziu, look. Look at all what I hold, and all what's in me. 'A z'a Vincenza said I let the knife fall and held tight to the worm. That was the sign at my birth. Let it be how we now live our lives. No more a just eye for eye. First, Blasiu. Now, you. No, we got to be good. We got to wash our hearts clean of all the evil inside."

The carter pushes the girl away. "She...is...gone!"

"The evil we do, the evil they do...what evil is greater? Evil is evil, Mastru Nonziu, one no more than the other. Sì, 'a z'a Vincenza, she's gone, and I suffer for it. The sinners burning in the fires of hell, they don't suffer no more than me. But that's no cause to do more wrong."

"Gratia, my brave Mamsella. You speak words that are now your own, but you don't see. There's no more good for me to do. Look at me. See what casts a good man back to his evil ways." He rips through his pocket and grabs a few yellow flower buds. He waves them at the Duchinu. "The pure and kind Vincenza's gone. The savages you call *men* killed her." He crushes the buds in his palm. "This is the last of Vincenza's miracles. It is the last of Vincenza and her love for me, born and gone in one small day like the bright lake fly in early spring. Here, in my hands, are the ways of her goodness. Goodness like this what saved your cousin." He flings them at the Duchinu's face. "And for a trade, and in your name, your savages killed. Is this how titled men shower gratitude on those that do them good?"

The surgeon rushes to the carter ready to slap him or worse, his fingers tight, the flesh of his palm red and stretched.

"Lucien, there'll be no violence in this room!"

"As you wish, my lord." The surgeon bows and shuffles to the window's ledge, his fists clenched in his high slit pockets.

"*God protect me from my friends.* Listen to my words, Voscenza," the carter throws a sneering look at the surgeon and the cousin, "like the Angelus bells, they'll ring in your heart all through the day 'til you plead for the truth to be silenced. *God protect me from my friends.* The friends that drink from jugs of vinegar. The friends that lurk in the night. *God protect me* got to be your daily prayer. But power blinds you. You are blind to the friends that betray you. Your Papà's savage men, even the ones with titles, even the ones," he gets down on his knee and bows to the surgeon, a big and taunting bow, "even the ones that got no more titles, they all betrayed you."

The surgeon springs from the ledge and lunges at the carter. *"Even the ones that got no more titles?* I'll show you what the ones *that got no more titles* can do!" He wraps his hands 'round the carter's neck and shakes him. He knocks him down. He pounds his head on the green flower rug. The girl leaps on the surgeon's back and tightens her grip on the knife, the struggle shining in the blade.

"Animal!" the cousin screams. That's when I howl like a mad dog, the brown dog howling with me. The cousin cups her ears. She lets out a cry, the kind of cry creatures of the forest make when their young ones are in danger, a cry that shoots out in the air and, when it fades, leaves the air sick and trembling. The Duchinu slaps his hand over his cousin's mouth and stomps his foot.

"Grace, I command you."

The girl raises the knife higher.

"Grace, I implore you…"

"My Papà was a good man. This Papà brought sorrow to my Mamma. He seen her at the lava cross. He seen what he done! This Papà is the Devil!"

*"Papà?"* the Duchinu jumps back.

*"Papà?"* the cousin gasps.

*"Papà?"* the surgeon flicks his head and eyes the girl on his back, his lips, tight and trembling.

I hold my belly and laugh at the panicky birds, screeching their *Papà* cries 'til the surgeon's back shoots up. The carter rolls out from 'neath him. The girl slides off and holds out her arms and wraps the carter in them.

"Mastru Nonziu, you're hurt." She kisses the carter's hand and wipes the blood that drips in his hollow eyes. She runs to the window and pinches a small boy spider crawling 'long the ledge. She whispers to it and closes her hand. When she opens it, there, in her palm, the spider spins his web. The web covers her palm. She rushes back to the carter and fastens it to his head like a fine bandage.

"Mamsella, your Papà..."

"*Sst...sst*," she presses her finger to her mouth. "No more, Mastru Nonziu. No more. I know all what there's to know of that evil Papà, things even you don't know, things he tried to do to me, things I bring to mind and things I can't. But I know all what I got to do now. No twist or turn of your words got to spare me. I know there's no more kindness here. I know Mamma blesses vengeance. Still I got to do the good. I got to do the good for 'a z'a Vincenza and for all what grows inside me. Good for good, but if he hurts you more..."

"What goodness beats inside your heart that shrivels inside of mine? You forgive, and, still, there's room in your heart to care for me, the one that can't forgive."

"I never known my Papà. This Papà, I don't want to know. But, you, Mastru Nonziu, you come to be like my..."

At the sound of the words, his chest rises. When it falls what issues forth is a long, quivering sigh and a rush of tears that washes clean the dirt on his face and the black tinge on his beard. But I can no more laugh at the sight of the white beard and the black tinge dripping down his brown velvet jacket, not now when my own eyes fill with water.

"Gratia Maria, my dear child, like a Papà, I got to keep you safe from harm. I got to take away your sorrows. Look at him, the great surgeon, curled up like a dog over there. What can he do to me? If he wants to stay in the Duchinu's good graces, he dares not do nothing to you. Your Mamma, she's safe. She's sleeping. None can harm her. You see, all what I say is true. Now, there are no more sorrows in your life."

"What madness is this?" The cousin drops to the green flower rug and tugs at the surgeon's jacket all while the brown dog, quiet and happy, licks the ficarindia juice on her fingers. "What madness is this?"

The Duchinu leans rigid over the two of them. "Lucien, I, too, wish to be informed. What genre of madness is this?"

"You are right, Alec. This *is* madness. All this drivel of sudden parental recognition. The girl is mad. Quite stupid, as well. She claims to be one of my own which, verily, she is not. Yet, at the same time, she has admitted to being that *Saitta* woman's daughter…"

"Dear God! Lucien, am I to believe you had a dalliance with her mother?"

"Dr. Gale!" the cousin cries out. "She's *your*…"

The Duchinu throws his hands in the surgeon's hair pulling at the red strands, "And this…is *this* the proof?"

He shakes off the Duchinu and moves to the window's ledge. "That is not the point. The girl you claim accomplishes so much good is equally culpable regarding your loss of revenue in the pistachio groves. *That*, the Duke of Bronte would say, *is* the point. I shall give her this: she plays the innocent quite well." He reaches in his vest pocket and pulls out the jewel flask. The girl jumps back. "My mistake," he says with a tight smile and slips it back, "this is neither the time nor the place for such indulgences, is it, peasant girl?" He fumbles in the pockets of his vest 'til he tugs at a small branch and pulls it out. "My lord, this *is* the evidence." He shuffles to the girl, waving the branch 'til it brushes past her cheek. The Duchinu's mouth drops open. He points at the branch where small red husks spring forth.

"Grace…how…did…you…?"

"Alec, allow me to answer for the girl. It is how demons work their magic." The surgeon waves the branch back in the girl's face. "You, peasant girl, do you know what this is?"

"Lucien, should you not be the one to enlighten us?"

"Very well, my lord. It is damaging proof of the pistachio grove her parents cultivated on your land."

"Dr. Gale, let us put an end to all your tiresome speculation. Take it, Grace. Assure me that you do not recognize it."

She closes her eyes and whispers a prayer and holds the branch to her chest. The red husks turn to white.

The Duchinu throws his hands over his mouth. "My God, Grace, who are you?"

"A witch," the surgeon whispers, "and not a very good one as she must rely on a bag of tricks."

"Lucien, this is not the time. Give me a moment to reflect." He takes in a breath. "Perhaps my interest in the grove shall peak one day, but, at the moment, we are dealing with more pressing matters."

"You are right, Alec. Now is the time to take pity on the girl and her madness."

She slips the branch in her apron and wraps the carter in her arms. The surgeon holds out his hand. She slaps it away.

"Come now, Grace, be civil. Allow the good doctor to assist you. We are all in a state of *bouleversement*. It is obvious that both you and Joseph…"

The carter breaks free of the girl's hold. "My name is *Nonziu!*"

"As I was saying, it is obvious you are experiencing emotional crests regarding the untimely loss of your Venice."

"Vincenza! Her name is *Vincenza!*" The carter crosses himself each time he says her name. "Vincenza, holy Vincenza…holy, holy Vincenza…"

"I stand corrected, Joseph. Viiiceeenzaaahhh. I have already given my word to Grace. If my men prove implicated in Viiiceeenzaaahhh's unfortunate death, they shall be punished. However, for the moment, let us bow our heads and say a prayer for the good woman's soul. Good. Now, I believe a hymn would be most appropriate." He clasps his hands, his lid flutters, and in a loud, deep voice, he sings out, "Things that once were wild alarms cannot now disturb my rest!"

"Rest?" The carter spits on the rug. "What do you know of rest? Not the rest what makes you do nothing and live off a title, but the rest a man earns when he finds his peace with a good woman."

"Joseph, I shall ignore the insolence of grief." Slow, slow, the Duchinu opens his eye and casts a long look at the girl. "However, allow me to inform you a turbulent soul is not exclusive to the peasant man. Who amongst us does not long for such a woman who may comprehend our…*desires?*"

"Vincenza made me a decent man, but her death throws me back to the Devil's clutches. *Ahi!*" he cries out and grabs his chest. "*Ahi!*" he leaps at the Duchinu and throws his hands 'round his neck. "The Devil's clutches! That's where I find my peace! That's where I find my rest!"

Quick, the surgeon jabs his elbow in the carter's side. He slaps his face and pounds his chest 'til the carter breaks free of the Duchinu. He pushes him to the door. "I have listened to verily all I can stomach. You, Carter, go back to your kind. You were never one of us. Nonetheless, you took great pains to distance yourself from *them*. Answer me, Carter, where *is* your kind?"

The carter falls to his knees. "Vincenza's gone. This body longs for a soul. Without a soul, it has no kind..."

"Come now, good man," the surgeon pats the carter's back, "we are not heartless. Perhaps if you have some goods of quality to offer us in the future, a fine pair of leather boots, that is your specialty, is it not? At the appropriate time, we shall receive you quite warmly. And, naturally, you must partake in your *Voscenza's* generosity as all *peasants* do on the first of May."

"Dr. Gale!"

"My lord, my apologies. Carter, should you like to regale us once more with your tale of the boy who became a fish? Should that bring you joy... and peace? In the future, perhaps. However, at the moment, we must bid you a fond adieu."

The carter jumps up and claws at his chest. "She was my soul! What's a man without his soul but a clean slate for the Devil's deeds?"

"Carter," the surgeon hisses, "you...*creatures*...have...no...soul."

"*Ahi!*" The carter lunges for the girl's knife. She holds to it fast. "Give it to me!"

"Mastru Nonziu!"

He grabs the knife and pounces on the surgeon. The girl punches the carter's hands. She bites them 'til they bleed, but still he don't lose his grip.

"Ppi piaciri! Please, Mastru Nonziu!" He slaps her away.

With a strength I never seen in no man, one hand holds the surgeon down. The other rubs the blade 'long the scars on his throat. The Duchinu tightens his grip 'round the wide leaf carvings. The cousin hides her face 'neath the brown dog's pillow. The girl lets out a howling cry.

"*Ahi!* Who is the one that got no soul?" the carter cries louder. "Who is the one that got to suffer the fires of hell for all time? Holy Savior, take the evil, not the good! Take the evil, not the good!" He crosses himself and slits the surgeon's throat.

The surgeon lets out a slaughter cry. He presses his palm to his throat. He moans and gurgles, the bright red foam spreading from 'neath his fingers. His nostrils flare. The smell of iron fills the air. When the surgeon's hand drops to his chest, the carter raises the knife and stabs at the throat again, again, again, 'til he throws his head back in near collapse. The surgeon's head reels back, too, his eyes fixed on the high ceiling, his mouth limp, his face pale, a criminal, at long last, punished for his crimes.

"Dare to speak a word, *Duchinu!*" the carter shouts.

The Duchinu opens his mouth, but his lips do none but tremble. He slaps at his throat, pulls it, punches it 'til his face is wet with tears, but the sound it makes is none but a whimper.

"Dare to say I'm a man condemned. This I know. Dare to say I'm a hunted man. I pray for Vincenza to hunt me down and comfort me in my dreams…but I am like the others now and kill like the others now…"

"Basta!" the girl cries out. "Maronna 'a Nunziata, help your suffering child. Z'a Vincenza, wrap him in *love* and not…and not…" The girl grabs the knife and hurls it out the window. "Let this be the end to all the evil that marks our lives." The knife flies past the courtyard and the lava cross. It flies south past the new carriage road and south past the vineyards and olive groves and the crowd of birch and oak trees. It flies east past the dry lands and the fertile lands and the lava rocks that pile high at Mungibellu's feet. And it flies all the way to the beautiful mountain's halo of smoke 'til it reaches her mouth, there, where Mungibellu swallows the glistening knife whole.

"Voscenza," the girl whispers, "I gave my word no harm comes to you this day. You see before you a good man what causes harm and punishes his own self in his heart." She strokes the carter's jaw that makes its own desperate speech of clicks and moans. "Show mercy on Mastru Nonziu, a man with sorrow for blood and grief for bones."

The Duchinu pries his fingers from the post of the bed, the carved leaves pressed in the lines of his palm like the ancient markings of a slave. He holds out his hands and stumbles to the body. "Lucien, Lucien, my God, Lucien! You were a fine man. This is how an animal dies, not a gentleman like you." The girl holds out her hands, but the Duchinu spits at them. "Now, *peasant girl*, now I understand the venom of your people." He digs his hand in the robe pocket and holds tight to the pistol. "Dr. Gale understood. I chose not to believe. You are as mad as the one on whose behalf you speak. That one muttering his prayers for salvation is not a man. He is nothing but a beast. And, you, with your clarion cry for mercy, you have pledged your loyalty to a murderer. Who are you, *peasant girl*, but a murderer's accomplice?" He turns up the wide collar like he got a chill inside him. The hem of the silk robe sweeps 'cross the green flower rug where the body lies, the deep red color of the robe soaking up the surgeon's blood. He stomps his foot. "You cannot bear witness to the murder of a loyal friend and plead for the murderer!" He pounds his fist in his hand. "Plead all you like, neither of you shall receive the balm of mercy from the fifth great Duke of Bronte."

The cousin throws off the pillow at the sound of the words. "The Duke of Bronte...The Duke of Bronte...The Duke of Bronte..." She whispers the words, her eyes closed, her hands clasped to her heart, like this is the prayer to save her.

"You're right, Voscenza. I pledged my loyalty, but not to Mastru Nonziu. I pledged it to my Mamma. But I didn't cause the pain she desired for you. I healed you. I healed your cousin. All in the name of 'a z'a Vincenza. In her name, this day, your life was spared. In 'a z'a Vincenza's name, I spared my Papà's life."

The Duchinu rushes to the great stairway. "Are you mad, peasant girl? He is *not* your father."

"He *was*. He knew it...and you know it, too."

"*He has not been spared!* Look at him! He is dead! Dead!" He teeters on the first steps, shouting and grabbing at the walls. The servants scream and swarm at the bottom of the stairway, their arms held up and out. He takes in one last breath and waves to his room. "Guards! Servants! Come quickly! Shackle the murderers and bring them to justice!"

*

In a corner of the Duchinu's room, the carter crouches, his face pale, his eyes lifeless 'til he shuts them tight. When he opens them, a light burns there, the light of truth burning in the eyes of all our kind. It's the truth of all what we live for, what Alfiu died for, what Agata aches for 'til her dying day. The Duchinu's kind, they live for warm lemon cakes and streams of color lights that illuminate the sky and documents with raised gold seals and *marionettes*

| |

and flasks of *green fairy*. But not our kind. Justice. That's what burns in all our eyes. That's what brings us hope. That's what we live for. That's how we die.

*

The Duchinu rushes back to the room, his arms held out to the cousin. She rubs her belly and tells him she got much to say, but first she got to understand it all herself. "Forgive me," she whimpers.

"Elizabeth, I, too, must beg your forgiveness for ever believing that another…"

An army of shiny boots and buckles pound the stairs. The cousin cups her ears. She crushes her face in the Duchinu's chest.

"Mastru Nonziu, they're coming," the girl whispers. "For all that's good and holy, shake off the spell the Devil casts on you. In the name of the one you hold dear and blessed in your heart, slip to the window and wait 'til I give the word. I know it's far, but I'll help you. Don't look at me with such eyes. I can help you. Chiazza, too. All you done for me, now, I got to take care of you. And I give you my word, I'll take care of Chiazza, too."

He takes the cross from his neck and slips it over the girl's head. "I got no more need for such a holy thing."

"'A z'a Vincenza worn this," she says and kisses it, "now, I got to wear it all the days of my life. Grazii, Mastru Nonziu, grazii. For all what you given me, grazii."

"Gratia Maria Saitta," he sobs, "for all what you given back to me, grazii."

The girl eyes the Duchinu and the one folded in his arms. She throws up her hands and makes a fist, then opens her hands and spreads her fingers wide. She crawls to the door. "Now, Mastru Nonziu!" she cries out and slams the door. "*Fora! Fora! Get out!* Run quick as your feet can bear!" The hands and arms and legs that built the dwelling for the shepherd boy now throw themselves 'cross the door, the army of shiny boots and buckles, try as they might, with no power to break it down.

"Run, Mastru Nonziu. May 'a Maronna 'a Nunziata protect you where you go!"

The Duchinu lunges at the carter's feet and grabs hold of his ankles. I shriek and howl. The cousin screams and rushes to the Duchinu's side. He got no way out but to loosen his grip and comfort her. The carter breaks free. His eyes shut tight, he leaps out the window. There, below, Chiazza waits for him. He lands in the back of the cart, cushioned by the fancy dresses. He jumps out and shouts "grazii" to Chiazza. In a flash, he's gone. The girl crosses herself and smiles. The shiny boots and buckles kick the door open. They push her 'cross the room, at the Duchinu's feet.

"After him!" the Duchinu shouts. "Seize him as you would any beast. Hurl him into a cage. Bind him. Shackle him. Parade him through the town. Toss him like refuse into a deep, dark hole where he shall await his trial, though trial may prove too good for him. If he cannot be restrained, kill him on sight as you would any wild beast. As for the peasant girl, I shall take charge of her myself."

"And, I, as well," the cousin says, brushing her cheek 'long the Duchinu's face like a dog that longs for petting. "From this day, dear Alec, we shall act as one and dole out punishment as one."

"From this day, my delicate Elizabeth…" She grabs his hand and kisses it. "Elizabeth…Elizabeth…"

"Yes, my lord."

"There is a service I must ask of you to which you must comply."

"Anything! Everything!"

"Elizabeth, you must return to your room."

"No, Alec, not now…not when…"

"Immediately."

She eyes the girl at the Duchinu's feet. "Animals, each and every one of them."

"Nonetheless, I implore you."

The cousin brings his hand to her chest. "Alec, I…"

"My heart rejoices that you wish to remain by my side. However, you cannot assist me. Shield your eyes. I shall lead you out the door."

The cousin shuts her eyes. "Dear God," she whimpers and taps her way 'cross the surgeon's carcass.

"Take my arm."

"Alec, what shall become of…?"

"Our beloved Dr. Gale? I assure you he shall be treated with the utmost respect and dignity awarded a man of his caliber…"

"*Caliber*," she chokes out the word, holding tight to the Duchinu's arm. "And the peasant girl?"

"As she is so fond of saying, *a just eye for eye*."

*

The girl stays. Where can she go? When the Duchinu comes back, she's sitting on the window ledge, smiling and holding her heart.

"Too late for that," he says. "Too late for all your *beguiling* ways." The air puffs hard from his nose, the openings flare out wide like Chiazza's when the carter drives her too hard. He wraps his fingers 'round the girl's wrists and lifts her up, small and light the way she is now, her red hair whipping 'round her, protecting her like armor.

The sun's journey ends behind the west mountains. In the darkening room, the Duchinu drags the girl 'cross the green flower rug where her feet kick the side of the carcass. He slaps her face. "Respect!" She falls down and knocks the jewel flask out of the surgeon's vest pocket. "My God!" The Duchinu rips off his eye patch, his sea eyes fixed on hers. "What have you done? Peasant girl, what have you made me do? It is beyond my comprehension how you have made everything so wrong."

She struggles to get up. He pushes her back down. "Voscenza, your cousin eats the raw meat when none watches her the way a beast gorges on his prey. All what's in her belly now got to make her change her ways or u vermu can come back to her."

"More dreams," he shouts, dragging her by the hair, "is that how it unravels? More dreams to see and undo us all?"

"Voscenza, they can come back to her."

"Worms? You said you cured her."

"Sì, but u vermu can come back. They come back first with the fright. There was much in the Castle to give Dunna Eeelisabetta fright 'though she can't bring it all to mind to tell you. Like me, all what the surgeon done I can't bring to mind. The specter she feared, Mastru Nonziu seen him in Dunna Eeelisabetta's room, he was of flesh and blood, and you called him a loyal friend. He's gone now, but he left his mark in her. It grows. Soon, all got to know, even you that don't want to know, you got to know when the innocent one screams for breath, and you look in his eyes, even you that don't want to know, you got to know."

He turns 'round. "What in God's name are you suggesting?" He falls on his knees and grabs her shoulders. "No! I shall not hear one more desperate lie!"

"Heed the truth, Voscenza. If u vermu comes back, you can help. 'A z'a Vincenza's basket does Dunna Eeelisabetta no more good. The plants are old and dry now, but there's a girl in the kitchen, the one with the round face. If you show her the dried boy filici, the young gardener got to help her find the plant. None in the Castle knows the prayers, but there's an old woman in Bronti…she's 'a z'a Vincenza's cummari and…"

"Enough!" He shakes her and loses his footing, the two falling on the green flower rug. He hovers over her, his robe like a big, red bird of prey, spreading its wings and hiding her from view. All what I see now is the girl's small face and the Duchinu's fingers, ten long, trembling fingers digging in the rug by her shoulders, desperate to keep his body straight and still. "You disparage Elizabeth," he whispers, breath to breath. "You disparage Dr. Gale. Yet, in such venomous speech, there is kindness in your voice. Do not be kind, not at this moment, not when I must… My God!" he cries out when his fingers curl and he topples to her side.

"You speak of kindness like it's a cloak I put on and take off when the sun shines or the moon shines. This is who I am. Voscenza, you know of kindness but when it suits you. And, now, you're not kind," she pushes herself up, "and, now, you got to kill me."

He grabs the girl's hand. "Kill you? How can I kill you when I… Signurina, land of hair…Signurina, land of… Grace, oh, my Grace…" He presses her hand in his palms and brings it to his cheek. He brings it to his lips. He kisses the precious jewel, him, a thief, wanting more kisses and stealing more kisses 'til she pulls her hand away.

"No! No! No!" He swipes his hand 'cross his mouth. "Dr. Gale, you were right! This is sorcery, pure and simple!" He throws himself on the green flower rug and thrashes 'round like he got a spell that grows in him and he got to shake it off. "Look at me! Look at me, peasant girl!" He takes in a breath, his hands on his knees. He takes in a breath and stands. "This is who you say you are, kind and good…well, this is who *I* am." He reaches in the pocket of his red silk robe and draws out the pistol. He waves it at the door. "As rational beings, there is always a choice to be made. At this hour, you leave me none."

# PART V:
# THE FOREST

*To love the one who does not love you is a waste of time.*

At the end of the long, blue hallway in the north, 'cross from the cousin's room, in the room where the cousin said the Duchinu locked away his splendors, there, from full moon to full moon, he locked away the girl. No one, not the servants, not the cousin, ever dared to enter. After the household fell to sleep, that was when he brought the girl food and fancy clothes and spoke to her of his home by the sea that now she can no more hope to visit. He spoke of Orlannu, the mad Orlannu, and the fury that coursed through the blood of epic knights and Bronti peasants. He talked of this and that. Always the girl stayed silent. And this September night when he slips a necklace with a ruby heart 'round her neck, still, she don't utter a word.

"The two of you...the difference is remarkable," he whispers and scratches the crest of his sand color beard. "Elizabeth must have emeralds to temper her hair, but, *you*, you must have rubies to deepen it. Promise me you shall never remove this necklace. It shall goad me to imagine...when the light shines on it, it shall reflect your own light or perhaps my light in you." He lets out a sigh, the white vapors of his breath sheathing the bones that jut from his cheeks. "Perhaps no light at all, madness on my part. Perhaps the only light of late is that which Dr. Gale's *green fairy* proffers me." He throws his head back and takes a swig from the surgeon's jewel flask, the sweet green smell filling the air. "Signurina, beautiful land of hair. Grace, beautiful Grace, it is time..."

All night, the full moon been shining, there, in the east where the sun lit the sky. Now, a dark yellow veil makes its way 'cross the moon. What happens in the sky this night is rare. I seen it last with my own Papà when I was but a boy. He told me of men in foreign lands that watched the yellow veil hide the moon. This frightened them, and, so, they threw swords in the air to slice the veil and make the moon shine once more. But there's no fear in the Duchinu's eyes. He wants the sky dark.

Alone, he carries out the deed. No guard shackles the girl. No Notary waves documents and makes bold speeches of *restitution and revenue*. In his long black jacket, black pants, black vest and stiff white shirt, he looks dressed for a celebration in the dark of night. He brushes away the wet from both his eyes, now that he don't wear no eye patch no more. He hands the girl a sack of food and three fancy dresses in green and yellow and rose and speaks but one word. In her Mamma's blue marriage dress and apron, washed and sewn up like new, she follows him down the great stairway and through the courtyard to the lava cross.

"Banished," he whispers in the cold, quiet air and waits 'til she says the word, too.

"Baaaneeeshaaa," she says and shudders.

He takes off his jacket and throws it over her shoulders. "It is by order of King Ferdinand I who gave our great Admiral and his heirs full penal jurisdiction over life and death…and banishment."

"Baaaneeeshaaa."

He gazes down at her, his low lip quivering. "A man stands before you crushed by the weight of his title."

"Baaaneeeshaaa."

"*Merum et mistum imperium*. It dates back to ancient times. Granted, this is not of your concern. It is the curse of privilege and power which the Duke of Bronte must bear."

"Duca? No, Voscenza, that man you can never be."

He kneels at the lava cross and rubs the chiseled words at the base. *Eroi Immortali Nili*. He stands back up, leaning rigid over the girl. "Immortal Hero of the Nile. My coat of arms is the great Vice-Admiral Lord Viscount Horatio Nelson's coat of arms. His motto is my motto: Let him wear the palm who has deserved it."

"Voscenza," she throws a look to the rooms in the north, "you kept me safe where none could find me. Your blood is not of their kind."

"*I deserve it*! Banished I say and banished it shall be! Do you understand? Banished from Bronte, indeed, from any town in close proximity to the Duchy."

"Baaaneeeshaaa?"

"Banished from the town, from the mountain…"

"Baaaneeeshaaa?"

"From your home."

"Baaaneeeshaaa from *your* home."

He throws his arms in the air and stomps 'round her. "No. *You* are banished. *You* are banished from *your* home. *You* are banished from your home and from all who live there."

"Mamma lives there. Baaaneeeshaaa from Mamma?"

"At long last! Yes, Grace, banished from your home and your mother."

"No! You keep me away from her for too long. Who cares for her now, now, that your men killed 'a z'a Vincenza and, now, that Mastru Nonziu…? Mamma, she got to be sick with worry."

"Grace, my fiancée has of late enlightened me as to the woman's madness. How can you care for a creature like that?"

"She's my Mamma."

He folds his arms, slapping them with his palms and blowing out puffs of cold air. "You claim Dr. Gale was your father, why had you not cared for him?"

She slips off the jacket and holds it out to him. He grabs it and wraps himself in the warmth. "He was my Papà from blood. But she's my Mamma from blood…and heart."

"You speak with such devotion. If I hadn't known better, I should say *love*."

"Avaja! All children got to love their Mammas."

"Perhaps out of duty."

"Out of love."

"Love," he whispers with a shudder. "And…her duty to you?"

"*Duty*…to a child?"

"Very well, devotion…*love*."

She smoothes down the new seams of the blue marriage dress washed and sewed by the *'nglisi tailor* that swore his loyalty to the Duchinu long ago.

A small man with the height and voice of a child, he slipped in and out of the Duchinu's room with satin and lace and silk in his small arms, his small fingers mending the girl's dress and sewing new dresses for her, too, fancy dresses in green and yellow and rose and all before the Duchinu sent him on a big ship back to Lundra.

"All Mammas got to love their children, if not this day, then on the morrow. Before they die, all Mammas got to love their children."

"Love and Honor!" He grabs her shoulders and shakes her 'til her foot slips and she falls. The sack opens and the bread and the cheese and the chicken and the lemon cake scatter on the cobble stones. "Love and Honor, the two precepts of your island, or, so your class would have us believe." He stomps on the bread and the chicken. "Here, in Sicily, we nobles suffocate from the lack of love and honor in your world."

"There *is* love, Voscenza. There *is* honor." She pushes herself back up.

"Not in the God-forsaken world you live in! In your world, no one loves anyone. Children are born. Children die. Where is the joy? Where is the sorrow? No one weeps at a baby's lifeless body tossed in the dirt, least of all the mothers who dispose of yet another mouth to feed."

She buries her face in the dresses. "I weep. I weep for the innocent ones, not like Mamma when they sought her out and threw coins at her feet and she wept and mourned for their dead." She holds out her arms and fixes her eyes on the Duchinu 'til he holds out his own trembling arms where she lays the three fancy dresses. "Me, I weep in silence. I weep for the innocent ones and for my sister and for Mamma that loved her too much."

He cradles the dresses. "It is as I have always surmised, Grace, you stand apart."

"'A z'a Vincenza said I am like no other."

"Yes," his voice, now, low and quivering, "*you* are like no other…"

"Voscenza, be kind and send me back to Mamma."

"No! No!" He shakes his head like the cross-eyed lunatic that shakes clean his old thoughts before he rants the new. "In your world, children leave no imprint. If they survive, what do they grow to be? Peasants with no imprint. Look at you, the way you stare at me with your mouth agape… *wide open, wide open.* You have no concept of the truths of which I speak nor the favor I grant you. I am saving you from further dealings with a woman of stone who cannot love you. Be grateful and leave. Banished! Banished from your home and from all who live there! Banished before I can no longer…"

She throws herself at his feet. She kisses his hand and calls him *good.* She pulls at his hand and calls him *fair* and *just.* She smiles like she already heard the Duchinu say he changed his way of thinking and she can care for her Mamma 'til her dying day. But he stands rigid and silent. She bites her lip 'til the small corner of her mouth is red and raw. And, then, like a great thought come to mind, she slaps her brow, and that's when she shouts out, "Voscenza, the fifth great Duca of Bronti!" and shouts out all his praises to the fading yellow veil that shadows the moon.

He shakes his hand free. "*Merum et mistum imperium.* Judicial power over life and death and banishment. Banished! That is how it must be."

"No! Voscenza, no!"

He throws his shoulders back and whispers that living on the Duca's land is no more what the girl can hope for, the cousin, doubting the girl's innocence in "ravaging priceless paintings and furniture," and, more, doubting the Duchinu's tale of her bold escape. "Banished…as your death is more than I can bear."

"But…"

"Dr. Gale was my father's friend and confidant. My father expects nothing less of me."

"I got to stay."

"If you do not leave, you shall serve as an example, a public deterrent, as my father would say, the way that Saitta peasant you call your *Papà* was made an example."

"The great Alfiu Saitta?"

"All the information I needed regarding him has always been at my disposal. Grace, you look confused. Have you not yet comprehended that I, too, have people to do my bidding?"

"People? *Ppù! Ppù!* People like the kind what killed 'a z'a Vincenza? You call such beasts *people?* They're stupid and selfish. There got to be a time when they sleep or look to satisfy their nature. That got to be the time for me to go to the dwelling and take care of Mamma."

"They have orders to shoot you."

"They got to find me."

"If you are *that* foolish, they shall."

"When I was but a child," the girl clasps her hands, "Mamma taught me a prayer. Not a holy one like the prayers to 'a Maronna 'a Nunziata that 'a z'a Vincenza taught me. No, this was Mamma's special prayer. I said it 'til the words took hold in my heart. Now, I say it to you. *Two are powerful. The one with everything and the one with nothing.* Now, who stands there with a mouth wide open? Now, who can't understand? I got to take care of my Mamma, and, then, she got to…one day, if not this day, but, one day, before she dies, one day, she got to…" She beats her chest. "And what do you want to do?" she cries out. "You want to take away all what I hope for! You, the Duchinu of the peasants, you got to know what a peasant can do when there's no more to hope for!"

He slaps the air with the back of his hand like the girl's threat is a swarm of flies he got to swat away. "*Duchinu*! I know what this nobleman can do to peasants who refer to me by that disparaging sobriquet!" He stomps his way to the west of the Castle and turns 'round. "Come to the stables and say your farewells expeditiously to Chiazza."

"Chiazza?"

"Did you not believe I had a special affection for the murderer's mare?"

"I gave my word to Mastru Nonziu to take care of her."

"Chiazza stays. Do not interpret such magnanimity as weakness. Her murdering master shall be punished!" The Duchinu marches with long, pounding strides.

"But I gave my word to Mastru Nonziu," the girl says walking fast behind.

He turns 'round and throws the dresses on the ground. "Your vow to a murderer is meaningless! As we speak, my men hunt the criminal down. When they find him…"

She takes in a breath and rushes past him. "Mastru Nonziu finds himself in a better place! None can find him there!"

The Duchinu marches quick behind her to the stable door, and, there, he takes in his own strong breaths. "Grace," he leans on the door, wiping his brow, "that is quite impossible, especially as the field guards close in on him."

She grabs the latch. "All what's in my dreams is all what I know. You, the Duchinu of the peasants, and you don't see and you don't hear a peasant's dreams. So, now, I got to tell you. Mastru Nonziu is safe. But sorrow and vengeance pour from his heart like blood from a gaping wound. I tell you, *he* is the one to close in on your men. And when he finds them, he got to kill them one by one 'til the last one dies."

"Grace, I am setting you free, and your recompense is yet another idle threat."

She pushes up the latch and throws the door open. "*Gggrrraaaccceee?* Basta with all what you call me! I know my name. It's not what you say. I know all what I am. It's not what you say I am."

He throws his hand back and slaps her face. "Judas! Judas I call you now. You and your red hair! You and your betrayals of kindness and…"

I ready myself to howl, but the girl lets out a laugh, louder than the sound of the blow. "*Giuda?* This is what you call me? Gratia Maria Saitta is my name. Gratia Maria Saitta. Now, you show me the moment is right to say all what I know beats in your heart. Day to night for the rest of your days, *Gratia Maria Saitta* got to be the one name what brings you comfort and pain. It's the one *disziu* you dare not utter."

"*Desire? Desire? For you?* How dare you!"

"Sì, desire for a peasant girl. Duchinu, how dare *you?*"

The Duchinu digs in his vest pocket and hurls the surgeon's flask at the stable door. Chiazza's head shoots up. Alone in the stable, bigger than the biggest square in all of Bronti, Chiazza trots 'round, happy and proud 'neath a crown of bright red roses. Behind her in the cart, new goods pile high, jugs and pots and beddings and looms, new goods mixed with the carter's old goods. Such a heavy load, and Chiazza drags it, the Duchinu says, 'round the Castle before the light of day, 'round and 'round the Castle 'til the sky turns black and she makes her way back to the stable to eat and rest. But it's no more the cart I know. The Duchinu seen to that when his men painted over the panels of the brave Orlannu with new scenes of the *hero* Nelson's victories at sea.

When the girl holds out her hand and whispers, the mare knickers soft and low and shakes her head clean of the Duchinu's flowers. In her nakedness, I see how strong and beautiful she is. The Duchinu holds out his hand. The mare squeals. The Duchinu jumps back. Through his teeth, he spits out the order. "Bring Chiazza to the gates!"

*

The girl leads Chiazza to the iron gates. The Duchinu holds out his hand again, but the mare kicks and jacks her front legs in the air. The cart jerks back. A low moaning comes from 'neath the blankets. Hands shoot up, gripping the sides of the cart and ripping at the blanket that hid the face of a boy that now got no more cause to hide. He opens his eyes. He takes in the iron gates and the new carriage road and lets out a cry. He cups his cheek, but the mark, once the shape of a broad bean, once red and hollow, is now none but a tiny pea that fades before my eyes.

"It's *you*." The girl's eyes fill with water.

The Duchinu swipes his hand 'cross her cheek and flicks the tears from her face. "What is this? Affection? Affection for a shepherd boy?" The tears in his hand harden and shine like tiny jewels. He rubs his thumb down the smooth flesh of each finger 'til the tears fall and shatter on the cobble stones. "Affection…"

"The shepherd boy done none but love your sheep, and what do you do? You keep him prisoner."

"Prisoner? On the contrary, he was overcome with grief when my men happened upon him. For the last month, he has been recovering at the manor, in his own fashion, as the driver of Chiazza's cart. When he is well, he shall return to the remaining sheep or choose a better livelihood, the choice is his, although I do hope he remains at the manor. He has the makings of a fine manservant, honest and loyal as he has proven to be."

"He got to stay with me."

"He is disheartened and weak. Do you intend to carry him?"

The girl kisses the shepherd boy's hands. "Blasiu that blazes the sky, the sorrow still got a hold in you. Let me be the one to do your healing."

"Gratia," the shepherd boy sobs, "Gratia that graces the earth."

The Duchinu narrows his eyes and lets out a weak laugh. He swallows hard and lets out a louder one. "Forgive me. This is simply too amusing. You peasants are quite fond of legends, are you not? Very well, here is one upon which you may reflect, as you, Grace, aptly stated, *day to night for the rest of your days*." He throws a look to the east where the shadows of mountains come in view. "According to the Greeks, the Cyclops, your one-eyed monster, was the progeny of the god of the sky and the goddess of the earth. *Blasiu that blazes the sky...Gratia that graces the earth...*" He laughs louder, a gasping, choking laugh. "Do I infer that the pair of you intend to create some new world order as...as *gods*?" A loud crackle like a thunder rises in his throat and near drowns out his words. "If, indeed, this is your intention, I should only imagine your progenies. Poor, ignorant, ungrateful monsters!"

The girl grabs the boy's hand. She kisses it, holds tight to it. "I make no sense of your words, Duchinu, but the dark in you, that I know. That I make sense of. This is no more the world for Blasiu and me."

"Blaise stays in my charge. Now, leave!"

"You speak like the surgeon. You laugh like him, too. I see what always been in you, for, now, it takes root...it grows...it thrives. You don't want to stop it no more, the dark in you. That got to make Dunna Eeelisabetta's own heart fill with joy."

He pats the pistol in his long jacket. "Blaise remains with me. Chiazza, as well."

"And Gratia Maria Saitta!" She waves her hand at the Castle and the sky. "Look! The moon fades. The sky's near bright. The Mattutinu bells got to ring soon. Dunna Eeelisabetta got to wake soon from her dreams and see me here. *A prisoner or a guest* she got to wonder. Nothing in your eyes got to make her believe your words, try as you might to keep the truth at bay."

He slips his hand in his pocket and clenches his teeth. "Truth? Truth? Yes, at long last, I clearly see the truth." He marches 'round her, his boots pounding on the cobble stones like a lunatic knocking at a door. "As quickly as you beguiled me when I first encountered you, that is how quickly I am free of you. There is but *one* truth, and it lies in *duty*. I lost sight of it and was made to forget how duty called to me. It calls to me now!" He draws the pistol and wraps his fingers 'round the wood handle. He runs through the South portico and the courtyard. "Guards!" He runs 'round the lava cross, waving the pistol. "Guards!"

A shudder rises through my body. I seen it all before. The guards, the Castle, the pistol. I seen it all in Alfiu's ball of light. And, now, I know it's for this hour that he come to me and that he begged me to keep the girl safe from harm. This is *my* duty! But how did I keep the girl safe in spring and summer? If truth be told, with howling to serve my own needs. No more. This is the hour I stand brave. This is the hour my word to Alfiu rings true.

I howl like a mad dog. Again, again, again, I howl, loud, wild, all while I gain ground. So quick I am, racing past solemn cypress trees. So close I am on the new carriage road. In bare a breath, I reach the iron gates and lie in wait.

The Duchinu runs back to the iron gates, his finger curled and tight on the trigger. I crouch at the Duchinu's feet. He looks down, and I show him all my teeth. What creature is this, animal or man, the Duchinu got to wonder. I leap up, standing tall, eye to eye with him. *Muntagna* they called me. *Muntagna* I am. When he stares in the eyes of this mountain of a man, his lips tremble, his pistol shakes in his hand. He got to think the *green fairy* plays tricks on his eyes, no peasant got to be so tall, no peasant got to stand so brave. I raise my arms and show him the thick fur on my hands and the claws at the ends of my fingers, the sharp, curved weapons ready to scratch out his heart, but Alfiu, he holds me back. *Keep the girl safe from harm,* he whispers 'cross my heart, *but let her show her mettle.* Quick, I drop to the ground. Like a madman, the Duchinu looks here, there, and 'round and 'round. But too late. At the first sight of candles flickering and shadows racing in hallways and at the first sound of boots pounding the stairs, I am long past gone.

"Gratia…Maria…Saitta," he stammers, the short barrel of the pistol shaking at her chest, "you are cunning and caught."

The girl sinks low to the ground on a patch of smooth earth where laborers tore up chipped cobble stones but yet to lay down the new. The Duchinu eyes the girl on the smooth earth. Who don't take it for defeat? He stands over her, but the foreign wind blows him back and blows his jacket up 'round his face and blows his pistol out of his hand.

And it whirls 'round him, too, and fills the air with the smell of orchard fruit, part apple, part pear. And it fills the air with the smell of blood and all the smells of life, the hope and death and madness and love and justice and bravery of life. They fight in the air and whirl through the South portico, the wind and the smells of life, 'round the iron gates and 'round the girl. And 'round the girl, the wind whips the earth in a thick, black eddy and seizes her inside. The guards rush to the Duchinu's side, their guns aimed at the whirling darkness. They wait for orders from the Duchinu, but he waves them back to the Castle. There, at the iron gates, the Duchinu cries out for the girl in the eddy, where safe as safe can be, she grabs the pistol.

Quick, it starts. Quick, it ends. How quiet the wind now, how faint the smells of life now, how steady she holds the gun, now, when she rolls on the ground, her hair flying 'round her. There, 'neath the Duchinu, she crouches. Silent and steady, she aims the short barrel, right at his heart.

"Judas!" he cries out. He digs deep in his pocket and throws the strand of the girl's hair in the air. It sparks and fires like the brightest illuminations. "Judas, every last one of you, and, you, the greatest Judas of all! Go! Run! Hide! My father's men shall find you. At the foot of Mount Etna, they shall find you. At the edge of the forest, they shall find you. Be it for snow or wood, be it for the Duchy or their own profits, they are there. And they shall find you. Run, hide, my manor guards, my field guards, each and every one of them, shall find you, and, when they bring you back at my command, they shall..."

"Chiazza, take us where we got to go!" the girl cries out. The mare gallops to the forest, unburdened by age or breed. The girl makes a fist, opens her hand and spreads her fingers wide. Swift, she races down the new carriage road to a narrow path west of the Castle, a path thick with beech and chestnut trees, wild pear and broom. There, she leaps in the cart and takes hold of the reins.

Far from the town and far from the Castle, they come 'on the edge of the forest. A bright red fox waits for them, her thick tale sweeping 'cross the earth, her gold eyes gazing at the sun. There, at the edge of the forest, beads of warm morning light shine through the trees. There, the fox bows to the girl and disappears 'neath the ancient beeches.

The girl turns 'round and eyes the path she traveled on. She makes a fist. She opens her hands. There, in her palms, in a smoking ball of light, the only world she ever known comes in view: the low lava road and the town she called home, the rocky paths to the mountains and to the threshold of her Mamma's dwelling, the new carriage road that led to the Castle and its crimes. "Chiazza, we got to bid farewell to all what we know." She pats the mare's sweaty flanks. "'A z'a Vincenza always spoke of where our neighbor's journey ends. She knew the town and the mountains were all but a resting place for me. Here is my path." She eyes the thick trees, the narrow path. "*Ahi*! How my heart hurts to leave Mamma, but, here and now, my journey starts."

*

She whips the reins. In the forest, the mare glides 'cross the path gentle and swift like a pet bird in the Duchinu's pond. She glides past the pines and birches, the maples and elms, past the chestnut and walnut trees, the thorn bushes and hawthorns that bow and uproot themselves, the lot of them, and fall to the sides of the path 'til the cart passes through like the story Patri Radici acted out of the prophet and the sea that takes on the color of fire.

Not one pebble digs in the mare's shoes. Not one gnarled branch scratches the girl or the shepherd boy, now that the forest protects them and keeps the world at bay. The girl and the shepherd boy safe. The mare safe. All safe and out of harm save the panels on the cart. The branches see to that. They slash all the sea battles and wash clean all the deeds of the *hero* Nelson. The girl turns 'round and bows to the trees that bent and swayed 'til the cart rode past them and, now, root themselves back in the ground, their thick, ancient trunks strong and firm in the crowded earth.

"This is how the forest welcomes us," she tells the boy.

"Where are we?" The boy leans back and eyes the narrowing columns of bark that all but graze the sky.

"*Bacenza, ni vori bacenza*. Patience…we need patience. And after time and patience, all got to be well."

"Gratia…"

"Sì. She is all what I am."

"Gratia that graces the earth…"

"*Sst…sst…*rest…all got to be well." She reaches in her apron and pulls out the branch the surgeon waved in her face. She peels back the white husks. Inside the husks are the shells she breaks open. Inside the shells are the purple skins she brushes away. And, there, in her hand, shine the *green gold* of Bronti, brighter than a king's jewels. She places one nut on the boy's tongue and one on her own, the others she places in the carter's box with the clasp of gold where once he said we keep our jewels and our most loved possessions.

The girl and the shepherd boy hold their hearts and swallow. This is the fruit of our land, born of the fire of Mungibellu and the prayers and the sweat of the peasants and the miracle of 'a Maronna 'a Nunziata, her blessing and her curse. Stubborn like the Bruntiszi, that's what they say of the tree that grows where none ought to thrive, that yields the fruit that got to satisfy the hunger of the peasants, the hungriest on earth.

"My Mamma and Papà planted trees, but they were blind to the harvest of their labor." She takes the branch and kisses it. "For my Mamma and Papà and for our sake, we got to take new branches and graft new trees and harvest new fruits. This is love. This brings honor, but this…" she holds tight to the pistol in her hand, "this that the Duchinu prized so much… and this," she rips the ruby from her neck, "this that burns my flesh, they got no place in the forest with us." She flings them high, past the smooth stones and birch trees, high, past the hills of black lava rocks huddled at Mungibellu's feet all the way to the beautiful mountain's halo of smoke and her wide open mouth that swallows the ruby and the pistol whole. The girl leaps from the cart and twirls 'round, her hands lifted to the sky. "And this," she rips the cap from the shepherd boy, "this got no place here."

"No!" the shepherd boy cries out when the girl digs a hole and buries it. "Naked like I am," he whispers and falls back down.

"Calmu, Blasiu, look at me, naked like I am, too. But, here, who sees us? The ones that mocked us? The ones that brought us shame? No, now, we are rid of them for all time."

"Shame or not, it's all what I know."

"Blasiu, look what the forest gives us, all what's new and good. We're safe. We're nourished." She runs from tree to tree and digs out mushrooms from the earth and picks berries from the branches and lays the mushrooms and berries inside her apron. She runs to a small clearing and gathers 'a *sparacogna*, the wild spring asparagus, and rushes back to the cart, her arms filled with the long stalks, part brown, part green, and knotted like tangled hair. She brushes the pointed tips 'cross the boy's face. "Look! What ought not to grow in this season…grows. It grows! It thrives! And it's here, all here, for the taking!" She pulls out a few wild berries from her apron and hands them to the boy. "Eat, Blasiu. A sweeter taste has yet to cross our lips."

The leather-laced boots the carter prized so much still swing at the back of the cart. The shepherd boy stretches. They fall on his chest. The girl slides them on the shepherd boy's feet. "A good home they have now with thanks to Mastru Nonziu. We bless him for the fancy dresses and the shoes and the pots and the blankets and all what he leaves for us, the old and the new. Most of all, we bless him for his songs that one day we got to sing to our own innocent ones, songs and tales of our brave heroes, the old heroes and the new." She kisses the cross 'round her neck. "May 'a Maronna 'a Nunziata keep our Mastru Nonziu safe from harm." She wipes the wet from her eyes. "And may she keep Mamma safe from harm."

The boy crawls to the bench and slides down from the cart. He crosses himself. "May 'a Maronna 'a Nunziata keep your Mamma safe from harm."

She smoothes down the blue marriage dress. "She *is* safe. Like a dream before my eyes, I see…" She grabs tight to the shepherd boy's hand. "She *is* safe 'though now I can no more care for her."

He kisses her hand and folds her in his arms. "All what you done for her. You been a good daughter, more you been a son to her. You made her proud as proud can be."

She breaks free of him and falls on the earth. "Mamma, you never seen what Blasiu sees! How could you when your heart burst from all your sorrows? So, how, with all your sorrows…how could you ever *love* me?"

The boy kneels beside her, his hand folded on hers. "Gratia," he whispers, "in her heart, she loved you, 'though none could see it for sorrow made a greater home there."

"Blasiu, no more." She pulls herself up and holds out her hand to the boy. "We got all our lives to talk of Mamma and Mastru Nonziu and 'a z'a

Vincenza, but, now, you got to rest." Her hand in his, she helps him to the bench. He takes in a breath and falls to the back of the cart. There, his hand tangles in the blanket. When he throws the blanket off, he knocks over a big basket filled with leaves and buds and rootstalks. He peeks inside and lowers it to the girl. She grabs the basket and kisses it a hundred times and more. With each kiss, she breathes in the bitter and the sweet of the plants. "Blasiu, this is 'a z'a Vincenza's basket, her big basket, the one I left in the Castle... But how is it here?"

*But how?* I wonder, too.

The boy leans over the side of the cart. "Can the plants heal?"

"At the Castle, they healed the girl like me."

"But they're fresh. They can't be the plants..."

She raises her eyes to the heavens, a bright smile on her face. "Sì, it's her basket and her plants, and they're all from my z'a Vincenza!"

"Gratia that graces the earth, I'm weak and full of shame. I taught you of the healing ways, and, now, I know no more of what I see before me."

"*I* know them. You got to know them, too, soon enough. Here, 'round us, there got to be new plants with new secrets and new prayers to rid us of all the sickness." She hugs the basket. "And, together, we got to learn them all."

"I can't..."

"Blasiu...you're sick with sorrow, but, one day, you got to be well. You need to be well for there's much work to do here."

The girl leaps back in the cart and tightens the reins, but Chiazza pays them no mind. She gallops through the darkest regions of the forest where tree trunks are thick, and boughs, heavy, where crowns of leaves hide the light and warmth of the sky. With all what the boy gone through, none dares call him *vigliaccu,* but, still, like a coward, he throws the blanket over his head.

"It's too dark! I know nothing but the dark!"

The girl makes a fist. She throws her hands up. She opens them and spreads her fingers wide. Quick, the leaves spread, and the light shines through. "Fear not, Blasiu. We have the light, and the mare knows where to guide us."

Chiazza races through the forest and breaks free from the girth and breast straps and throws off the harness, too, but, still, the shafts stay in place. I swear on my eyes, she pulls the cart...*but how...but how...but how?* She gallops with silent breath deep, deep in the forest 'til her hooves splash 'cross the earth. Covered in mud, they slow to a trot and rest.

"Maronna mia! Blasiu, look! 'A z'a Vincenza sends us more gifts, small and clear and pure. There, behind the trees, see how the water flows, down it flows to a small path, down to us, here, where none can find it. *The end of the journey for our neighbor is but a resting place for us.* 'A z'a Vincenza spoke all what's true. We had to journey far to reach the purest water. This water's ours, not no field guard's and not no Duca's. Ours! 'A z'a Vincenza knew. She knew I'd find my path, and on my path, drink the purest water, and on my path, be blessed."

The shepherd boy takes a breath. He falls back down and reaches for the girl's hand.

She turns 'round and reaches back for his. "Rest, now, Blasiu that blazes the sky. Bon riposu. This day our journey starts."

# 1 MAY 1880

*Whoever is born is reborn.*

"Who are you to tell such tales?" Agata gazes in my eyes. Quick, Alfiu gave me gifts, but, slow, slow, these years with Agata, he took the gifts away. No more does he haunt me in my dreams. No more do I hold in me the strength of a beast. Slow, slow, I watched the fur shed from my body and heard the howls turn to speech, again. Slow, slow, I watched the claws grow to hands and feet and the last curved nail fall away. I am a Bronti man once more. A peasant through and through, but, still, Agata don't know me.

She sits in a chair I made of thick branches but a day past. Her white hair pulled back, her round red knuckles smoother each day, she drinks a tea I prepare that makes her strong. She says it's too dark. She can't see the flower buds for now her great joy is to count each one of them. I pour oil in the tin cup and twist a piece of cloth and light it. In the glow, she studies my face and taps my eyes and cheeks. I am a man again, a peasant Agata cursed for cowardice. Slow, slow, these years with Agata, I seen her madness drive out all the hate. And in her madness, now, there is no more sorrow.

"Who am I to tell such tales? I'm a friend," I whisper, "come to take care of you."

"You have Alfiu's big, black eyes."

"We're of the same blood."

"*Oooooo*," she sighs, "you're my maritu come back to me."

"I been a maritu to a good woman. Vincenza was her name. She's gone. I know she got to find it good now that I take care of you."

She throws her head back and raises her hand high. "You're so big."

"They call me Muntagna."

"Muntagna, the food smells good."

The creature I killed was small and orphaned. The flesh grizzles in the hearth where the flames spark and rise. She cups her eyes.

"Does the light hurt you?" I pull branches from the fire to dull the flame 'til Agata smiles. All what she asks, I do for her.

She rocks side to side. "A hunger gnaws in my belly."

Before the stars shine in the sky this first of May, Agata got to eat a good meal. And 'though I never gave my word to Alfiu, who got to take care of her now that the girl can't come back? She makes me cry with all her thankfulness to me and kisses my hand like I'm the Duchinu. The tears run down my cheek. She smiles and wipes it clean. "You cry like the sick woman and the girl and the coward in the tale. They all cried…and the girl, she cried too much, but who can fault her? Tell me, was her hair so red like Mungibellu's fire? Were her eyes so gold?"

"Agata," I say and pinch the flesh on her arm, "when did you know a Bruntiszi peasant to widen the truth?"

She lets out a laugh but chokes on it. She grabs her throat and sticks her fingers in her mouth. *Mbu…mbu…mbu…mbu…*

The wide mouth jug's near empty. I know before the light of day, I got to make my way to Mungibellu and satisfy her longings with pure water, none but pure water Vincenza said that got to enter the home.

"When did I know a Bruntiszi peasant to widen the truth?" Agata laughs and slaps her knee. "Sing your tale, Muntagna, and I'll name the giant what widens the truth." I stomp my foot and tell the tale I tell each night. "*Bravu!*" she shouts out when the hero kills the evil one. "*Bravu!*" she shouts out when the girl flees to the forest with her shepherd boy. She crosses herself and prays for the sick woman in the tale. "The Mamma wasn't kind and good," she says. "All Mammas got to be kind and good and love their daughters. The girl was a good figghia. O, to call her *figghia mia*…O, to have a good daughter like the girl in the tale and to *love* her for my own…"

She blesses the girl and throws kisses in the air. And, me, I can no more hold back the rush of tears.

"Don't weep…*ninnananna…ninnananna…ninnananna…*"

"No, Agata, no more weeping," I say and slap the tears from my eyes. "All the sorrow's gone."

"Sì, all the sorrow's gone." She reaches for the meat. "No, Agata, before we eat, let's say a prayer for my Vincenza and your Alfiu."

She throws her hands in the air and sings in a high voice and loud, too, 'til creatures in far-off caves start to howl. "Tonight I dreamed I was in the Castle. I had a fine little wood dove. I wanted to gain her trust. I dealt a blow. It hit her in the belly. She dealt a blow. It hit me in the heart. Our presence long remains inside each other."

"*Sst. Sst.* Agata, a good notion you got to sing the carter's song, but…"

"He sang like no other."

"Sì, Agata, and all the island loved his songs, but…"

"I long to see him."

"One day, he got to come back. 'Til then, he makes his way to near and far-off towns. '*A chiazza*! the people cry. *To the square*! They crowd 'round and wait for him. And when he nears, their eyes and mouths open wide, bound by the spell he casts singing out the tales of the brave Orlannu."

"The carter's brave like the brave Orlannu."

"Sì. All are brave. My Vincenza and your Alfiu, too. Now, let's say a prayer for the good woman that was once my wife and a prayer for your *maritu*, too. They left the earth to live in the heavens. They're brave, brave like Mastru Nonziu and brave like the brave Orlannu."

Each night, we sing the carter's songs and pray. I sing out *the tale of the girl in the forest*. And when Agata's quiet once more, she eats all what I hunt to keep her belly full. This is how we live our lives 'neath the spotted moons and the bright full moons. How many more moons got to shine in the sky before we both are called to paradise? I hold out my hand. She rests hers in mine. I help her to bed and sleep 'neath the stars like the shepherd boy when the girl slept in his cave.

The girl. I bless the girl for this fine dwelling, far from the Duca and his men. I bless her for the care a good daughter showered on her Mamma. *The girl.* What beats inside her now? The soothing voice of Vincenza, the bleating of the lamb, the madness of her Mamma, the songs of the carter, the Castle and its crimes…or are there new beatings inside her? "This is what I hope for!" I cry out. "With all my heart, this is what I hope for the girl! Gratia, Gratia Maria," I sob, "you made your mark, you found your path, 'though it's a path only the brave dare travel on!"

Agata hears my cries. She rushes to my side and quiets me.

"It's nothing," I tell her, "none but the dreams of an old man."

She takes hold of my hand. "You're not old, Muntagna," she whispers. "You're *brave*."

I throw my head back and take in a breath. The air feels cold in my throat. She says the word again. I look up at her lost smile and say it with her. *Brave*. I swallow it. It rushes through my blood, warming me like the Duca's finest wine.

*Brave* she calls me. *Brave. Brave.* Who dares to call me a coward now? I gave my word to Alfiu, and I kept it. *Brave*, I lie 'neath the stars. 'Neath the stars, the girl lies, too, this night and each night to come, safe from harm, deep in the forest, with the shepherd boy.

CPSIA information can be obtained at www.ICGtesting.com
Printed in the USA
BVOW07s1455290913

332346BV00002B/88/P